IT TAKES 2

AN ONI PRESS PUBLICATION

IT TAKES 2

2

WRITTEN AND ILLUSTRATED BY **YEHUDI MERCADO**

COLOR ASSISTANCE BY
Andrea Bell, Sophia Foodis,
Mary Bellamy, and Dave Wheeler
EDITED BY
Grace Scherpeter
DESIGNED BY
Kate Z. Stone

Published by Oni-Lion Force Publishing Group, LLC

JAMES LUCAS JONES president & publisher
CHARLIE CHU e.v.p. of creative & business development
STEVE ELLIS s.v.p. of games & operations
ALEX SEGURA s.v.p. of marketing & sales
MICHELLE NGUYEN associate publisher
BRAD ROOKS director of operations
AMBER O'NEILL special projects manager
MARGOT WOOD director of marketing & sales
KATIE SAINZ marketing manager
HENRY BARAJAS sales manager
TARA LEHMANN publicist
HOLLY AITCHISON consumer marketing manager
TROY LOOK director of design & production
ANGIE KNOWLES production manager
KATE Z. STONE senior graphic designer
CAREY HALL graphic designer
SARAH ROCKWELL graphic designer
HILARY THOMPSON graphic designer
VINCENT KUKUA digital prepress technician
CHRIS CERASI managing editor
JASMINE AMIRI senior editor
SHAWNA GORE senior editor
AMANDA MEADOWS senior editor
ROBERT MEYERS senior editor, licensing
DESIREE RODRIGUEZ editor
GRACE SCHEIPETER editor
ZACK SOTO editor
BEN EISNER game developer
JUNG LEE logistics coordinator
KUIAN KELLUM warehouse assistant

JOE NOZEMACK publisher emeritus

ONIPRESS.COM
FACEBOOK.COM/ONIPRESS
TWITTER.COM/ONIPRESS
INSTAGRAM.COM/ONIPRESS

@YMERCADO
SUPERMERCADO.PIZZA

1319 SE Martin Luther King Jr. Blvd.
Suite #240
Portland, OR 97214

First Edition: April 2022
ISBN: 978-1-62010-783-6
ISBN COVER B: 978-1-63715-032-0
eISBN: 978-1-62010-804-8

10 9 8 7 6 5 4 3 2 1

Library of Congress Control Number: 2017948857

Printed in China.

DEDICATED TO THE KIDS AT THE
BROOKLYN PUBLIC LIBRARY

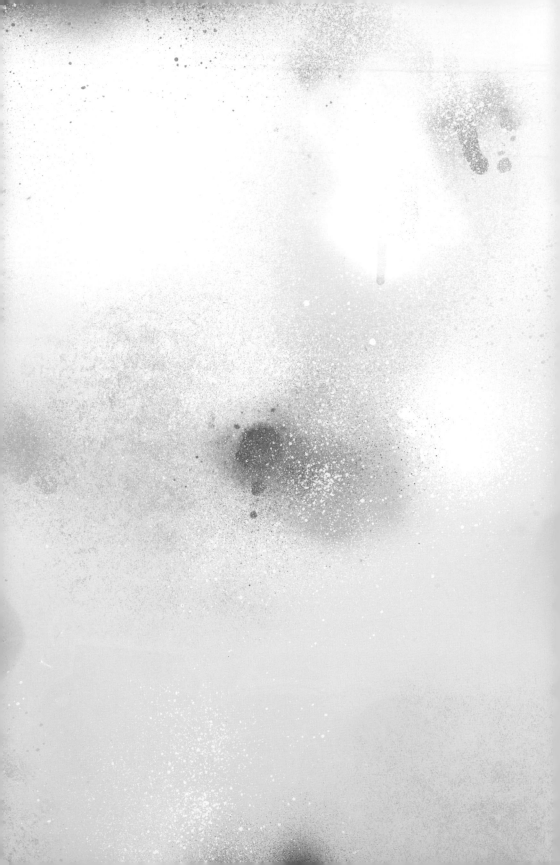

PRELUDE

MEGA HERTZ'S BIG BREAK

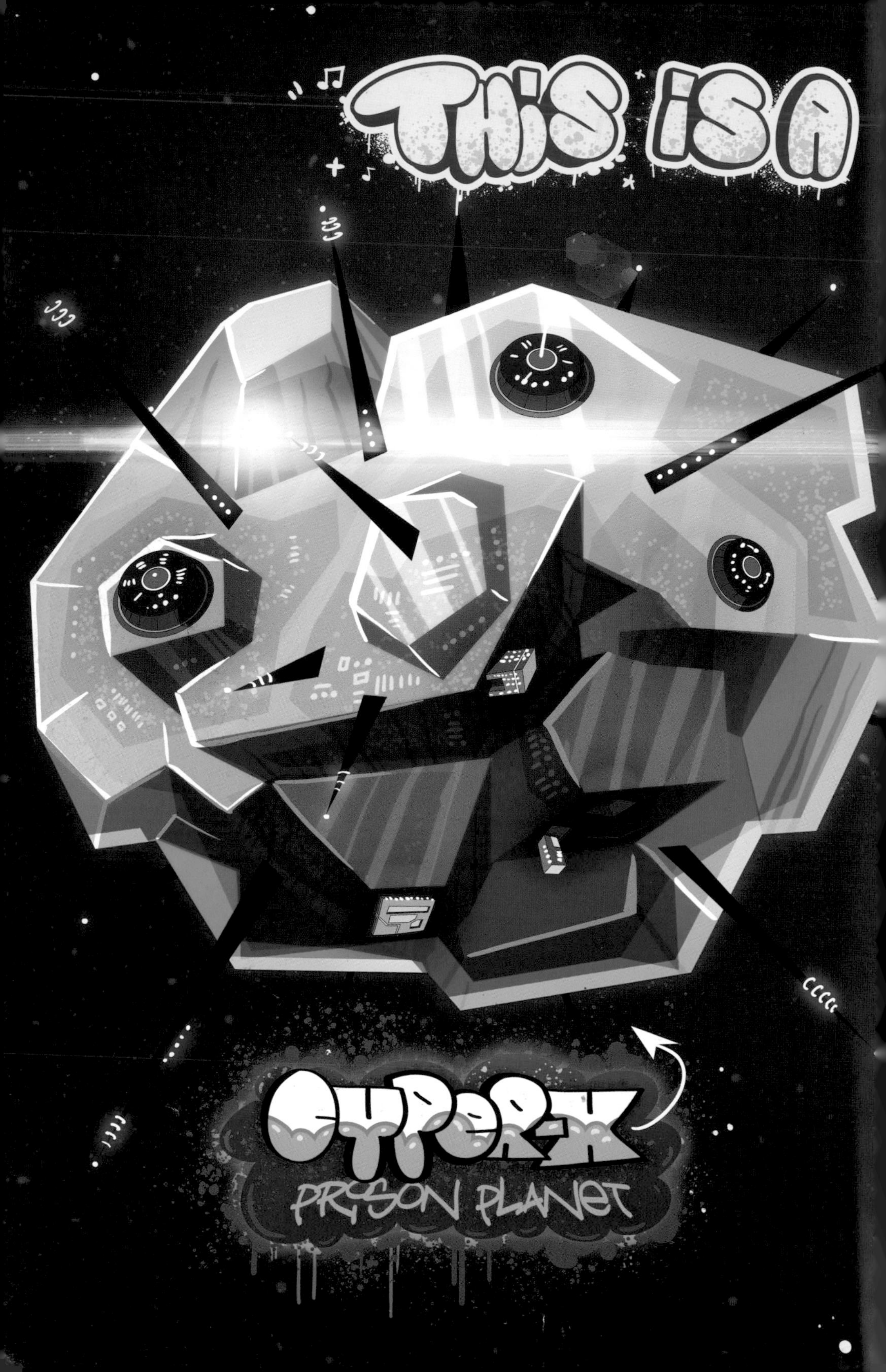

THIS IS A
CYPER-X
PRISON PLANET

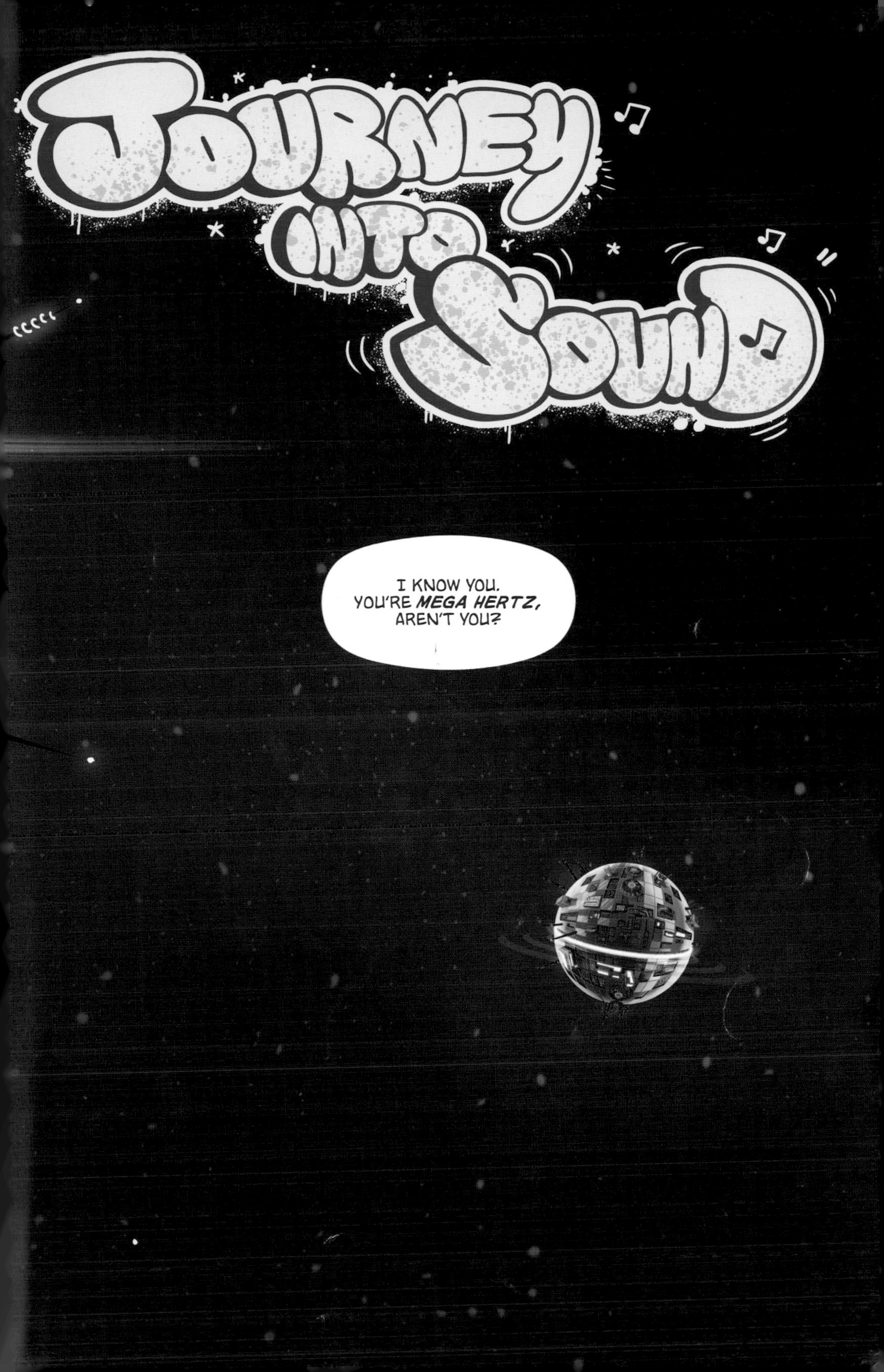
JOURNEY INTO SOUND
I KNOW YOU. YOU'RE *MEGA HERTZ,* AREN'T YOU?

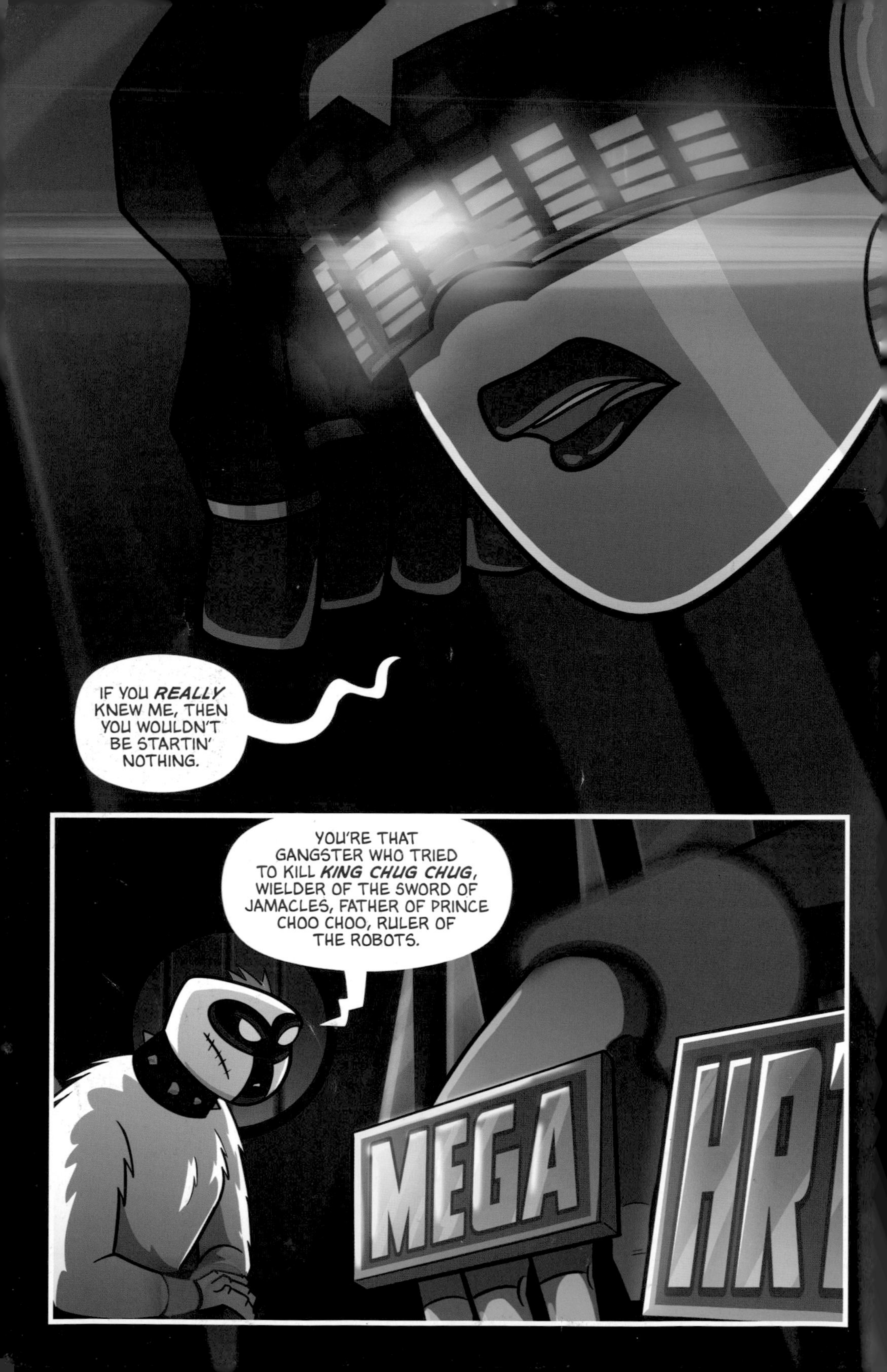

IF YOU *REALLY* KNEW ME, THEN YOU WOULDN'T BE STARTIN' NOTHING.
YOU'RE THAT GANGSTER WHO TRIED TO KILL *KING CHUG CHUG*, WIELDER OF THE SWORD OF JAMACLES, FATHER OF PRINCE CHOO CHOO, RULER OF THE ROBOTS.
MEGA

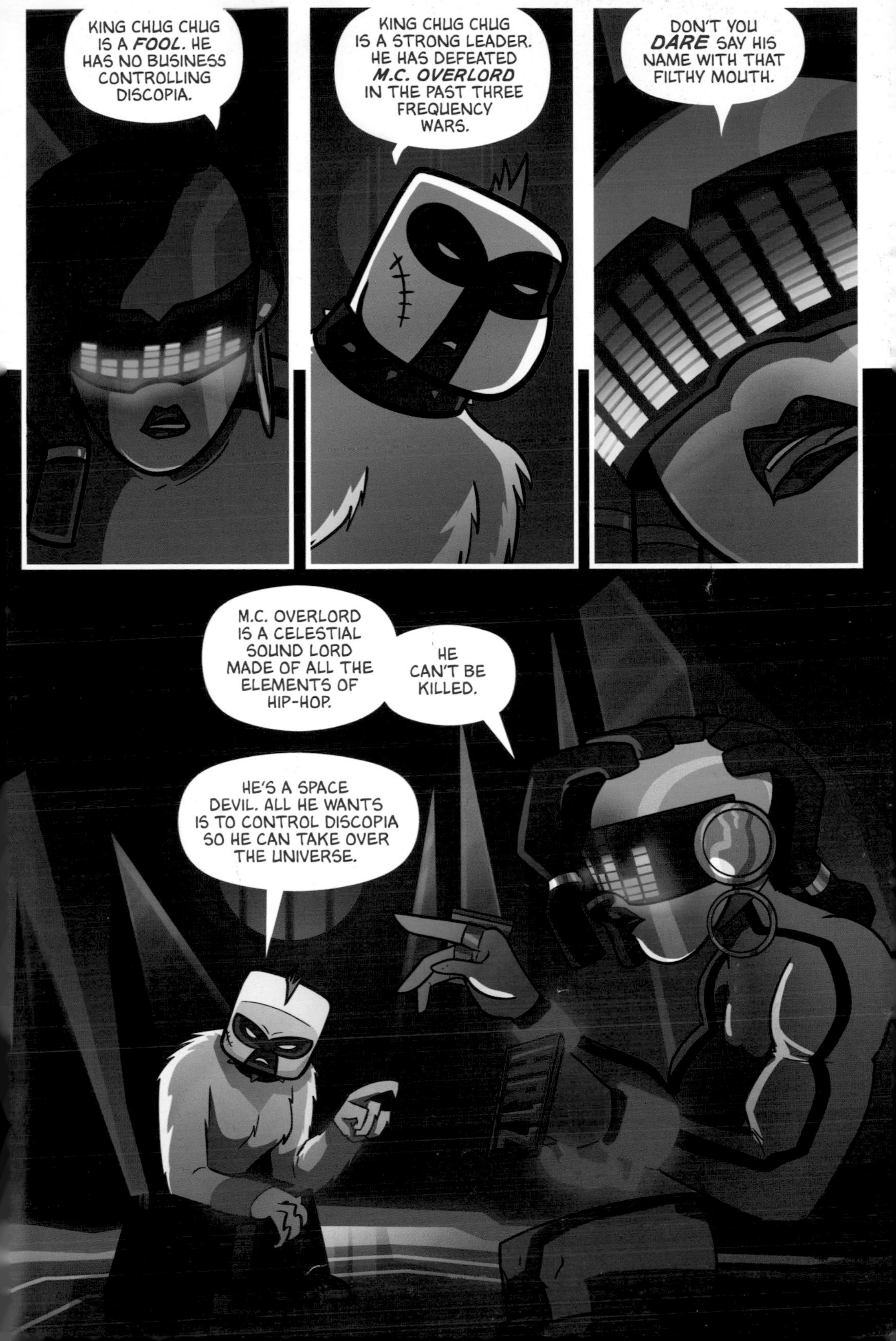
KING CHUG CHUG IS A FOOL. HE HAS NO BUSINESS CONTROLLING DISCOPIA.
KING CHUG CHUG IS A STRONG LEADER. HE HAS DEFEATED M.C. OVERLORD IN THE PAST THREE FREQUENCY WARS.
DON'T YOU DARE SAY HIS NAME WITH THAT FILTHY MOUTH.
M.C. OVERLORD IS A CELESTIAL SOUND LORD MADE OF ALL THE ELEMENTS OF HIP-HOP.
HE CAN'T BE KILLED.
HE'S A SPACE DEVIL. ALL HE WANTS IS TO CONTROL DISCOPIA SO HE CAN TAKE OVER THE UNIVERSE.

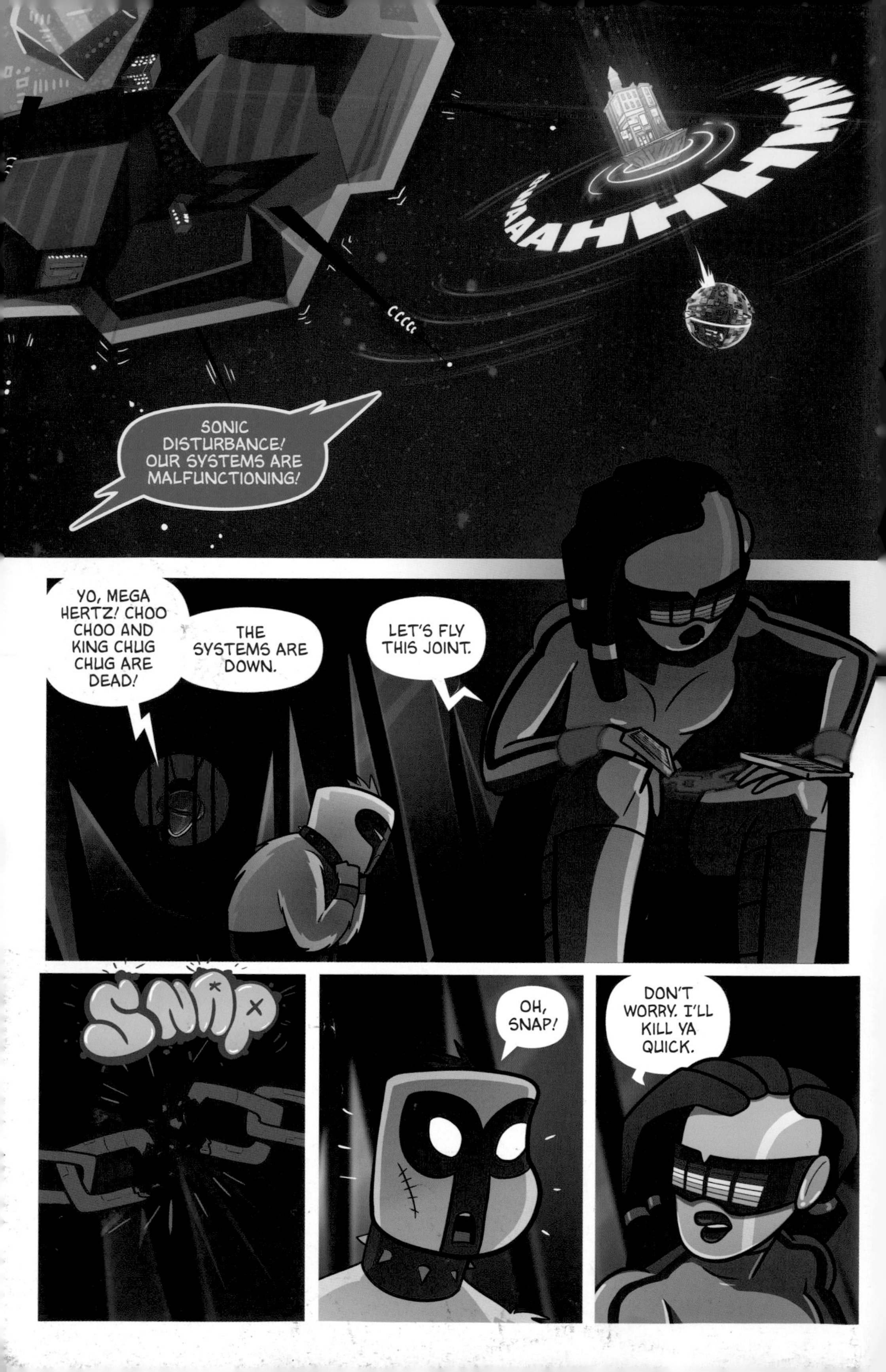
HHHHMMMM
AAAAHHHH
CCCC
SONIC DISTURBANCE! OUR SYSTEMS ARE MALFUNCTIONING!
YO, MEGA HERTZ! CHOO CHOO AND KING CHUG CHUG ARE DEAD!
THE SYSTEMS ARE DOWN.
LET'S FLY THIS JOINT.
SNAP
OH, SNAP!
DON'T WORRY. I'LL KILL YA QUICK.

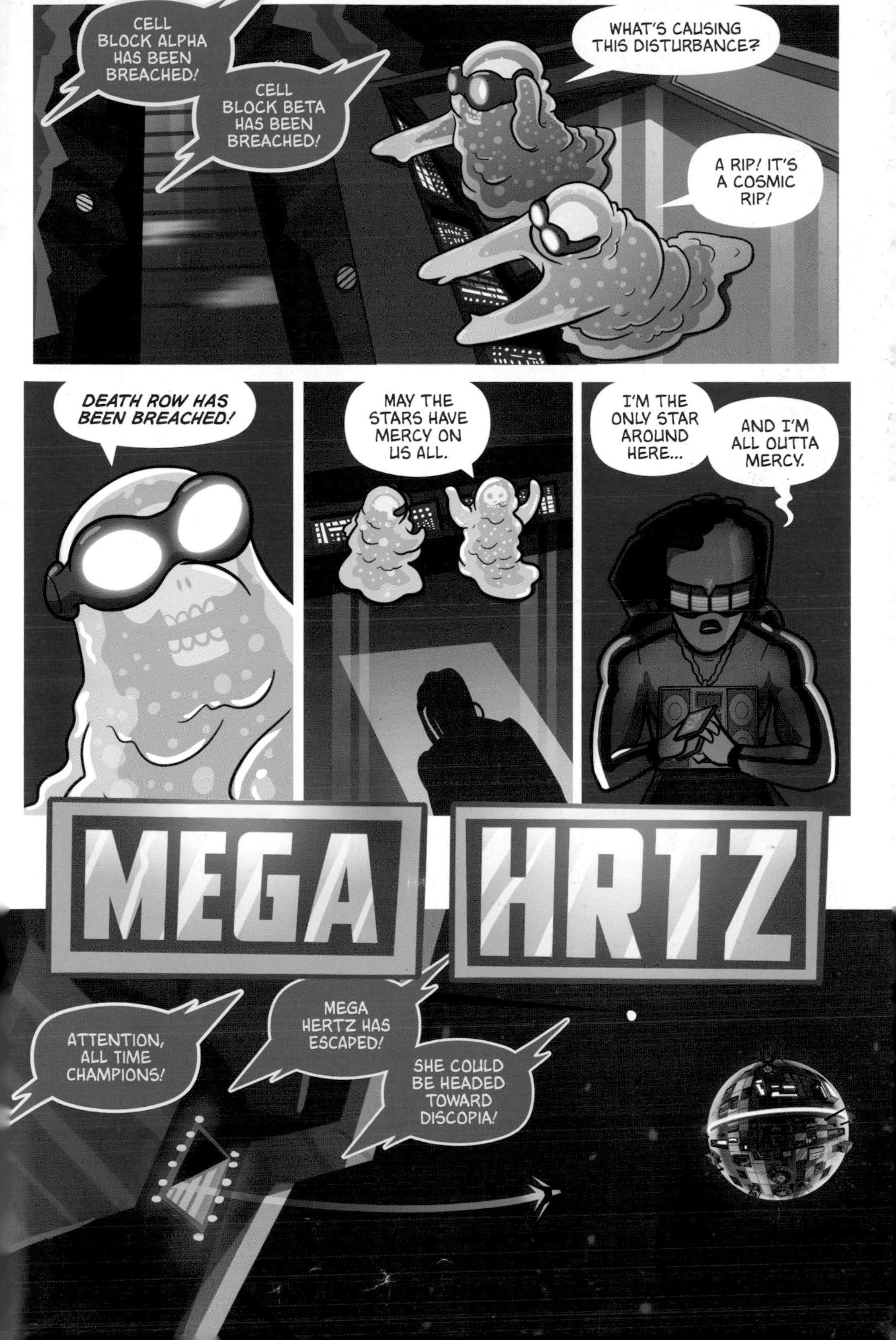
CELL BLOCK ALPHA HAS BEEN BREACHED!
CELL BLOCK BETA HAS BEEN BREACHED!
WHAT'S CAUSING THIS DISTURBANCE?
A RIP! IT'S A COSMIC RIP!
DEATH ROW HAS BEEN BREACHED!
MAY THE STARS HAVE MERCY ON US ALL.
I'M THE ONLY STAR AROUND HERE...
AND I'M ALL OUTTA MERCY.
MEGA HRTZ
ATTENTION, ALL TIME CHAMPIONS!
MEGA HERTZ HAS ESCAPED!
SHE COULD BE HEADED TOWARD DISCOPIA!

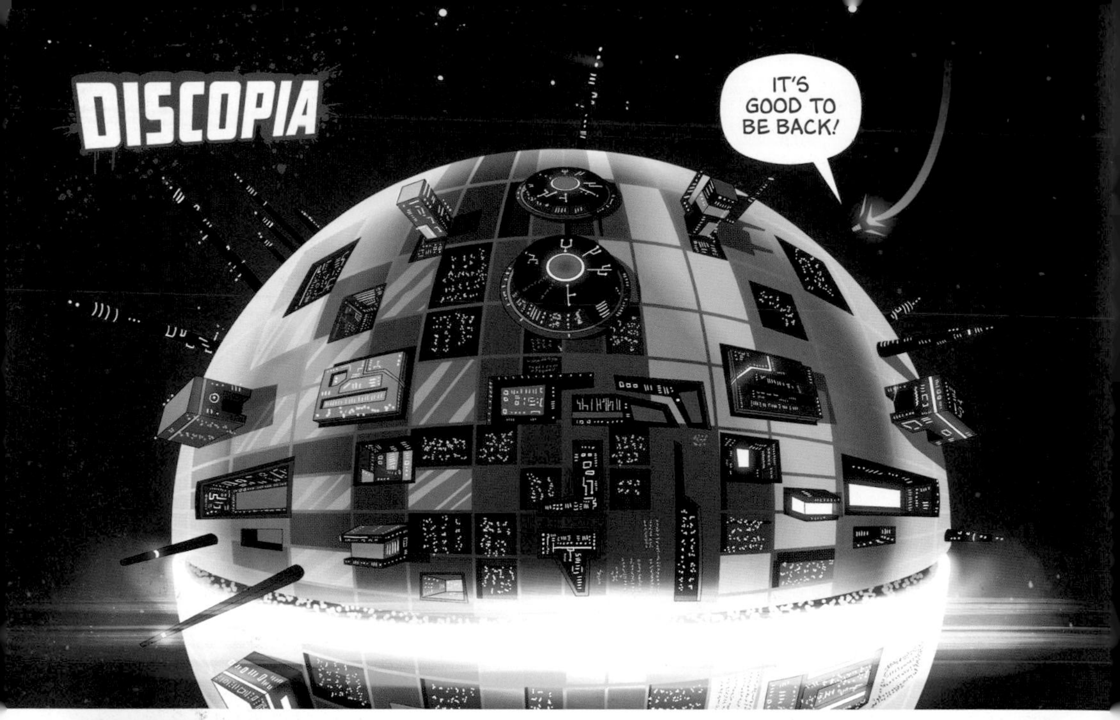
DISCOPIA
IT'S GOOD TO BE BACK!

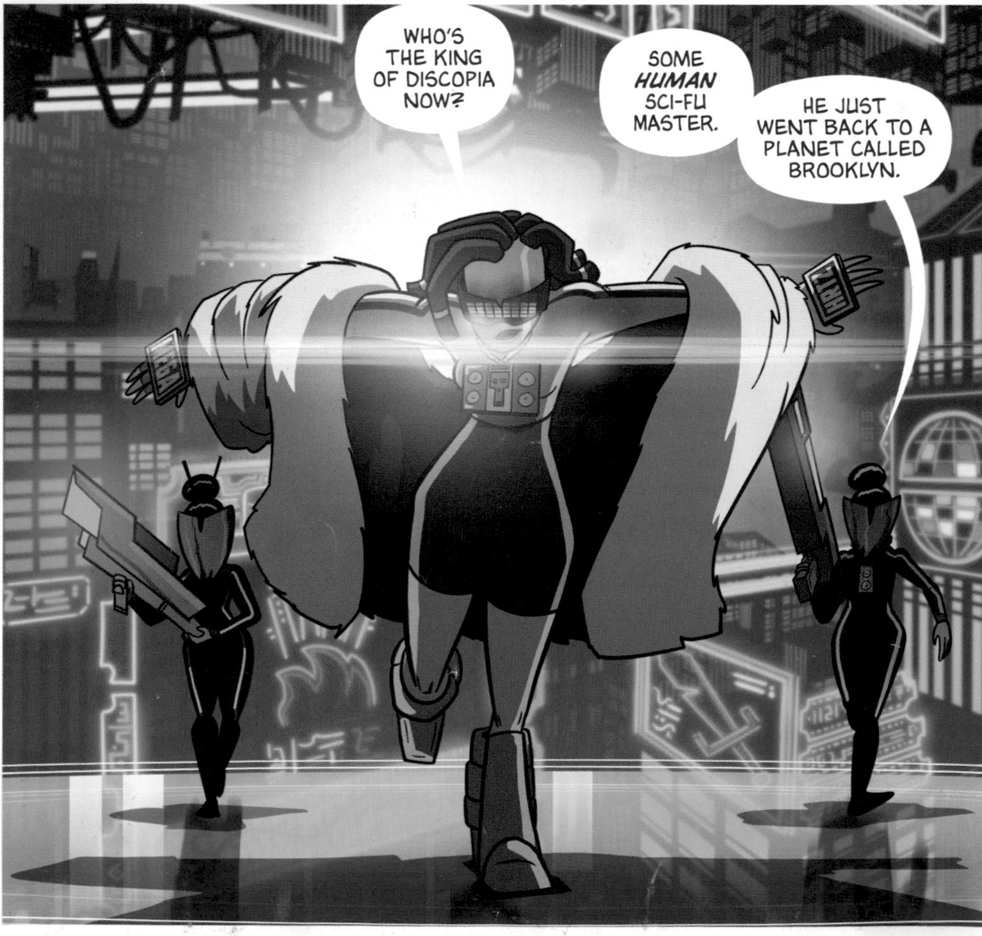
WHO'S THE KING OF DISCOPIA NOW?
SOME *HUMAN* SCI-FU MASTER.
HE JUST WENT BACK TO A PLANET CALLED BROOKLYN.

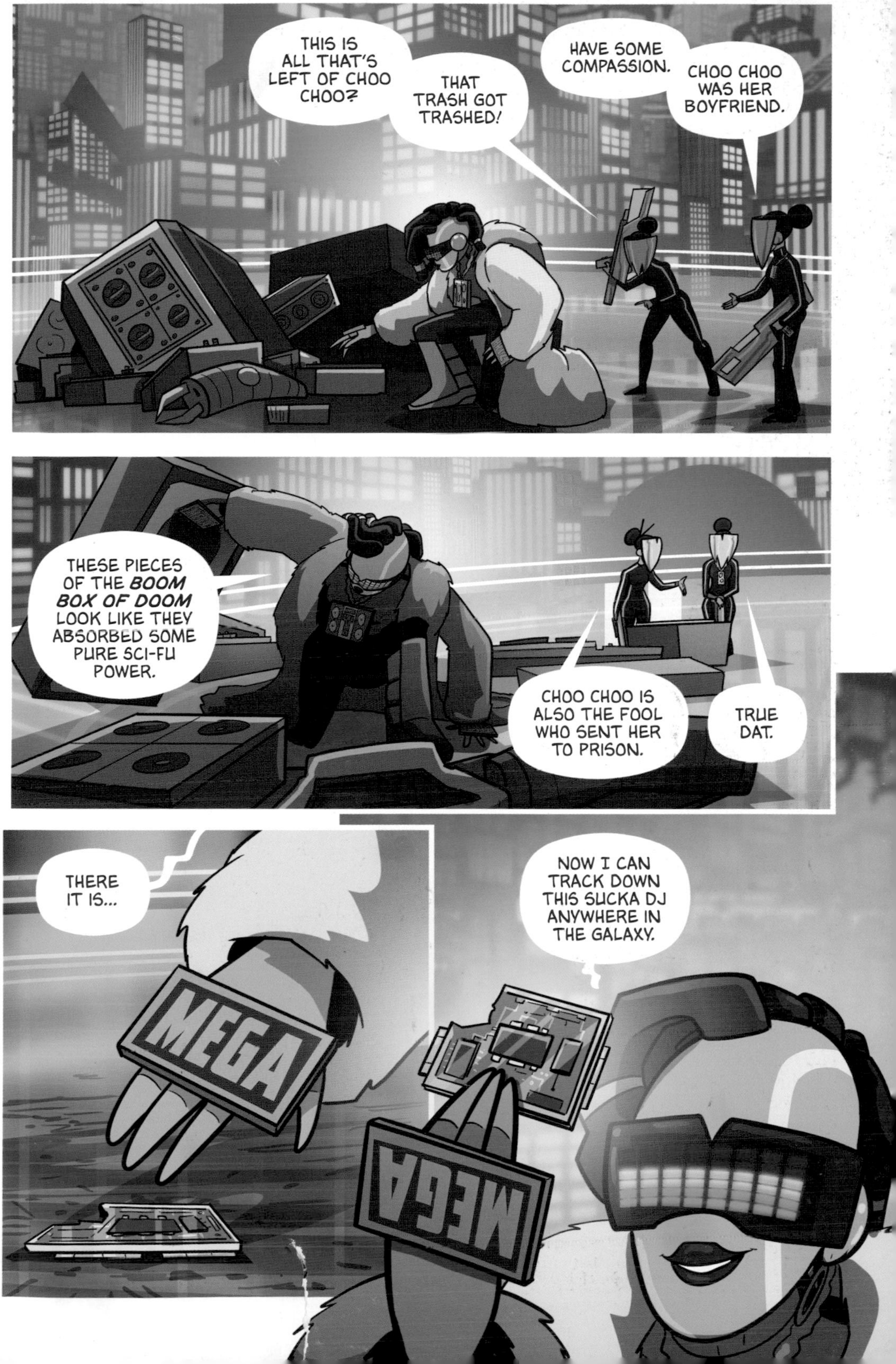
THIS IS ALL THAT'S LEFT OF CHOO CHOO?
THAT TRASH GOT TRASHED!
HAVE SOME COMPASSION.
CHOO CHOO WAS HER BOYFRIEND.
THESE PIECES OF THE **BOOM BOX OF DOOM** LOOK LIKE THEY ABSORBED SOME PURE SCI-FU POWER.
CHOO CHOO IS ALSO THE FOOL WHO SENT HER TO PRISON.
TRUE DAT.
THERE IT IS...
NOW I CAN TRACK DOWN THIS SUCKA DJ ANYWHERE IN THE GALAXY.
MEGA
MEGA

TRACK
1
STACKS ON STACKS

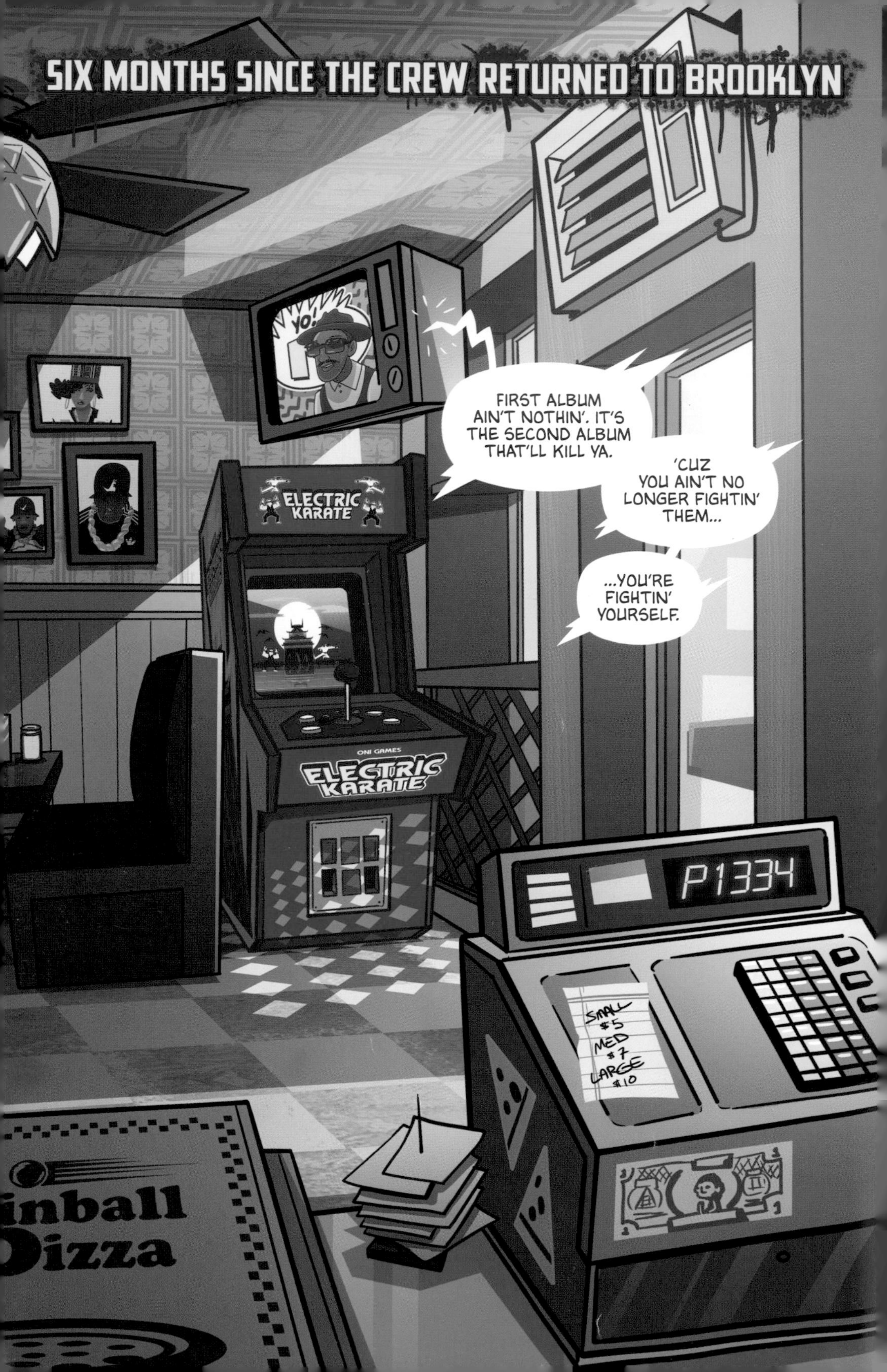
SIX MONTHS SINCE THE CREW RETURNED TO BROOKLYN
YO!
FIRST ALBUM AIN'T NOTHIN'. IT'S THE SECOND ALBUM THAT'LL KILL YA.
'CUZ YOU AIN'T NO LONGER FIGHTIN' THEM...
...YOU'RE FIGHTIN' YOURSELF.
ELECTRIC KARATE
ONI GAMES
ELECTRIC KARATE
P1334
SMALL $5
MED $7
LARGE $10
inball
Pizza

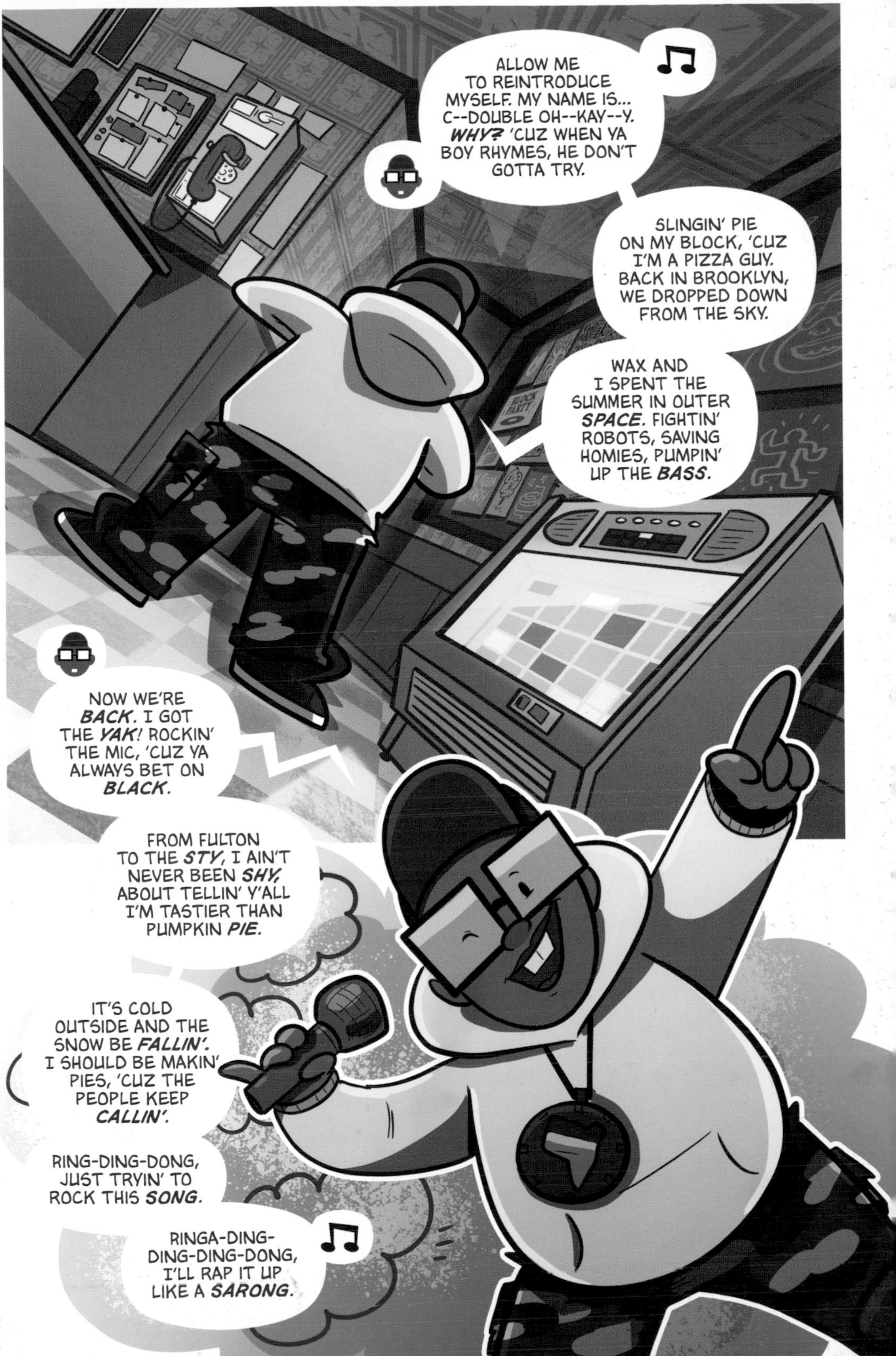
ALLOW ME TO REINTRODUCE MYSELF. MY NAME IS... C--DOUBLE OH--KAY--Y. WHY? 'CUZ WHEN YA BOY RHYMES, HE DON'T GOTTA TRY.
SLINGIN' PIE ON MY BLOCK, 'CUZ I'M A PIZZA GUY. BACK IN BROOKLYN, WE DROPPED DOWN FROM THE SKY.
WAX AND I SPENT THE SUMMER IN OUTER SPACE. FIGHTIN' ROBOTS, SAVING HOMIES, PUMPIN' UP THE BASS.
BLOCK PARTY
NOW WE'RE BACK. I GOT THE YAK! ROCKIN' THE MIC, 'CUZ YA ALWAYS BET ON BLACK.
FROM FULTON TO THE STY, I AIN'T NEVER BEEN SHY, ABOUT TELLIN' Y'ALL I'M TASTIER THAN PUMPKIN PIE.
IT'S COLD OUTSIDE AND THE SNOW BE FALLIN'. I SHOULD BE MAKIN' PIES, 'CUZ THE PEOPLE KEEP CALLIN'.
RING-DING-DONG, JUST TRYIN' TO ROCK THIS SONG.
RINGA-DING-DING-DING-DONG, I'LL RAP IT UP LIKE A SARONG.

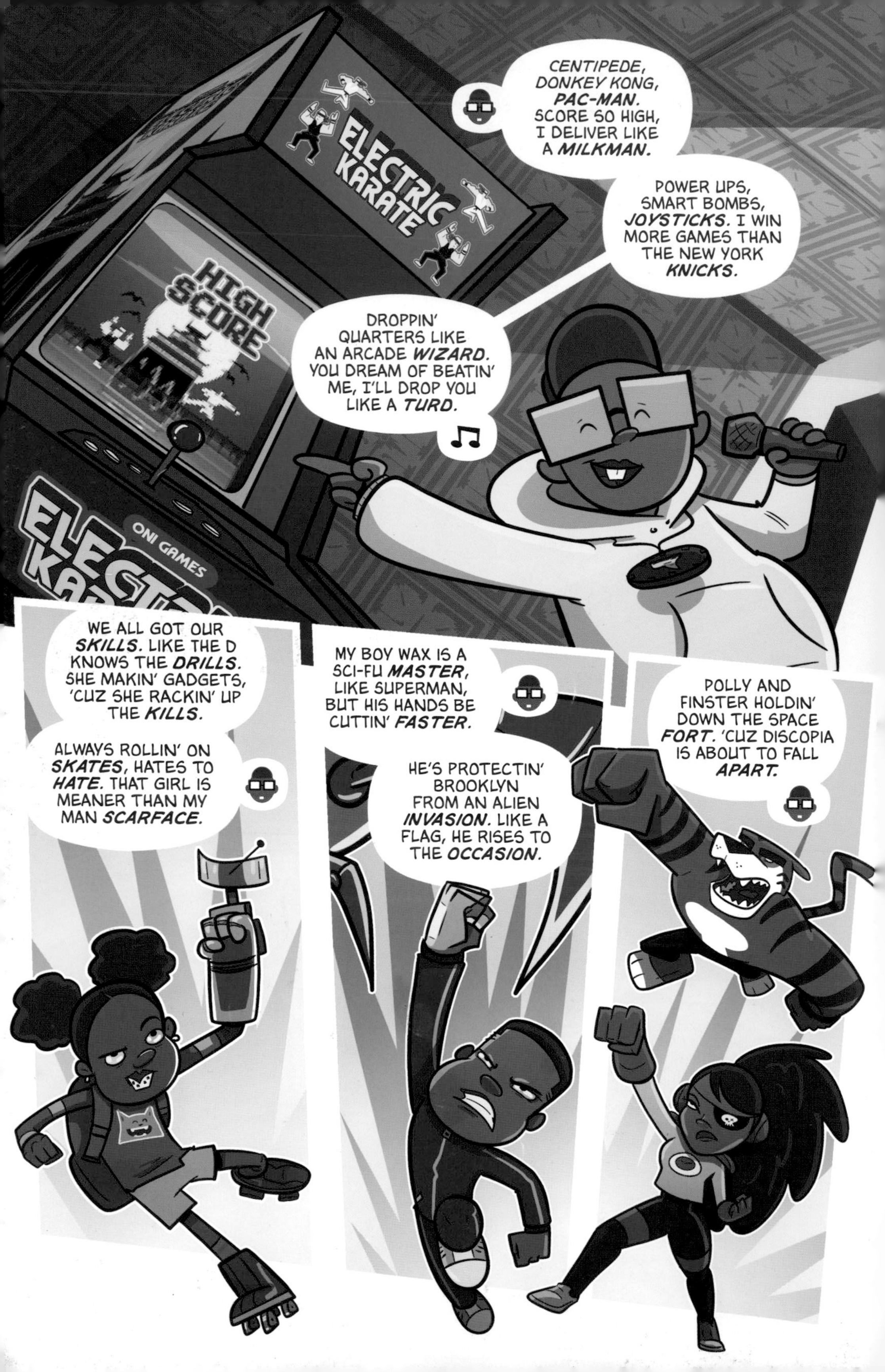
ELECTRIC KARATE
HIGH SCORE
CENTIPEDE, DONKEY KONG, PAC-MAN. SCORE SO HIGH, I DELIVER LIKE A MILKMAN.
POWER UPS, SMART BOMBS, JOYSTICKS. I WIN MORE GAMES THAN THE NEW YORK KNICKS.
DROPPIN' QUARTERS LIKE AN ARCADE WIZARD. YOU DREAM OF BEATIN' ME, I'LL DROP YOU LIKE A TURD.
ONI GAMES
WE ALL GOT OUR SKILLS. LIKE THE D KNOWS THE DRILLS. SHE MAKIN' GADGETS, 'CUZ SHE RACKIN' UP THE KILLS.
ALWAYS ROLLIN' ON SKATES, HATES TO HATE. THAT GIRL IS MEANER THAN MY MAN SCARFACE.
MY BOY WAX IS A SCI-FU MASTER, LIKE SUPERMAN, BUT HIS HANDS BE CUTTIN' FASTER.
HE'S PROTECTIN' BROOKLYN FROM AN ALIEN INVASION. LIKE A FLAG, HE RISES TO THE OCCASION.
POLLY AND FINSTER HOLDIN' DOWN THE SPACE FORT. 'CUZ DISCOPIA IS ABOUT TO FALL APART.

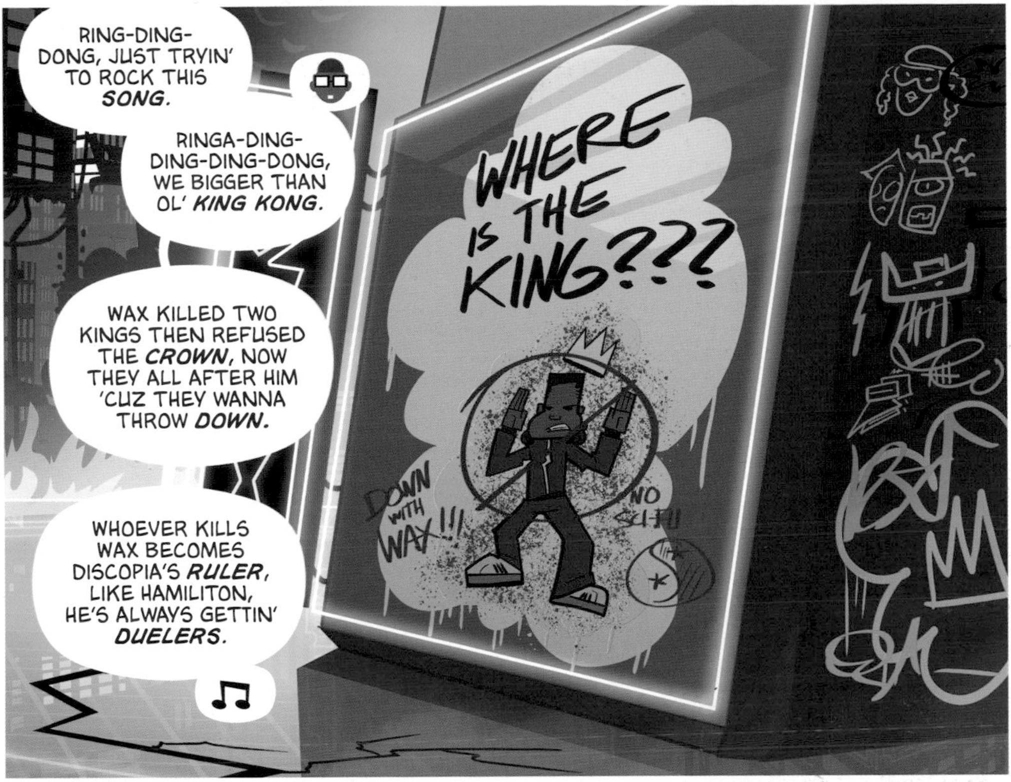
RING-DING-DONG, JUST TRYIN' TO ROCK THIS SONG.
RINGA-DING-DING-DING-DONG, WE BIGGER THAN OL' KING KONG.
WAX KILLED TWO KINGS THEN REFUSED THE CROWN, NOW THEY ALL AFTER HIM 'CUZ THEY WANNA THROW DOWN.
WHOEVER KILLS WAX BECOMES DISCOPIA'S RULER, LIKE HAMILITON, HE'S ALWAYS GETTIN' DUELERS.
WHERE IS THE KING???
DOWN WITH WAX!!!
NO
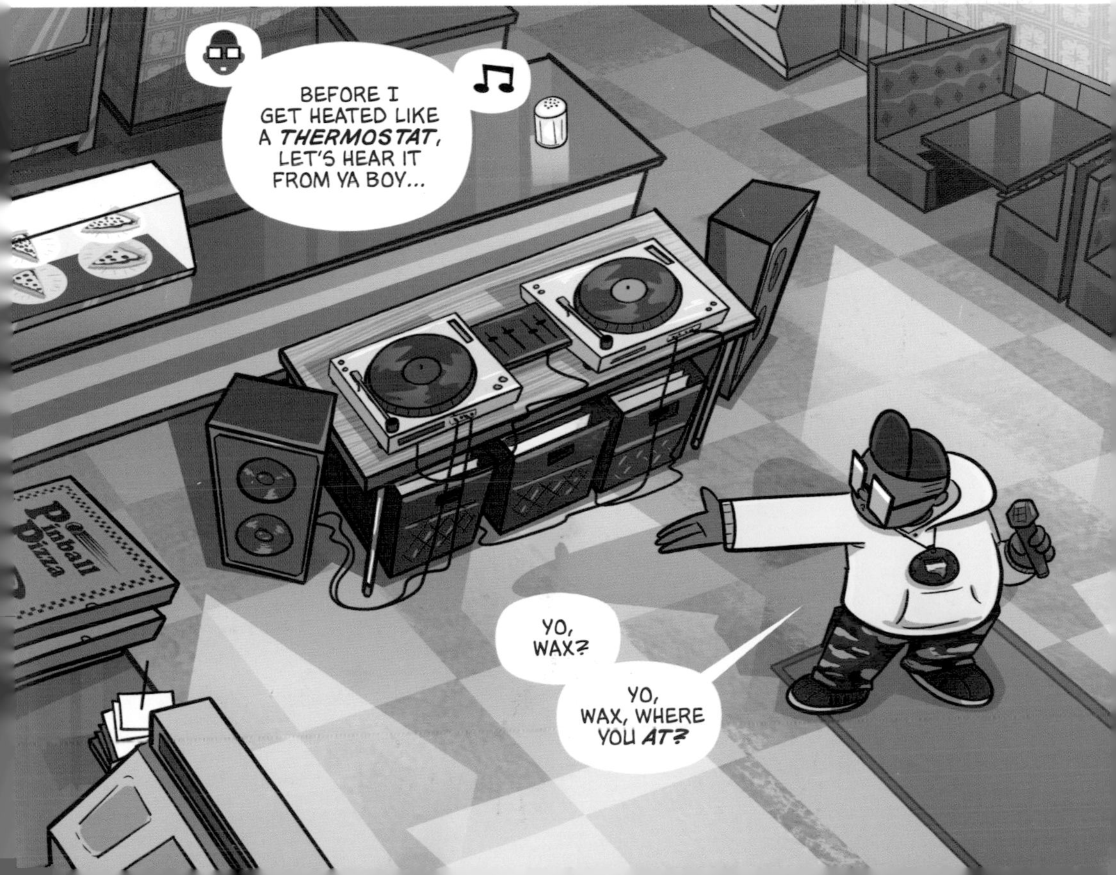
BEFORE I GET HEATED LIKE A THERMOSTAT, LET'S HEAR IT FROM YA BOY...
Pinball Pizza
YO, WAX?
YO, WAX, WHERE YOU AT?

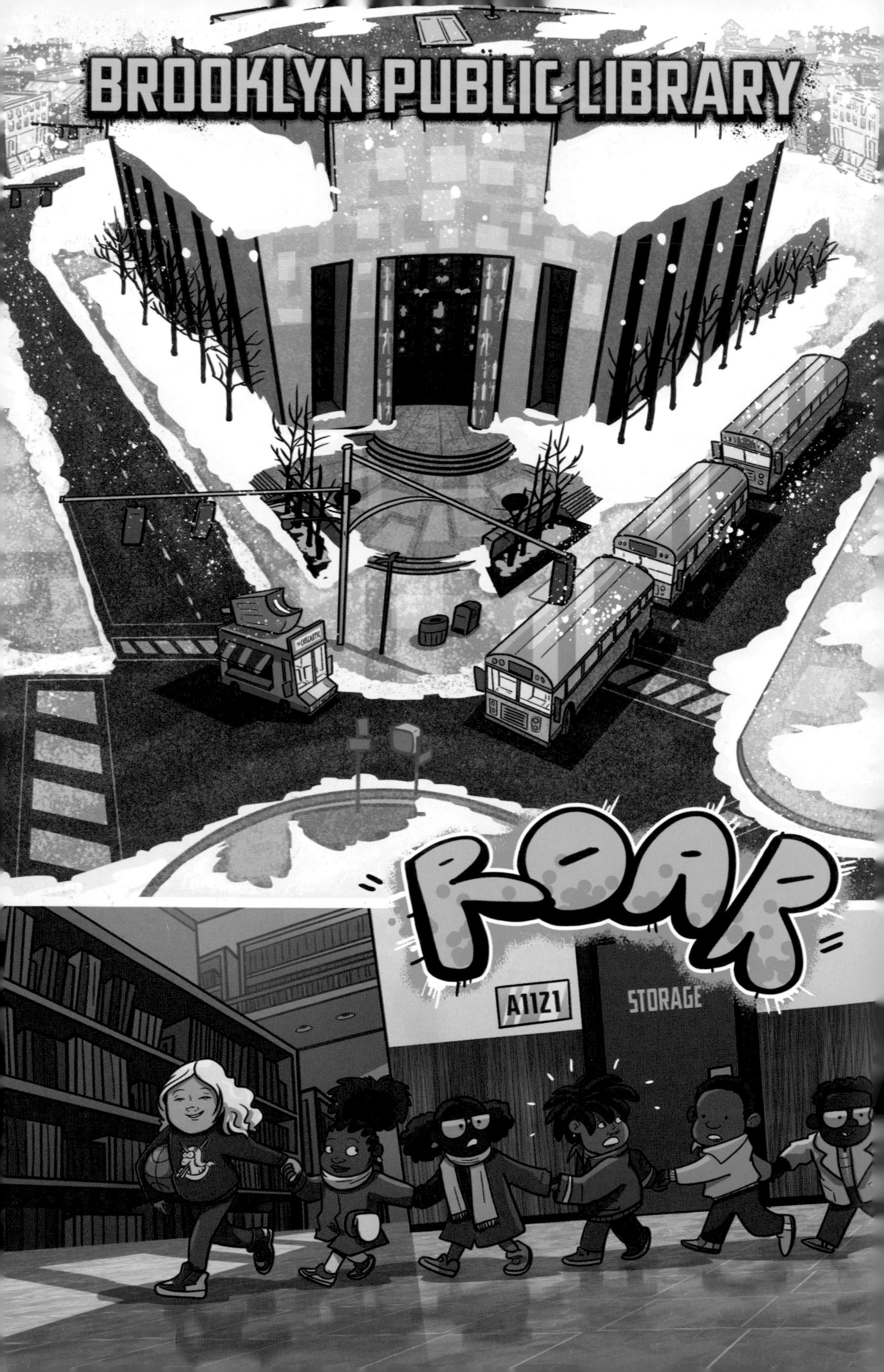
BROOKLYN PUBLIC LIBRARY
ROAR
A1121
STORAGE

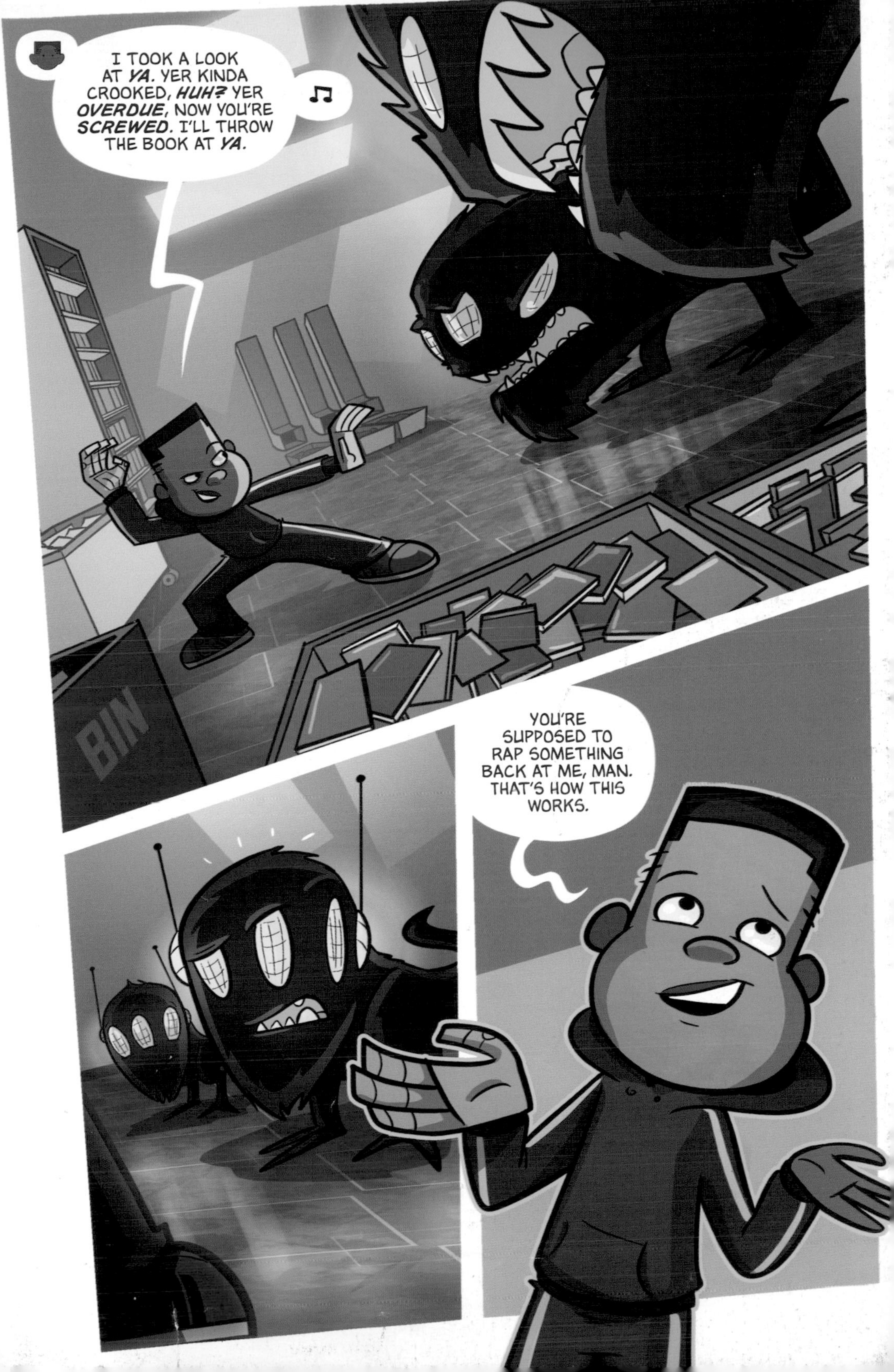
I TOOK A LOOK AT *YA*. YER KINDA CROOKED, ***HUH?*** YER ***OVERDUE***, NOW YOU'RE ***SCREWED***. I'LL THROW THE BOOK AT *YA*.
♫
BIN
YOU'RE SUPPOSED TO RAP SOMETHING BACK AT ME, MAN. THAT'S HOW THIS WORKS.

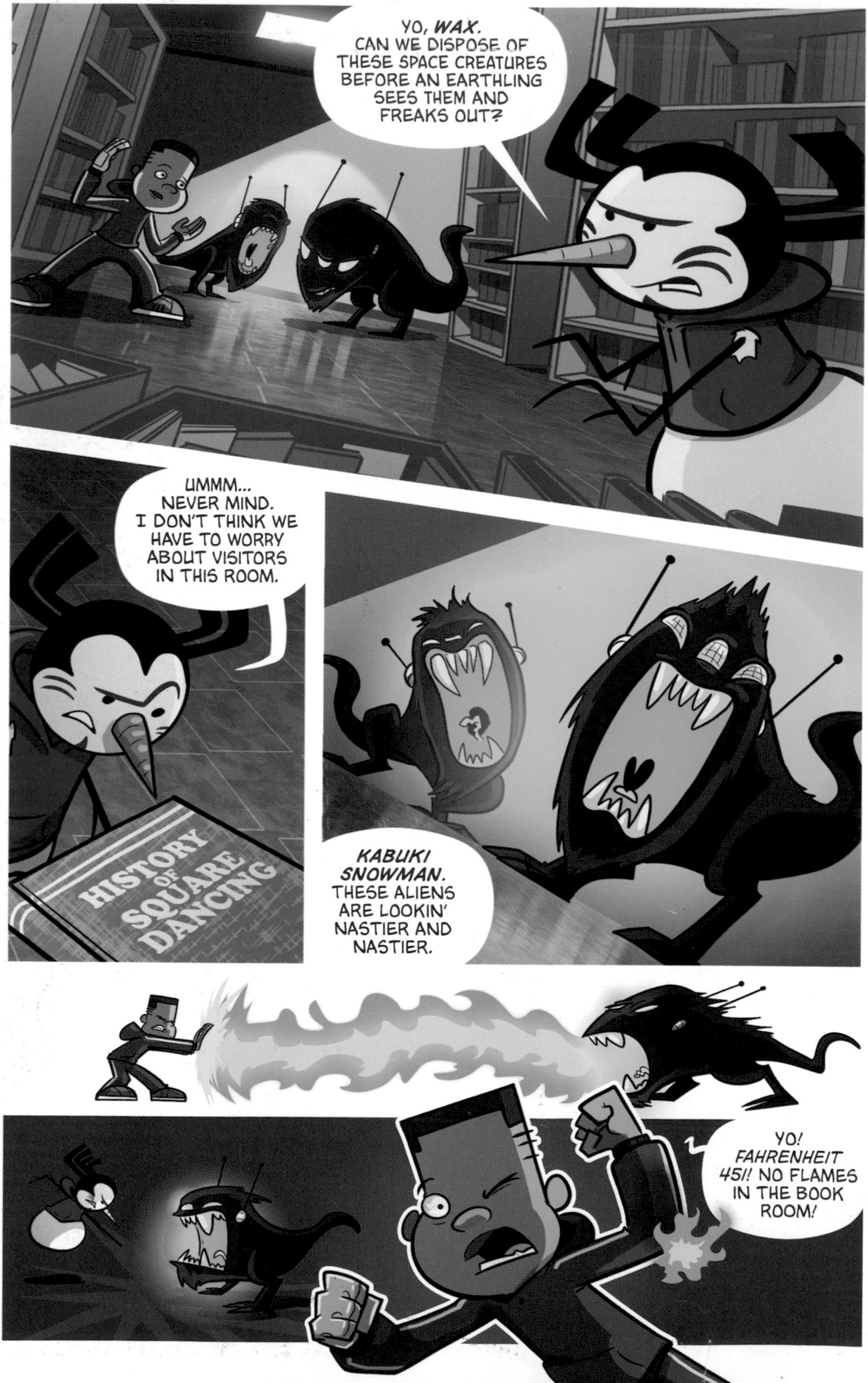
YO, WAX. CAN WE DISPOSE OF THESE SPACE CREATURES BEFORE AN EARTHLING SEES THEM AND FREAKS OUT?
UMMM... NEVER MIND. I DON'T THINK WE HAVE TO WORRY ABOUT VISITORS IN THIS ROOM.
HISTORY OF SQUARE DANCING
KABUKI SNOWMAN. THESE ALIENS ARE LOOKIN' NASTIER AND NASTIER.
YO! FAHRENHEIT 451! NO FLAMES IN THE BOOK ROOM!

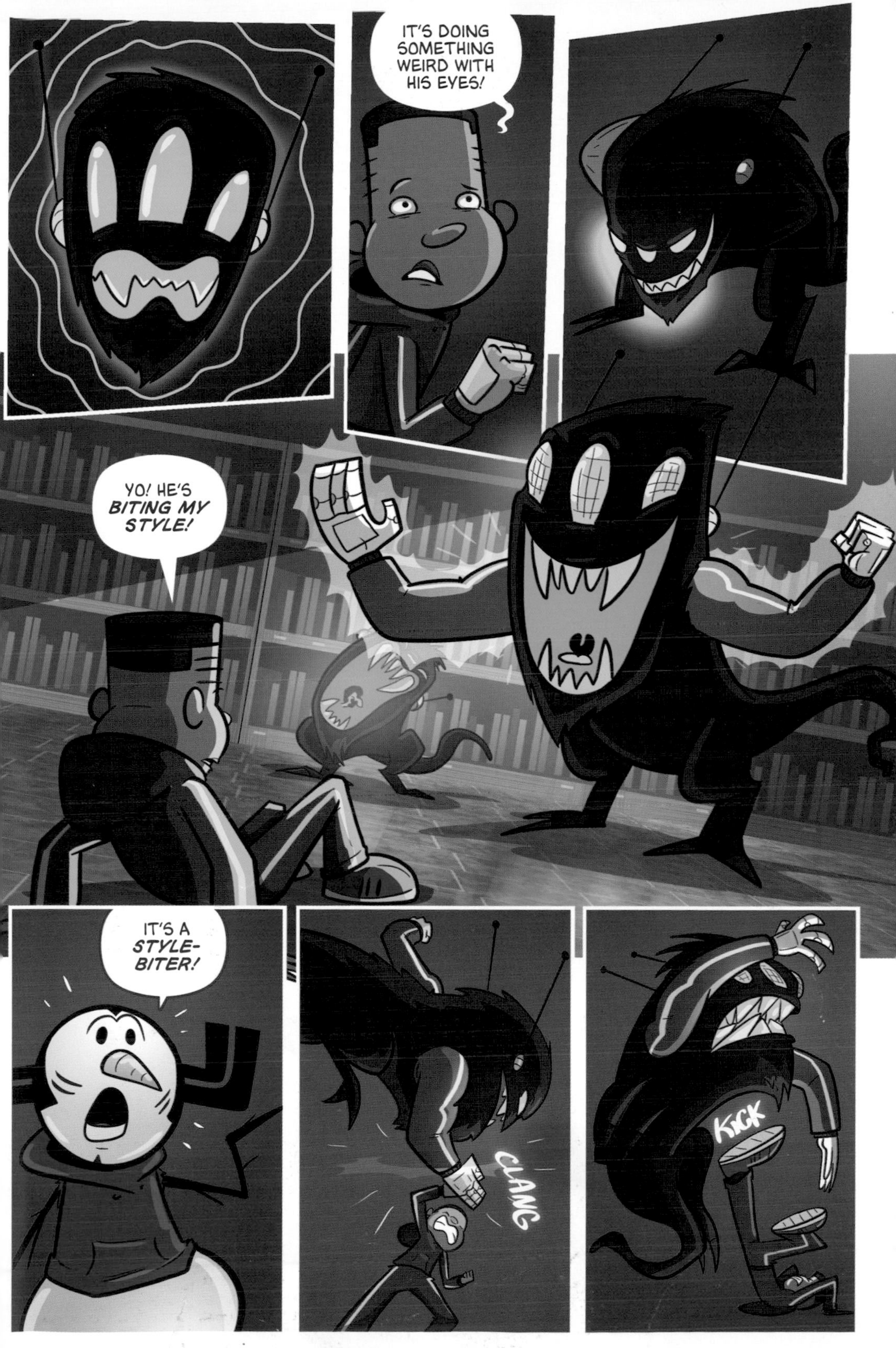
IT'S DOING SOMETHING WEIRD WITH HIS EYES!
YO! HE'S BITING MY STYLE!
IT'S A STYLE-BITER!
CLANG
KICK

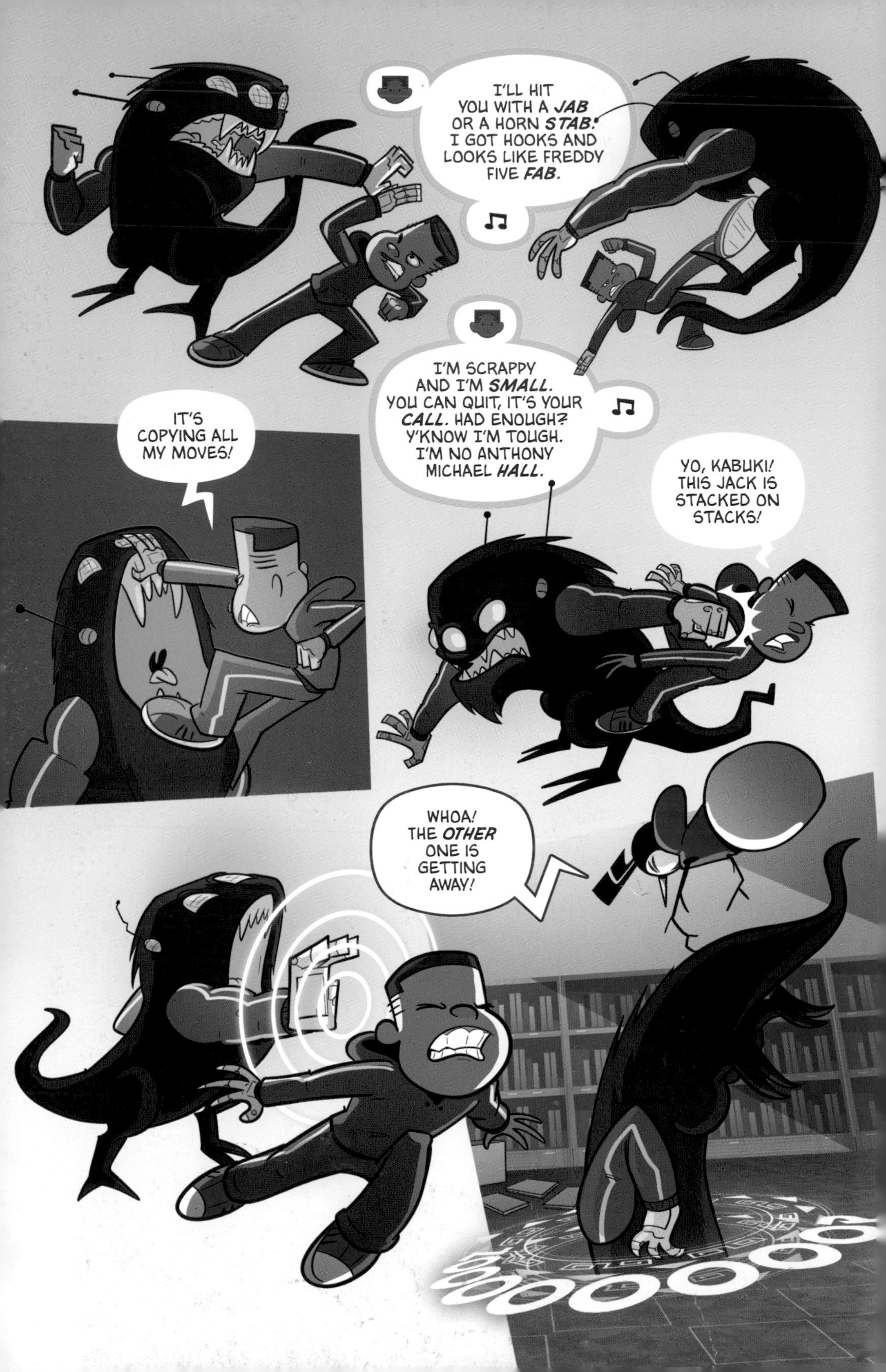
I'LL HIT YOU WITH A *JAB* OR A HORN *STAB!* I GOT HOOKS AND LOOKS LIKE FREDDY FIVE *FAB.*
I'M SCRAPPY AND I'M *SMALL.* YOU CAN QUIT, IT'S YOUR *CALL.* HAD ENOUGH? Y'KNOW I'M TOUGH. I'M NO ANTHONY MICHAEL *HALL.*
IT'S COPYING ALL MY MOVES!
YO, KABUKI! THIS JACK IS STACKED ON STACKS!
WHOA! THE *OTHER* ONE IS GETTING AWAY!
SOOOOOOOOOOOO

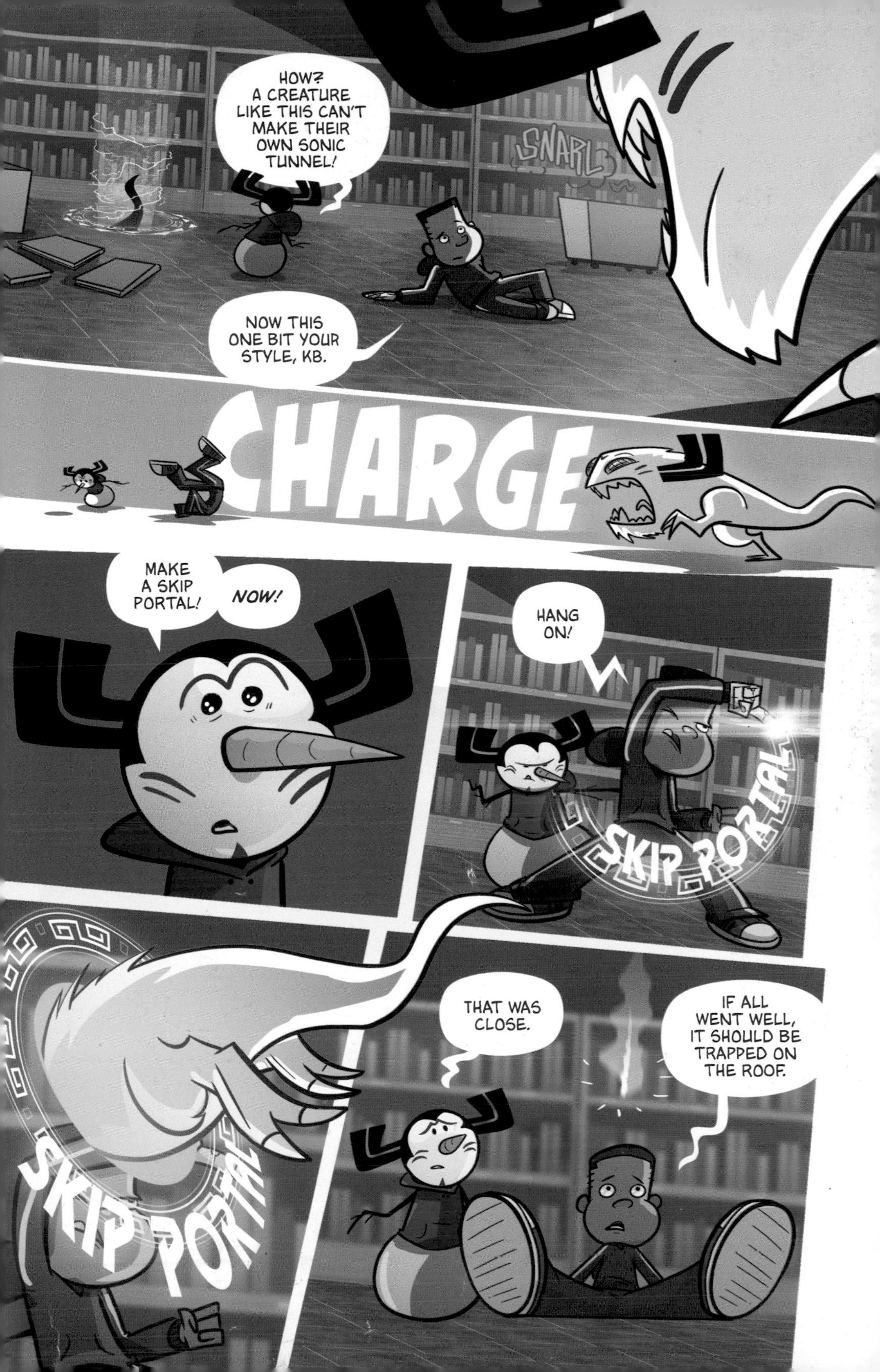
HOW? A CREATURE LIKE THIS CAN'T MAKE THEIR OWN SONIC TUNNEL!
SNARL
NOW THIS ONE BIT YOUR STYLE, KB.
CHARGE
MAKE A SKIP PORTAL!
NOW!
HANG ON!
SKIP PORTAL
SKIP PORTAL
THAT WAS CLOSE.
IF ALL WENT WELL, IT SHOULD BE TRAPPED ON THE ROOF.

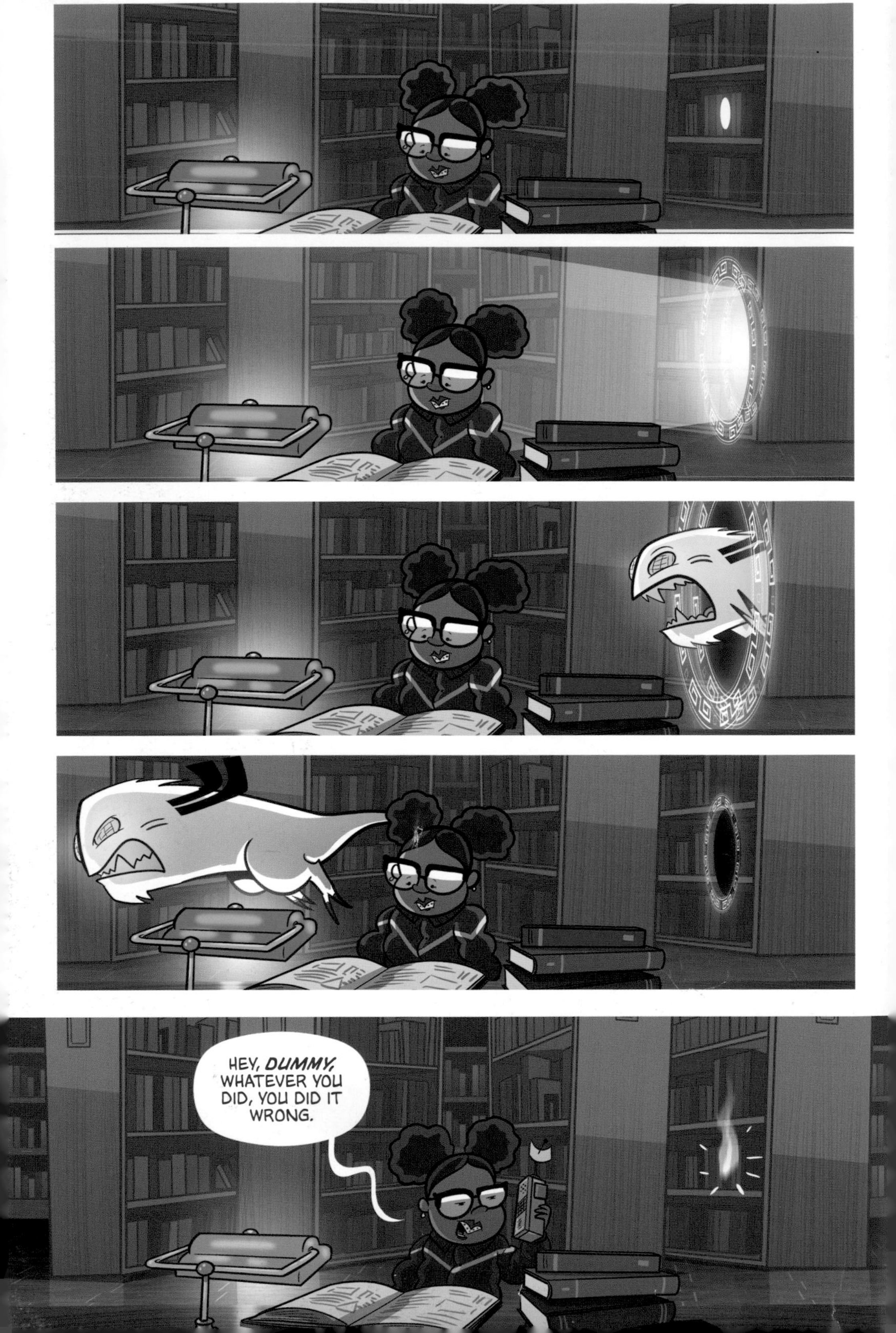
HEY, *DUMMY,* WHATEVER YOU DID, YOU DID IT WRONG.

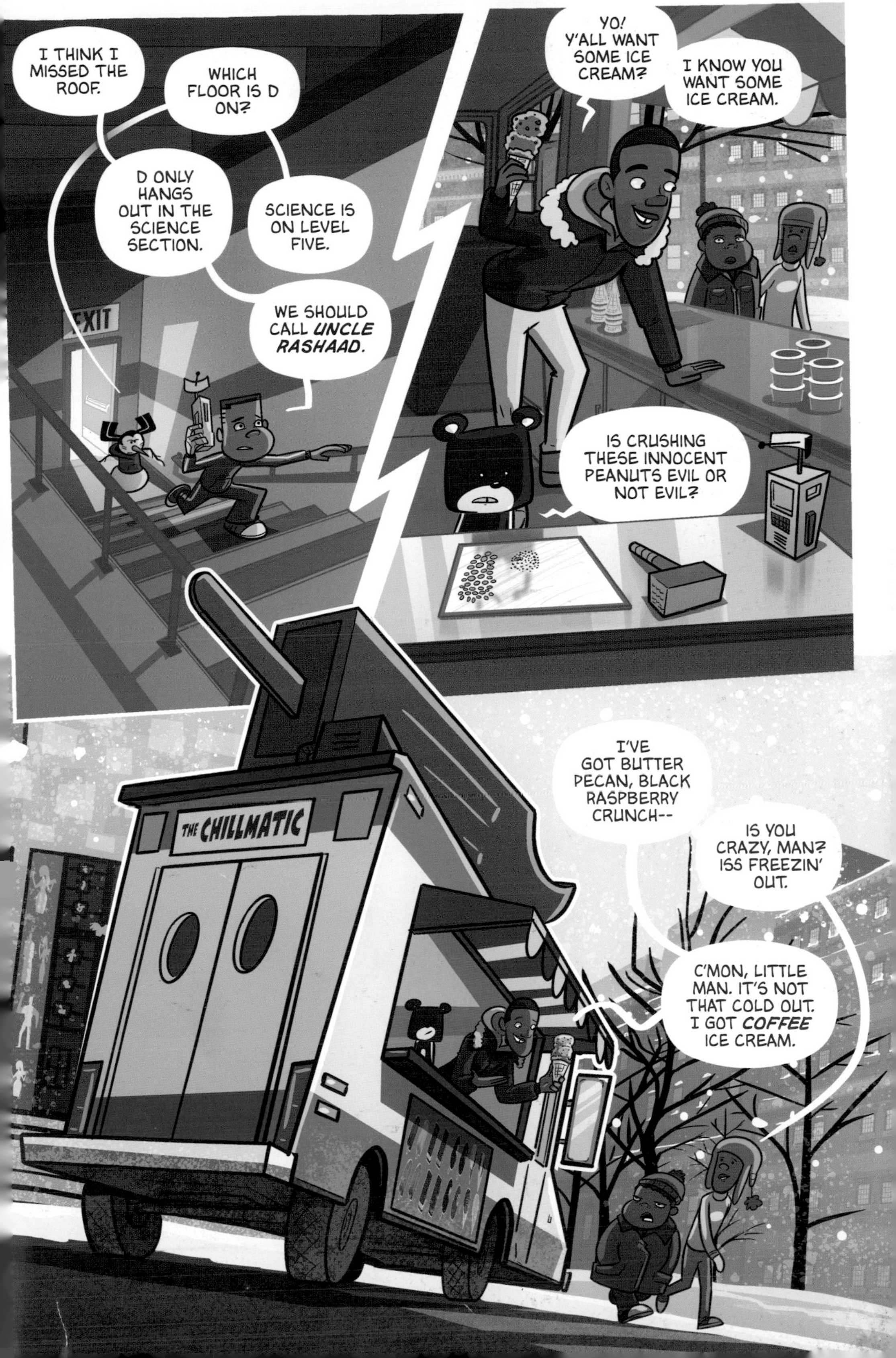
I THINK I MISSED THE ROOF.
WHICH FLOOR IS D ON?
D ONLY HANGS OUT IN THE SCIENCE SECTION.
SCIENCE IS ON LEVEL FIVE.
EXIT
WE SHOULD CALL *UNCLE RASHAAD.*
YO! Y'ALL WANT SOME ICE CREAM?
I KNOW YOU WANT SOME ICE CREAM.
IS CRUSHING THESE INNOCENT PEANUTS EVIL OR NOT EVIL?
THE CHILLMATIC
I'VE GOT BUTTER PECAN, BLACK RASPBERRY CRUNCH--
IS YOU CRAZY, MAN? ISS FREEZIN' OUT.
C'MON, LITTLE MAN. IT'S NOT THAT COLD OUT. I GOT *COFFEE* ICE CREAM.

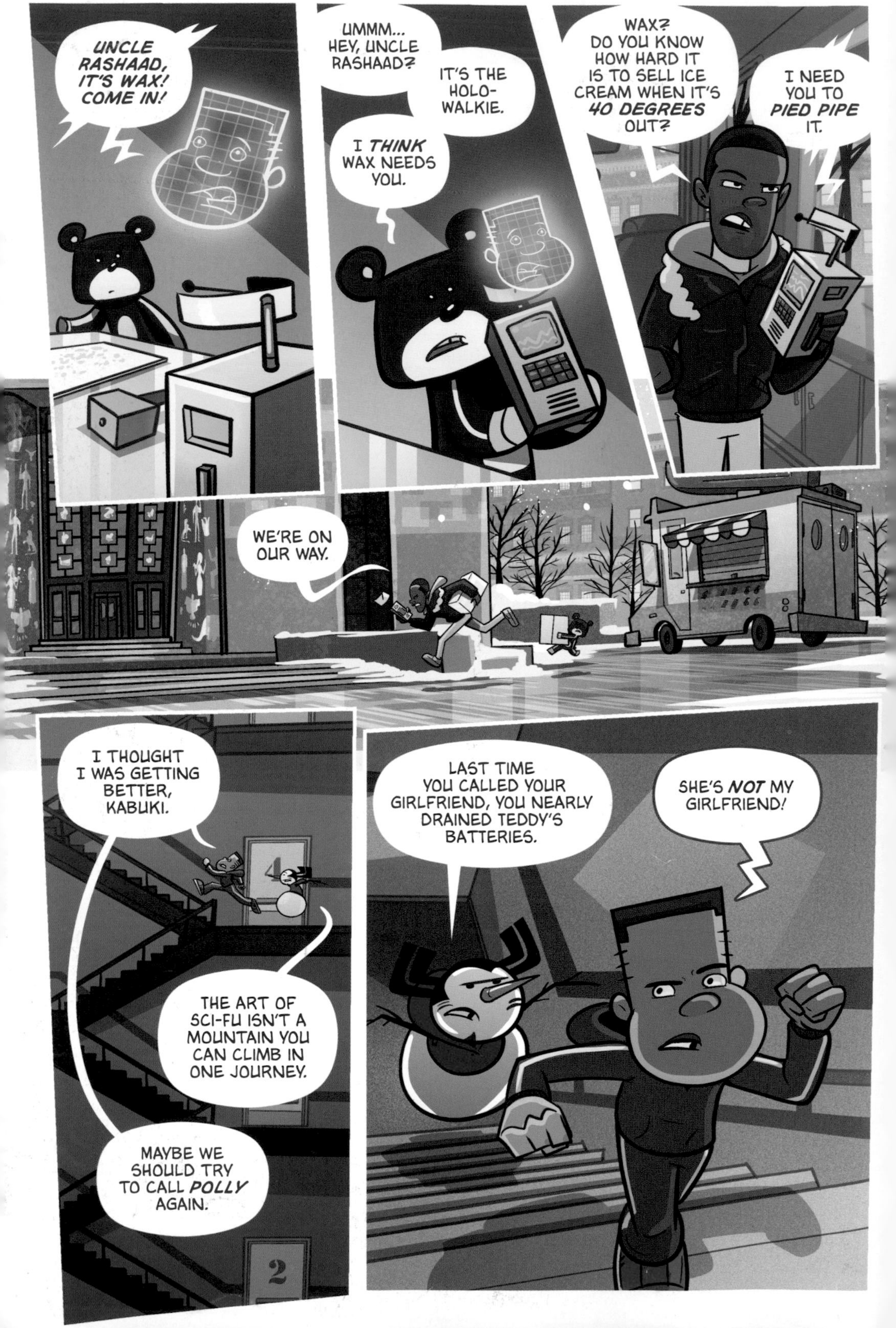
UNCLE RASHAAD, IT'S WAX! COME IN!
UMMM... HEY, UNCLE RASHAAD?
IT'S THE HOLO-WALKIE.
I THINK WAX NEEDS YOU.
WAX? DO YOU KNOW HOW HARD IT IS TO SELL ICE CREAM WHEN IT'S 40 DEGREES OUT?
I NEED YOU TO PIED PIPE IT.
WE'RE ON OUR WAY.
I THOUGHT I WAS GETTING BETTER, KABUKI.
THE ART OF SCI-FU ISN'T A MOUNTAIN YOU CAN CLIMB IN ONE JOURNEY.
MAYBE WE SHOULD TRY TO CALL POLLY AGAIN.
LAST TIME YOU CALLED YOUR GIRLFRIEND, YOU NEARLY DRAINED TEDDY'S BATTERIES.
SHE'S NOT MY GIRLFRIEND!
4
2

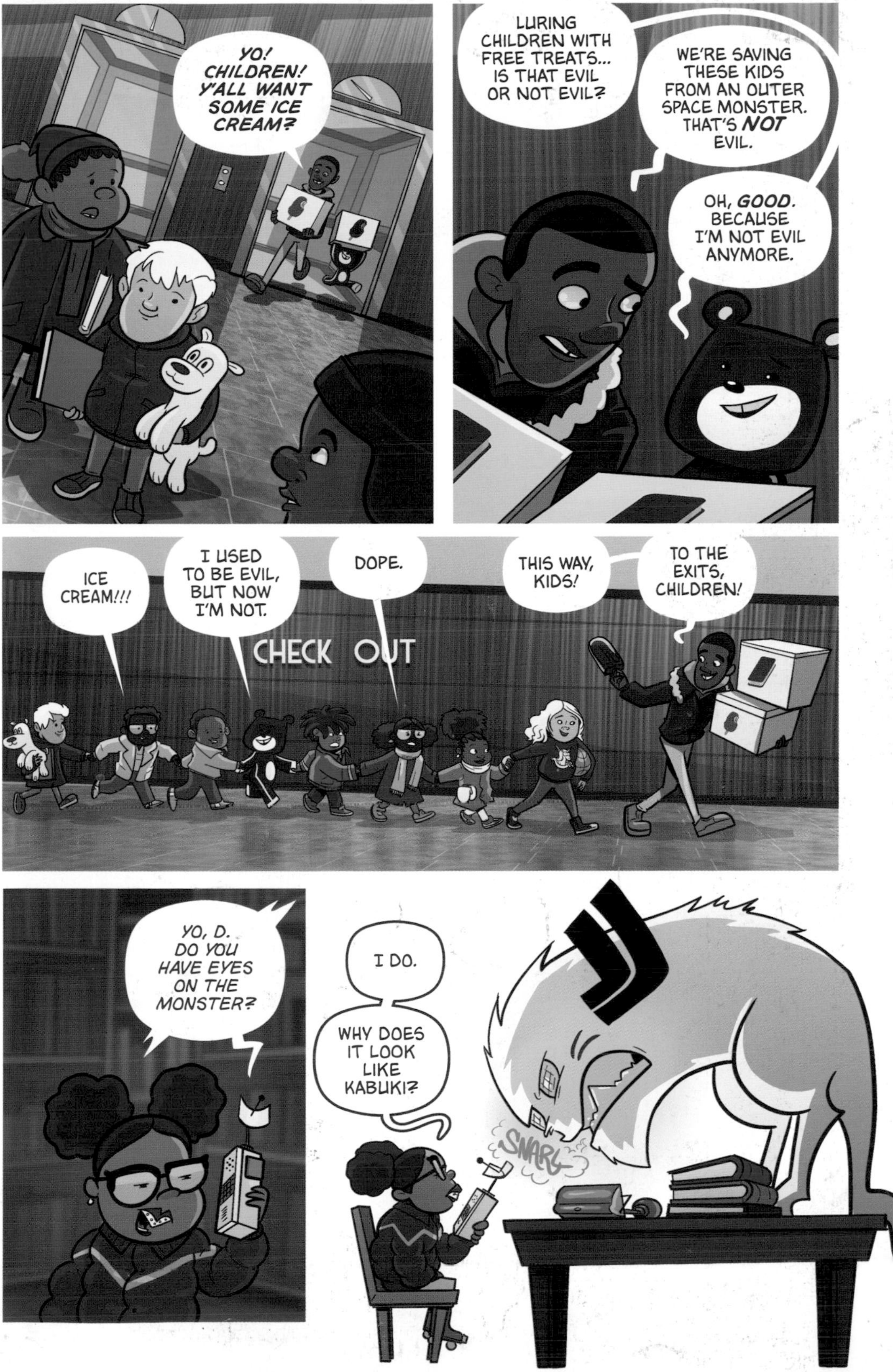
YO! CHILDREN! Y'ALL WANT SOME ICE CREAM?
LURING CHILDREN WITH FREE TREATS... IS THAT EVIL OR NOT EVIL?
WE'RE SAVING THESE KIDS FROM AN OUTER SPACE MONSTER. THAT'S NOT EVIL.
OH, GOOD. BECAUSE I'M NOT EVIL ANYMORE.
ICE CREAM!!!
I USED TO BE EVIL, BUT NOW I'M NOT.
DOPE.
THIS WAY, KIDS!
TO THE EXITS, CHILDREN!
CHECK OUT
YO, D. DO YOU HAVE EYES ON THE MONSTER?
I DO.
WHY DOES IT LOOK LIKE KABUKI?
SNARL

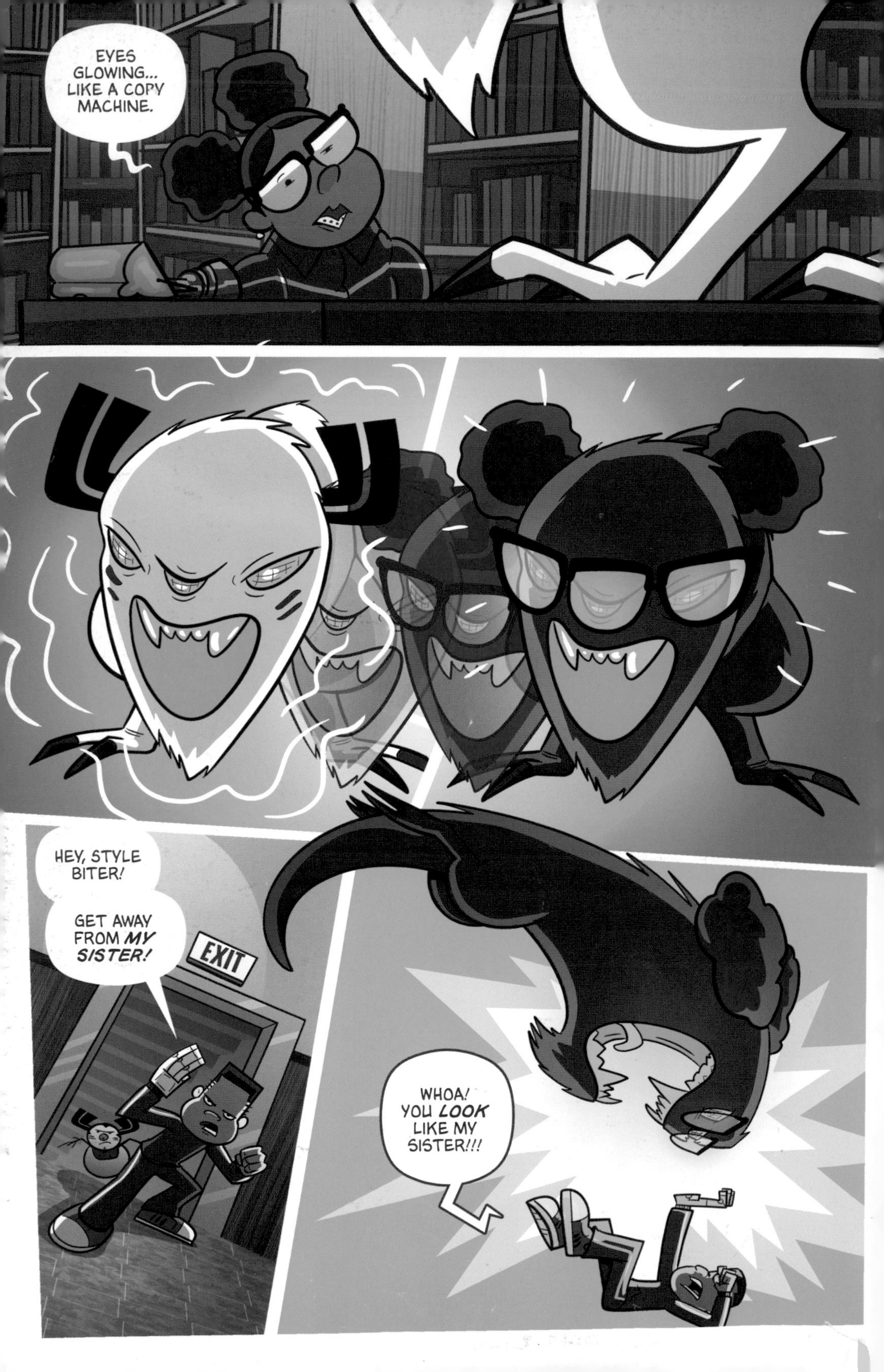
EYES GLOWING... LIKE A COPY MACHINE.
HEY, STYLE BITER!
GET AWAY FROM *MY SISTER!*
EXIT
WHOA! YOU *LOOK* LIKE MY SISTER!!!

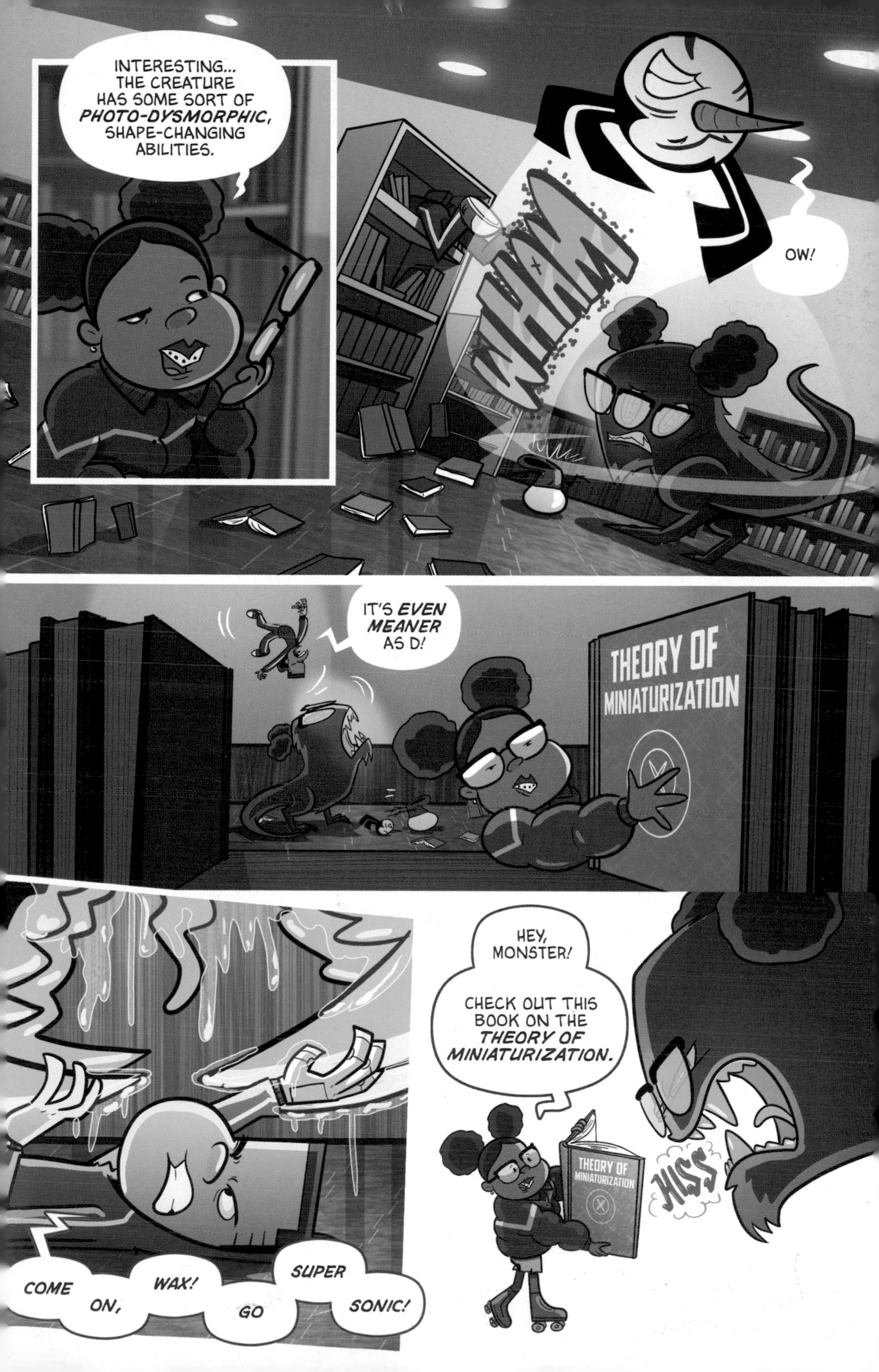
INTERESTING... THE CREATURE HAS SOME SORT OF PHOTO-DYSMORPHIC, SHAPE-CHANGING ABILITIES.
WHAM
OW!
IT'S EVEN MEANER AS D!
THEORY OF MINIATURIZATION
COME ON, WAX! GO SUPER SONIC!
HEY, MONSTER!
CHECK OUT THIS BOOK ON THE THEORY OF MINIATURIZATION.
THEORY OF MINIATURIZATION
HISS

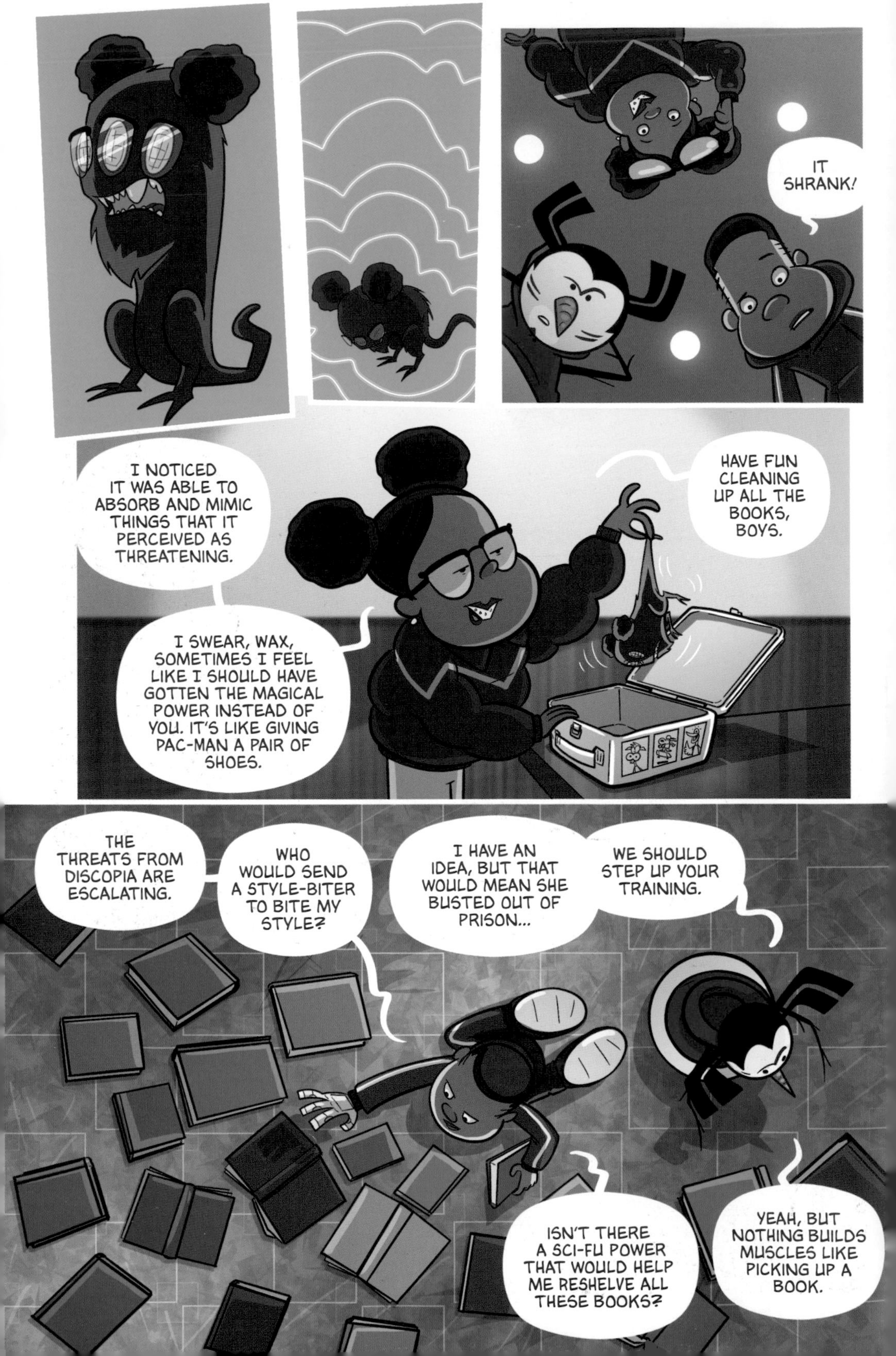
IT SHRANK!
I NOTICED IT WAS ABLE TO ABSORB AND MIMIC THINGS THAT IT PERCEIVED AS THREATENING.
HAVE FUN CLEANING UP ALL THE BOOKS, BOYS.
I SWEAR, WAX, SOMETIMES I FEEL LIKE I SHOULD HAVE GOTTEN THE MAGICAL POWER INSTEAD OF YOU. IT'S LIKE GIVING PAC-MAN A PAIR OF SHOES.
THE THREATS FROM DISCOPIA ARE ESCALATING.
WHO WOULD SEND A STYLE-BITER TO BITE MY STYLE?
I HAVE AN IDEA, BUT THAT WOULD MEAN SHE BUSTED OUT OF PRISON...
WE SHOULD STEP UP YOUR TRAINING.
ISN'T THERE A SCI-FU POWER THAT WOULD HELP ME RESHELVE ALL THESE BOOKS?
YEAH, BUT NOTHING BUILDS MUSCLES LIKE PICKING UP A BOOK.

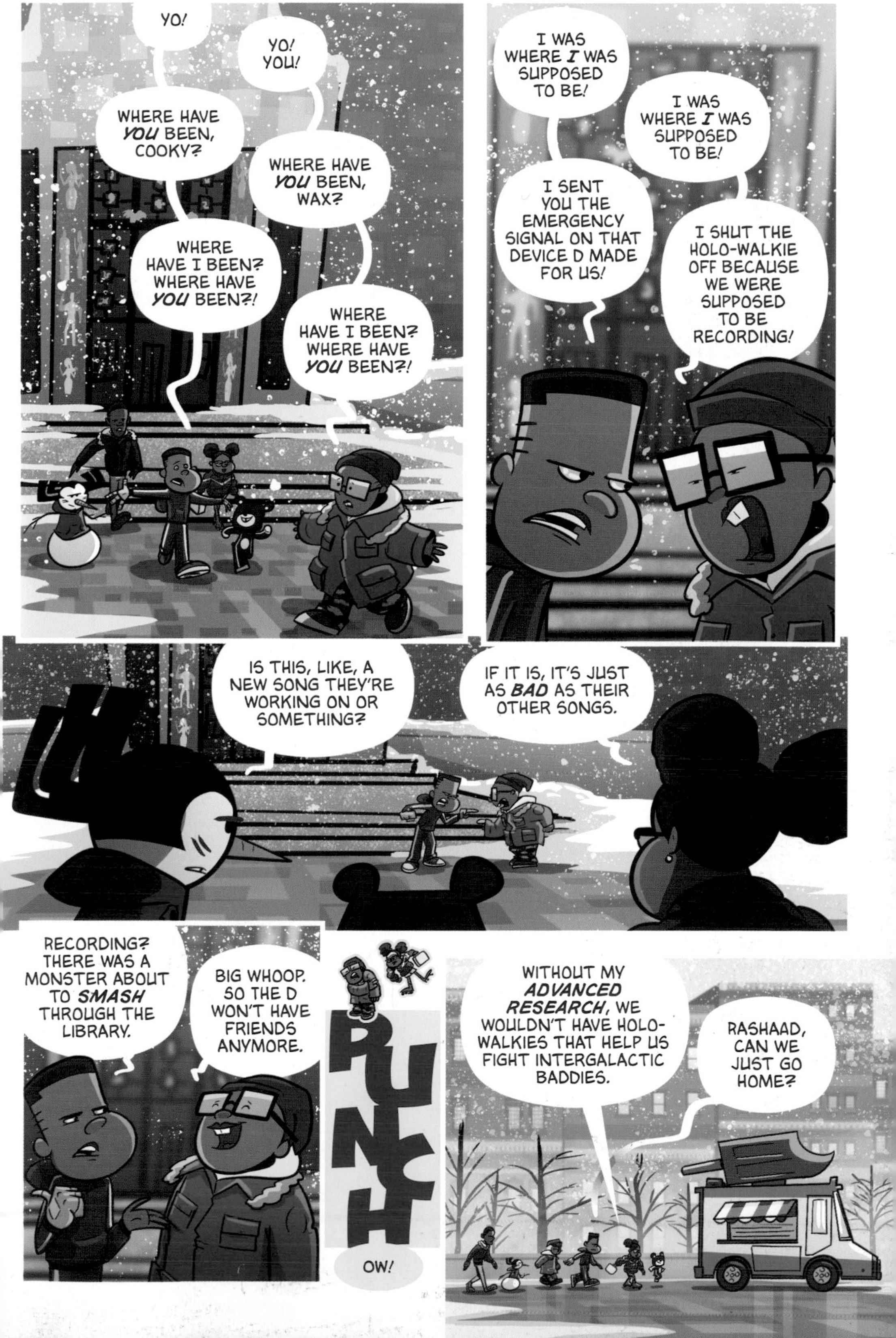
YO!
YO! YOU!
WHERE HAVE YOU BEEN, COOKY?
WHERE HAVE YOU BEEN, WAX?
WHERE HAVE I BEEN? WHERE HAVE YOU BEEN?!
WHERE HAVE I BEEN? WHERE HAVE YOU BEEN?!
I WAS WHERE I WAS SUPPOSED TO BE!
I WAS WHERE I WAS SUPPOSED TO BE!
I SENT YOU THE EMERGENCY SIGNAL ON THAT DEVICE D MADE FOR US!
I SHUT THE HOLO-WALKIE OFF BECAUSE WE WERE SUPPOSED TO BE RECORDING!
IS THIS, LIKE, A NEW SONG THEY'RE WORKING ON OR SOMETHING?
IF IT IS, IT'S JUST AS BAD AS THEIR OTHER SONGS.
RECORDING? THERE WAS A MONSTER ABOUT TO SMASH THROUGH THE LIBRARY.
BIG WHOOP. SO THE D WON'T HAVE FRIENDS ANYMORE.
PUNCH
OW!
WITHOUT MY ADVANCED RESEARCH, WE WOULDN'T HAVE HOLO-WALKIES THAT HELP US FIGHT INTERGALACTIC BADDIES.
RASHAAD, CAN WE JUST GO HOME?

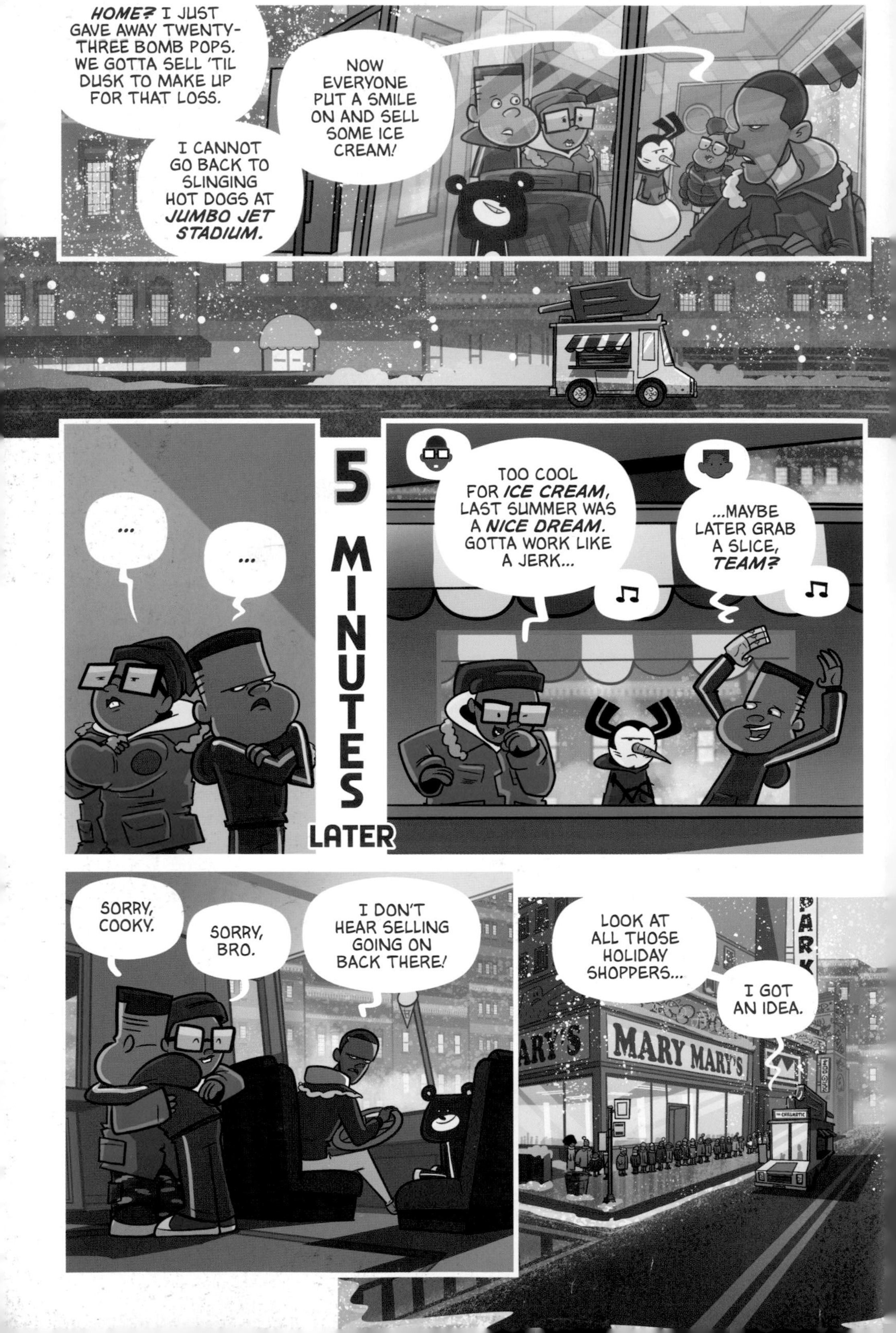
HOME? I JUST GAVE AWAY TWENTY-THREE BOMB POPS. WE GOTTA SELL 'TIL DUSK TO MAKE UP FOR THAT LOSS.
I CANNOT GO BACK TO SLINGING HOT DOGS AT JUMBO JET STADIUM.
NOW EVERYONE PUT A SMILE ON AND SELL SOME ICE CREAM!
...
...
5 MINUTES LATER
TOO COOL FOR ICE CREAM, LAST SUMMER WAS A NICE DREAM. GOTTA WORK LIKE A JERK...
♫
...MAYBE LATER GRAB A SLICE, TEAM?
♫
SORRY, COOKY.
SORRY, BRO.
I DON'T HEAR SELLING GOING ON BACK THERE!
LOOK AT ALL THOSE HOLIDAY SHOPPERS...
I GOT AN IDEA.
MARY MARY'S

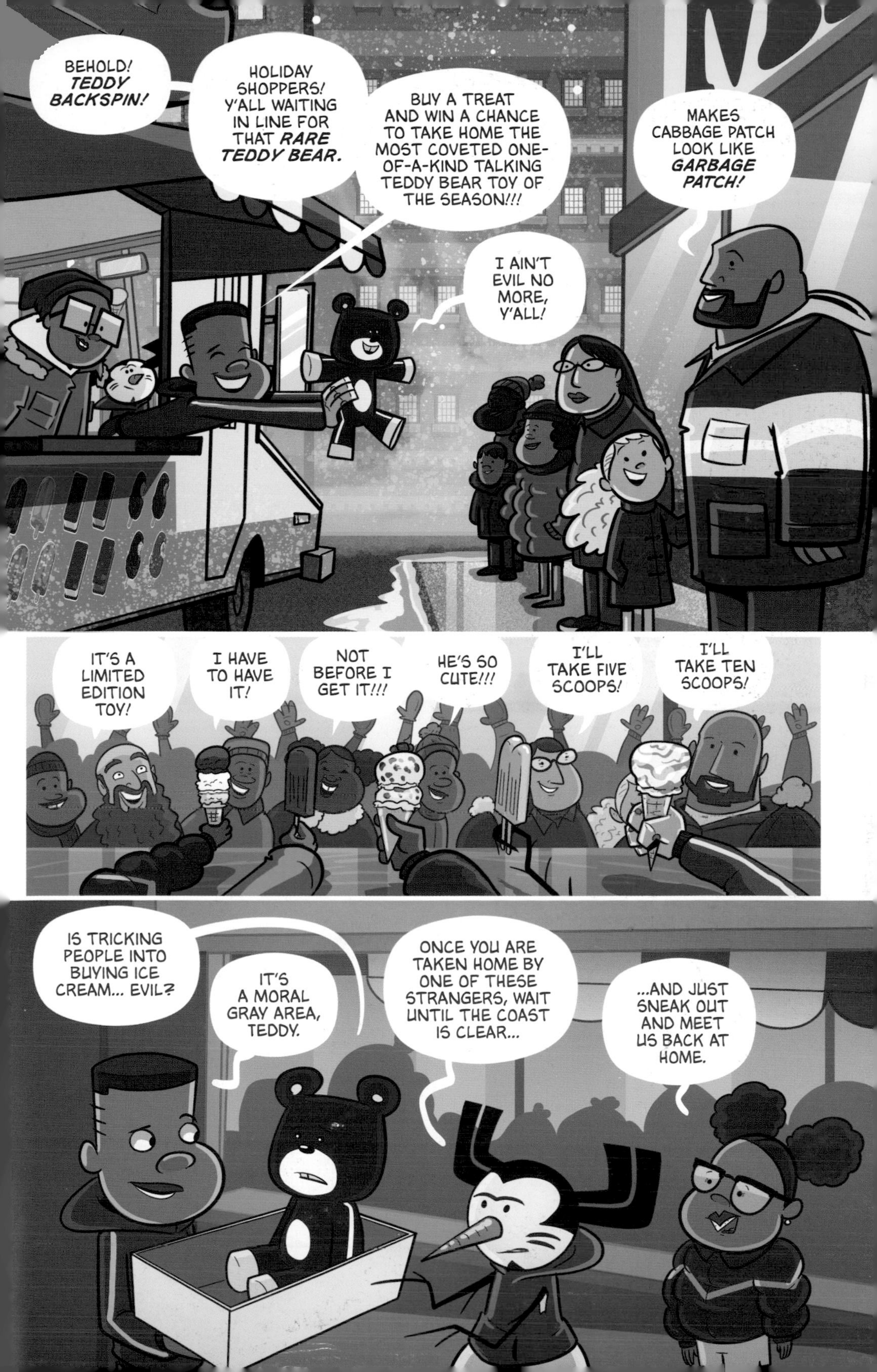
BEHOLD! TEDDY BACKSPIN!
HOLIDAY SHOPPERS! Y'ALL WAITING IN LINE FOR THAT RARE TEDDY BEAR.
BUY A TREAT AND WIN A CHANCE TO TAKE HOME THE MOST COVETED ONE-OF-A-KIND TALKING TEDDY BEAR TOY OF THE SEASON!!!
MAKES CABBAGE PATCH LOOK LIKE GARBAGE PATCH!
I AIN'T EVIL NO MORE, Y'ALL!
IT'S A LIMITED EDITION TOY!
I HAVE TO HAVE IT!
NOT BEFORE I GET IT!!!
HE'S SO CUTE!!!
I'LL TAKE FIVE SCOOPS!
I'LL TAKE TEN SCOOPS!
IS TRICKING PEOPLE INTO BUYING ICE CREAM... EVIL?
IT'S A MORAL GRAY AREA, TEDDY.
ONCE YOU ARE TAKEN HOME BY ONE OF THESE STRANGERS, WAIT UNTIL THE COAST IS CLEAR...
...AND JUST SNEAK OUT AND MEET US BACK AT HOME.

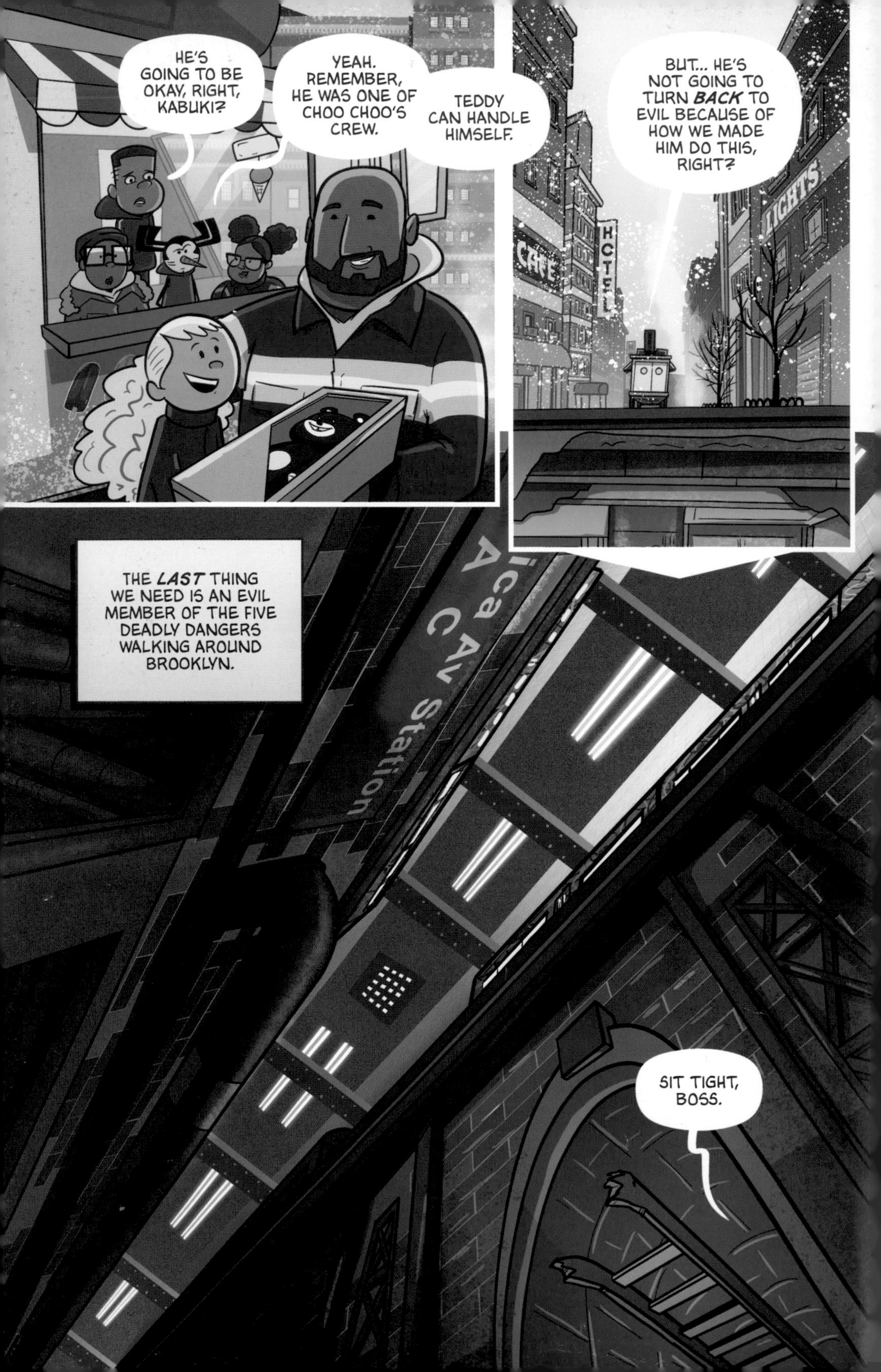
HE'S GOING TO BE OKAY, RIGHT, KABUKI?
YEAH. REMEMBER, HE WAS ONE OF CHOO CHOO'S CREW.
TEDDY CAN HANDLE HIMSELF.
CAFE
HOTEL
LIGHTS
BUT... HE'S NOT GOING TO TURN *BACK* TO EVIL BECAUSE OF HOW WE MADE HIM DO THIS, RIGHT?
THE *LAST* THING WE NEED IS AN EVIL MEMBER OF THE FIVE DEADLY DANGERS WALKING AROUND BROOKLYN.
ica A Av Station
SIT TIGHT, BOSS.

ONCE WE FIX YOUR BATTERY, YOU'LL BE BACK IN *FIGHTING SHAPE.*
ONCE YOU'RE IN FIGHTING SHAPE, YOU CAN GET *BACK THE CROWN.*
ONCE YOU HAVE THE CROWN, WE CAN GET *BACK TO DISCOPIA.*
HEY! LOOK AT THAT!
TEDDY IS AWAY FROM WAX AND THE REST OF THE CREW.
WE CAN TOTALLY USE HIS BATTERY.
5
TURN THE FIVE DEADLY DANGERS TRANSPONDER BACK ON.
YOU GOT IT, *CHOO CHOO.*
YOU'RE A GOOD FRIEND, *CHICKEN WICKED RHYMES.*

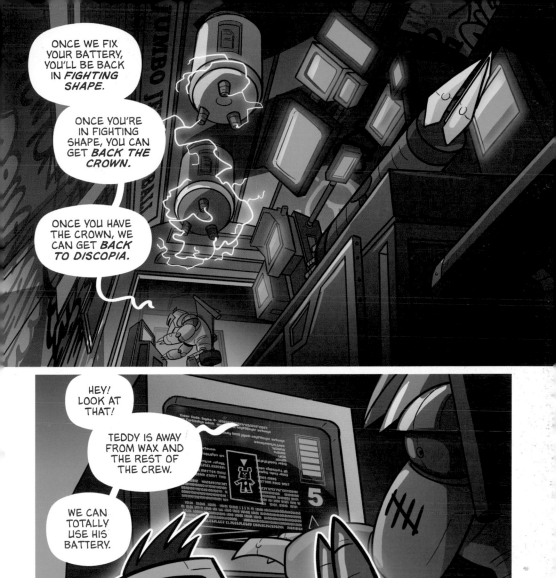

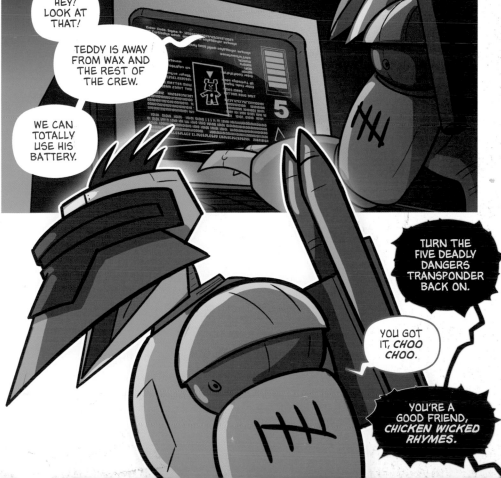

TRACK

2

ALWAYS ON TIME

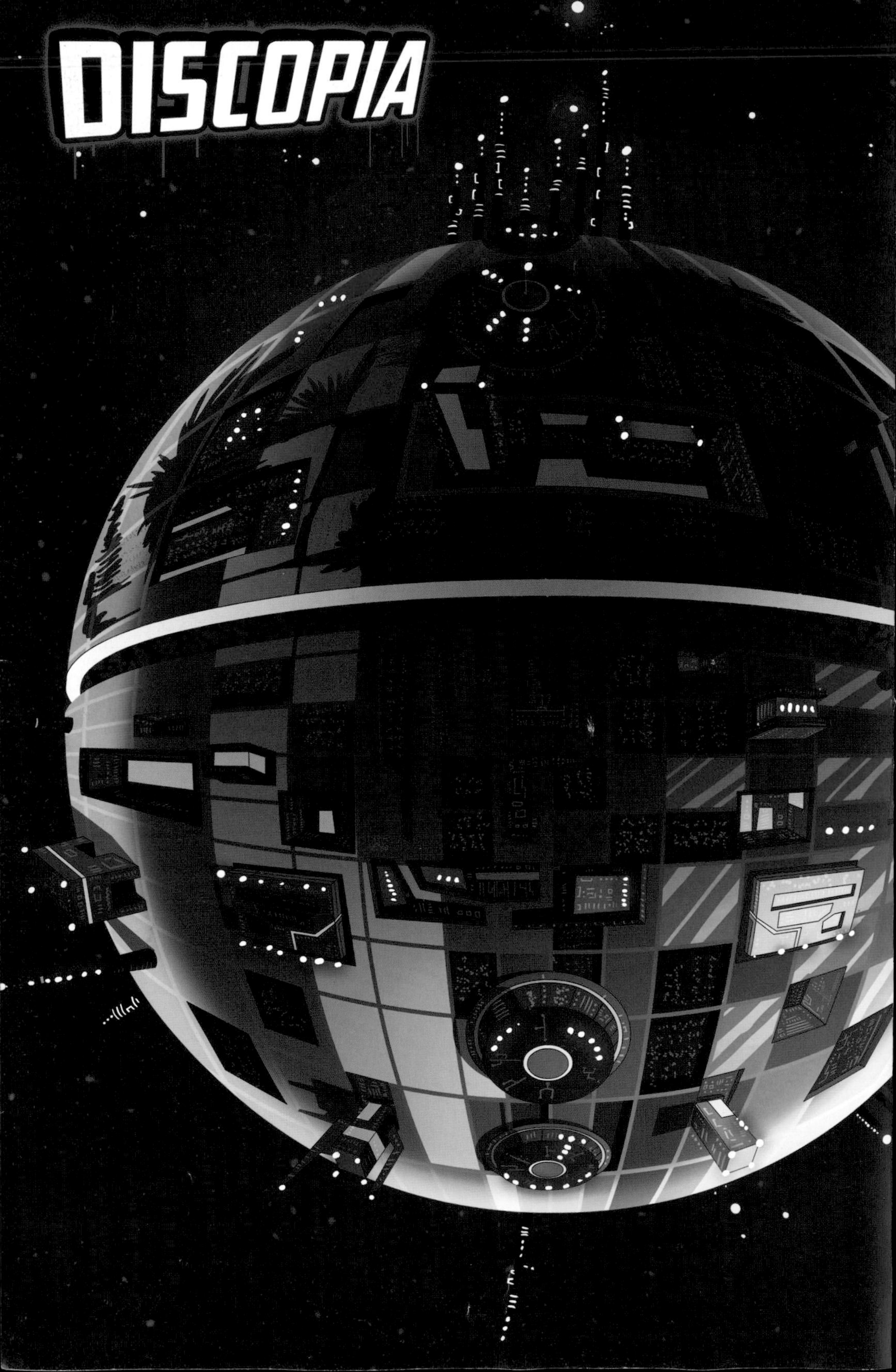
DISCOPIA

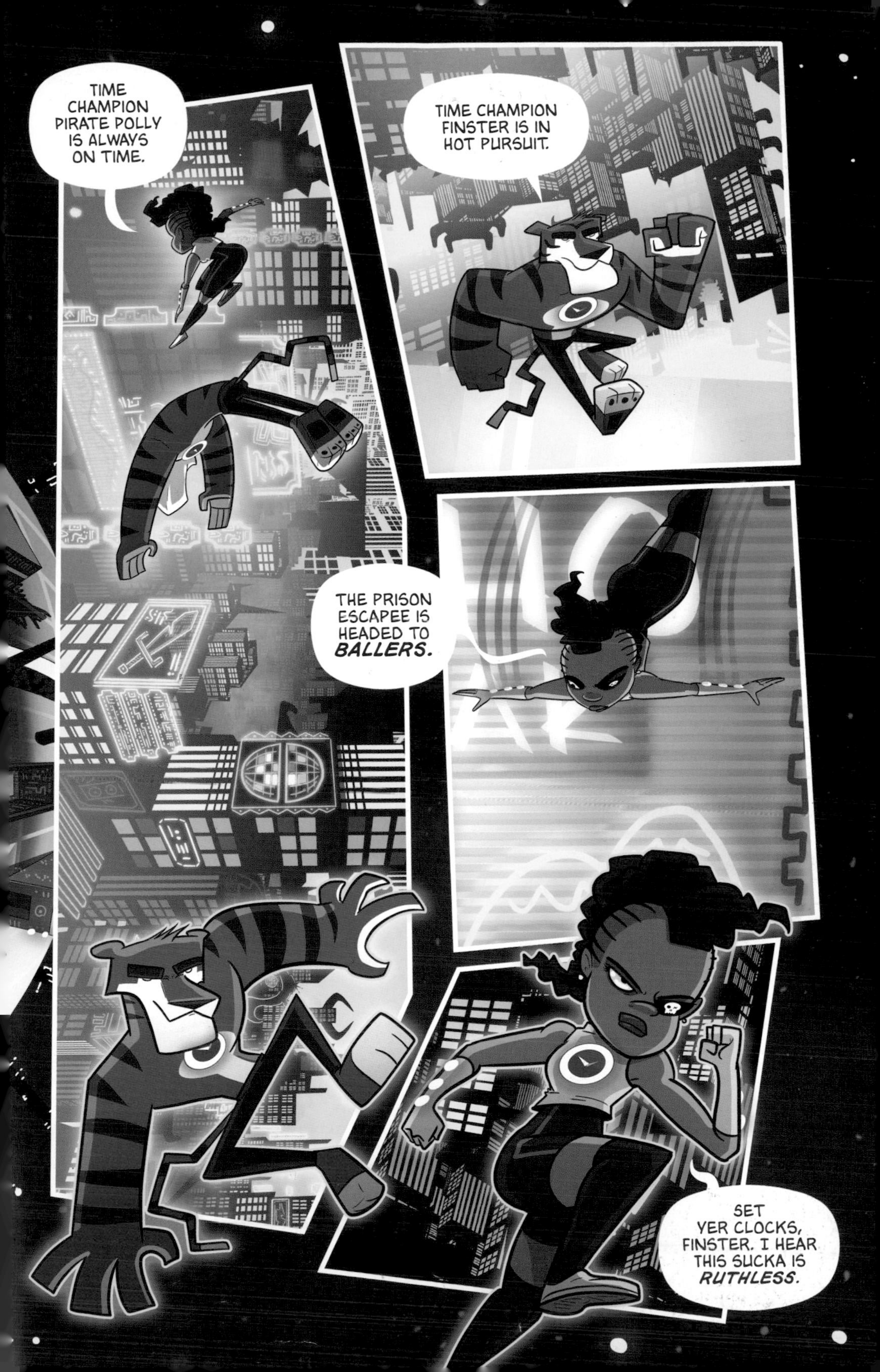
TIME CHAMPION PIRATE POLLY IS ALWAYS ON TIME.
TIME CHAMPION FINSTER IS IN HOT PURSUIT.
THE PRISON ESCAPEE IS HEADED TO **BALLERS.**
SET YER CLOCKS, FINSTER. I HEAR THIS SUCKA IS ***RUTHLESS.***

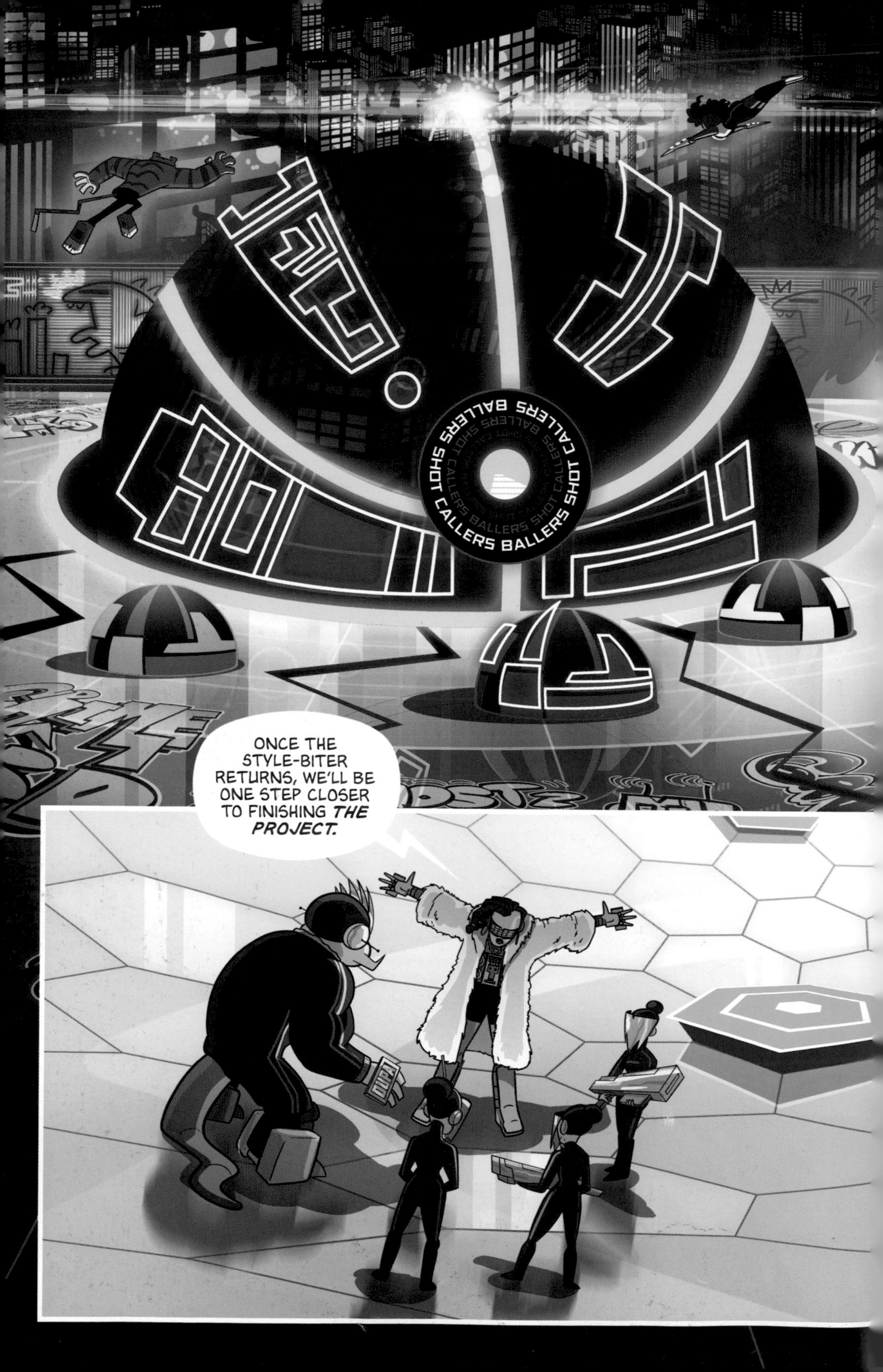
SHOT CALLERS BALLERS
ONCE THE STYLE-BITER RETURNS, WE'LL BE ONE STEP CLOSER TO FINISHING *THE PROJECT.*

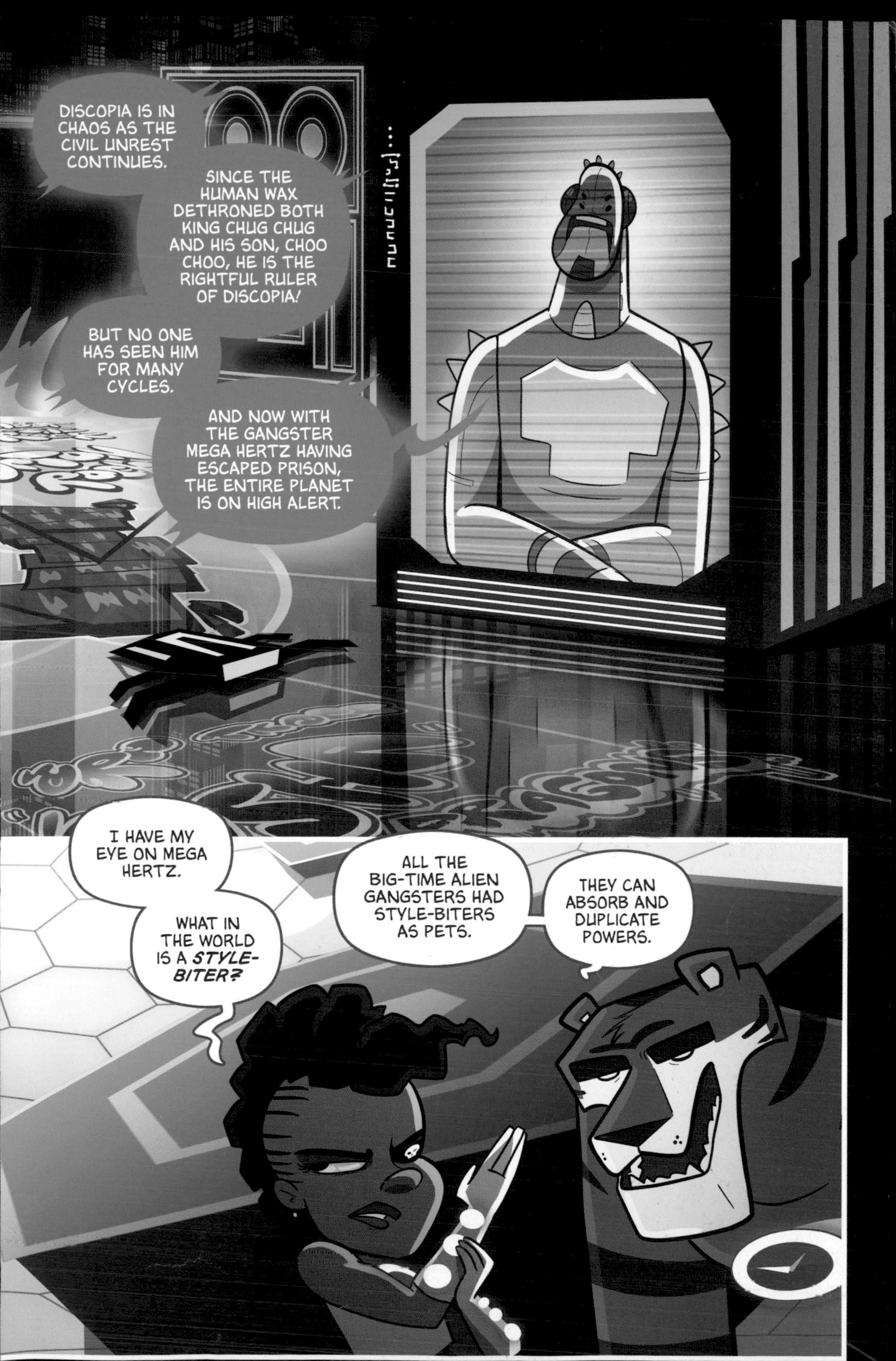
DISCOPIA IS IN CHAOS AS THE CIVIL UNREST CONTINUES.
SINCE THE HUMAN WAX DETHRONED BOTH KING CHUG CHUG AND HIS SON, CHOO CHOO, HE IS THE RIGHTFUL RULER OF DISCOPIA!
BUT NO ONE HAS SEEN HIM FOR MANY CYCLES.
AND NOW WITH THE GANGSTER MEGA HERTZ HAVING ESCAPED PRISON, THE ENTIRE PLANET IS ON HIGH ALERT.
I HAVE MY EYE ON MEGA HERTZ.
WHAT IN THE WORLD IS A *STYLE-BITER?*
ALL THE BIG-TIME ALIEN GANGSTERS HAD STYLE-BITERS AS PETS.
THEY CAN ABSORB AND DUPLICATE POWERS.

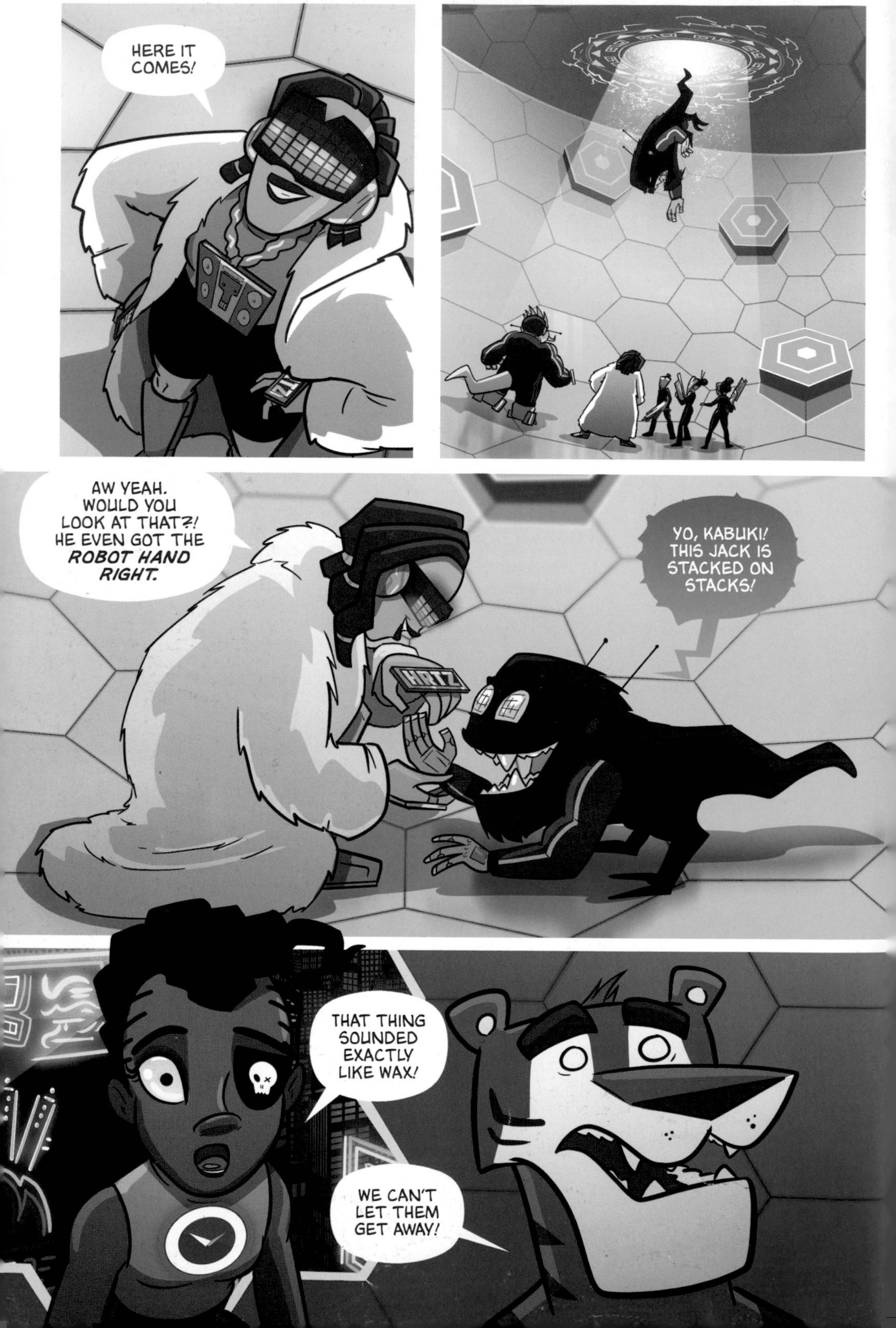
HERE IT COMES!
AW YEAH. WOULD YOU LOOK AT THAT?! HE EVEN GOT THE *ROBOT HAND RIGHT.*
YO, KABUKI! THIS JACK IS STACKED ON STACKS!
HRTZ
THAT THING SOUNDED EXACTLY LIKE WAX!
WE CAN'T LET THEM GET AWAY!

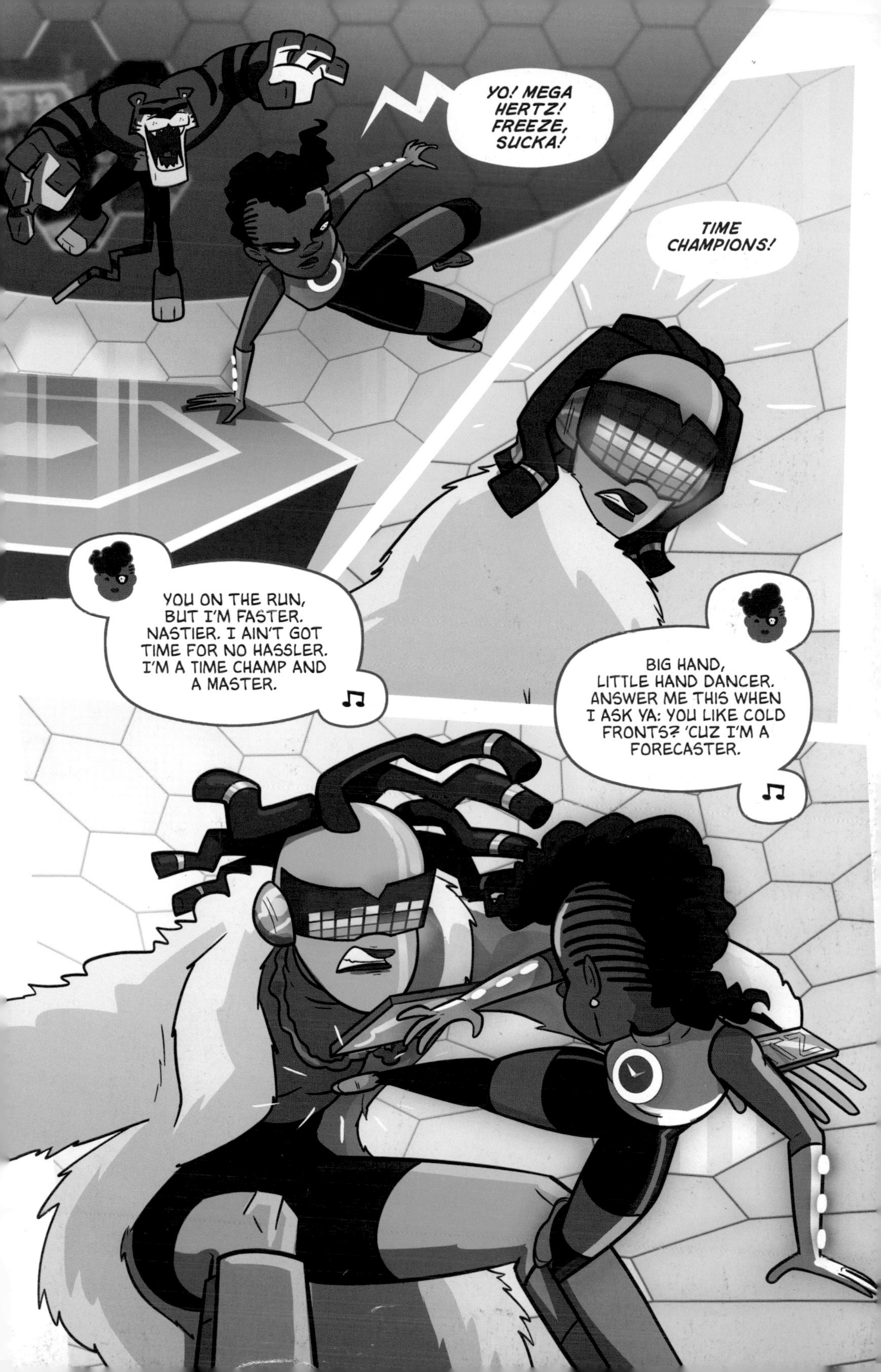
YO! MEGA HERTZ! FREEZE, SUCKA!
TIME CHAMPIONS!
YOU ON THE RUN, BUT I'M FASTER. NASTIER. I AIN'T GOT TIME FOR NO HASSLER. I'M A TIME CHAMP AND A MASTER.
BIG HAND, LITTLE HAND DANCER. ANSWER ME THIS WHEN I ASK YA: YOU LIKE COLD FRONTS? 'CUZ I'M A FORECASTER.

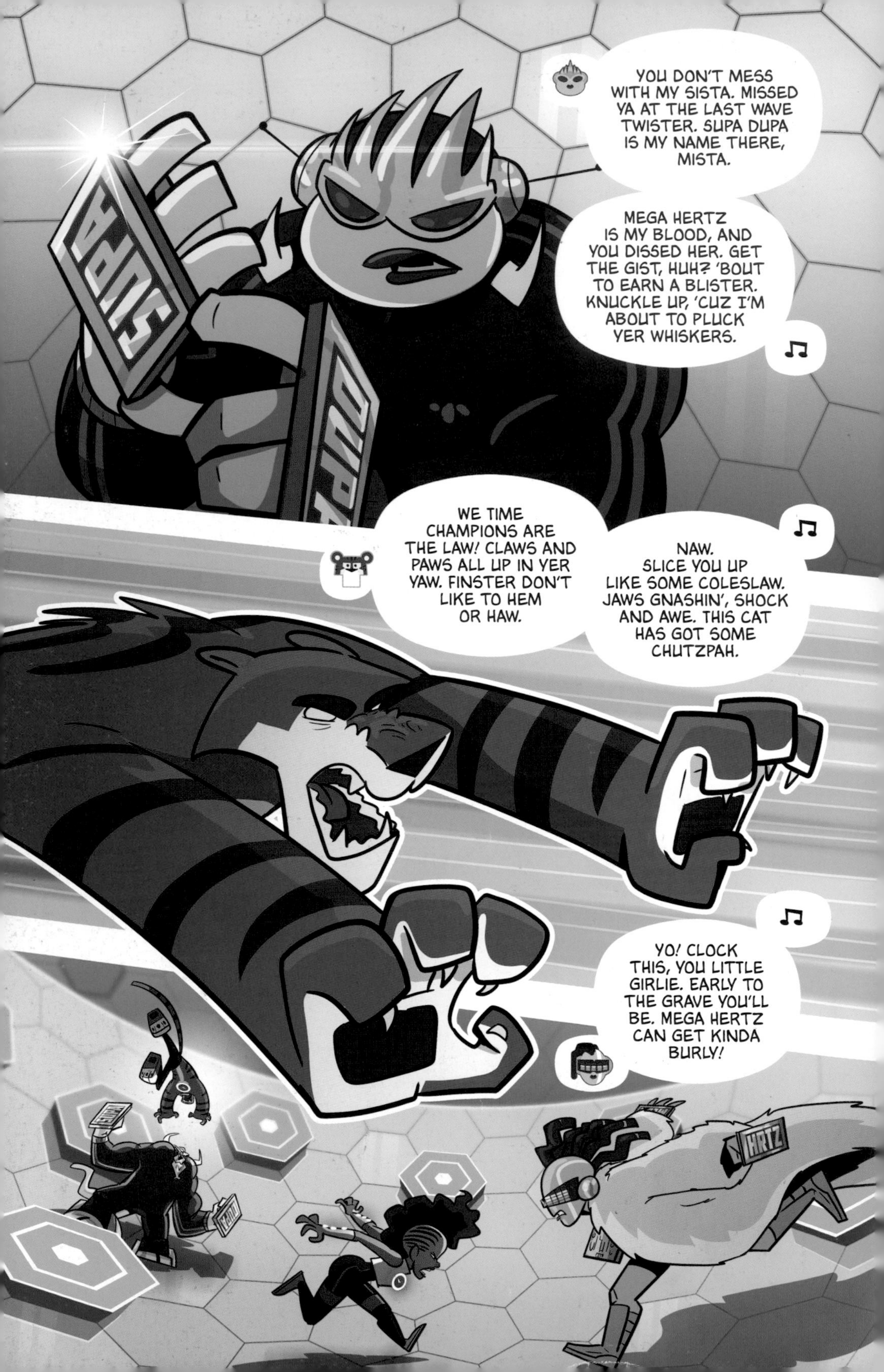

YOU DON'T MESS WITH MY SISTA. MISSED YA AT THE LAST WAVE TWISTER. SUPA DUPA IS MY NAME THERE, MISTA.
MEGA HERTZ IS MY BLOOD, AND YOU DISSED HER. GET THE GIST, HUH? 'BOUT TO EARN A BLISTER. KNUCKLE UP, 'CUZ I'M ABOUT TO PLUCK YER WHISKERS.
SUPA
DUPA
WE TIME CHAMPIONS ARE THE LAW! CLAWS AND PAWS ALL UP IN YER YAW. FINSTER DON'T LIKE TO HEM OR HAW.
NAW. SLICE YOU UP LIKE SOME COLESLAW. JAWS GNASHIN', SHOCK AND AWE. THIS CAT HAS GOT SOME CHUTZPAH.
YO! CLOCK THIS, YOU LITTLE GIRLIE. EARLY TO THE GRAVE YOU'LL BE. MEGA HERTZ CAN GET KINDA BURLY!
HRTZ

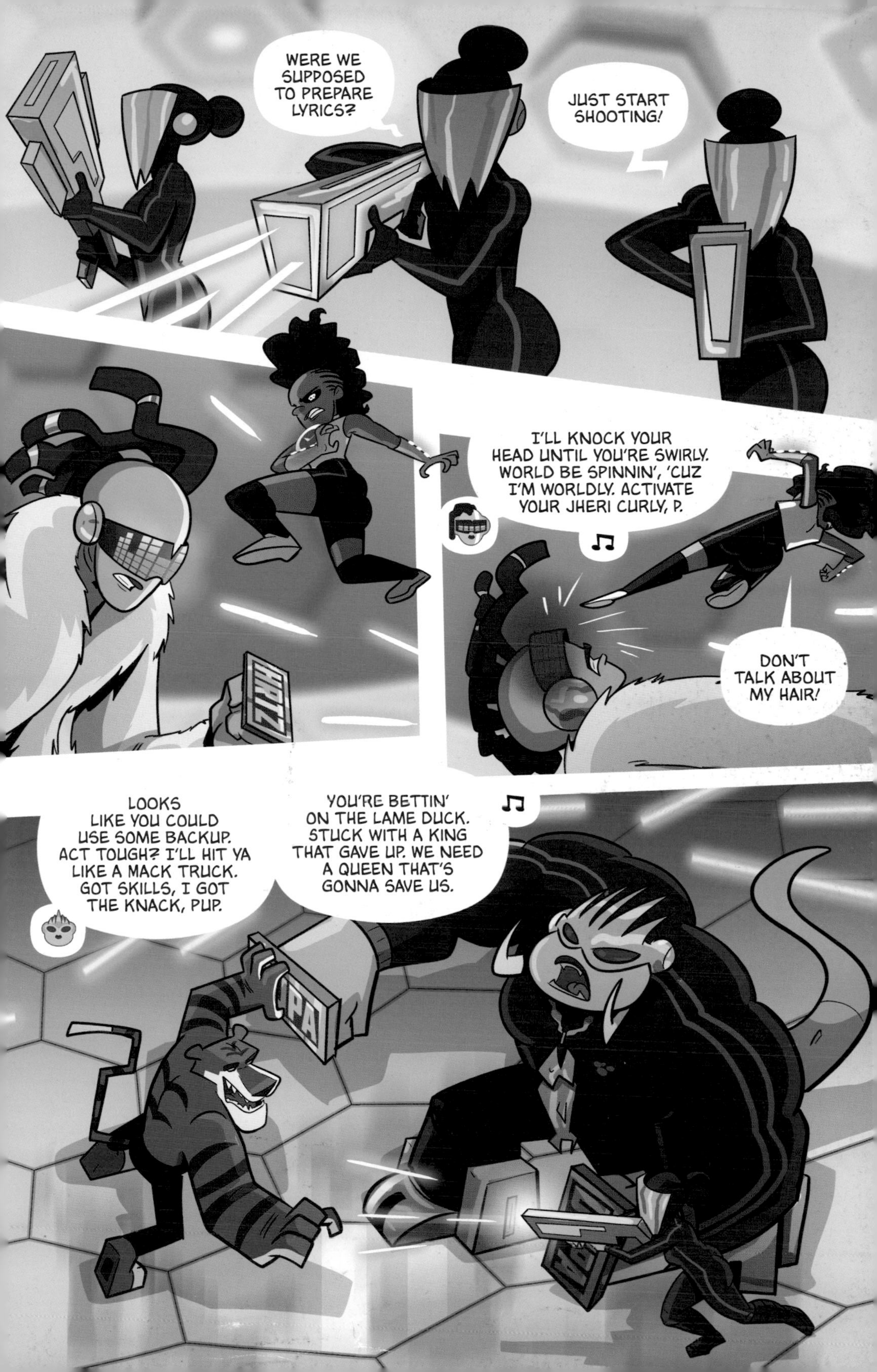
WERE WE SUPPOSED TO PREPARE LYRICS?
JUST START SHOOTING!
HRTZ
I'LL KNOCK YOUR HEAD UNTIL YOU'RE SWIRLY. WORLD BE SPINNIN', 'CUZ I'M WORLDLY. ACTIVATE YOUR JHERI CURLY, P.
DON'T TALK ABOUT MY HAIR!
LOOKS LIKE YOU COULD USE SOME BACKUP. ACT TOUGH? I'LL HIT YA LIKE A MACK TRUCK. GOT SKILLS, I GOT THE KNACK, PUP.
YOU'RE BETTIN' ON THE LAME DUCK. STUCK WITH A KING THAT GAVE UP. WE NEED A QUEEN THAT'S GONNA SAVE US.
PA

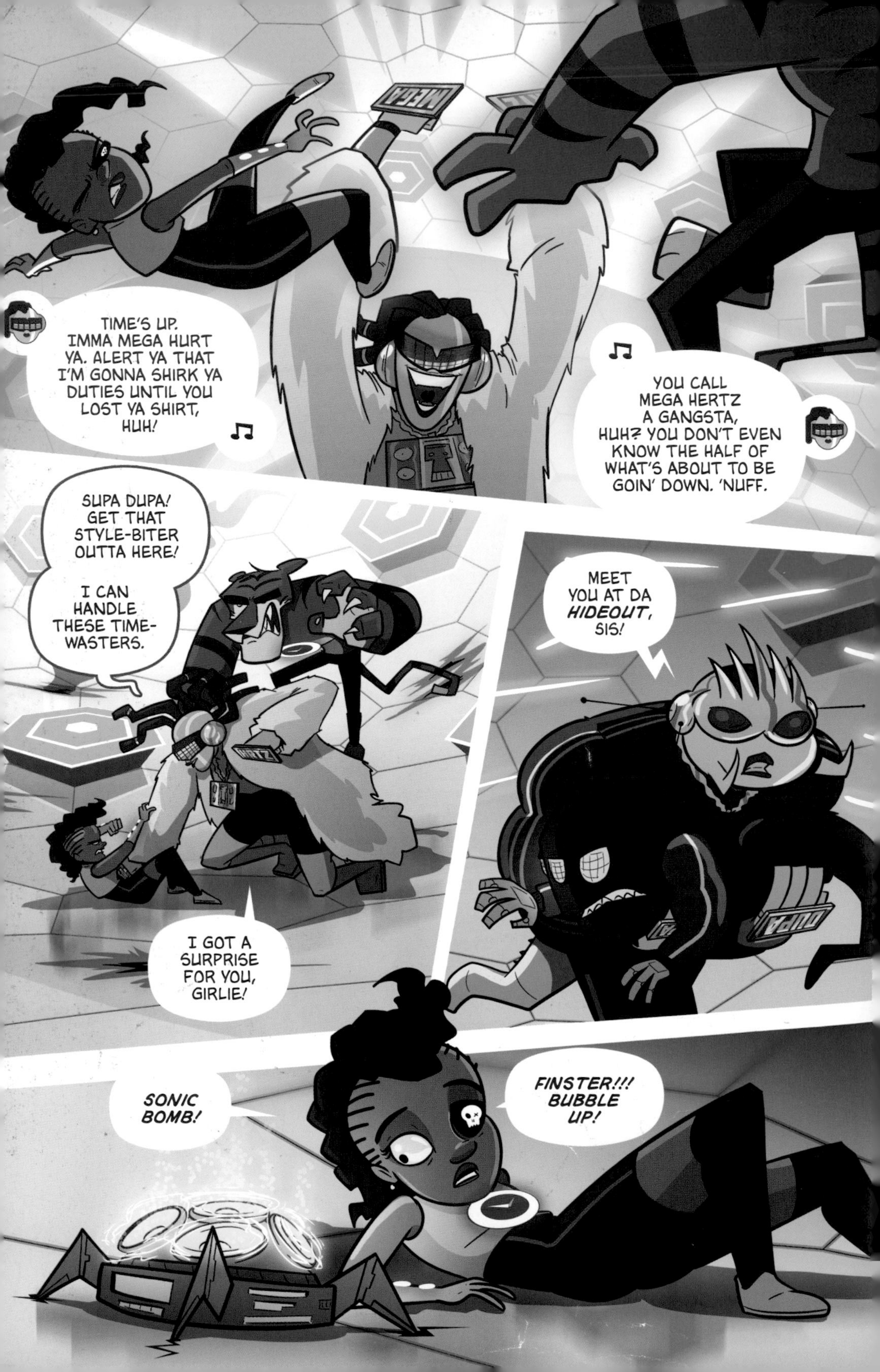
MEGA
TIME'S UP. IMMA MEGA HURT YA. ALERT YA THAT I'M GONNA SHIRK YA DUTIES UNTIL YOU LOST YA SHIRT, HUH!
YOU CALL MEGA HERTZ A GANGSTA, HUH? YOU DON'T EVEN KNOW THE HALF OF WHAT'S ABOUT TO BE GOIN' DOWN. 'NUFF.
SUPA DUPA! GET THAT STYLE-BITER OUTTA HERE!
I CAN HANDLE THESE TIME-WASTERS.
HERTZ
I GOT A SURPRISE FOR YOU, GIRLIE!
MEET YOU AT DA *HIDEOUT*, SIS!
DUPA
SONIC BOMB!
FINSTER!!! BUBBLE UP!

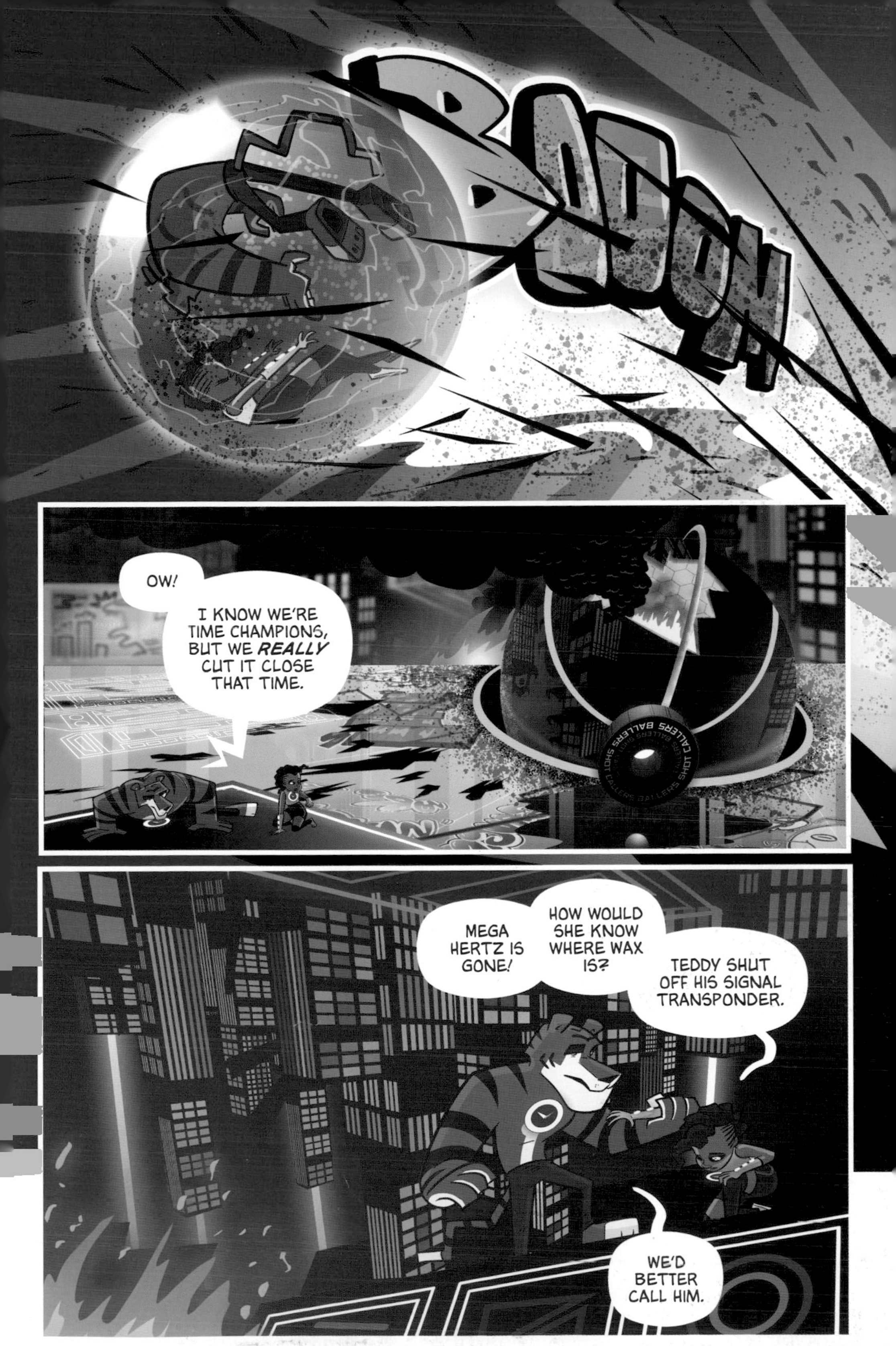
OW!
I KNOW WE'RE TIME CHAMPIONS, BUT WE *REALLY* CUT IT CLOSE THAT TIME.
SHOT CALLERS BALLERS
MEGA HERTZ IS GONE!
HOW WOULD SHE KNOW WHERE WAX IS?
TEDDY SHUT OFF HIS SIGNAL TRANSPONDER.
WE'D BETTER CALL HIM.

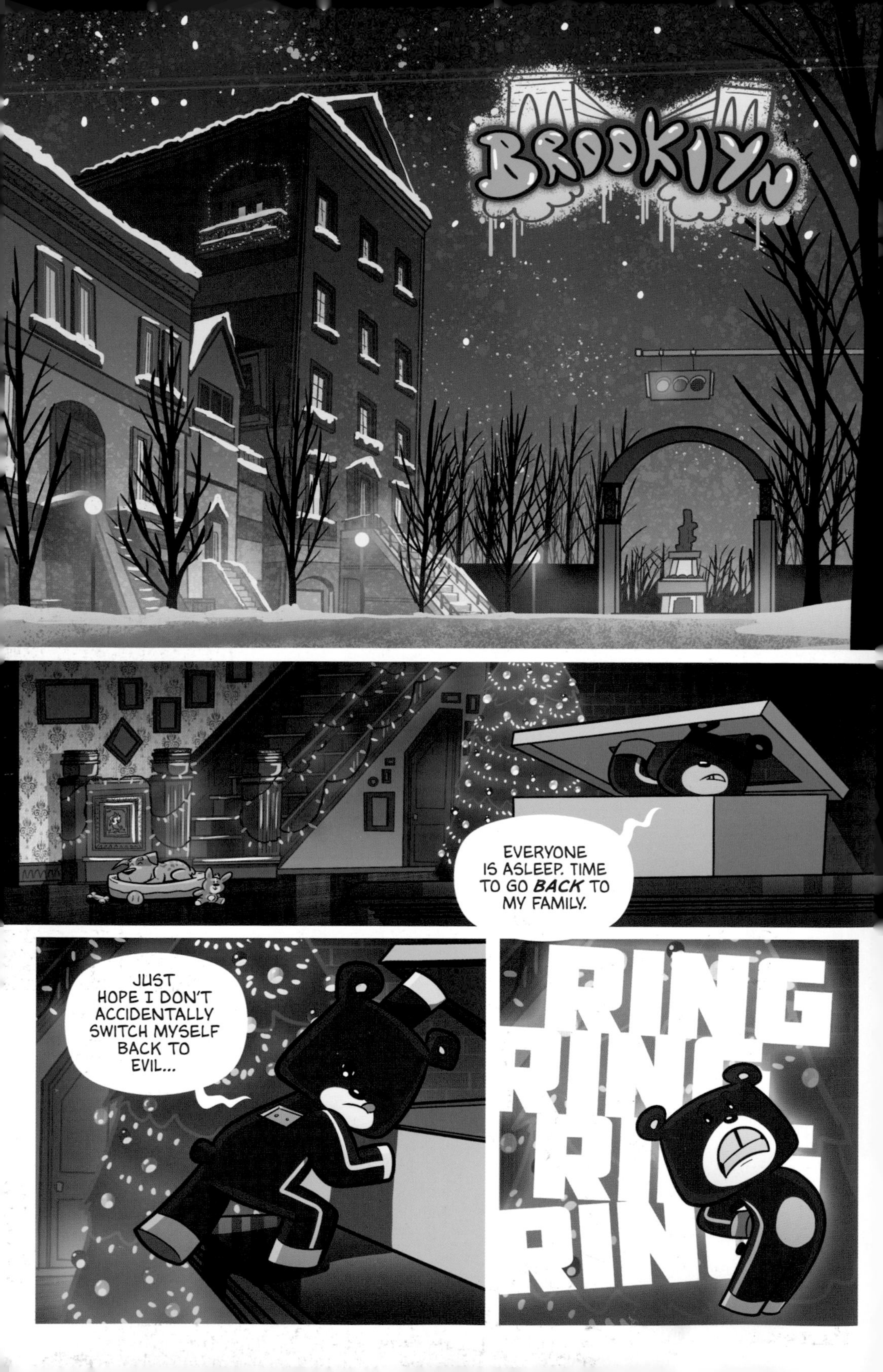
BROOKLYN
EVERYONE IS ASLEEP. TIME TO GO *BACK* TO MY FAMILY.
JUST HOPE I DON'T ACCIDENTALLY SWITCH MYSELF BACK TO EVIL...
RING RING RING RING

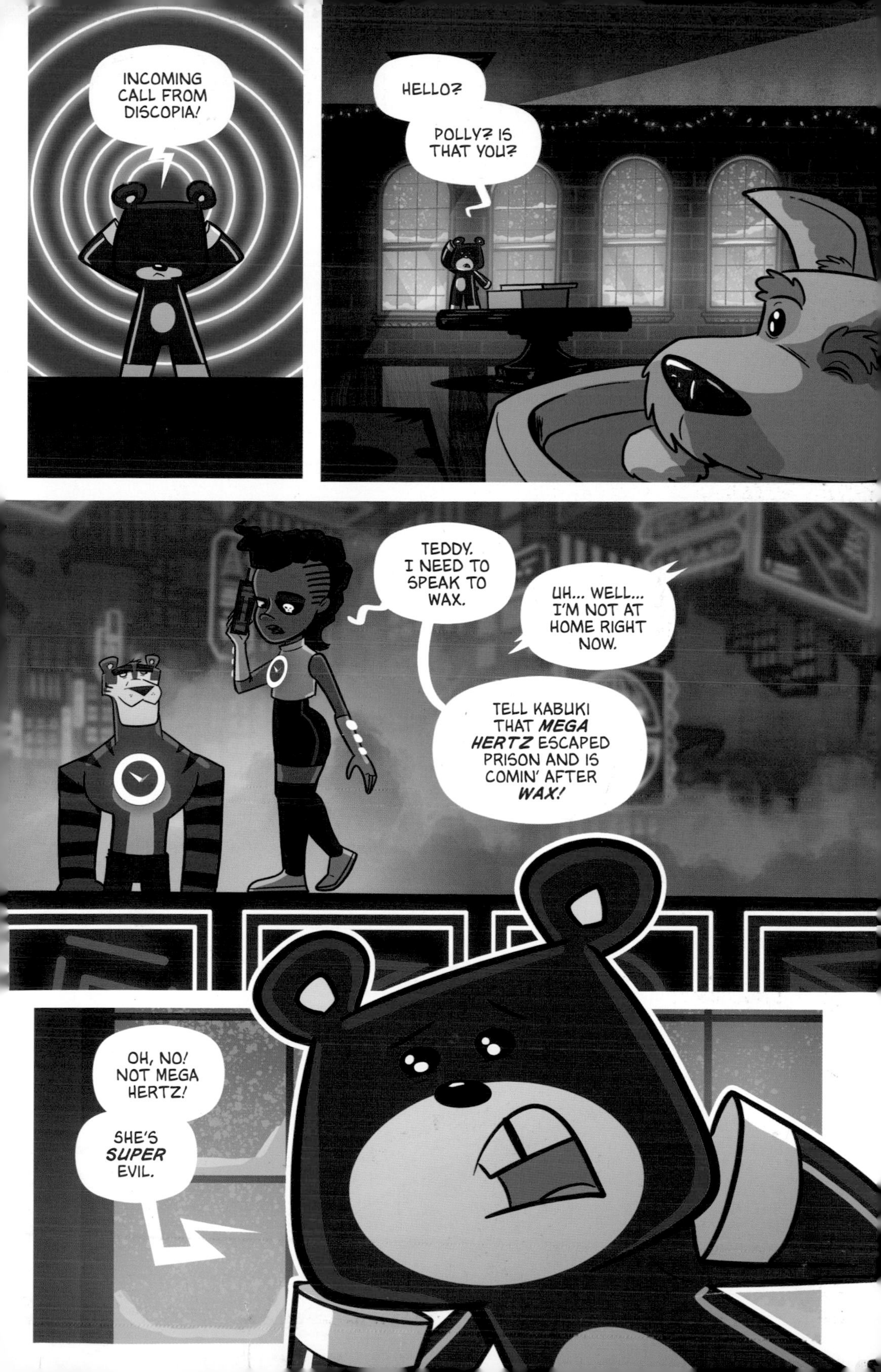
INCOMING CALL FROM DISCOPIA!
HELLO?
POLLY? IS THAT YOU?
TEDDY. I NEED TO SPEAK TO WAX.
UH... WELL... I'M NOT AT HOME RIGHT NOW.
TELL KABUKI THAT *MEGA HERTZ* ESCAPED PRISON AND IS COMIN' AFTER *WAX!*
OH, NO! NOT MEGA HERTZ!
SHE'S *SUPER* EVIL.

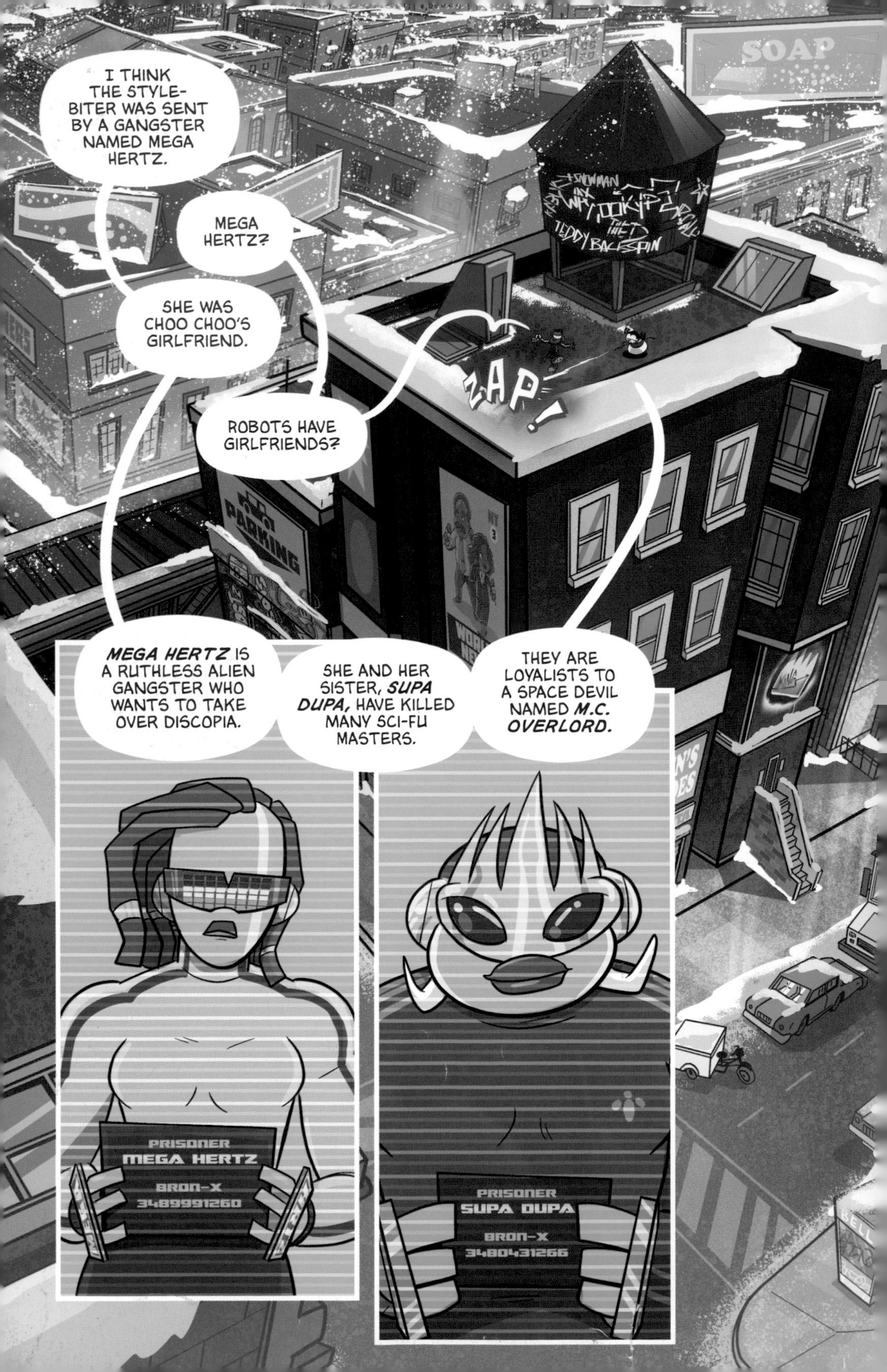
I THINK THE STYLE-BITER WAS SENT BY A GANGSTER NAMED MEGA HERTZ.
MEGA HERTZ?
SHE WAS CHOO CHOO'S GIRLFRIEND.
ROBOTS HAVE GIRLFRIENDS?
ZAP!
SOAP
PARKING
MEGA HERTZ IS A RUTHLESS ALIEN GANGSTER WHO WANTS TO TAKE OVER DISCOPIA.
SHE AND HER SISTER, *SUPA DUPA,* HAVE KILLED MANY SCI-FU MASTERS.
THEY ARE LOYALISTS TO A SPACE DEVIL NAMED *M.C. OVERLORD.*
PRISONER
MEGA HERTZ
BRON-X
3489991260
PRISONER
SUPA DUPA
BRON-X
3480431266

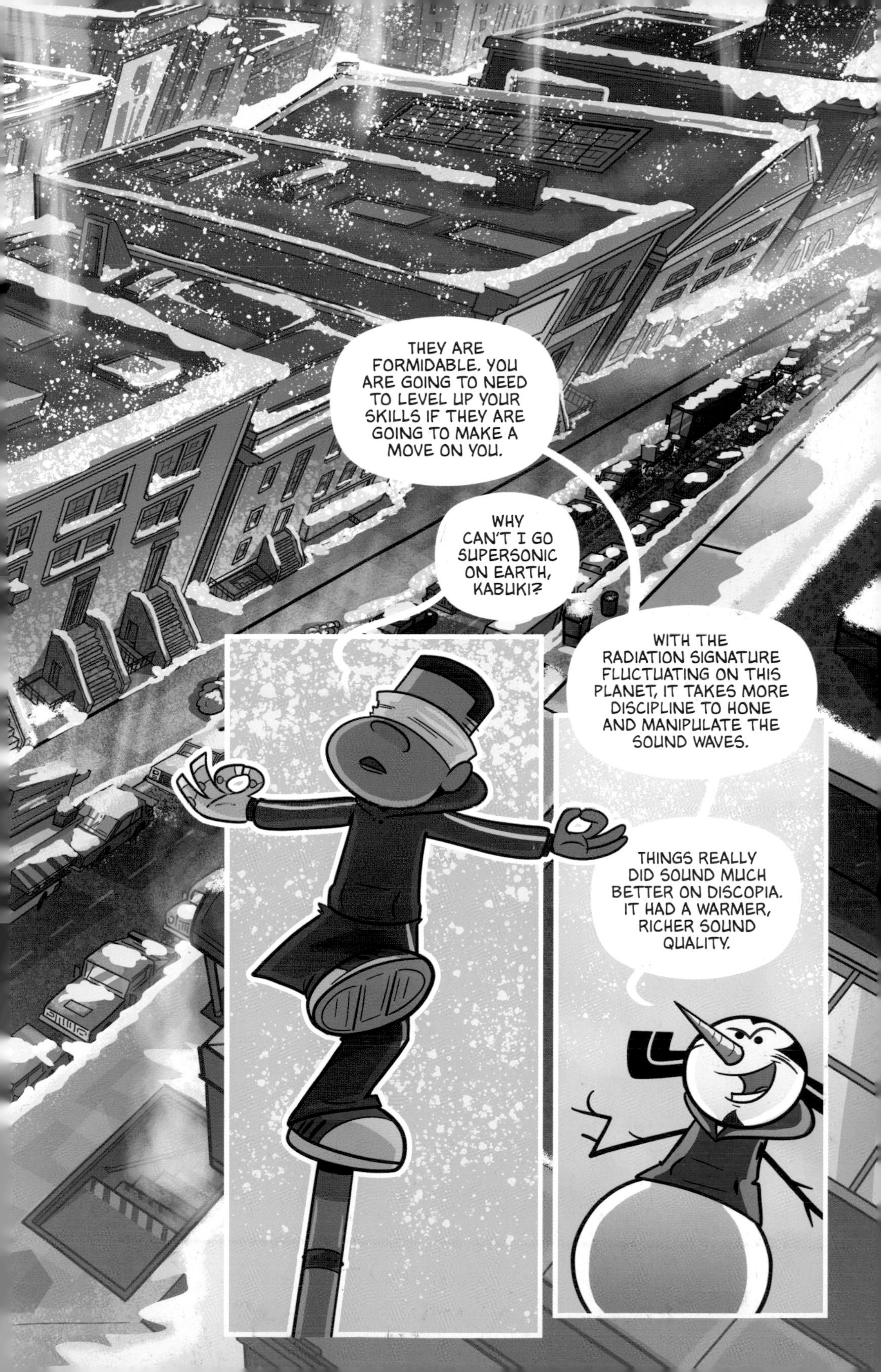
THEY ARE FORMIDABLE. YOU ARE GOING TO NEED TO LEVEL UP YOUR SKILLS IF THEY ARE GOING TO MAKE A MOVE ON YOU.
WHY CAN'T I GO SUPERSONIC ON EARTH, KABUKI?
WITH THE RADIATION SIGNATURE FLUCTUATING ON THIS PLANET, IT TAKES MORE DISCIPLINE TO HONE AND MANIPULATE THE SOUND WAVES.
THINGS REALLY DID SOUND MUCH BETTER ON DISCOPIA. IT HAD A WARMER, RICHER SOUND QUALITY.

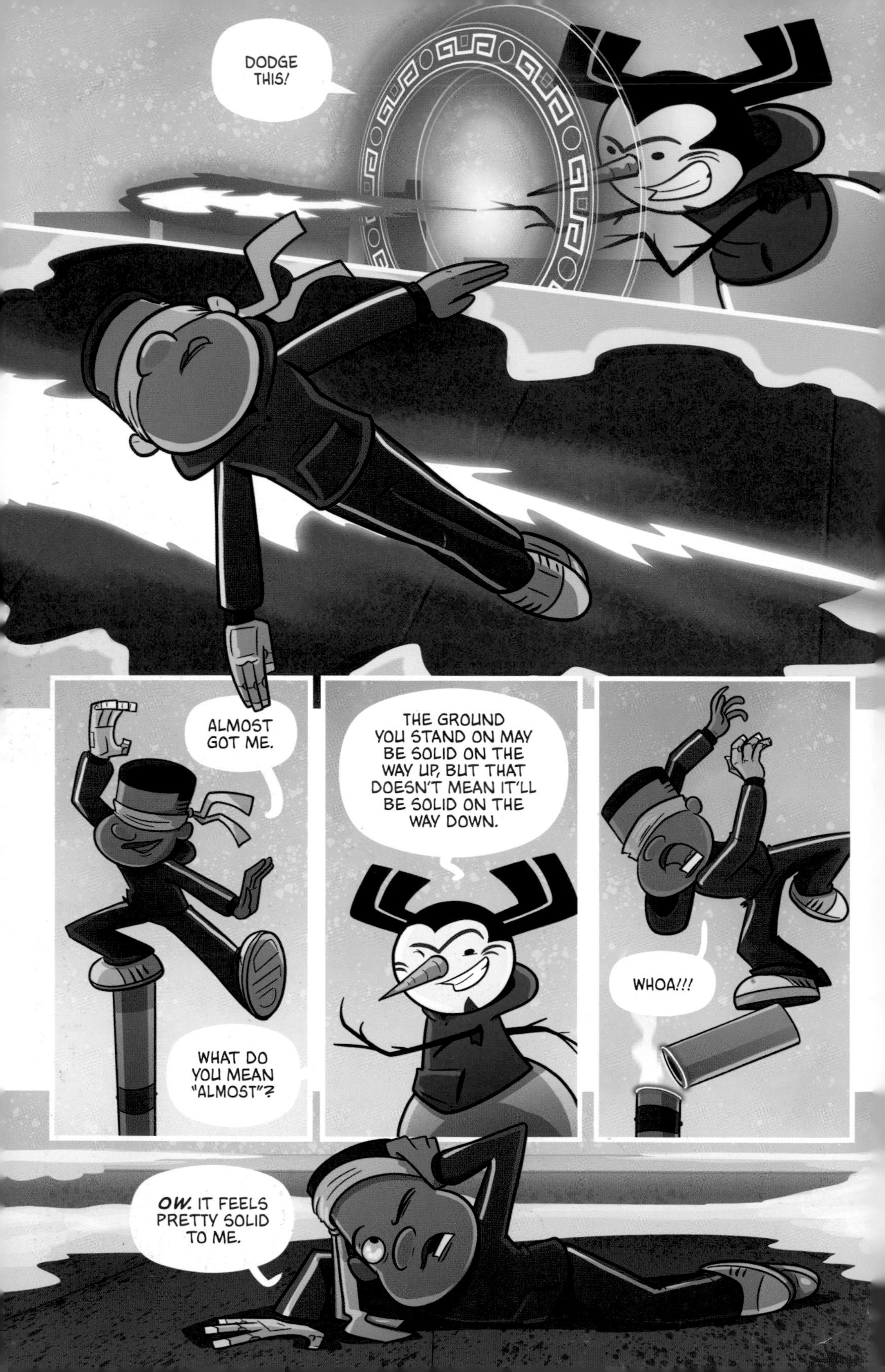
DODGE THIS!
ALMOST GOT ME.
WHAT DO YOU MEAN "ALMOST"?
THE GROUND YOU STAND ON MAY BE SOLID ON THE WAY UP, BUT THAT DOESN'T MEAN IT'LL BE SOLID ON THE WAY DOWN.
WHOA!!!
OW. IT FEELS PRETTY SOLID TO ME.

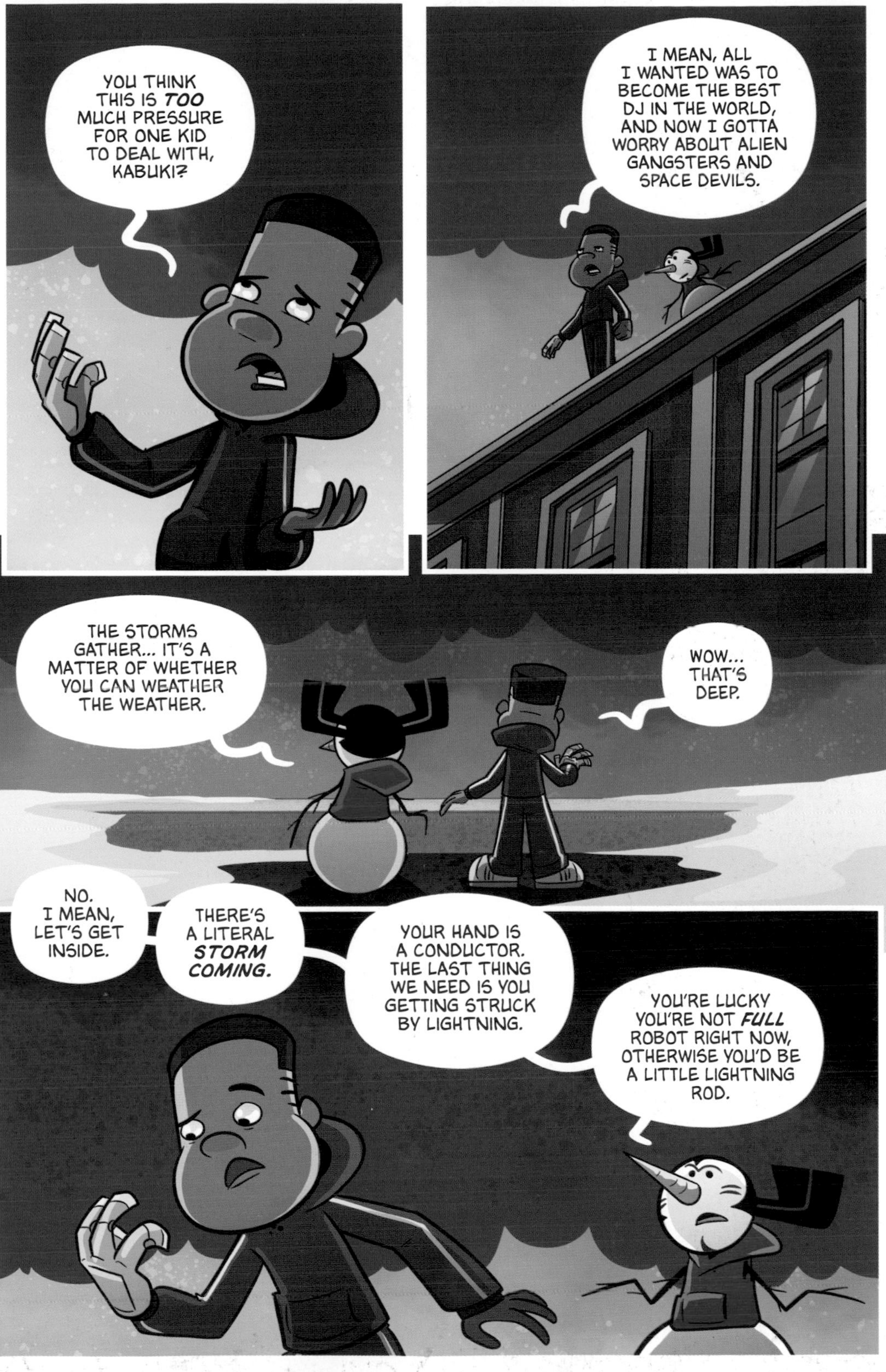
YOU THINK THIS IS TOO MUCH PRESSURE FOR ONE KID TO DEAL WITH, KABUKI?
I MEAN, ALL I WANTED WAS TO BECOME THE BEST DJ IN THE WORLD, AND NOW I GOTTA WORRY ABOUT ALIEN GANGSTERS AND SPACE DEVILS.
THE STORMS GATHER... IT'S A MATTER OF WHETHER YOU CAN WEATHER THE WEATHER.
WOW... THAT'S DEEP.
NO. I MEAN, LET'S GET INSIDE.
THERE'S A LITERAL STORM COMING.
YOUR HAND IS A CONDUCTOR. THE LAST THING WE NEED IS YOU GETTING STRUCK BY LIGHTNING.
YOU'RE LUCKY YOU'RE NOT FULL ROBOT RIGHT NOW, OTHERWISE YOU'D BE A LITTLE LIGHTNING ROD.

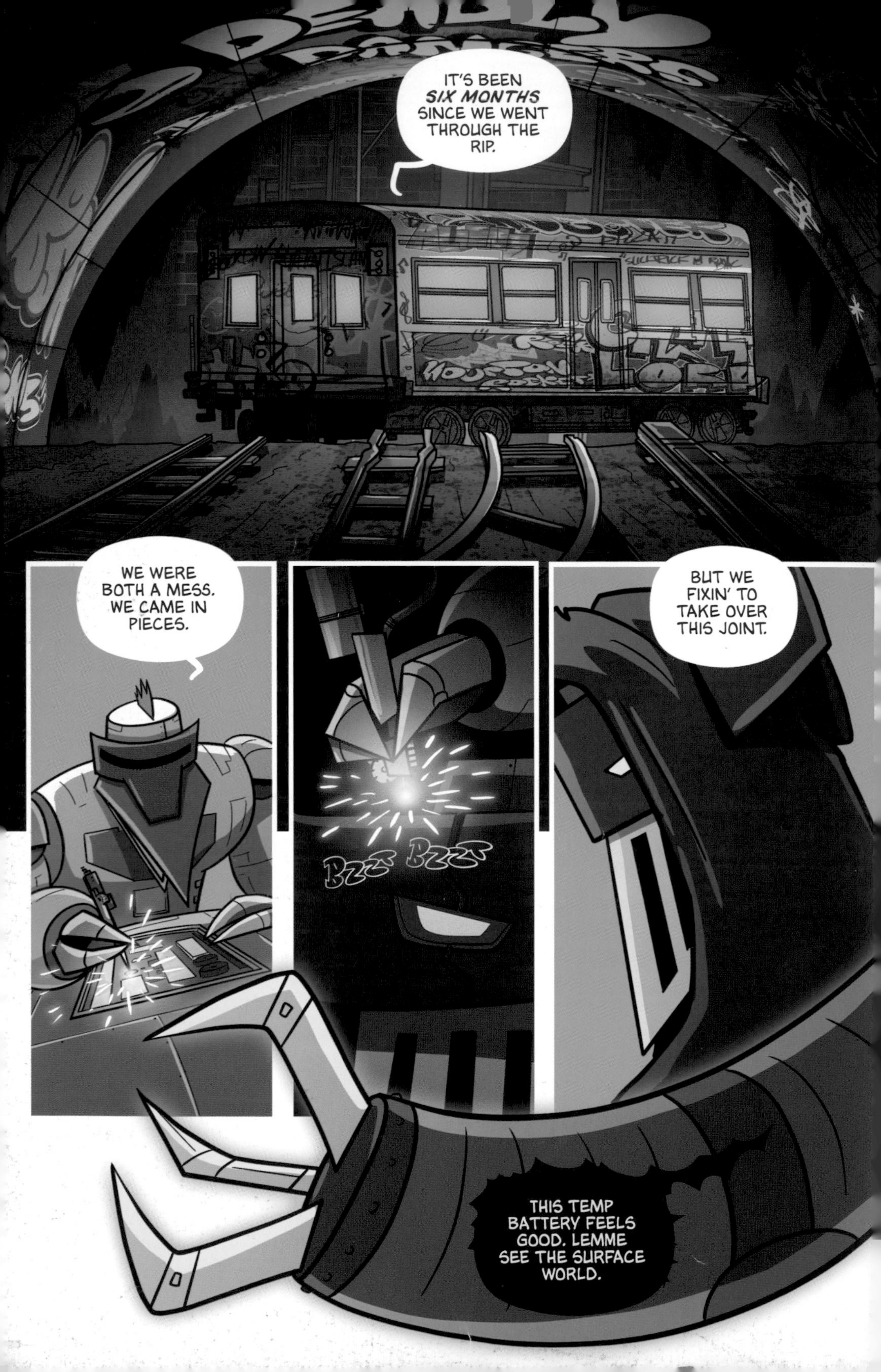
IT'S BEEN *SIX MONTHS* SINCE WE WENT THROUGH THE RIP.
WE WERE BOTH A MESS. WE CAME IN PIECES.
BZZT BZZT
BUT WE FIXIN' TO TAKE OVER THIS JOINT.
THIS TEMP BATTERY FEELS GOOD. LEMME SEE THE SURFACE WORLD.

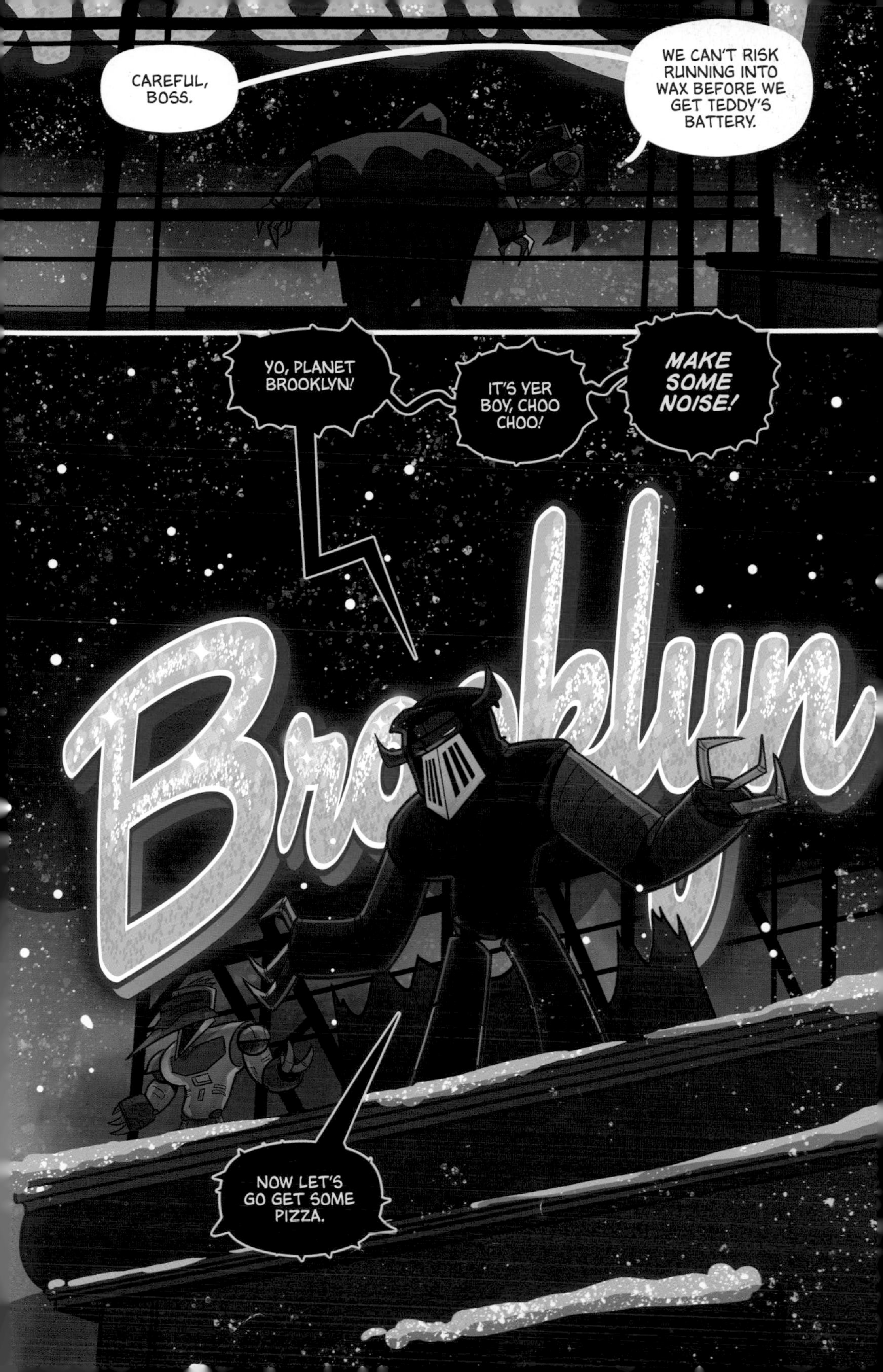
CAREFUL, BOSS.
WE CAN'T RISK RUNNING INTO WAX BEFORE WE GET TEDDY'S BATTERY.
YO, PLANET BROOKLYN!
IT'S YER BOY, CHOO CHOO!
MAKE SOME NOISE!
Brooklyn
NOW LET'S GO GET SOME PIZZA.

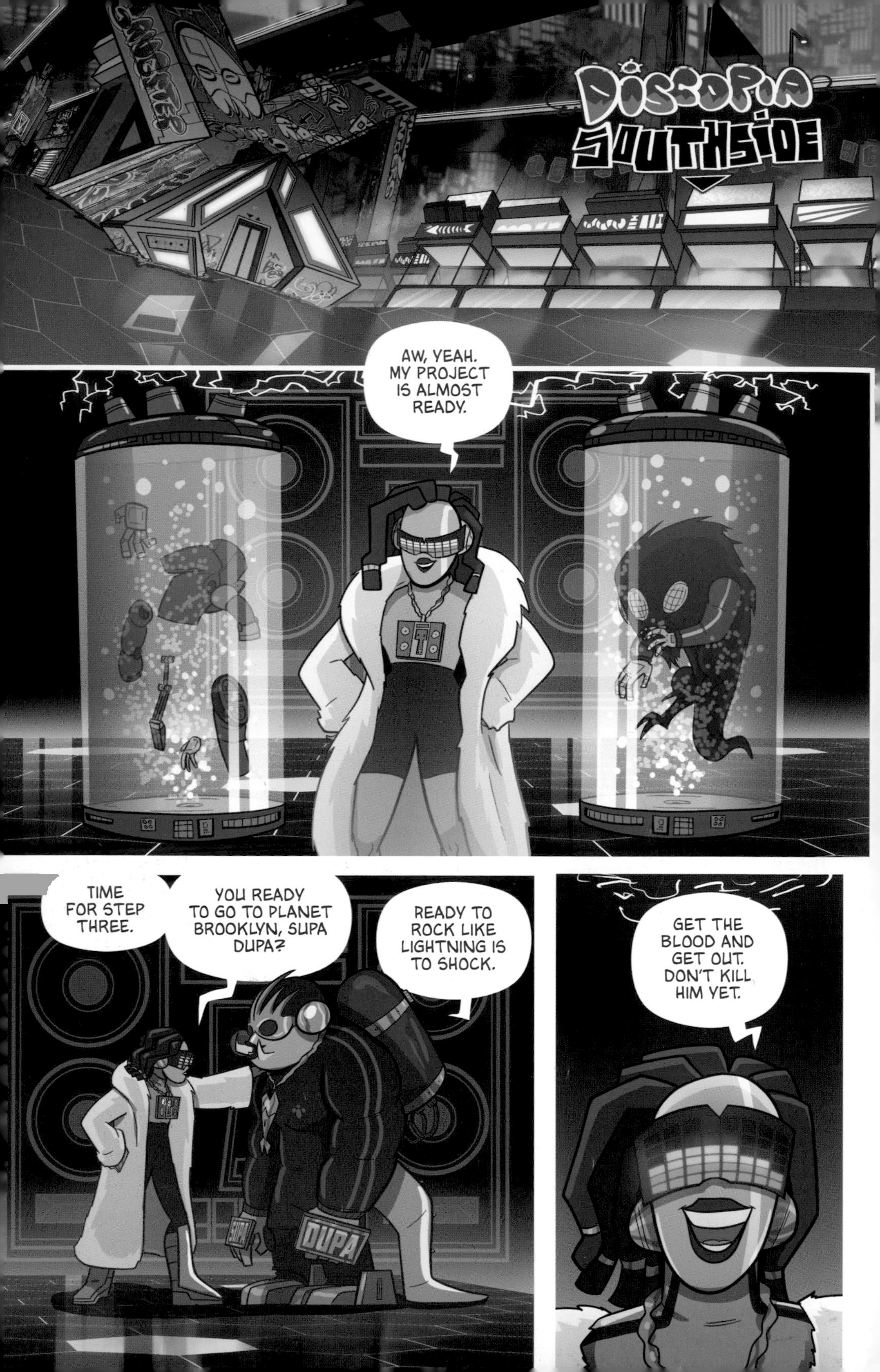
DISCOPIA SOUTHSIDE
AW, YEAH. MY PROJECT IS ALMOST READY.
TIME FOR STEP THREE.
YOU READY TO GO TO PLANET BROOKLYN, SUPA DUPA?
READY TO ROCK LIKE LIGHTNING IS TO SHOCK.
GET THE BLOOD AND GET OUT. DON'T KILL HIM YET.
SUPA
DUPA

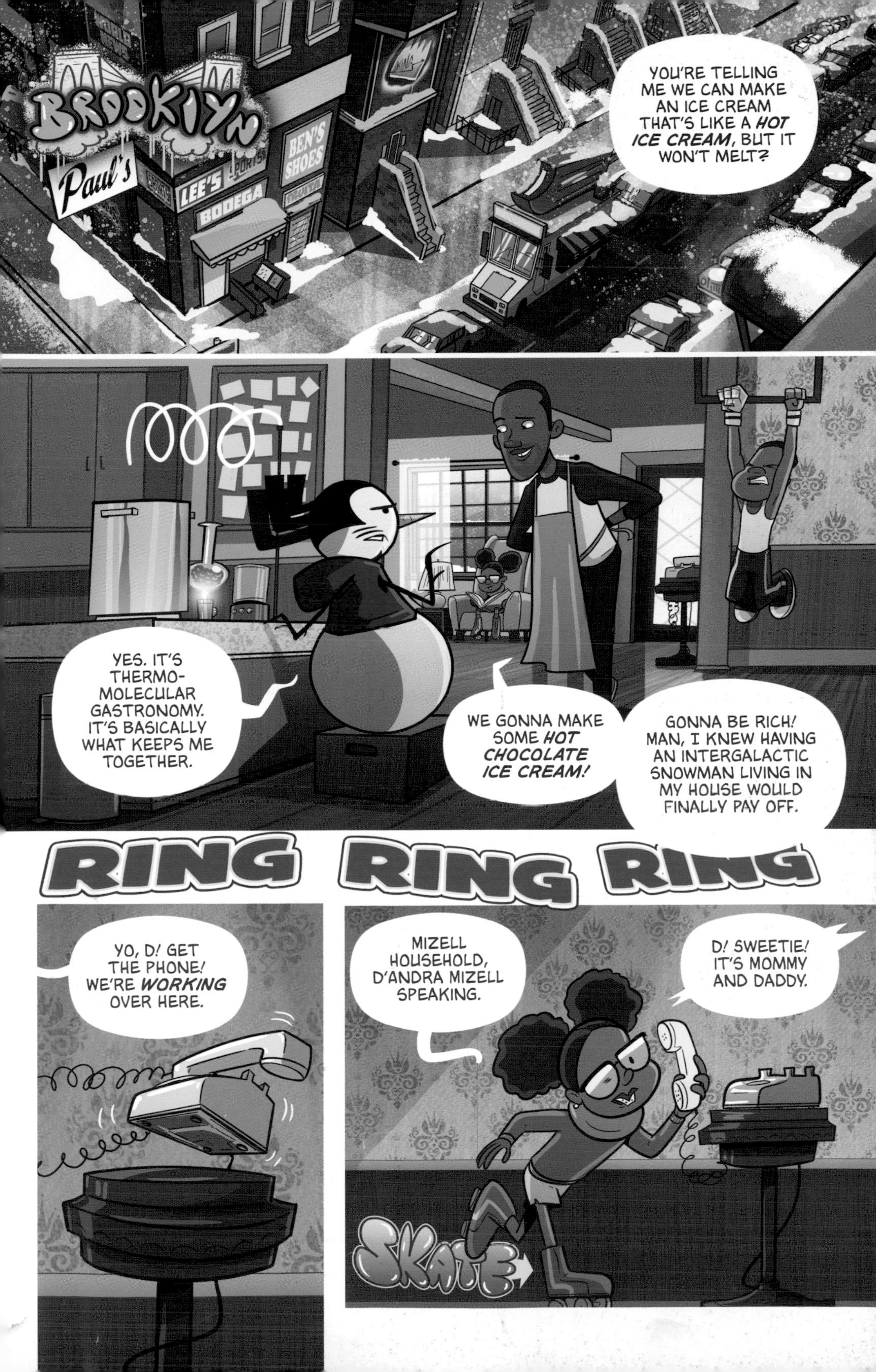
BROOKLYN
Paul's
LEE'S
BODEGA
BEN'S SHOES
YOU'RE TELLING ME WE CAN MAKE AN ICE CREAM THAT'S LIKE A *HOT ICE CREAM*, BUT IT WON'T MELT?
YES. IT'S THERMO-MOLECULAR GASTRONOMY. IT'S BASICALLY WHAT KEEPS ME TOGETHER.
WE GONNA MAKE SOME *HOT CHOCOLATE ICE CREAM!*
GONNA BE RICH! MAN, I KNEW HAVING AN INTERGALACTIC SNOWMAN LIVING IN MY HOUSE WOULD FINALLY PAY OFF.
RING RING RING
YO, D! GET THE PHONE! WE'RE *WORKING* OVER HERE.
MIZELL HOUSEHOLD, D'ANDRA MIZELL SPEAKING.
D! SWEETIE! IT'S MOMMY AND DADDY.
SKATE

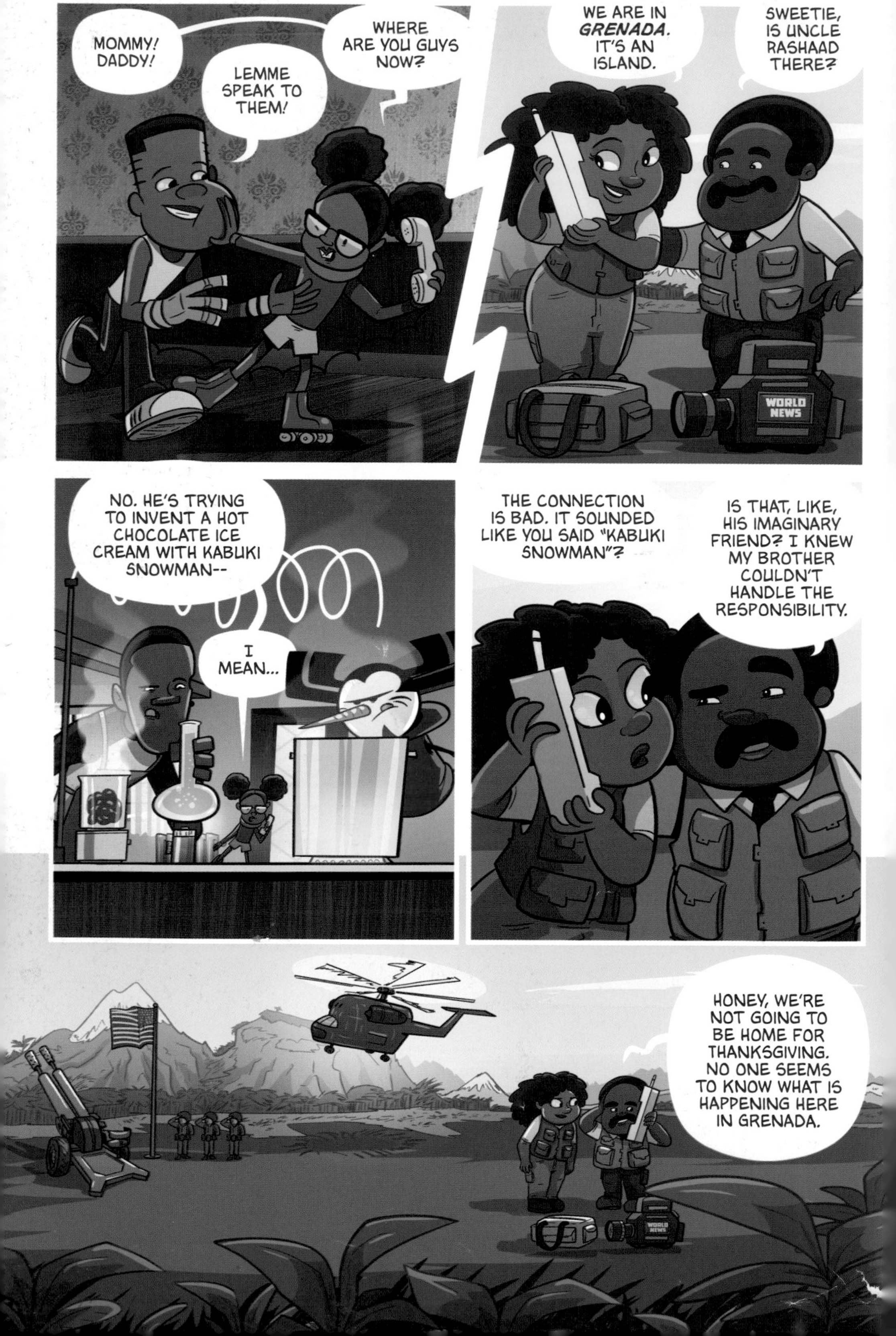
MOMMY! DADDY!
LEMME SPEAK TO THEM!
WHERE ARE YOU GUYS NOW?
WE ARE IN *GRENADA*. IT'S AN ISLAND.
SWEETIE, IS UNCLE RASHAAD THERE?
WORLD NEWS
NO. HE'S TRYING TO INVENT A HOT CHOCOLATE ICE CREAM WITH KABUKI SNOWMAN--
I MEAN...
THE CONNECTION IS BAD. IT SOUNDED LIKE YOU SAID "KABUKI SNOWMAN"?
IS THAT, LIKE, HIS IMAGINARY FRIEND? I KNEW MY BROTHER COULDN'T HANDLE THE RESPONSIBILITY.
HONEY, WE'RE NOT GOING TO BE HOME FOR THANKSGIVING. NO ONE SEEMS TO KNOW WHAT IS HAPPENING HERE IN GRENADA.
WORLD NEWS

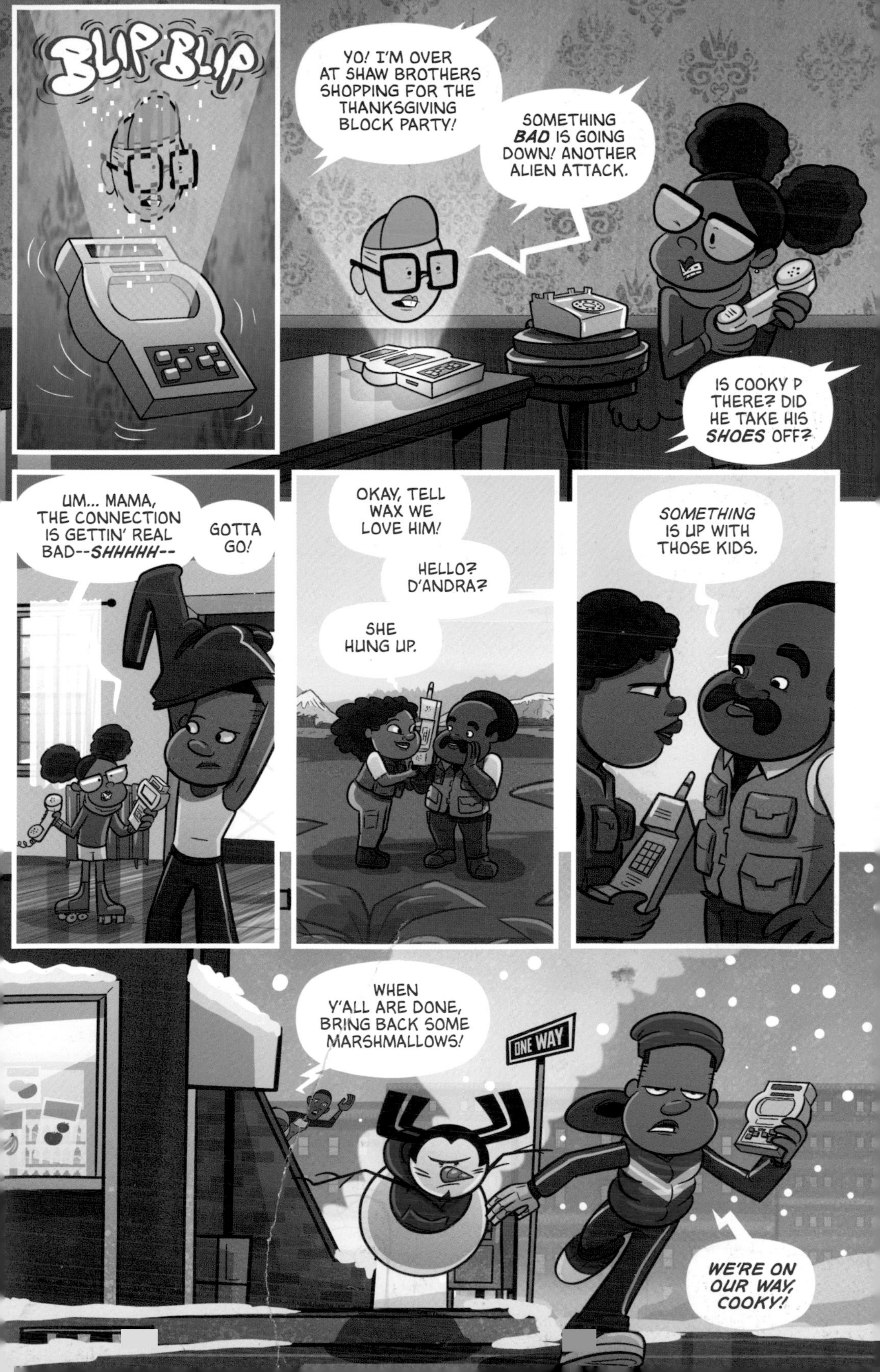
BLIP BLIP
YO! I'M OVER AT SHAW BROTHERS SHOPPING FOR THE THANKSGIVING BLOCK PARTY!
SOMETHING BAD IS GOING DOWN! ANOTHER ALIEN ATTACK.
IS COOKY P THERE? DID HE TAKE HIS SHOES OFF?
UM... MAMA, THE CONNECTION IS GETTIN' REAL BAD--SHHHHH--
GOTTA GO!
OKAY, TELL WAX WE LOVE HIM!
HELLO? D'ANDRA?
SHE HUNG UP.
SOMETHING IS UP WITH THOSE KIDS.
WHEN Y'ALL ARE DONE, BRING BACK SOME MARSHMALLOWS!
ONE WAY
WE'RE ON OUR WAY, COOKY!

TRACK
3

COLD CRUSH CREW

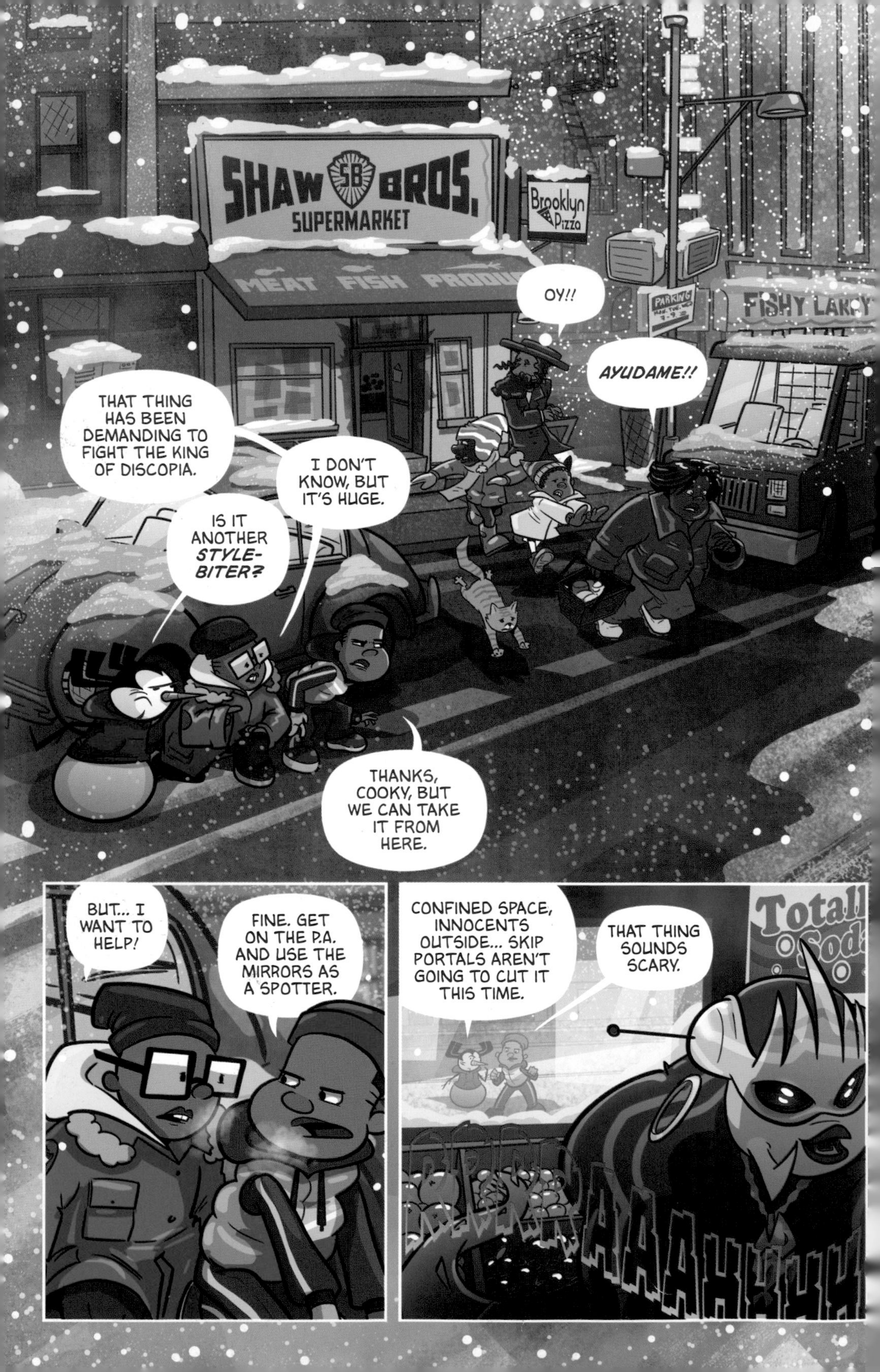
SHAW SB BROS.
SUPERMARKET
MEAT FISH PRODU
Brooklyn Pizza
FISHY LARRY
OY!!
AYUDAME!!
THAT THING HAS BEEN DEMANDING TO FIGHT THE KING OF DISCOPIA.
I DON'T KNOW, BUT IT'S HUGE.
IS IT ANOTHER *STYLE-BITER?*
THANKS, COOKY, BUT WE CAN TAKE IT FROM HERE.
BUT... I WANT TO HELP!
FINE. GET ON THE P.A. AND USE THE MIRRORS AS A SPOTTER.
CONFINED SPACE, INNOCENTS OUTSIDE... SKIP PORTALS AREN'T GOING TO CUT IT THIS TIME.
THAT THING SOUNDS SCARY.
AAAHHHH

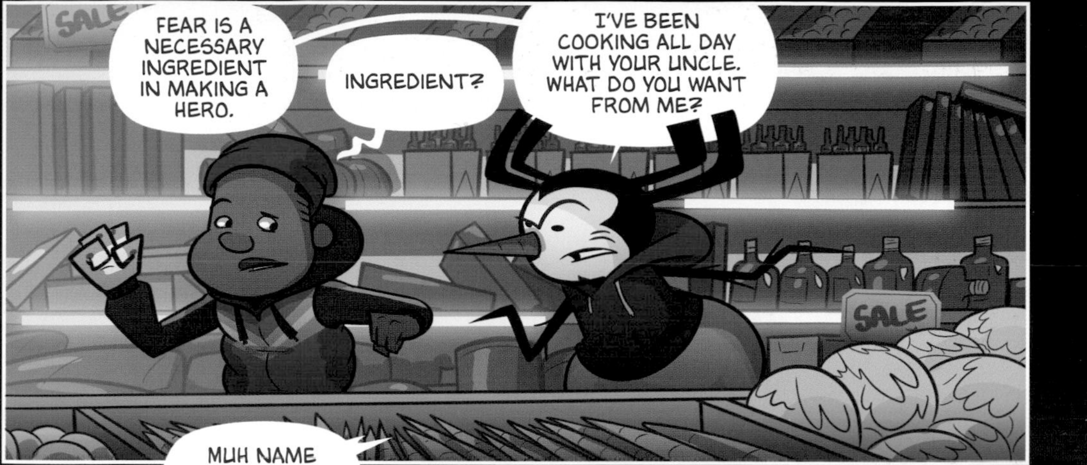
SALE
FEAR IS A NECESSARY INGREDIENT IN MAKING A HERO.
INGREDIENT?
I'VE BEEN COOKING ALL DAY WITH YOUR UNCLE. WHAT DO YOU WANT FROM ME?
SALE
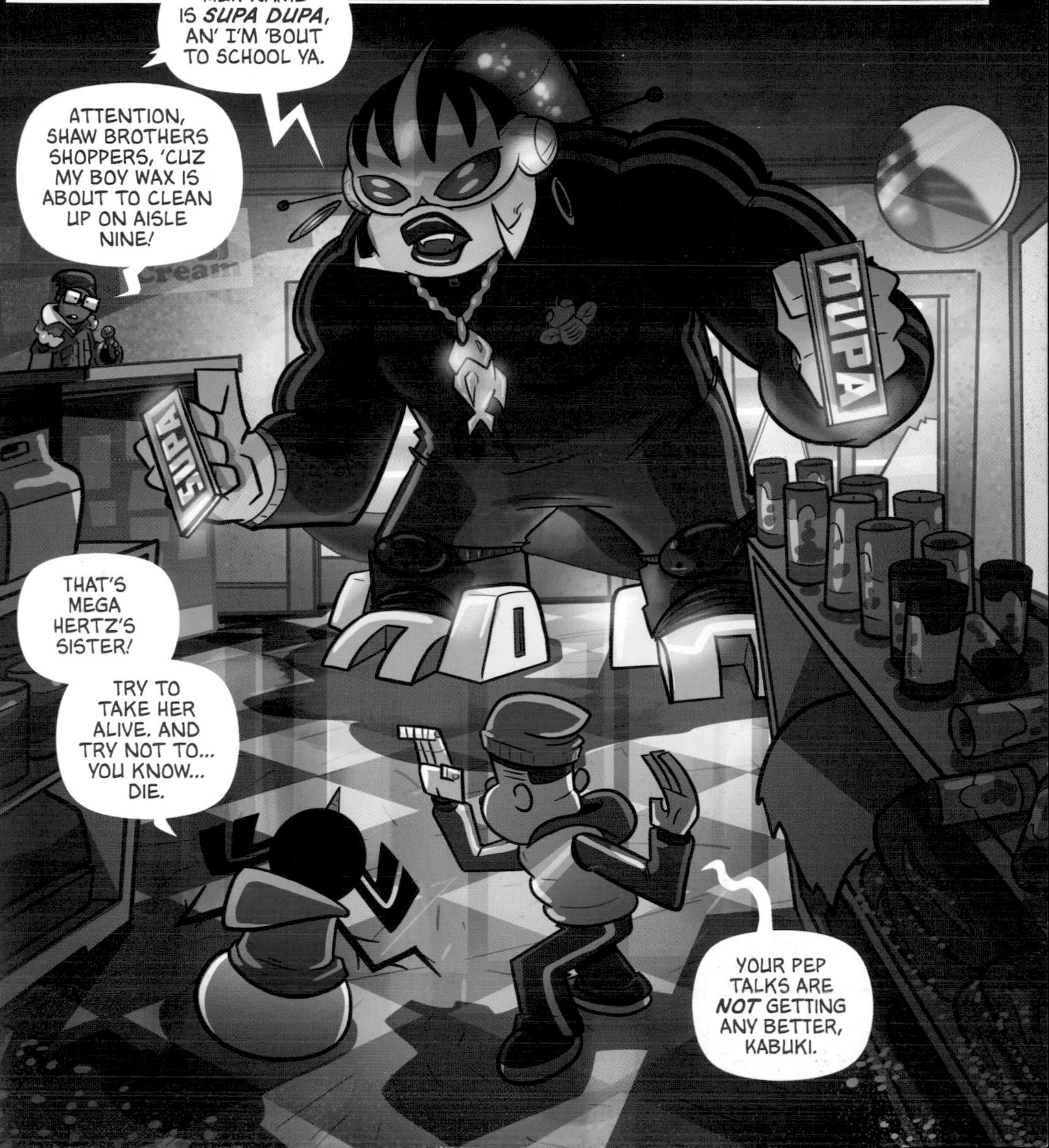
MUH NAME IS ***SUPA DUPA***, AN' I'M 'BOUT TO SCHOOL YA.
ATTENTION, SHAW BROTHERS SHOPPERS, 'CUZ MY BOY WAX IS ABOUT TO CLEAN UP ON AISLE NINE!
SUPA
DUPA
THAT'S MEGA HERTZ'S SISTER!
TRY TO TAKE HER ALIVE. AND TRY NOT TO... YOU KNOW... DIE.
YOUR PEP TALKS ARE ***NOT*** GETTING ANY BETTER, KABUKI.

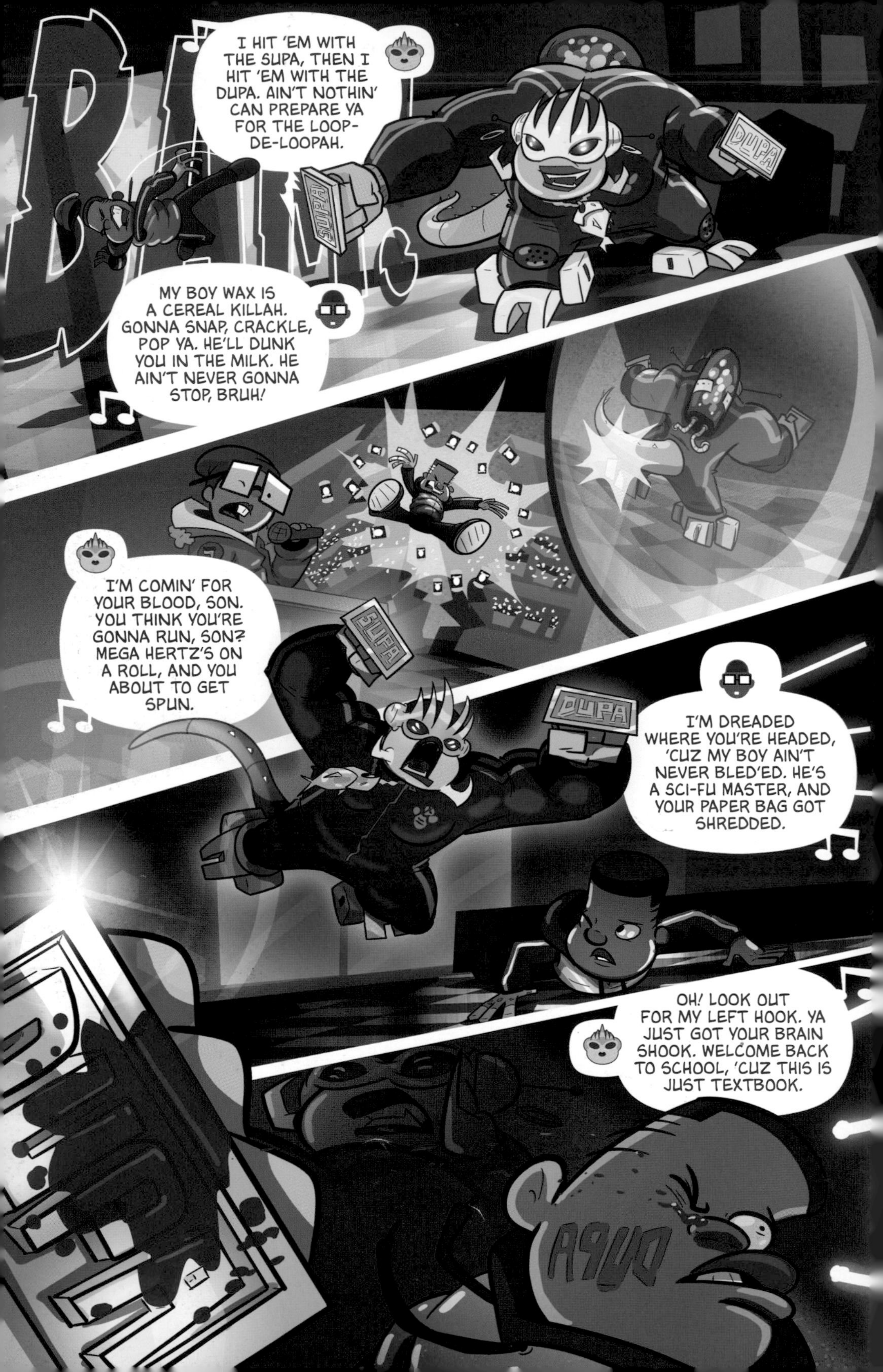
I HIT 'EM WITH THE SUPA, THEN I HIT 'EM WITH THE DUPA. AIN'T NOTHIN' CAN PREPARE YA FOR THE LOOP-DE-LOOPAH.
DUPA
SUPA
MY BOY WAX IS A CEREAL KILLAH. GONNA SNAP, CRACKLE, POP YA. HE'LL DUNK YOU IN THE MILK. HE AIN'T NEVER GONNA STOP, BRUH!
I'M COMIN' FOR YOUR BLOOD, SON. YOU THINK YOU'RE GONNA RUN, SON? MEGA HERTZ'S ON A ROLL, AND YOU ABOUT TO GET SPUN.
SUPA
DUPA
I'M DREADED WHERE YOU'RE HEADED, 'CUZ MY BOY AIN'T NEVER BLED'ED. HE'S A SCI-FU MASTER, AND YOUR PAPER BAG GOT SHREDDED.
OH! LOOK OUT FOR MY LEFT HOOK. YA JUST GOT YOUR BRAIN SHOOK. WELCOME BACK TO SCHOOL, 'CUZ THIS IS JUST TEXTBOOK.

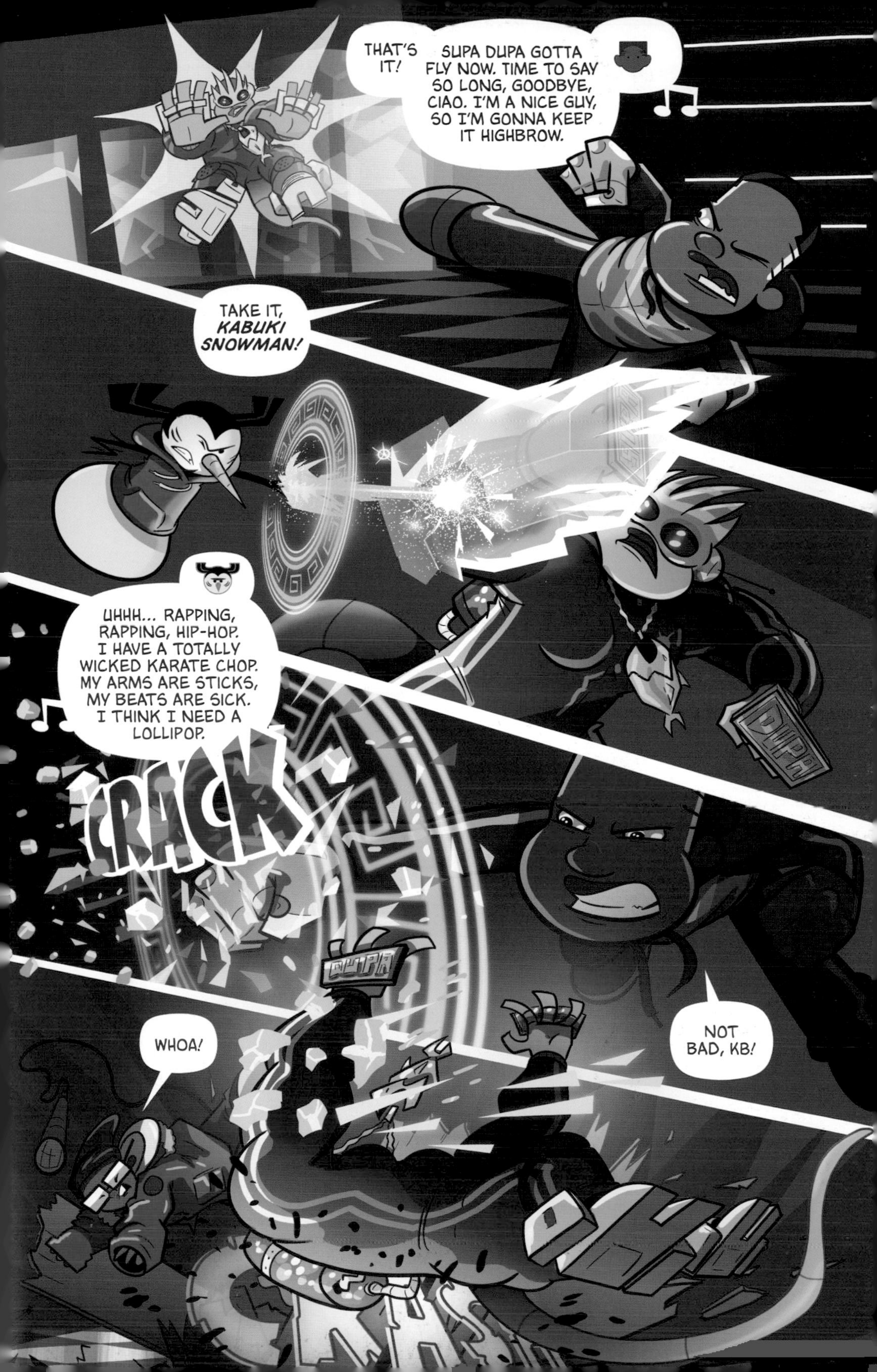
THAT'S IT!
SUPA DUPA GOTTA FLY NOW. TIME TO SAY SO LONG, GOODBYE, CIAO. I'M A NICE GUY, SO I'M GONNA KEEP IT HIGHBROW.
TAKE IT, *KABUKI SNOWMAN!*
UHHH... RAPPING, RAPPING, HIP-HOP. I HAVE A TOTALLY WICKED KARATE CHOP. MY ARMS ARE STICKS, MY BEATS ARE SICK. I THINK I NEED A LOLLIPOP.
DUPA
CRACK
DUPA
WHOA!
NOT BAD, KB!

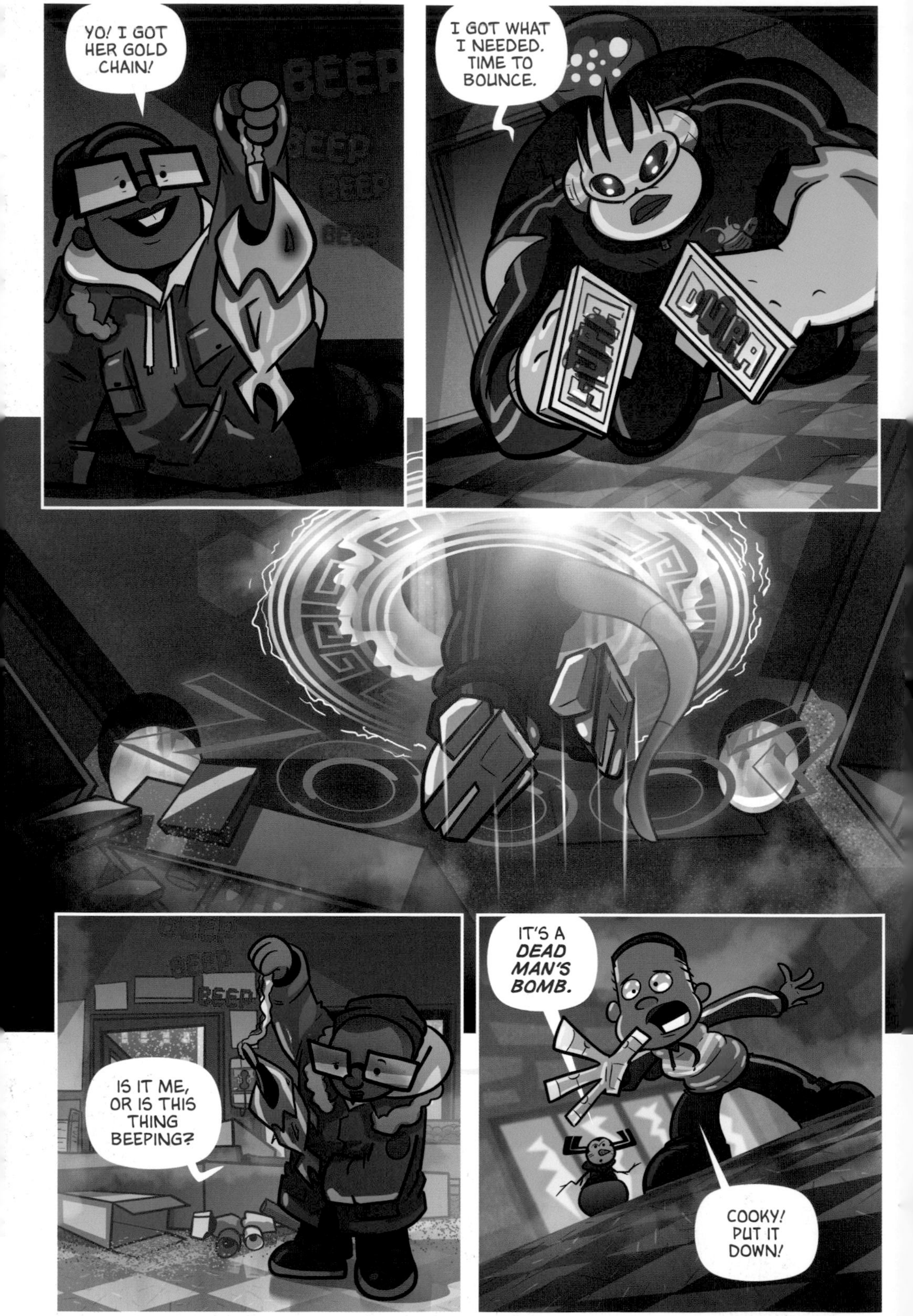
YO! I GOT HER GOLD CHAIN!
BEEP
BEEP
BEEP
I GOT WHAT I NEEDED. TIME TO BOUNCE.
IS IT ME, OR IS THIS THING BEEPING?
IT'S A *DEAD MAN'S BOMB.*
COOKY! PUT IT DOWN!

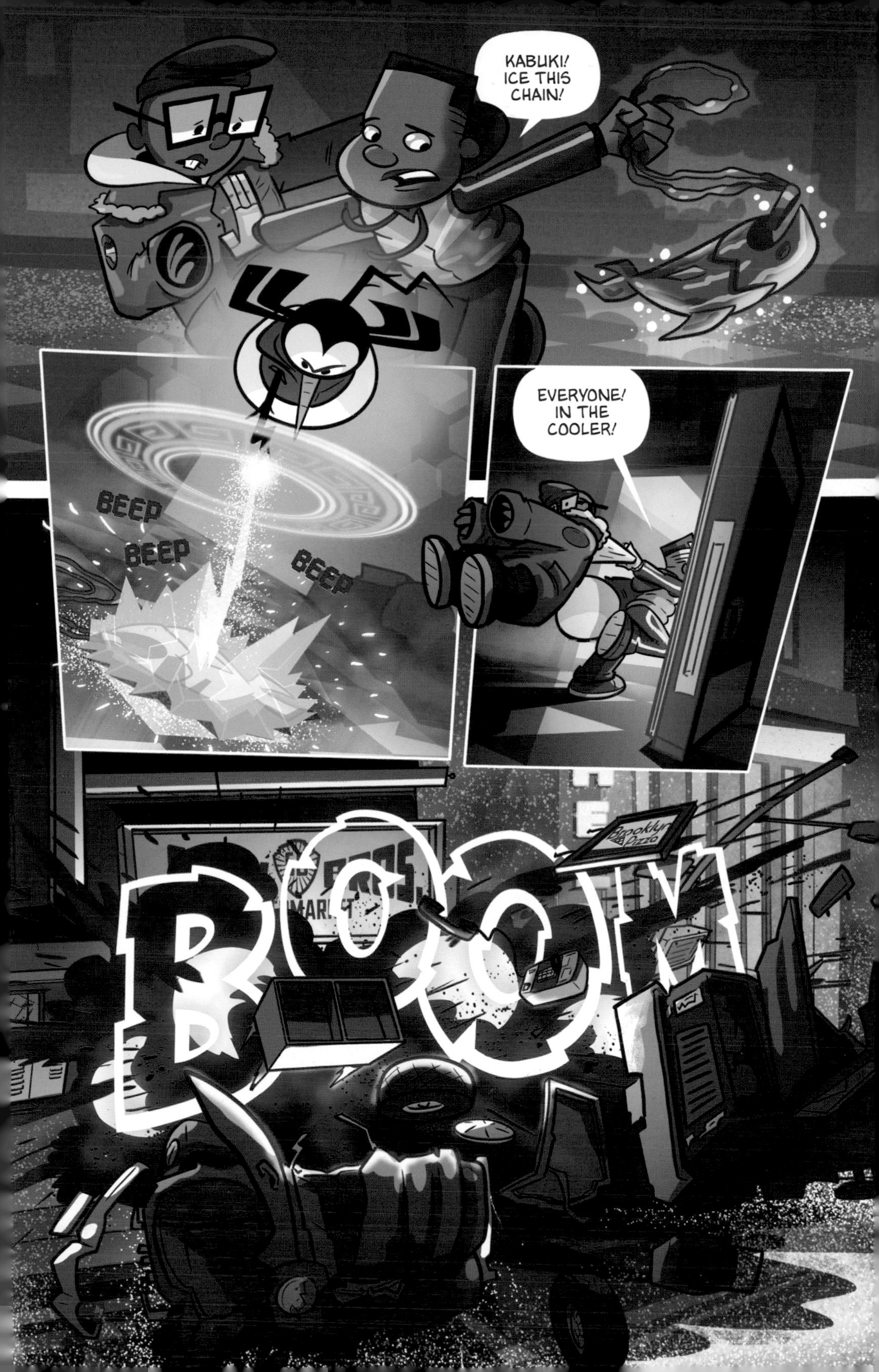
KABUKI! ICE THIS CHAIN!
BEEP
BEEP
BEEP
EVERYONE! IN THE COOLER!
BOOM
Brooklyn Pizza

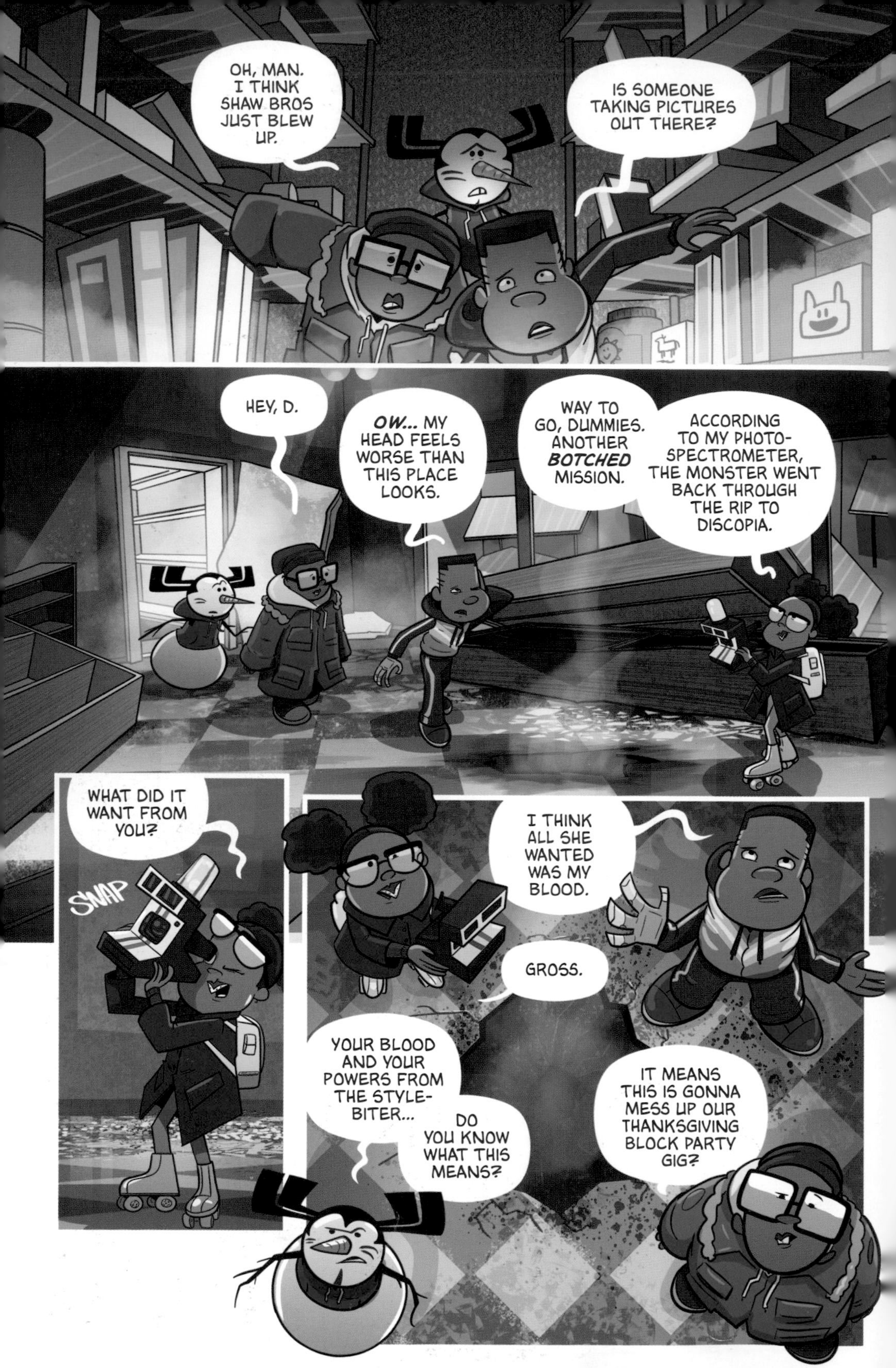
OH, MAN. I THINK SHAW BROS JUST BLEW UP.
IS SOMEONE TAKING PICTURES OUT THERE?
HEY, D.
OW... MY HEAD FEELS WORSE THAN THIS PLACE LOOKS.
WAY TO GO, DUMMIES. ANOTHER BOTCHED MISSION.
ACCORDING TO MY PHOTO-SPECTROMETER, THE MONSTER WENT BACK THROUGH THE RIP TO DISCOPIA.
WHAT DID IT WANT FROM YOU?
SNAP
I THINK ALL SHE WANTED WAS MY BLOOD.
GROSS.
YOUR BLOOD AND YOUR POWERS FROM THE STYLE-BITER...
DO YOU KNOW WHAT THIS MEANS?
IT MEANS THIS IS GONNA MESS UP OUR THANKSGIVING BLOCK PARTY GIG?

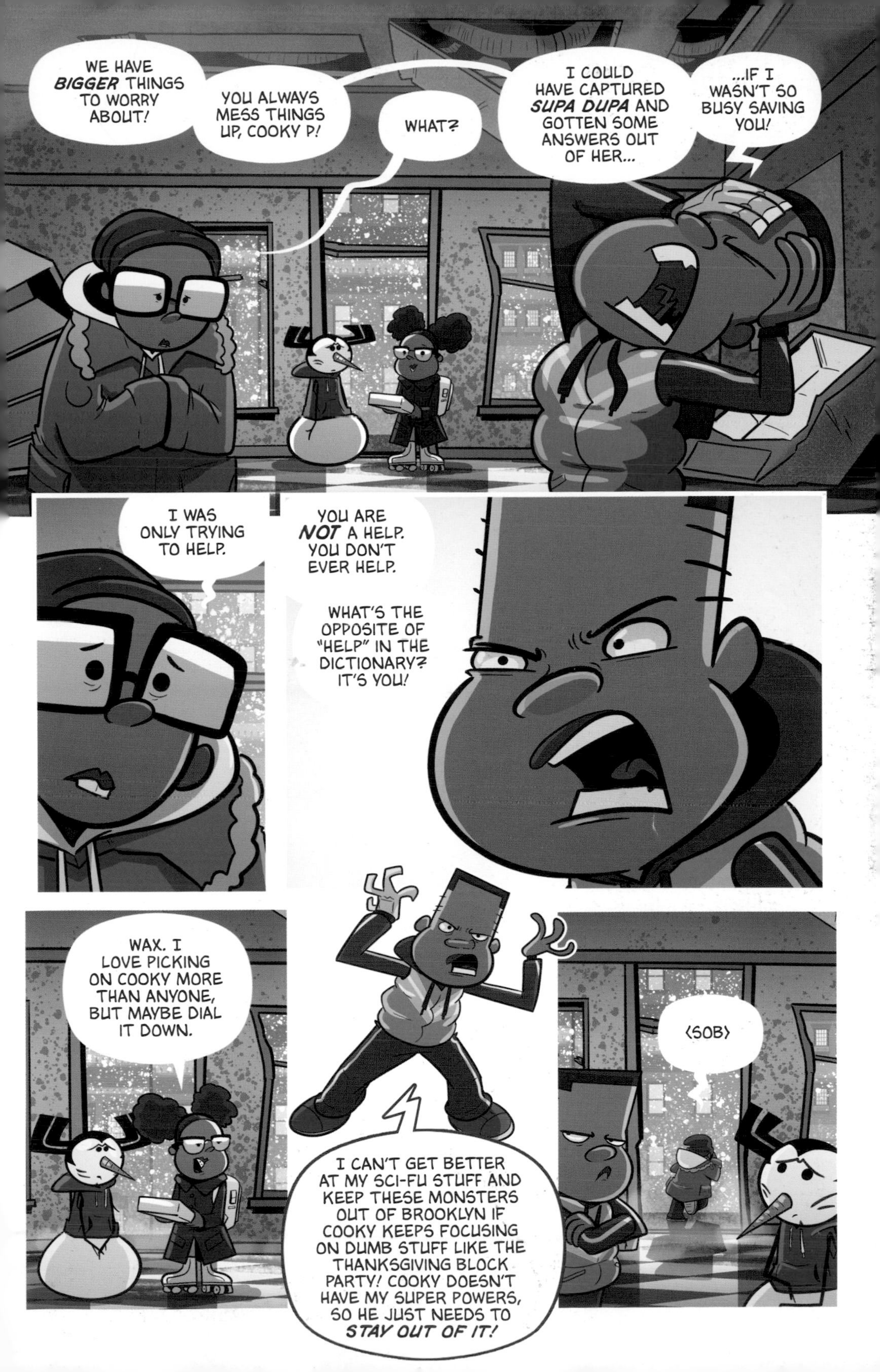
WE HAVE BIGGER THINGS TO WORRY ABOUT!
YOU ALWAYS MESS THINGS UP, COOKY P!
WHAT?
I COULD HAVE CAPTURED SUPA DUPA AND GOTTEN SOME ANSWERS OUT OF HER...
...IF I WASN'T SO BUSY SAVING YOU!
I WAS ONLY TRYING TO HELP.
YOU ARE NOT A HELP. YOU DON'T EVER HELP.
WHAT'S THE OPPOSITE OF "HELP" IN THE DICTIONARY? IT'S YOU!
WAX. I LOVE PICKING ON COOKY MORE THAN ANYONE, BUT MAYBE DIAL IT DOWN.
I CAN'T GET BETTER AT MY SCI-FU STUFF AND KEEP THESE MONSTERS OUT OF BROOKLYN IF COOKY KEEPS FOCUSING ON DUMB STUFF LIKE THE THANKSGIVING BLOCK PARTY! COOKY DOESN'T HAVE MY SUPER POWERS, SO HE JUST NEEDS TO STAY OUT OF IT!
<SOB>

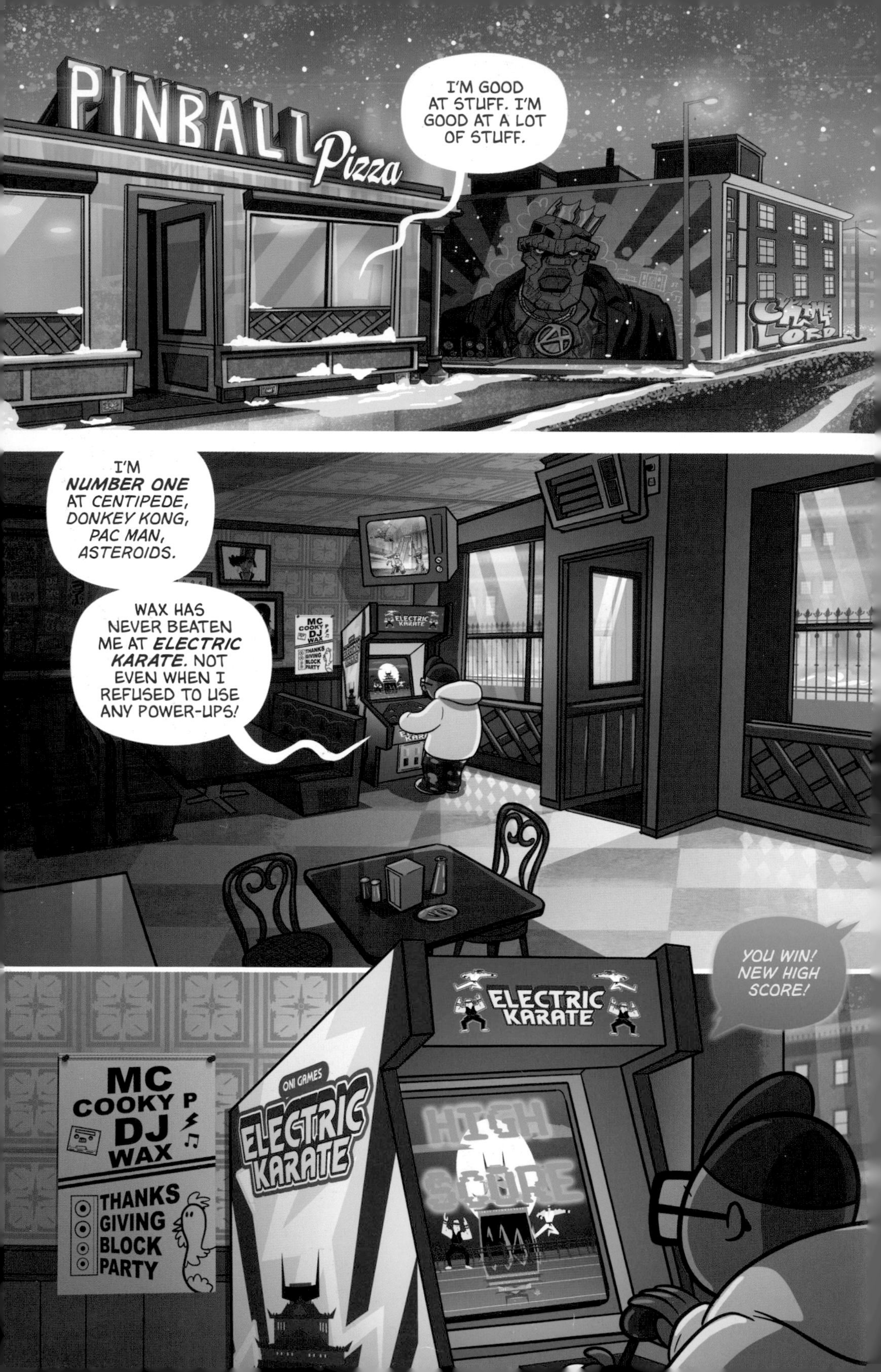
PINBALL
Pizza
I'M GOOD AT STUFF. I'M GOOD AT A LOT OF STUFF.
CRIME LORD
I'M *NUMBER ONE* AT *CENTIPEDE, DONKEY KONG, PAC MAN, ASTEROIDS.*
WAX HAS NEVER BEATEN ME AT *ELECTRIC KARATE.* NOT EVEN WHEN I REFUSED TO USE ANY POWER-UPS!
ELECTRIC KARATE
MC COOKY DJ WAX
THANKS GIVING BLOCK PARTY
ELECTRIC KARATE
ONI GAMES
ELECTRIC KARATE
HIGH SCORE
YOU WIN! NEW HIGH SCORE!

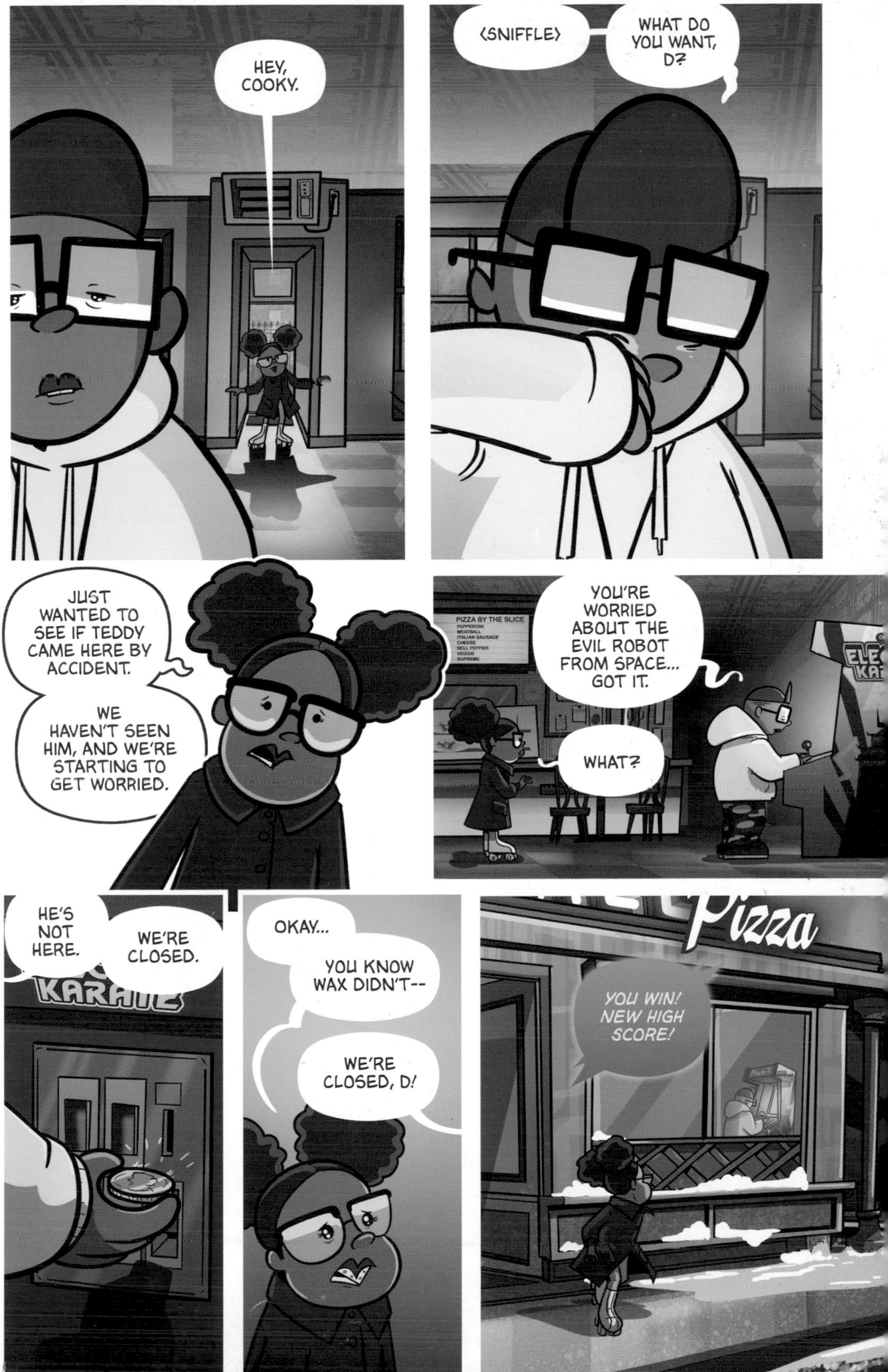
HEY, COOKY.
<SNIFFLE>
WHAT DO YOU WANT, D?
JUST WANTED TO SEE IF TEDDY CAME HERE BY ACCIDENT.
WE HAVEN'T SEEN HIM, AND WE'RE STARTING TO GET WORRIED.
PIZZA BY THE SLICE
PEPPERONI
MEATBALL
ITALIAN SAUSAGE
CHEESE
BELL PEPPER
VEGGIE
SUPREME
YOU'RE WORRIED ABOUT THE EVIL ROBOT FROM SPACE... GOT IT.
WHAT?
HE'S NOT HERE.
WE'RE CLOSED.
KARATE
OKAY...
YOU KNOW WAX DIDN'T--
WE'RE CLOSED, D!
Pizza
YOU WIN! NEW HIGH SCORE!

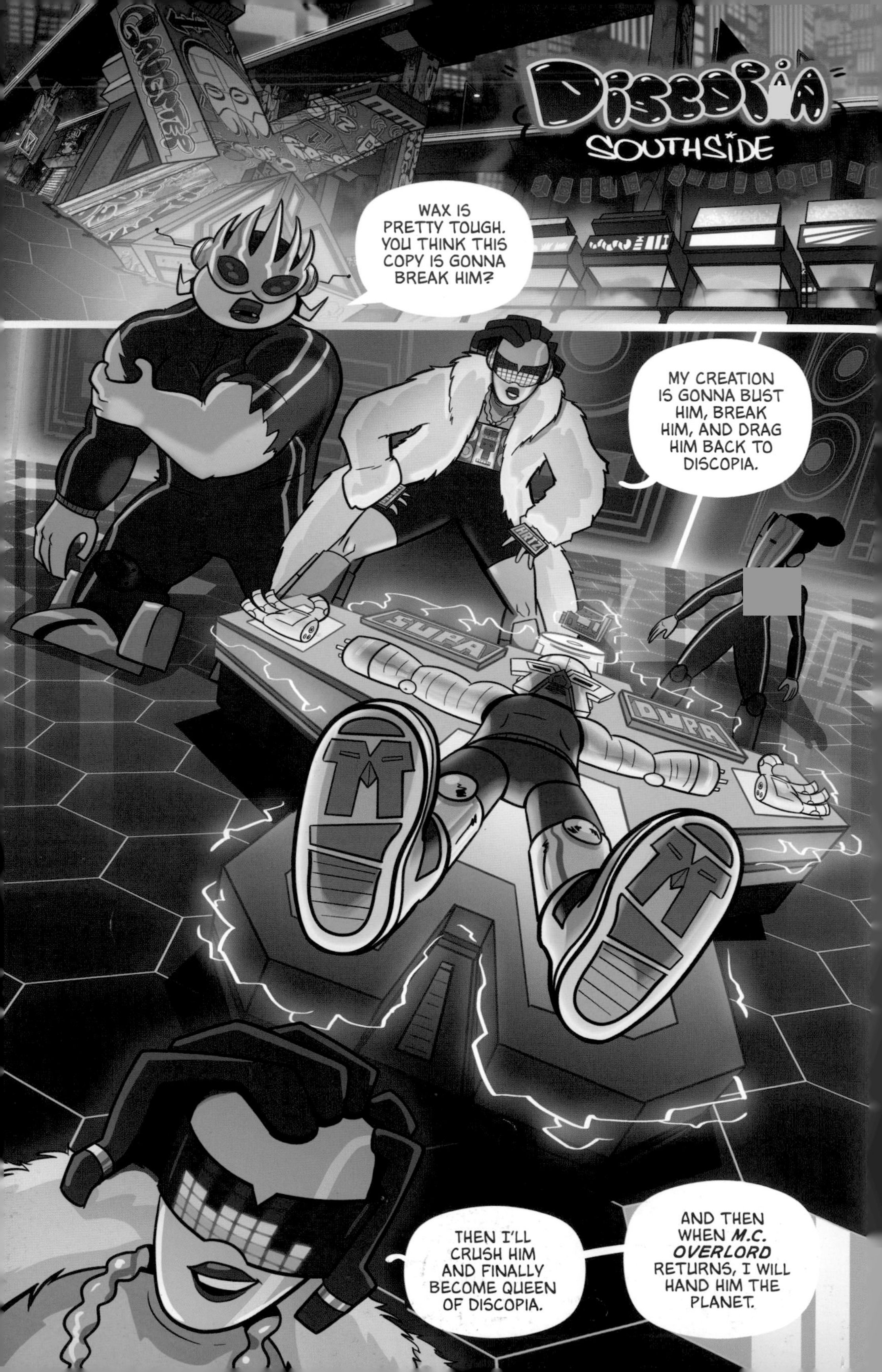
DISCOPIA
SOUTHSIDE
WAX IS PRETTY TOUGH. YOU THINK THIS COPY IS GONNA BREAK HIM?
MY CREATION IS GONNA BUST HIM, BREAK HIM, AND DRAG HIM BACK TO DISCOPIA.
SUPA
DUPA
THEN I'LL CRUSH HIM AND FINALLY BECOME QUEEN OF DISCOPIA.
AND THEN WHEN *M.C. OVERLORD* RETURNS, I WILL HAND HIM THE PLANET.

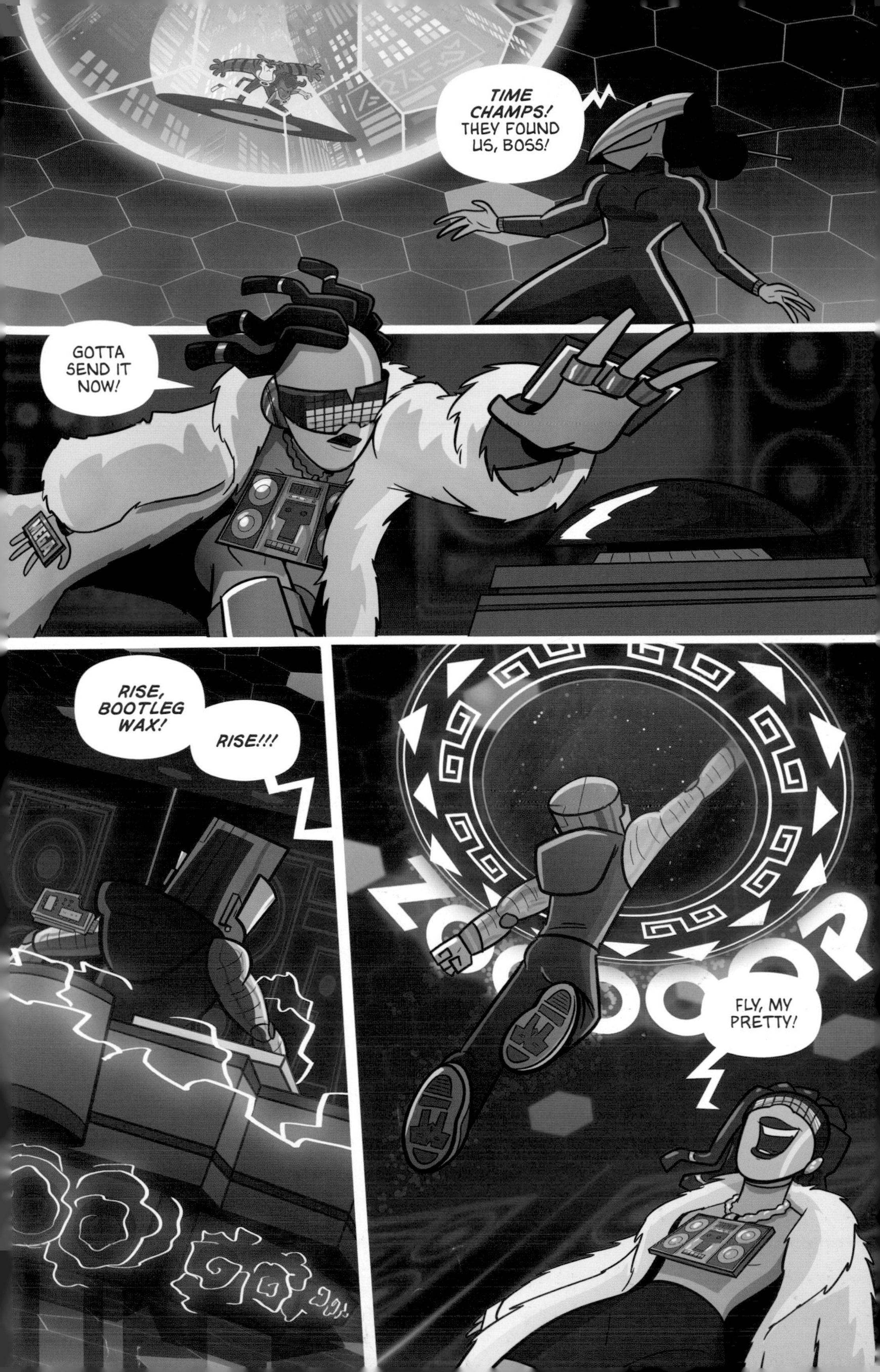
TIME CHAMPS! THEY FOUND US, BOSS!
GOTTA SEND IT NOW!
RISE, BOOTLEG WAX!
RISE!!!
FLY, MY PRETTY!

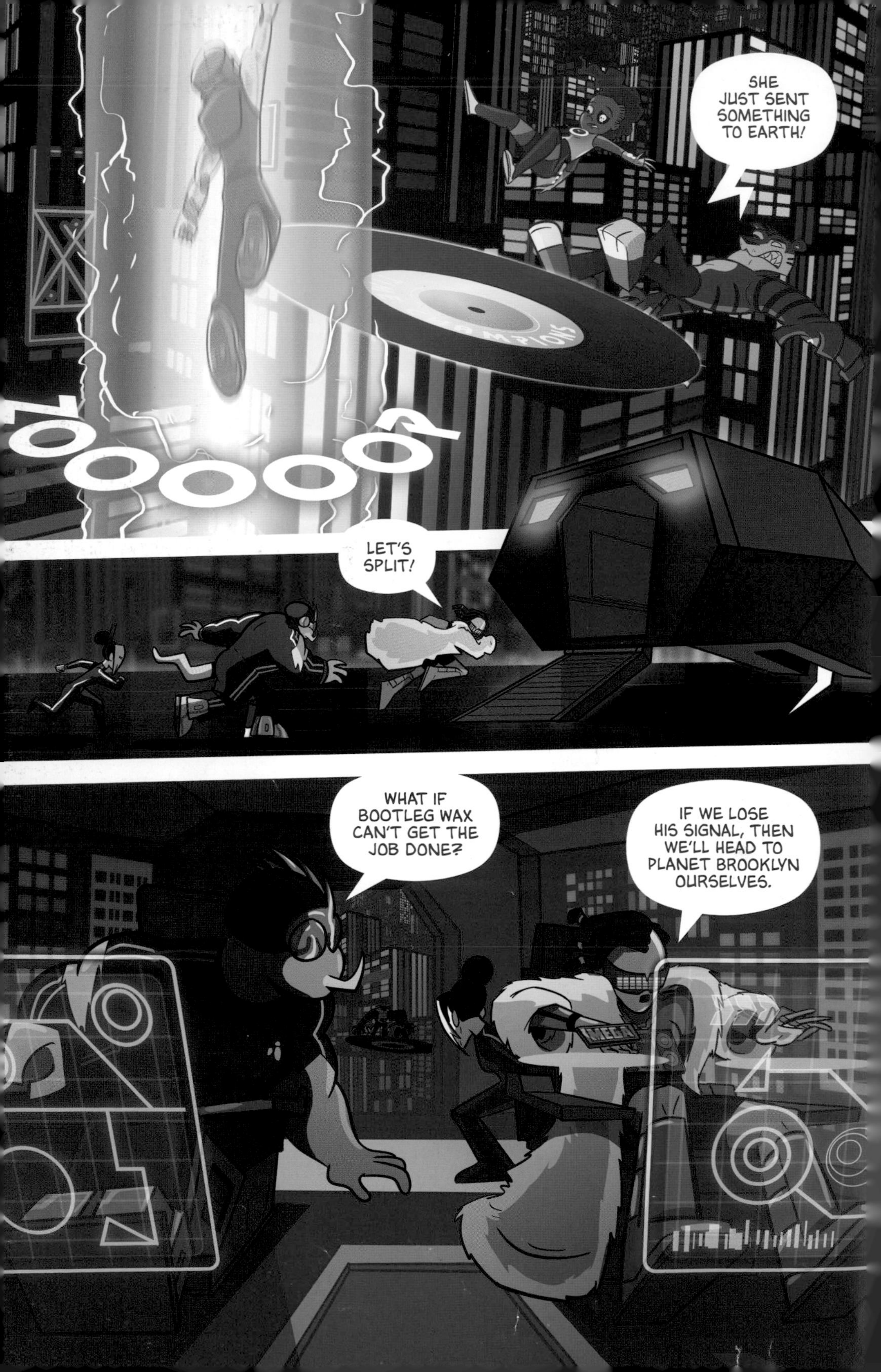
SHE JUST SENT SOMETHING TO EARTH!
TOOOOOOO
LET'S SPLIT!
WHAT IF BOOTLEG WAX CAN'T GET THE JOB DONE?
IF WE LOSE HIS SIGNAL, THEN WE'LL HEAD TO PLANET BROOKLYN OURSELVES.
MEGA

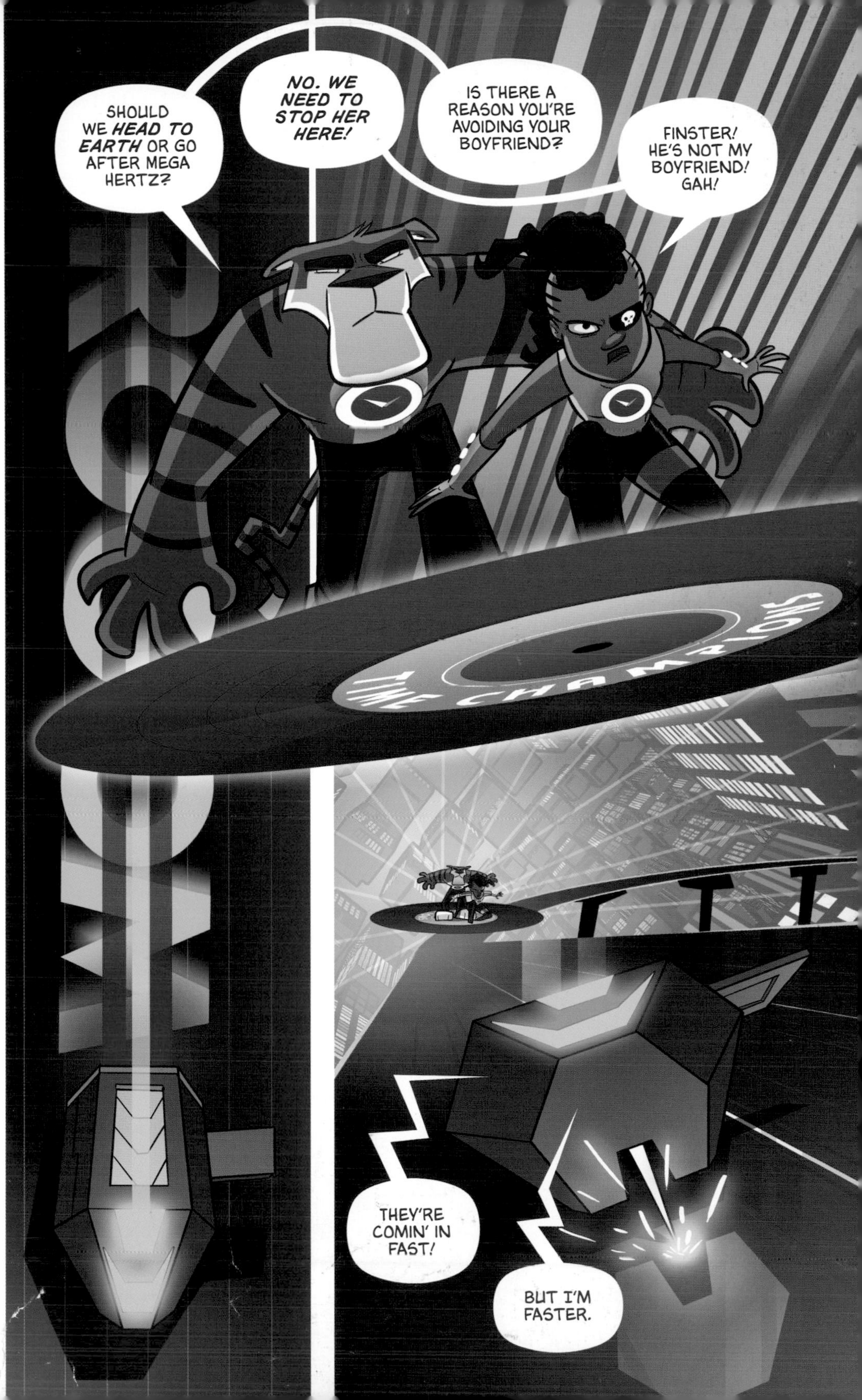
SHOULD WE *HEAD TO EARTH* OR GO AFTER MEGA HERTZ?
NO. WE NEED TO STOP HER HERE!
IS THERE A REASON YOU'RE AVOIDING YOUR BOYFRIEND?
FINSTER! HE'S NOT MY BOYFRIEND! GAH!
TIME CHAMELIONS
THEY'RE COMIN' IN FAST!
BUT I'M FASTER.

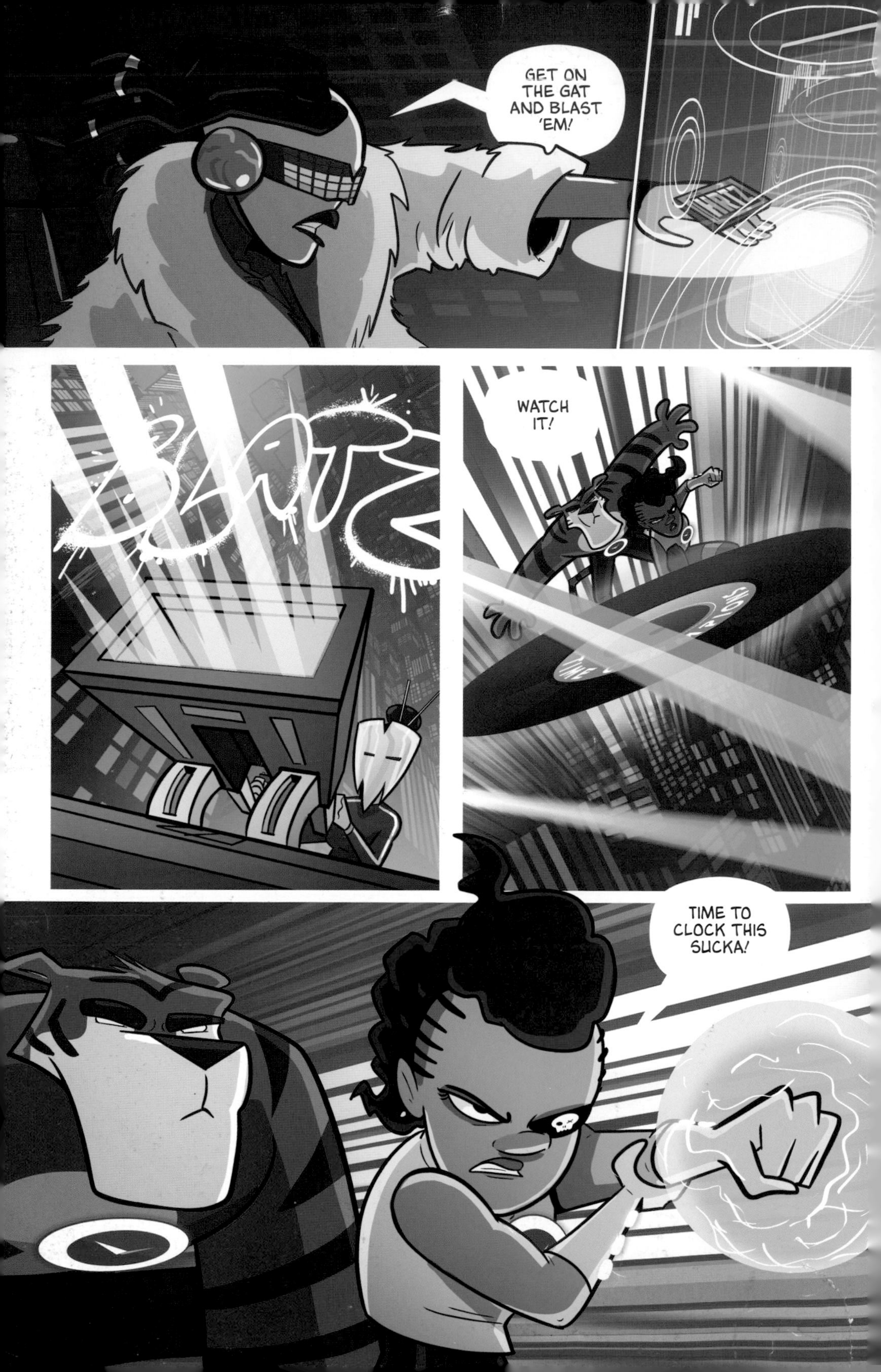
GET ON THE GAT AND BLAST 'EM!
WATCH IT!
TIME TO CLOCK THIS SUCKA!

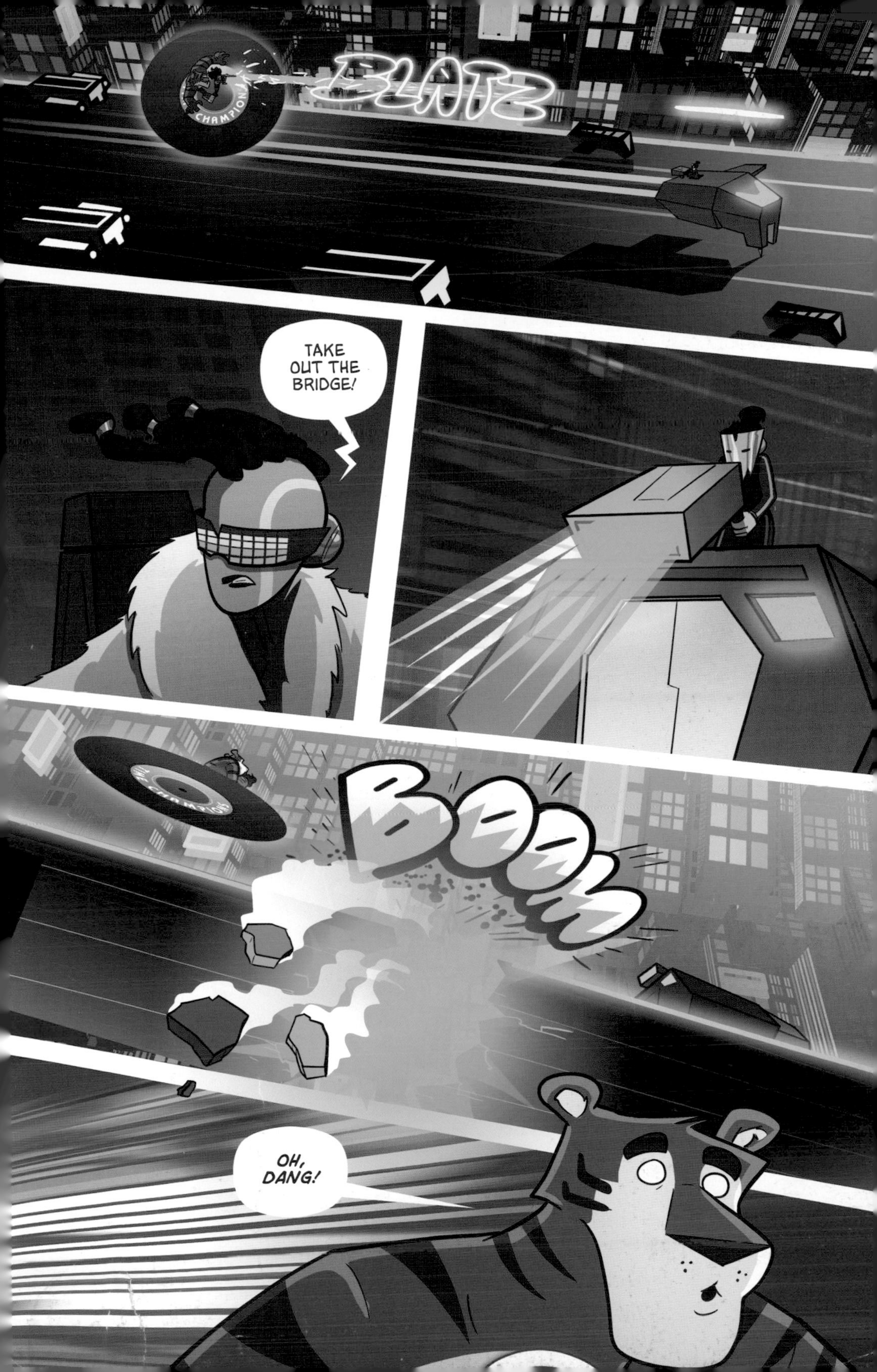

CHAMPIONS
BLATZ
TAKE OUT THE BRIDGE!
THE CHAMPIONS
BOOM
OH, DANG!

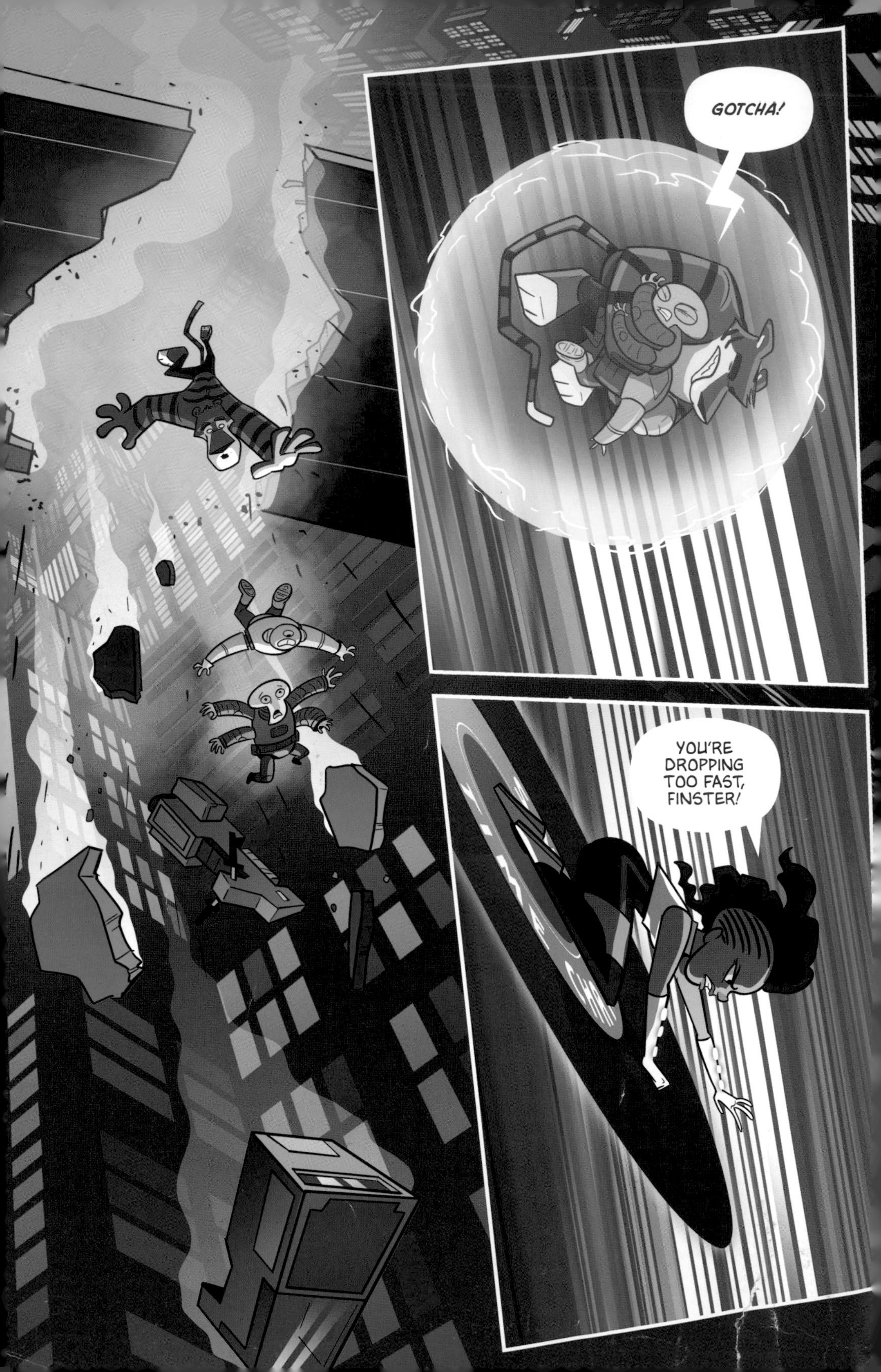
GOTCHA!
YOU'RE DROPPING TOO FAST, FINSTER!

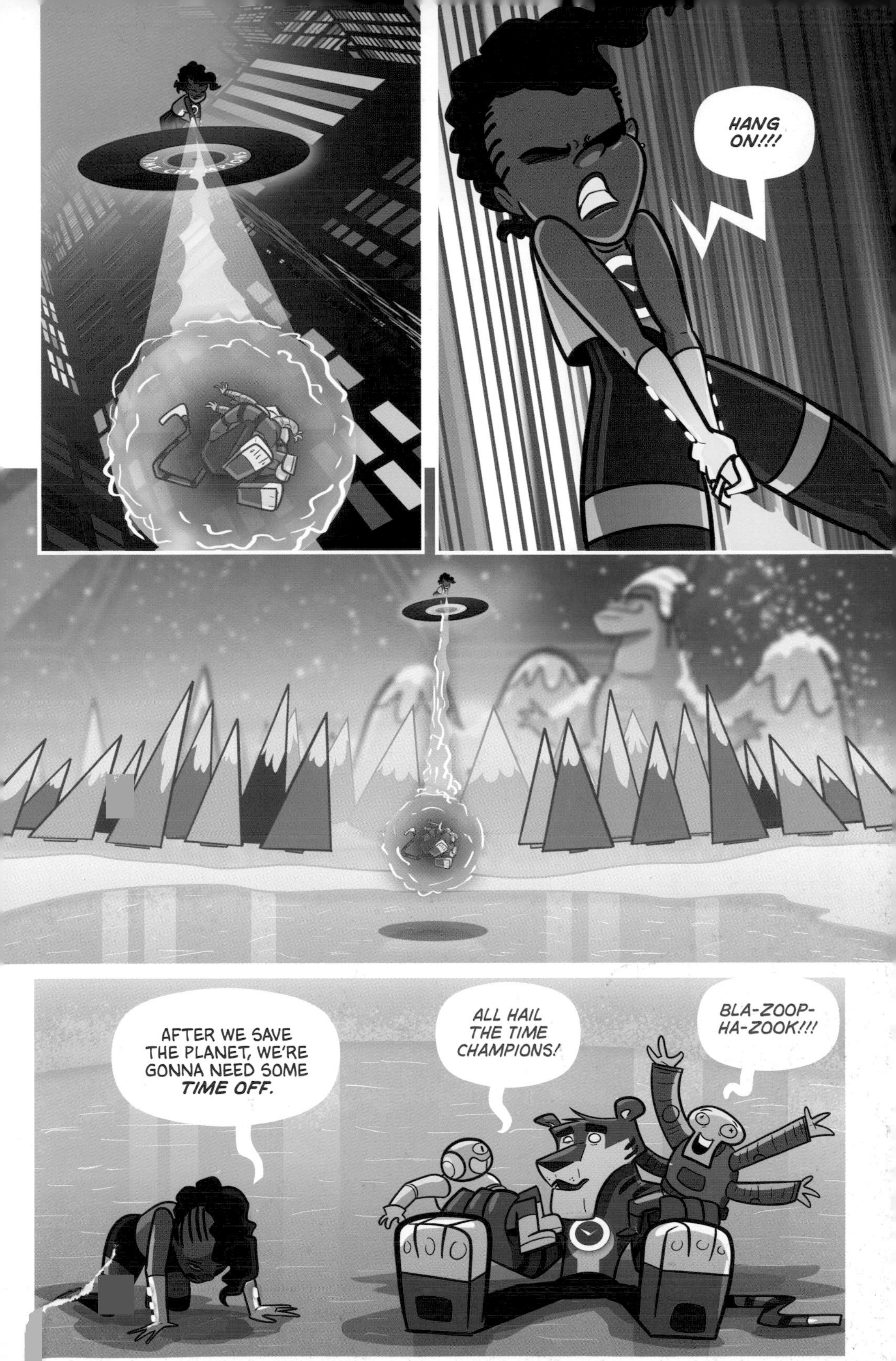
HANG ON!!!
AFTER WE SAVE THE PLANET, WE'RE GONNA NEED SOME *TIME OFF.*
ALL HAIL THE TIME CHAMPIONS!
BLA-ZOOP-HA-ZOOK!!!

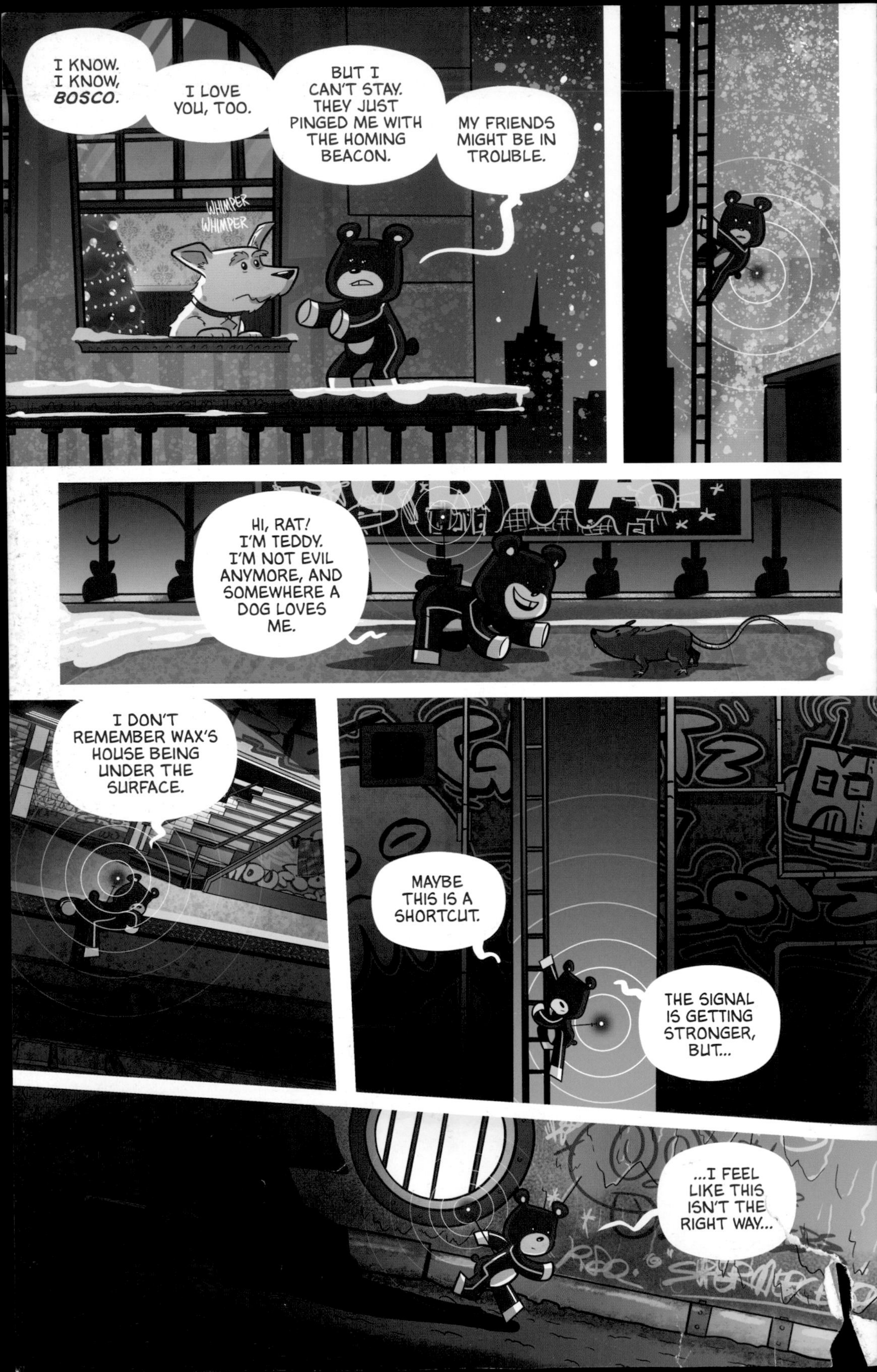
I KNOW. I KNOW, *BOSCO.*
I LOVE YOU, TOO.
BUT I CAN'T STAY. THEY JUST PINGED ME WITH THE HOMING BEACON.
MY FRIENDS MIGHT BE IN TROUBLE.
WHIMPER WHIMPER
HI, RAT! I'M TEDDY. I'M NOT EVIL ANYMORE, AND SOMEWHERE A DOG LOVES ME.
I DON'T REMEMBER WAX'S HOUSE BEING UNDER THE SURFACE.
MAYBE THIS IS A SHORTCUT.
THE SIGNAL IS GETTING STRONGER, BUT...
...I FEEL LIKE THIS ISN'T THE RIGHT WAY...

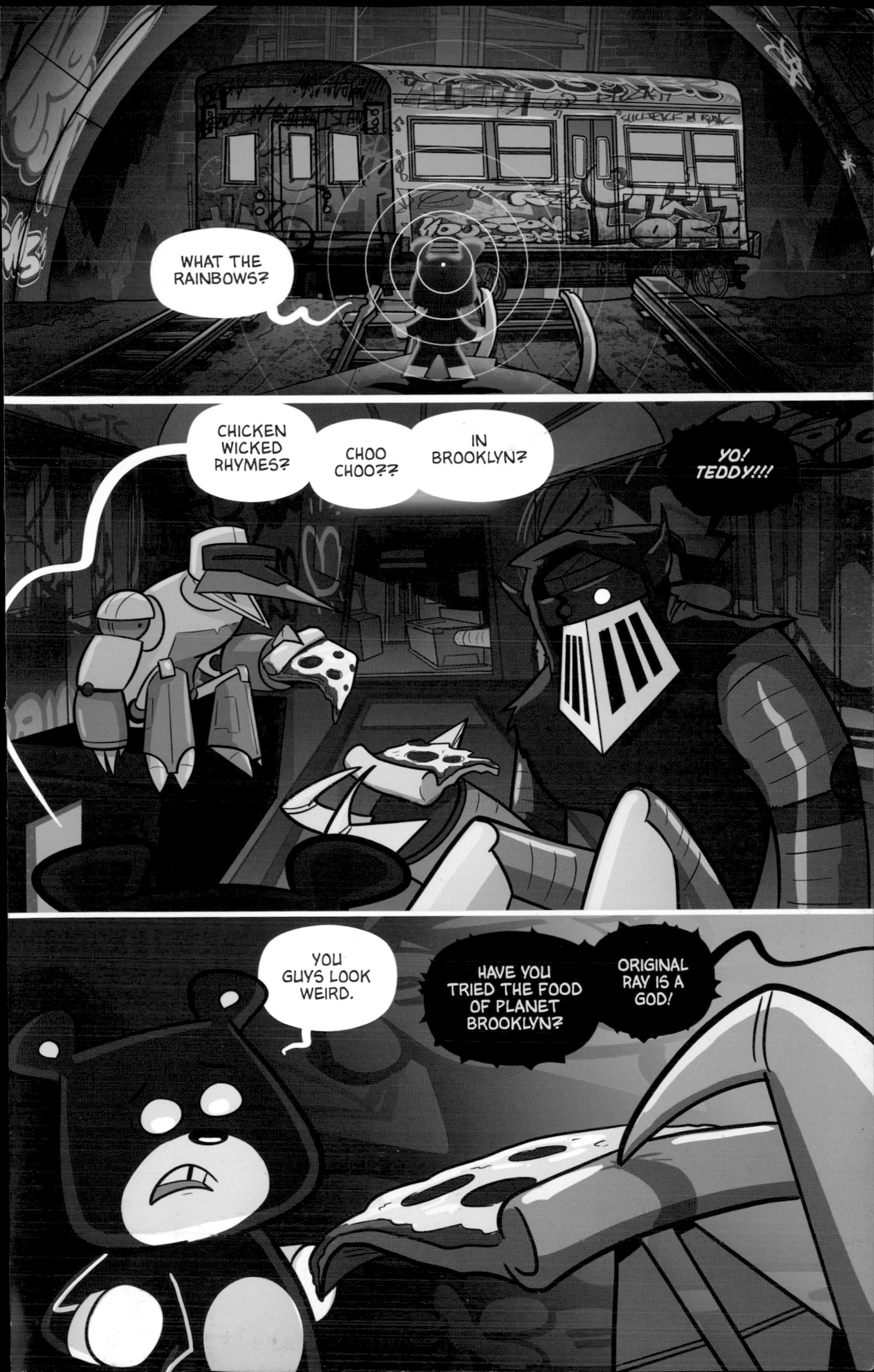
WHAT THE RAINBOWS?
CHICKEN WICKED RHYMES?
CHOO CHOO??
IN BROOKLYN?
YO! TEDDY!!!
YOU GUYS LOOK WEIRD.
HAVE YOU TRIED THE FOOD OF PLANET BROOKLYN?
ORIGINAL RAY IS A GOD!

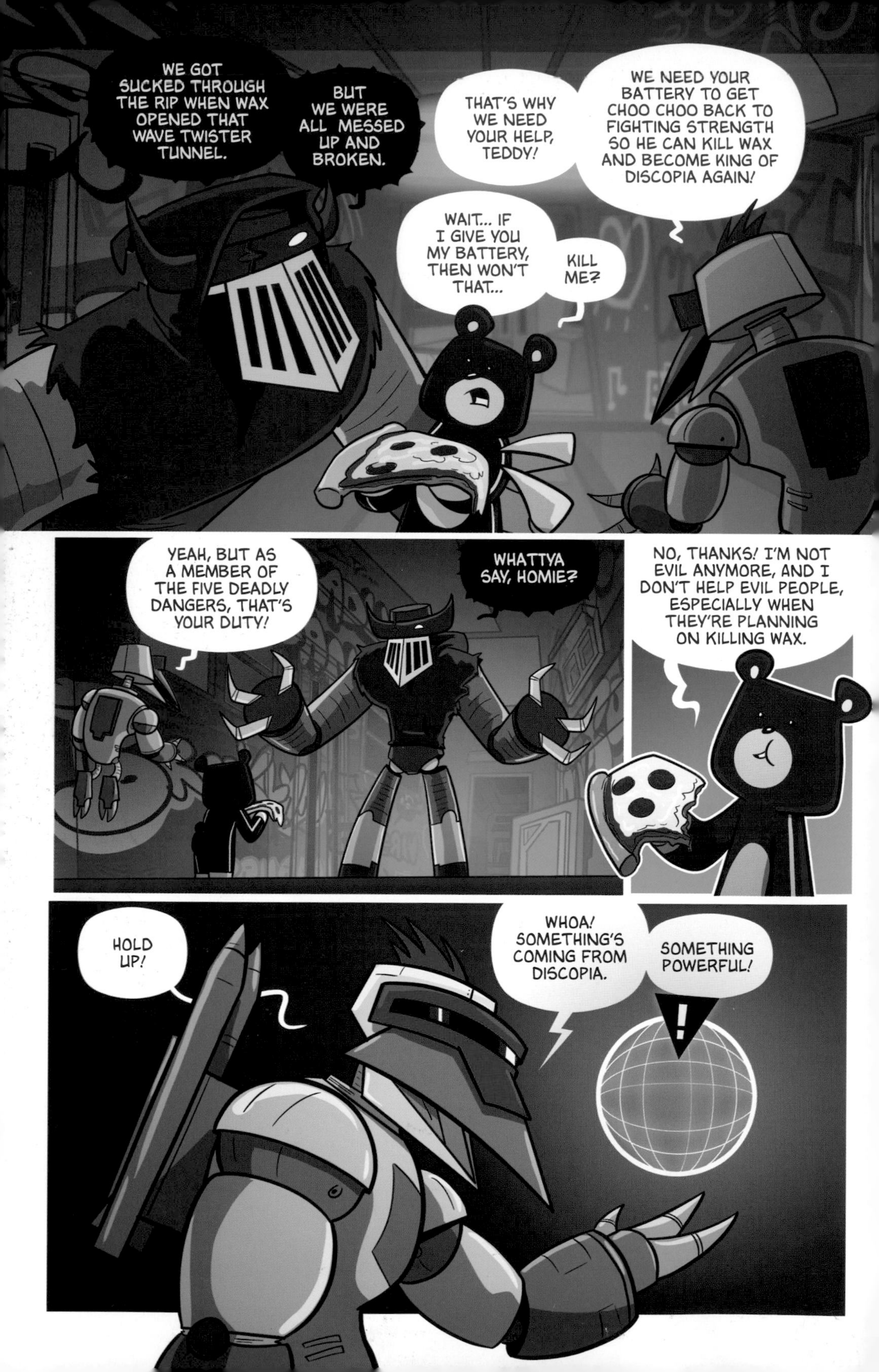

WE GOT SUCKED THROUGH THE RIP WHEN WAX OPENED THAT WAVE TWISTER TUNNEL.
BUT WE WERE ALL MESSED UP AND BROKEN.
THAT'S WHY WE NEED YOUR HELP, TEDDY!
WE NEED YOUR BATTERY TO GET CHOO CHOO BACK TO FIGHTING STRENGTH SO HE CAN KILL WAX AND BECOME KING OF DISCOPIA AGAIN!
WAIT... IF I GIVE YOU MY BATTERY, THEN WON'T THAT...
KILL ME?
YEAH, BUT AS A MEMBER OF THE FIVE DEADLY DANGERS, THAT'S YOUR DUTY!
WHATTYA SAY, HOMIE?
NO, THANKS! I'M NOT EVIL ANYMORE, AND I DON'T HELP EVIL PEOPLE, ESPECIALLY WHEN THEY'RE PLANNING ON KILLING WAX.
HOLD UP!
WHOA! SOMETHING'S COMING FROM DISCOPIA.
SOMETHING POWERFUL!
!

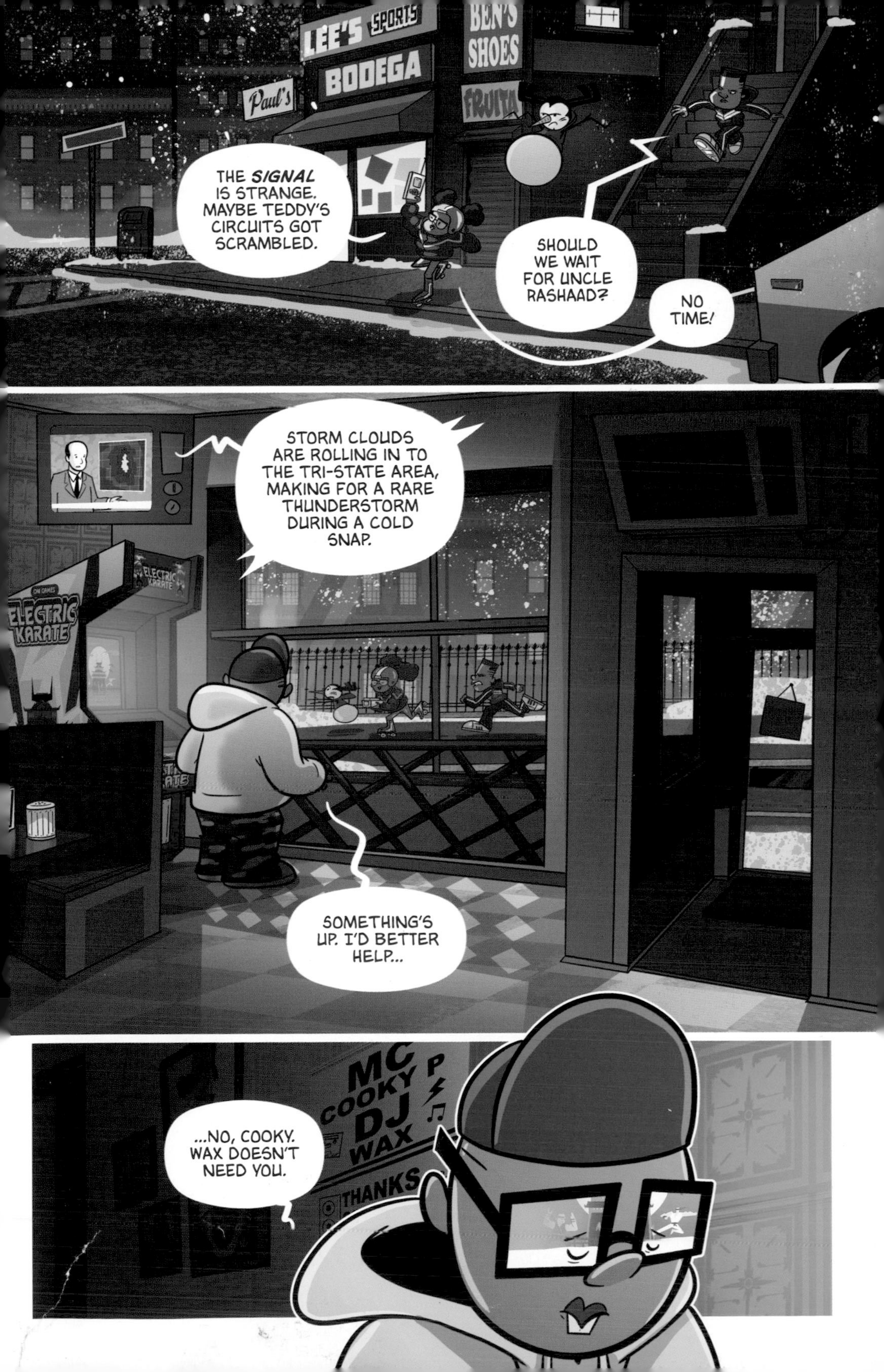
LEE'S SPORTS
BODEGA
BEN'S SHOES
Paul's
FRUITA
THE *SIGNAL* IS STRANGE. MAYBE TEDDY'S CIRCUITS GOT SCRAMBLED.
SHOULD WE WAIT FOR UNCLE RASHAAD?
NO TIME!
STORM CLOUDS ARE ROLLING IN TO THE TRI-STATE AREA, MAKING FOR A RARE THUNDERSTORM DURING A COLD SNAP.
ELECTRIC KARATE
SOMETHING'S UP. I'D BETTER HELP...
MC COOKY DJ WAX
THANKS
...NO, COOKY. WAX DOESN'T NEED YOU.

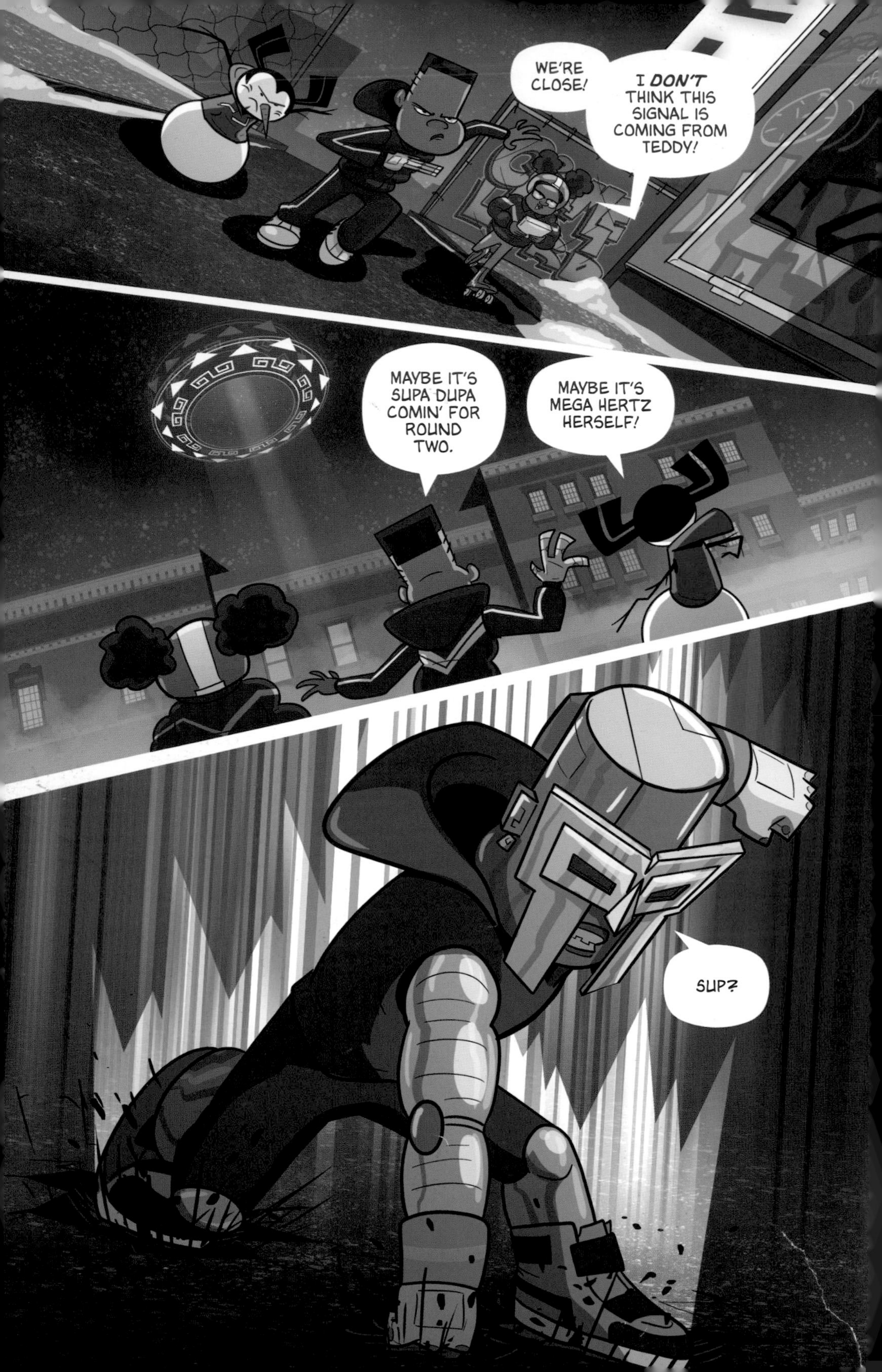
WE'RE CLOSE!
I DON'T THINK THIS SIGNAL IS COMING FROM TEDDY!
MAYBE IT'S SUPA DUPA COMIN' FOR ROUND TWO.
MAYBE IT'S MEGA HERTZ HERSELF!
SUP?

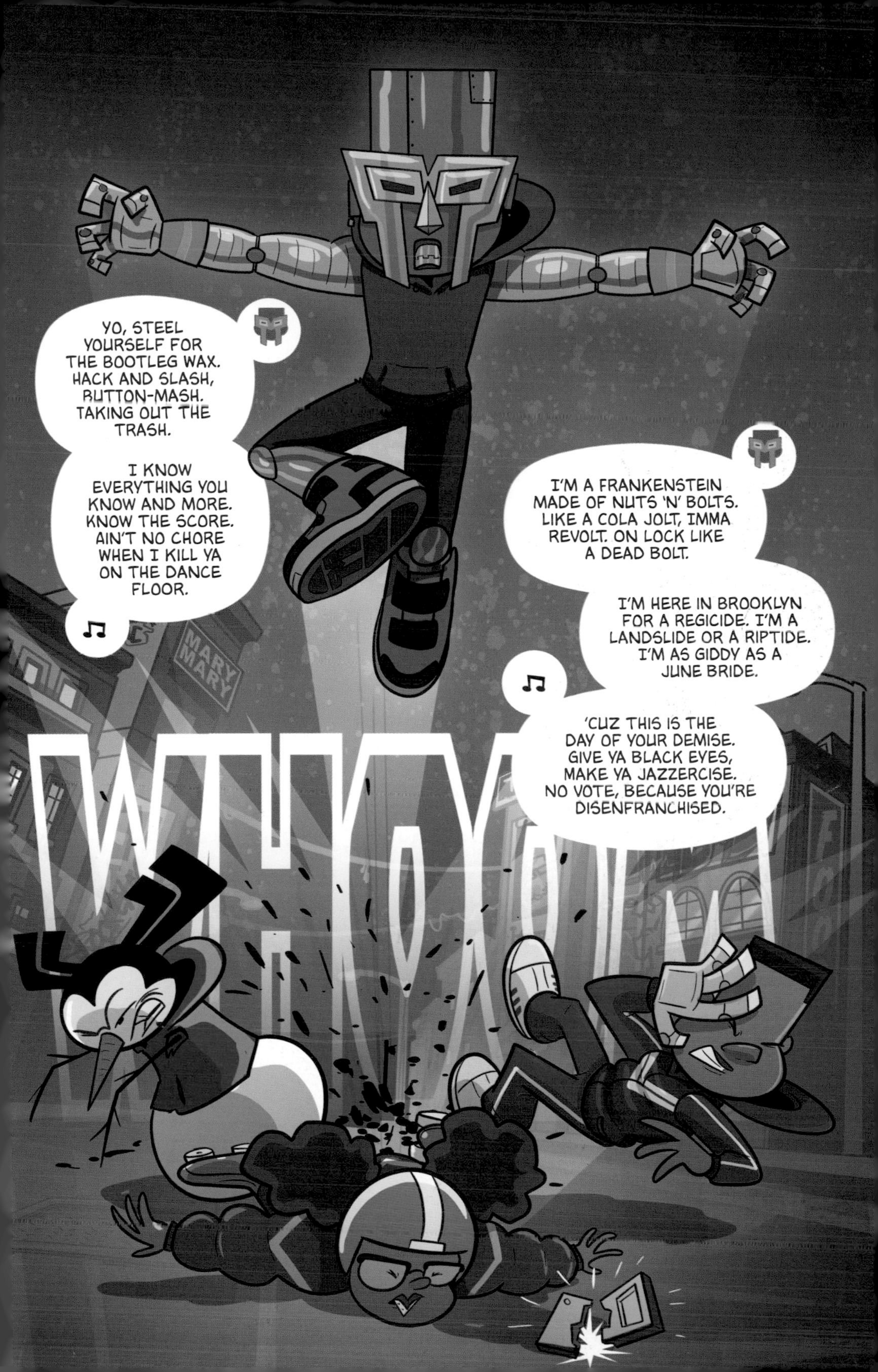
YO, STEEL YOURSELF FOR THE BOOTLEG WAX. HACK AND SLASH, BUTTON-MASH. TAKING OUT THE TRASH.
I KNOW EVERYTHING YOU KNOW AND MORE. KNOW THE SCORE. AIN'T NO CHORE WHEN I KILL YA ON THE DANCE FLOOR.
I'M A FRANKENSTEIN MADE OF NUTS 'N' BOLTS. LIKE A COLA JOLT, IMMA REVOLT. ON LOCK LIKE A DEAD BOLT.
I'M HERE IN BROOKLYN FOR A REGICIDE. I'M A LANDSLIDE OR A RIPTIDE. I'M AS GIDDY AS A JUNE BRIDE.
'CUZ THIS IS THE DAY OF YOUR DEMISE. GIVE YA BLACK EYES, MAKE YA JAZZERCISE. NO VOTE, BECAUSE YOU'RE DISENFRANCHISED.
MARY MARY

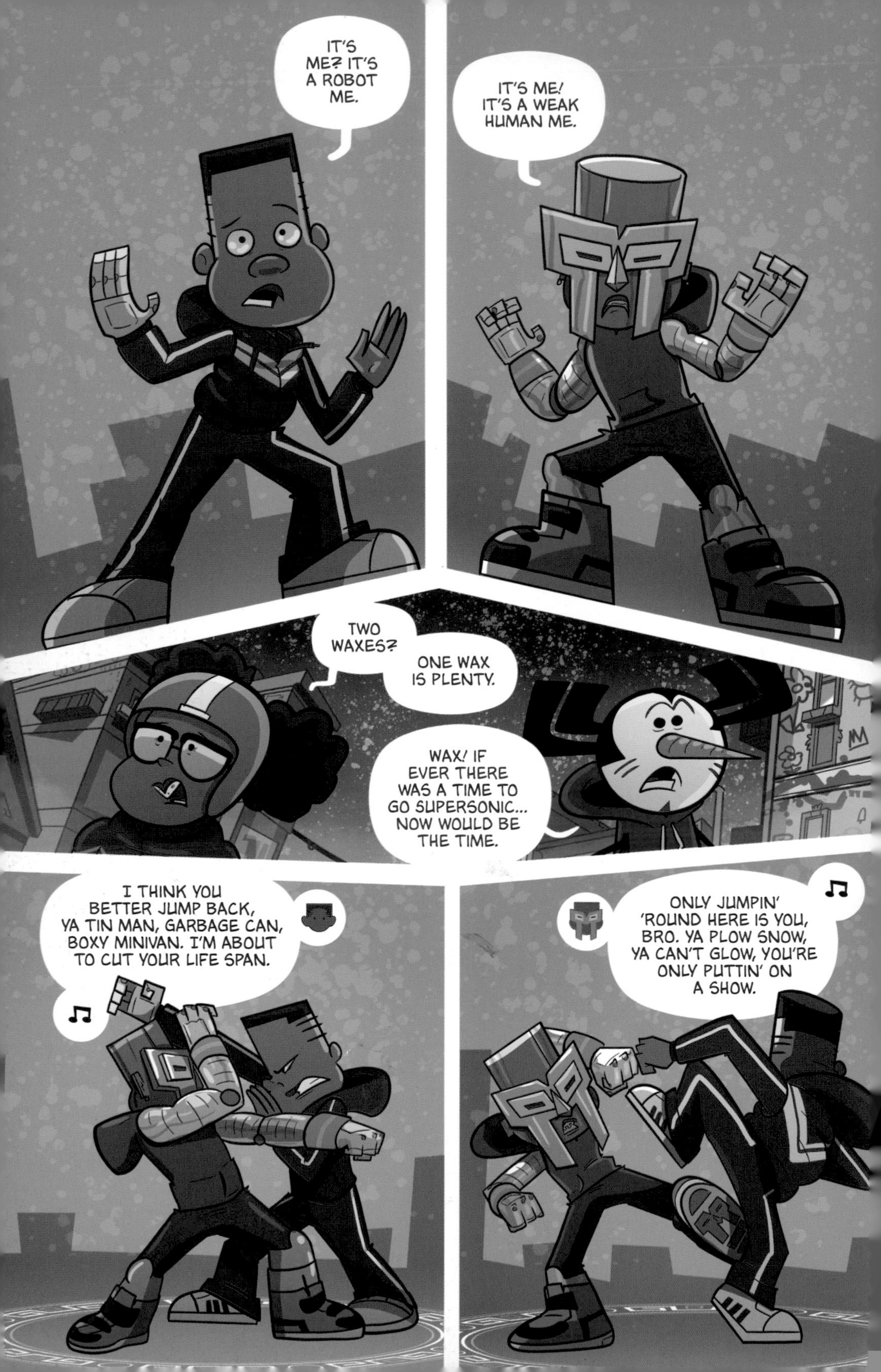

IT'S ME? IT'S A ROBOT ME.
IT'S ME! IT'S A WEAK HUMAN ME.
TWO WAXES?
ONE WAX IS PLENTY.
WAX! IF EVER THERE WAS A TIME TO GO SUPERSONIC... NOW WOULD BE THE TIME.
I THINK YOU BETTER JUMP BACK, YA TIN MAN, GARBAGE CAN, BOXY MINIVAN. I'M ABOUT TO CUT YOUR LIFE SPAN.
ONLY JUMPIN' 'ROUND HERE IS YOU, BRO. YA PLOW SNOW, YA CAN'T GLOW, YOU'RE ONLY PUTTIN' ON A SHOW.

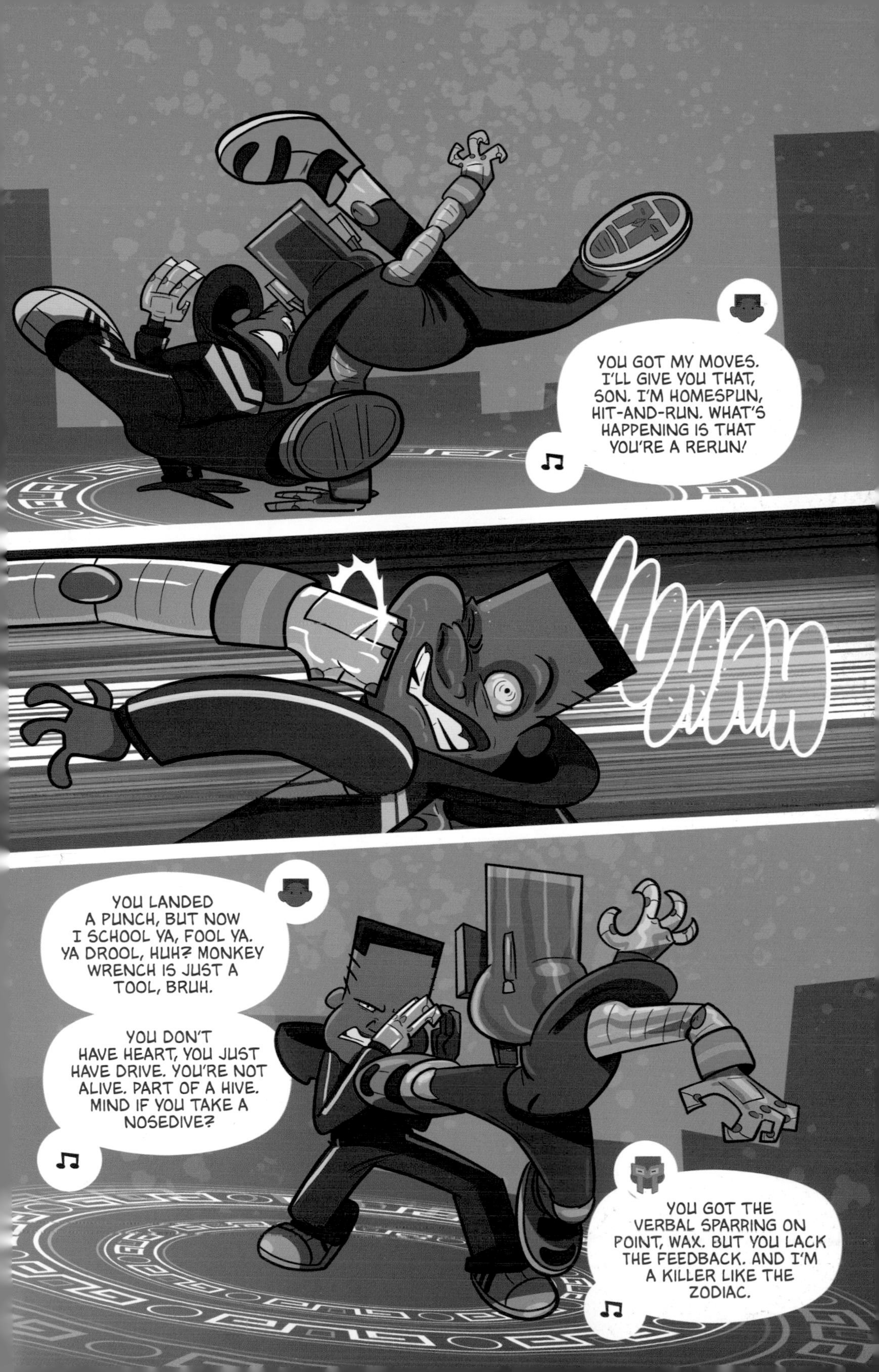
YOU GOT MY MOVES. I'LL GIVE YOU THAT, SON. I'M HOMESPUN, HIT-AND-RUN. WHAT'S HAPPENING IS THAT YOU'RE A RERUN!
WHAM
YOU LANDED A PUNCH, BUT NOW I SCHOOL YA, FOOL YA. YA DROOL, HUH? MONKEY WRENCH IS JUST A TOOL, BRUH.
YOU DON'T HAVE HEART, YOU JUST HAVE DRIVE. YOU'RE NOT ALIVE. PART OF A HIVE. MIND IF YOU TAKE A NOSEDIVE?
YOU GOT THE VERBAL SPARRING ON POINT, WAX. BUT YOU LACK THE FEEDBACK. AND I'M A KILLER LIKE THE ZODIAC.

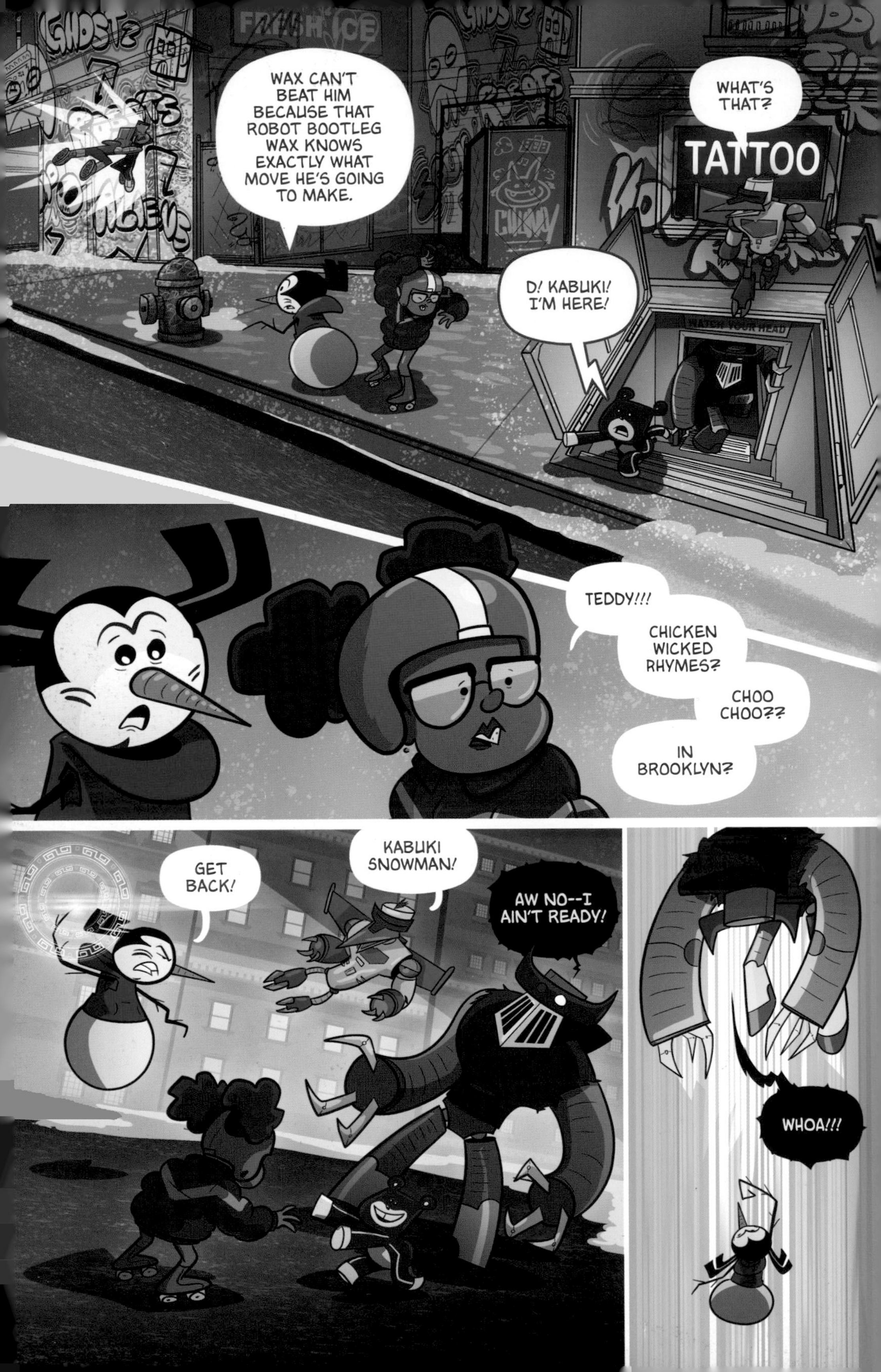
WAX CAN'T BEAT HIM BECAUSE THAT ROBOT BOOTLEG WAX KNOWS EXACTLY WHAT MOVE HE'S GOING TO MAKE.
WHAT'S THAT?
TATTOO
D! KABUKI! I'M HERE!
TEDDY!!!
CHICKEN WICKED RHYMES?
CHOO CHOO??
IN BROOKLYN?
GET BACK!
KABUKI SNOWMAN!
AW NO--I AIN'T READY!
WHOA!!!

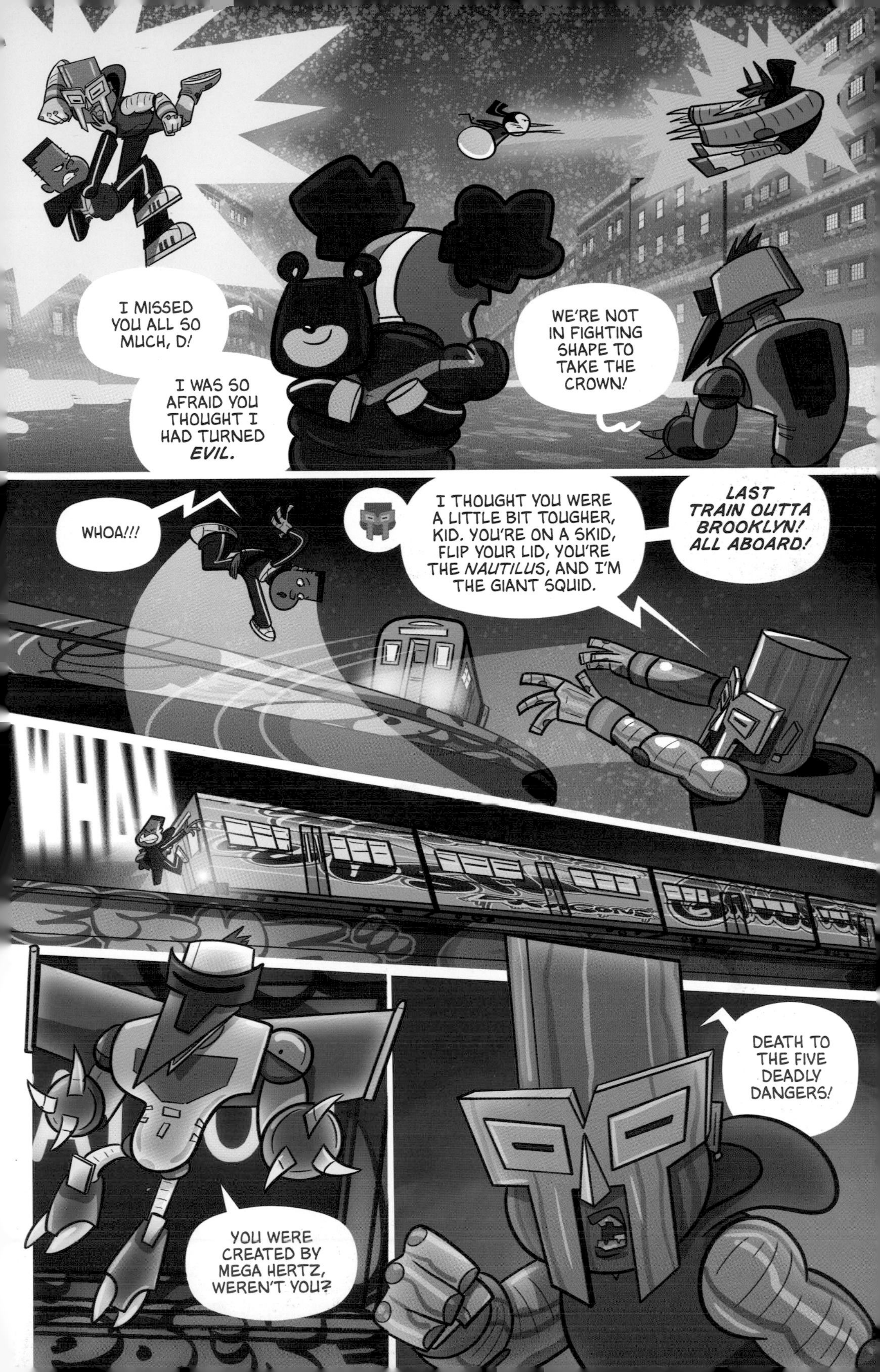
I MISSED YOU ALL SO MUCH, D!
I WAS SO AFRAID YOU THOUGHT I HAD TURNED *EVIL.*
WE'RE NOT IN FIGHTING SHAPE TO TAKE THE CROWN!
WHOA!!!
I THOUGHT YOU WERE A LITTLE BIT TOUGHER, KID. YOU'RE ON A SKID, FLIP YOUR LID, YOU'RE THE *NAUTILUS*, AND I'M THE GIANT SQUID.
LAST TRAIN OUTTA BROOKLYN! ALL ABOARD!
WHAM
DEATH TO THE FIVE DEADLY DANGERS!
YOU WERE CREATED BY MEGA HERTZ, WEREN'T YOU?

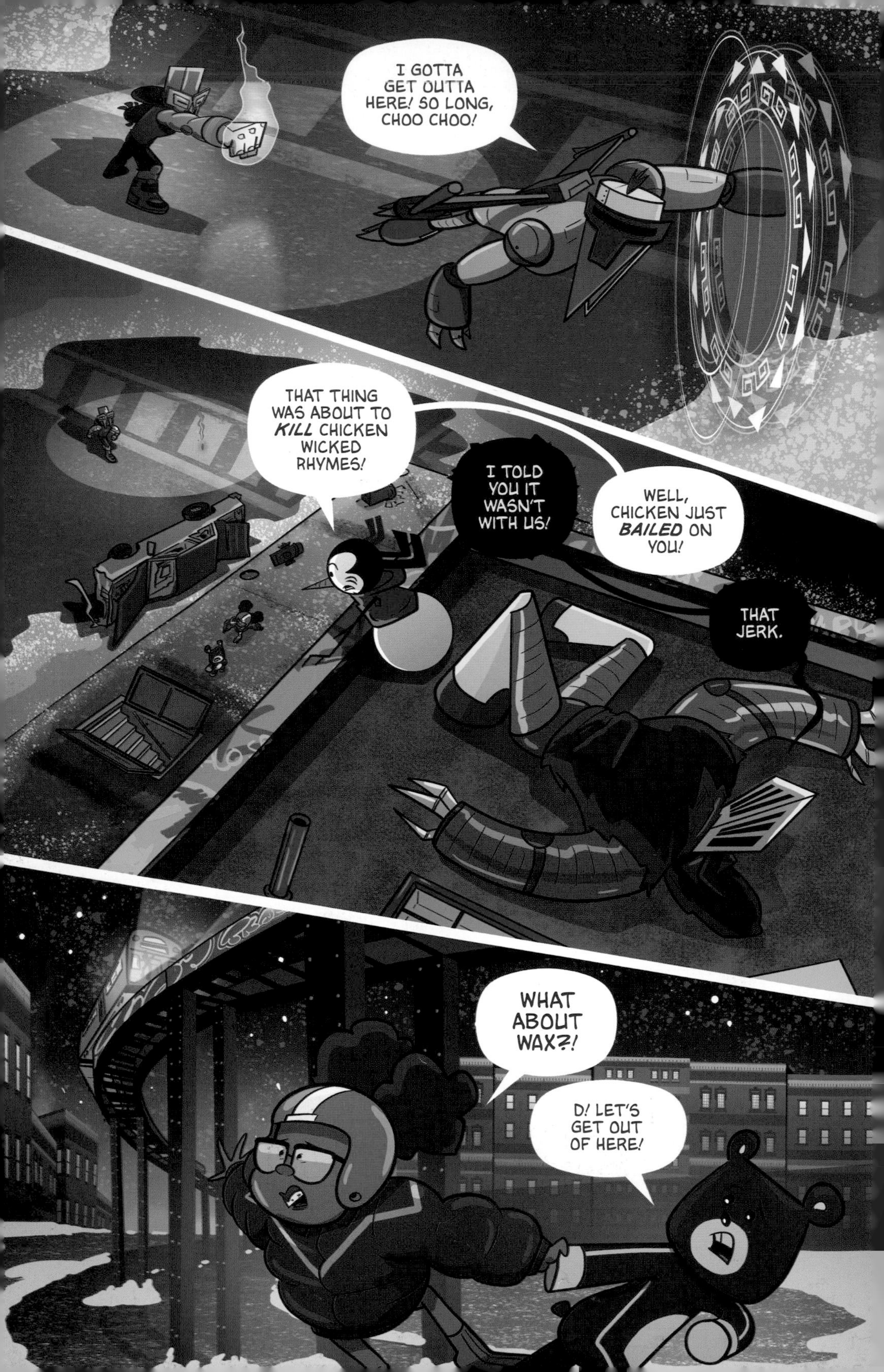
I GOTTA GET OUTTA HERE! SO LONG, CHOO CHOO!
THAT THING WAS ABOUT TO KILL CHICKEN WICKED RHYMES!
I TOLD YOU IT WASN'T WITH US!
WELL, CHICKEN JUST BAILED ON YOU!
THAT JERK.
WHAT ABOUT WAX?!
D! LET'S GET OUT OF HERE!

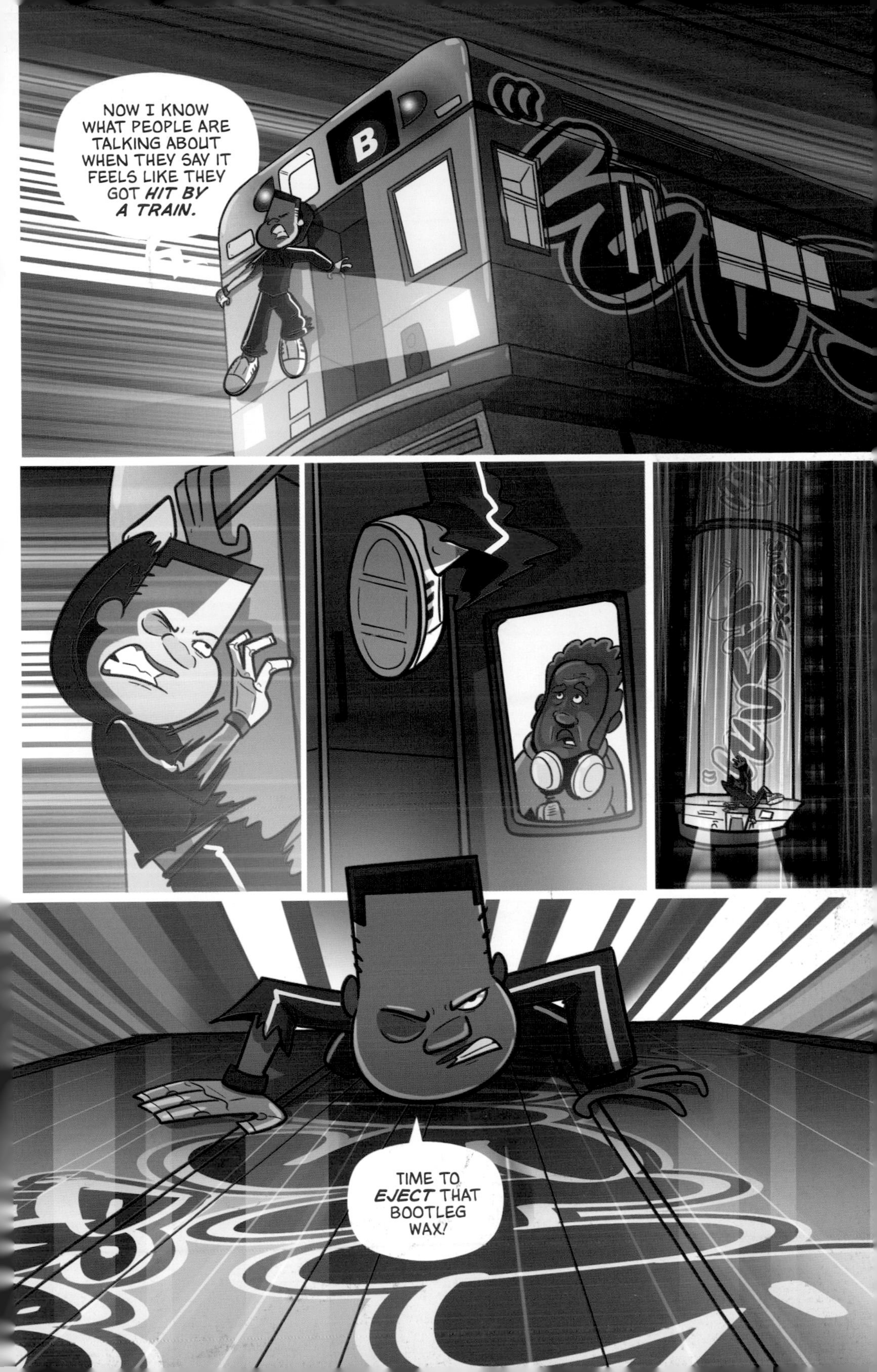
NOW I KNOW WHAT PEOPLE ARE TALKING ABOUT WHEN THEY SAY IT FEELS LIKE THEY GOT HIT BY A TRAIN.
B
TIME TO EJECT THAT BOOTLEG WAX!

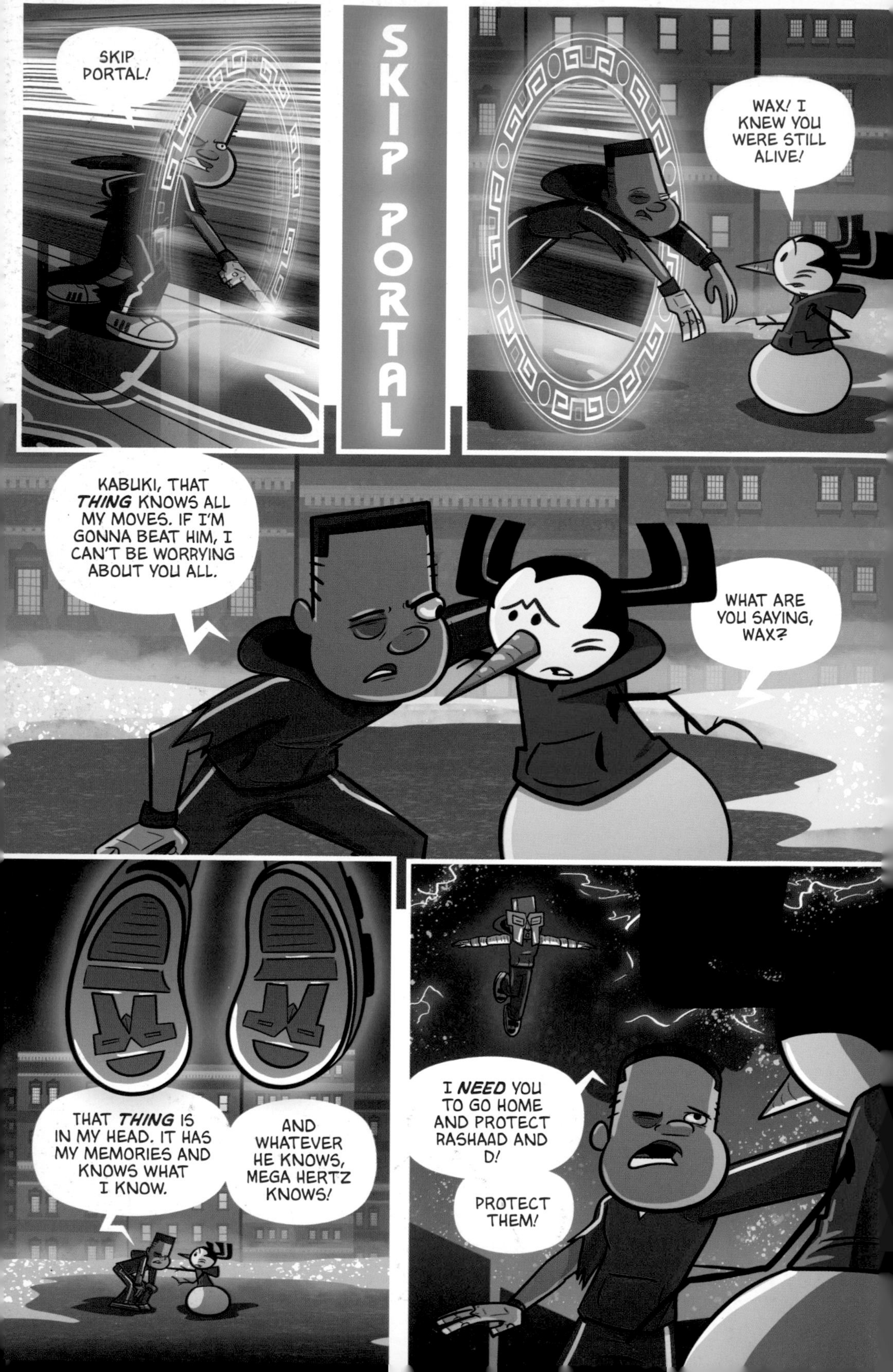
SKIP PORTAL!
SKIP PORTAL
WAX! I KNEW YOU WERE STILL ALIVE!
KABUKI, THAT *THING* KNOWS ALL MY MOVES. IF I'M GONNA BEAT HIM, I CAN'T BE WORRYING ABOUT YOU ALL.
WHAT ARE YOU SAYING, WAX?
THAT *THING* IS IN MY HEAD. IT HAS MY MEMORIES AND KNOWS WHAT I KNOW.
AND WHATEVER HE KNOWS, MEGA HERTZ KNOWS!
I *NEED* YOU TO GO HOME AND PROTECT RASHAAD AND D!
PROTECT THEM!

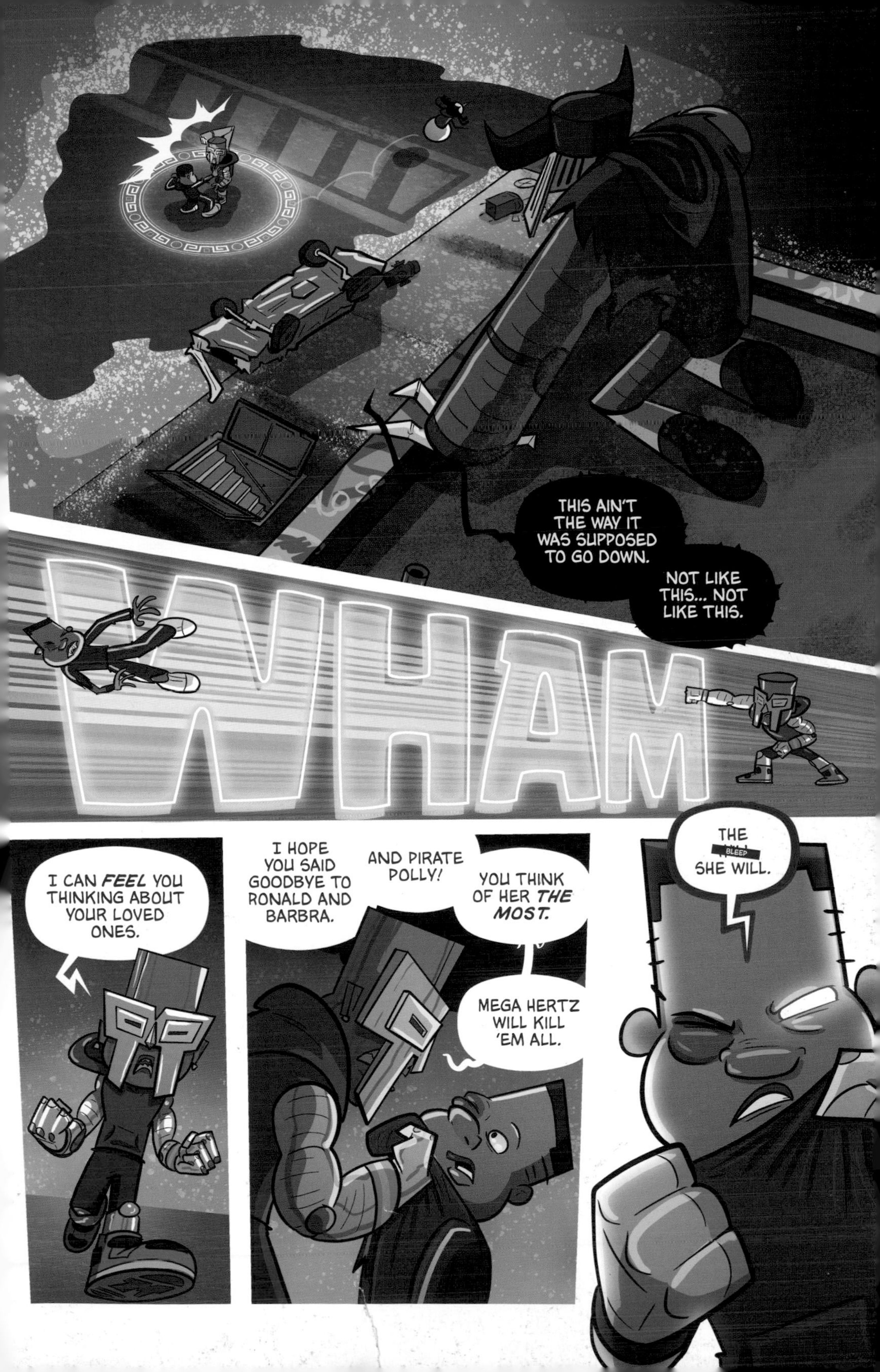
THIS AIN'T THE WAY IT WAS SUPPOSED TO GO DOWN.
NOT LIKE THIS... NOT LIKE THIS.
WHAM
I CAN *FEEL* YOU THINKING ABOUT YOUR LOVED ONES.
I HOPE YOU SAID GOODBYE TO RONALD AND BARBRA.
AND PIRATE POLLY!
YOU THINK OF HER *THE MOST.*
MEGA HERTZ WILL KILL 'EM ALL.
THE [redacted] SHE WILL.
BLEEP

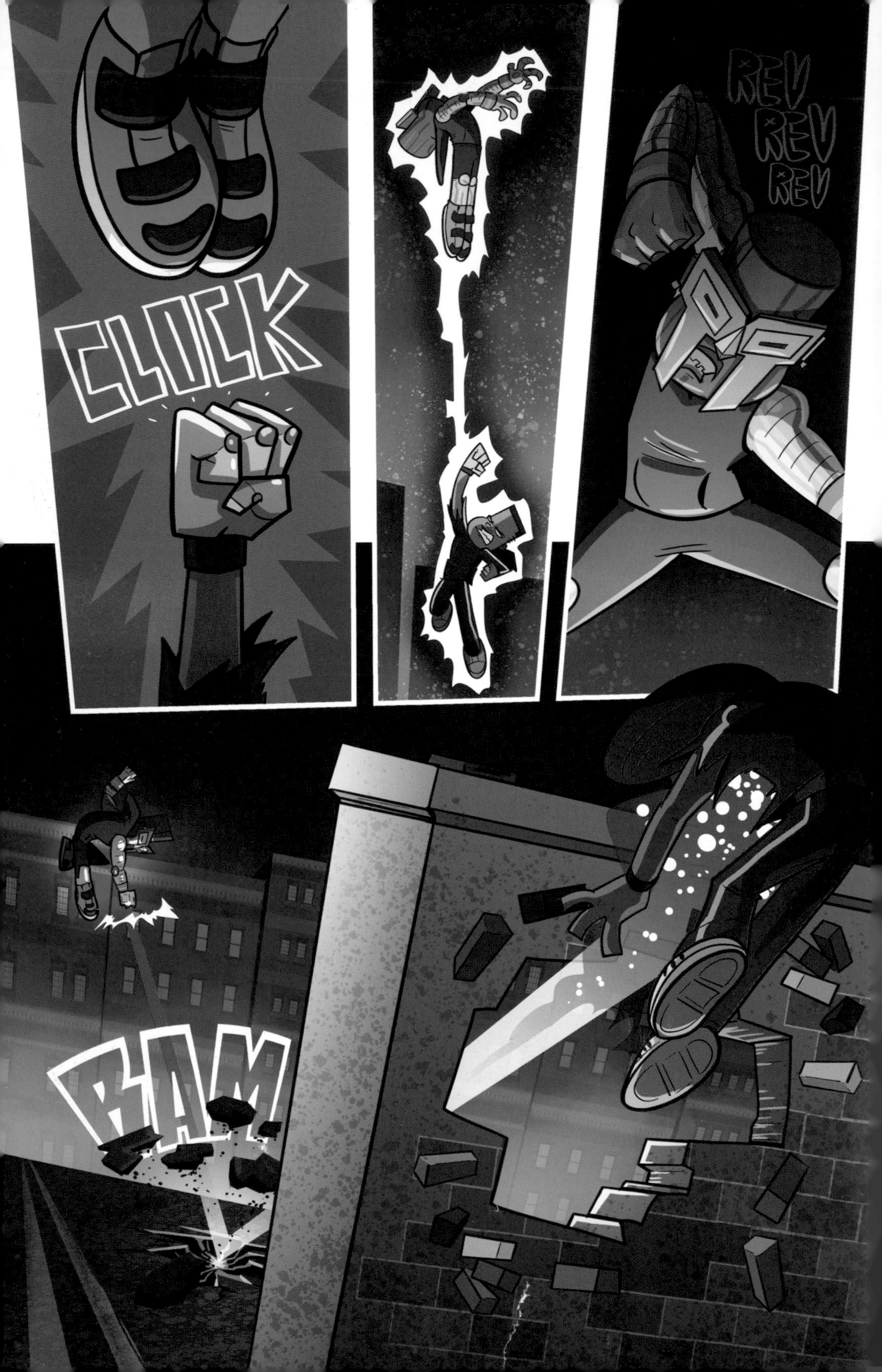
CLOCK
REV
REV
REV
BAM

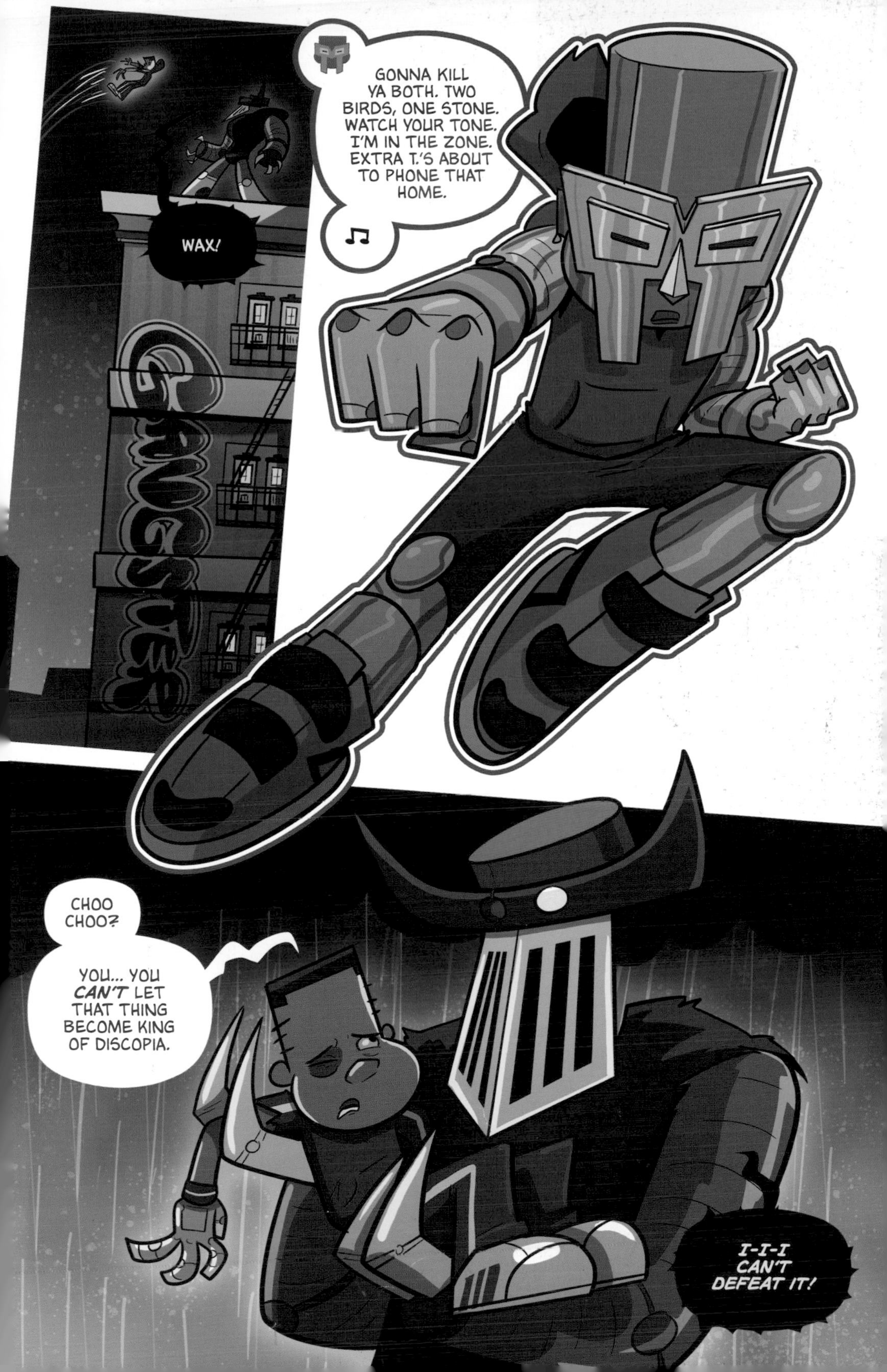
GONNA KILL YA BOTH. TWO BIRDS, ONE STONE. WATCH YOUR TONE. I'M IN THE ZONE. EXTRA T.'S ABOUT TO PHONE THAT HOME.
♫
WAX!
CHOO CHOO?
YOU... YOU *CAN'T* LET THAT THING BECOME KING OF DISCOPIA.
I-I-I CAN'T DEFEAT IT!

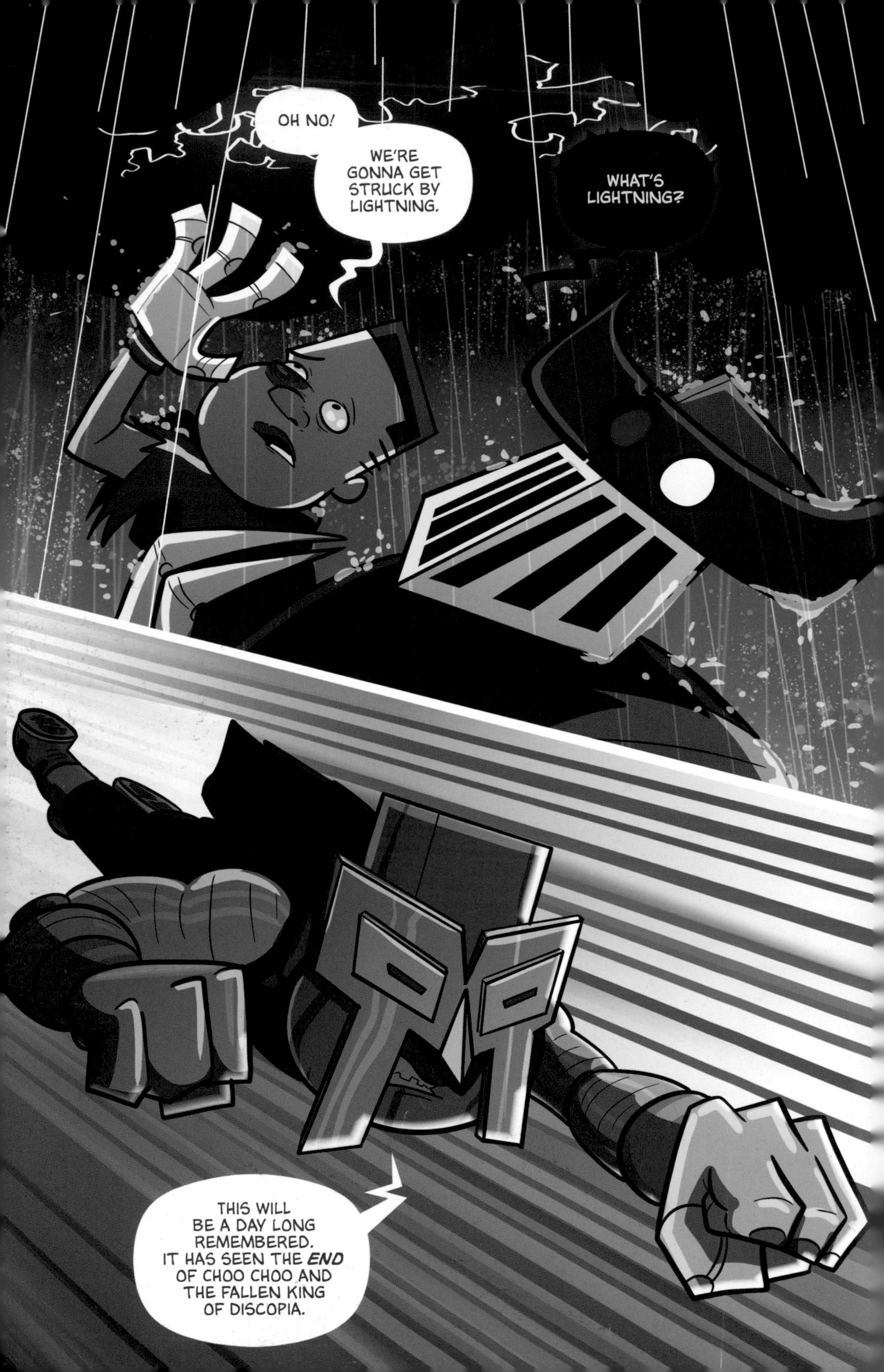
OH NO!
WE'RE GONNA GET STRUCK BY LIGHTNING.
WHAT'S LIGHTNING?
THIS WILL BE A DAY LONG REMEMBERED. IT HAS SEEN THE *END* OF CHOO CHOO AND THE FALLEN KING OF DISCOPIA.

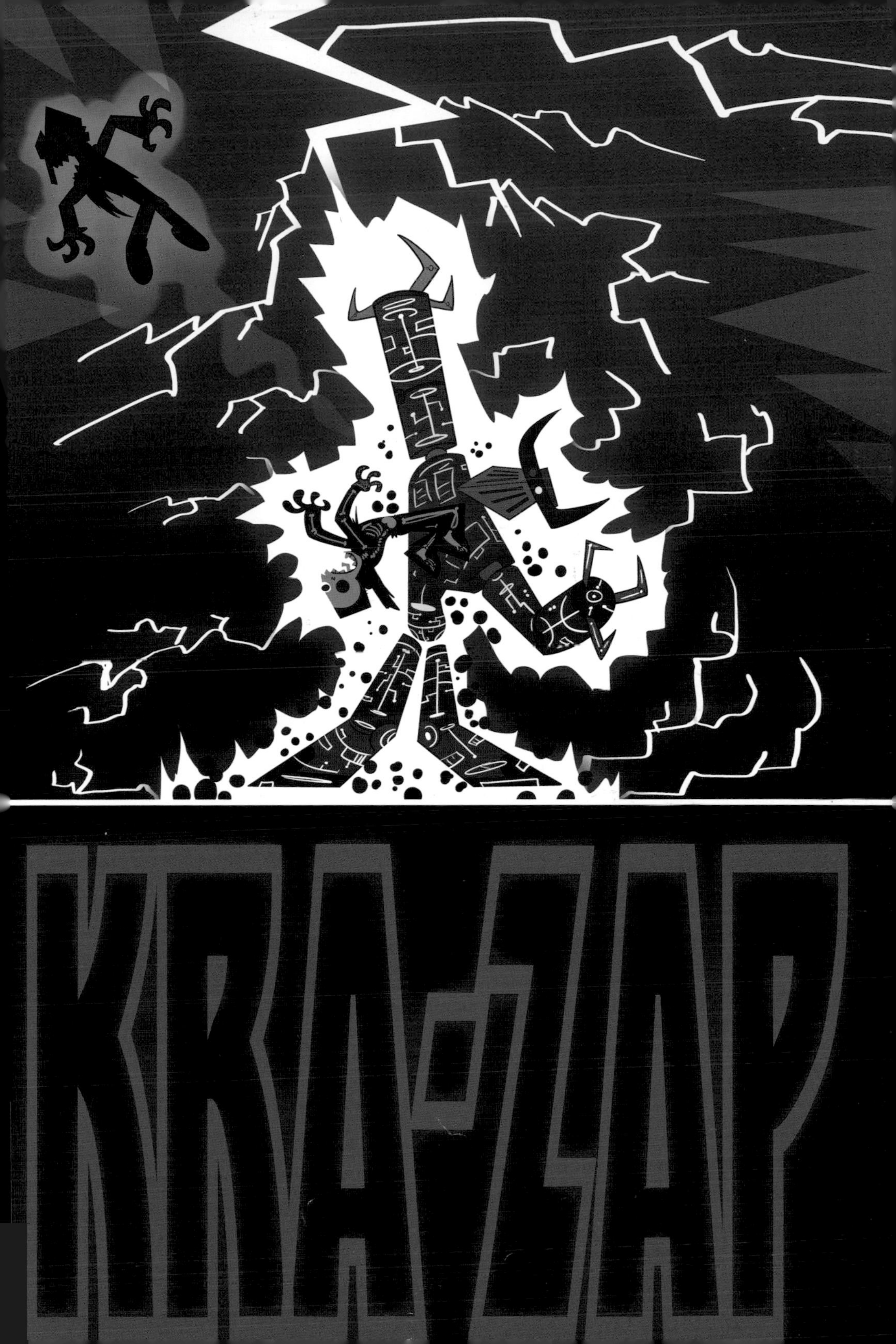
KRA-ZAP

TRACK
4

THE DIGITAL UNDERGROUND

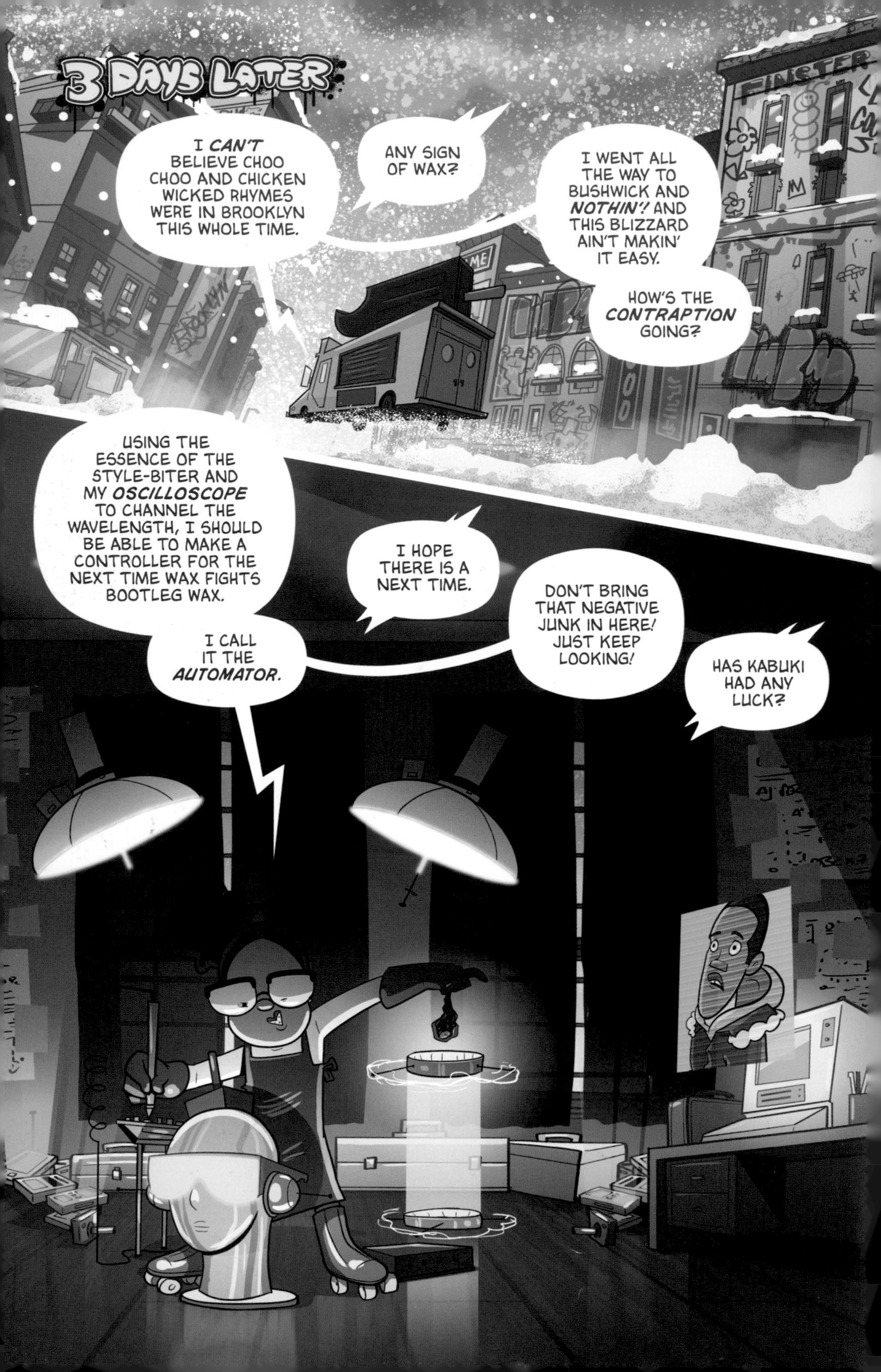
3 DAYS LATER
I *CAN'T* BELIEVE CHOO CHOO AND CHICKEN WICKED RHYMES WERE IN BROOKLYN THIS WHOLE TIME.
ANY SIGN OF WAX?
I WENT ALL THE WAY TO BUSHWICK AND *NOTHIN'!* AND THIS BLIZZARD AIN'T MAKIN' IT EASY.
HOW'S THE *CONTRAPTION* GOING?
USING THE ESSENCE OF THE STYLE-BITER AND MY *OSCILLOSCOPE* TO CHANNEL THE WAVELENGTH, I SHOULD BE ABLE TO MAKE A CONTROLLER FOR THE NEXT TIME WAX FIGHTS BOOTLEG WAX.
I CALL IT THE *AUTOMATOR*.
I HOPE THERE IS A NEXT TIME.
DON'T BRING THAT NEGATIVE JUNK IN HERE! JUST KEEP LOOKING!
HAS KABUKI HAD ANY LUCK?

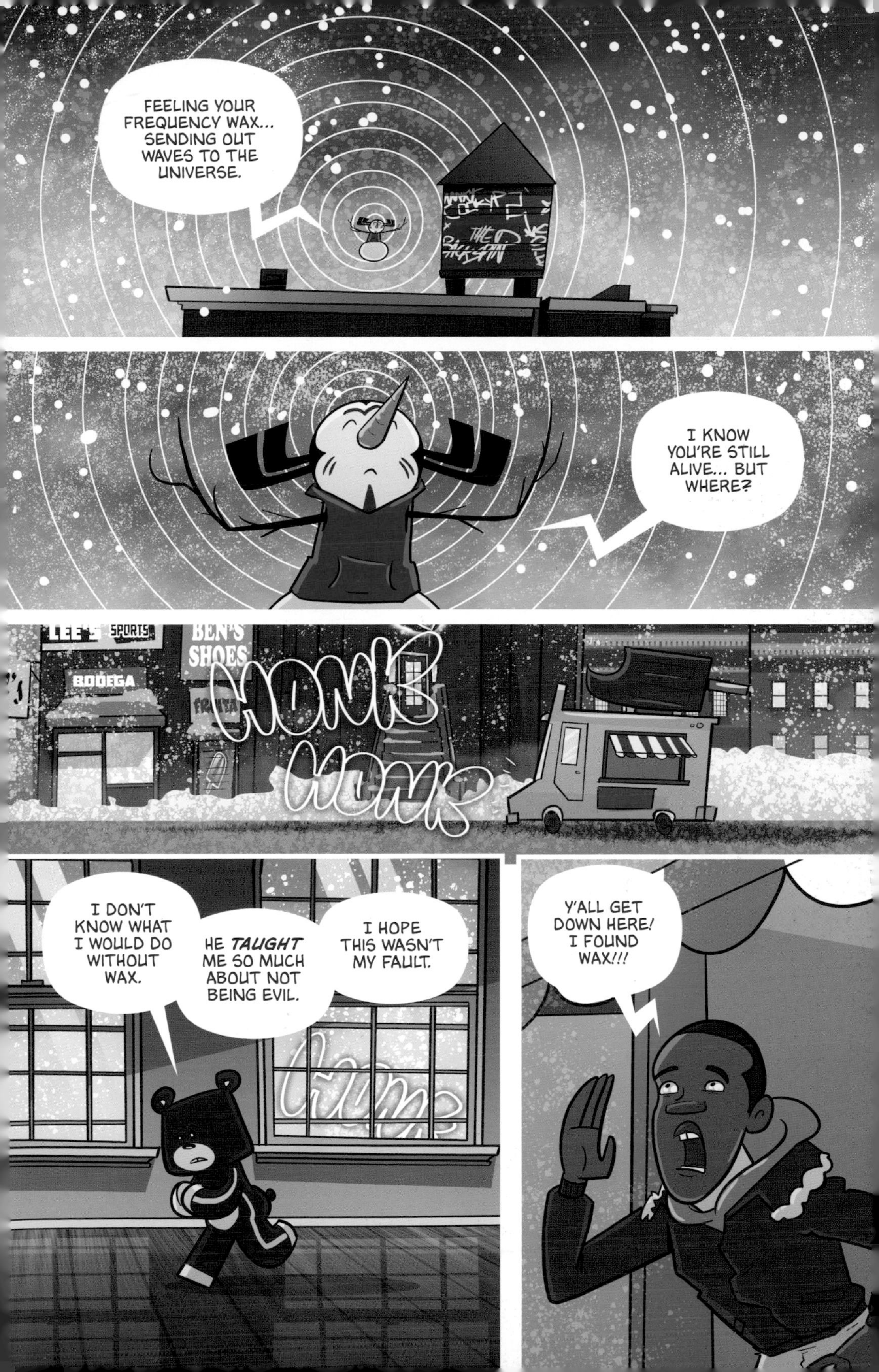
FEELING YOUR FREQUENCY WAX... SENDING OUT WAVES TO THE UNIVERSE.
I KNOW YOU'RE STILL ALIVE... BUT WHERE?
LEE'S
SPORTS
BEN'S SHOES
BODEGA
HONK
HONK
I DON'T KNOW WHAT I WOULD DO WITHOUT WAX.
HE *TAUGHT* ME SO MUCH ABOUT NOT BEING EVIL.
I HOPE THIS WASN'T MY FAULT.
Y'ALL GET DOWN HERE! I FOUND WAX!!!

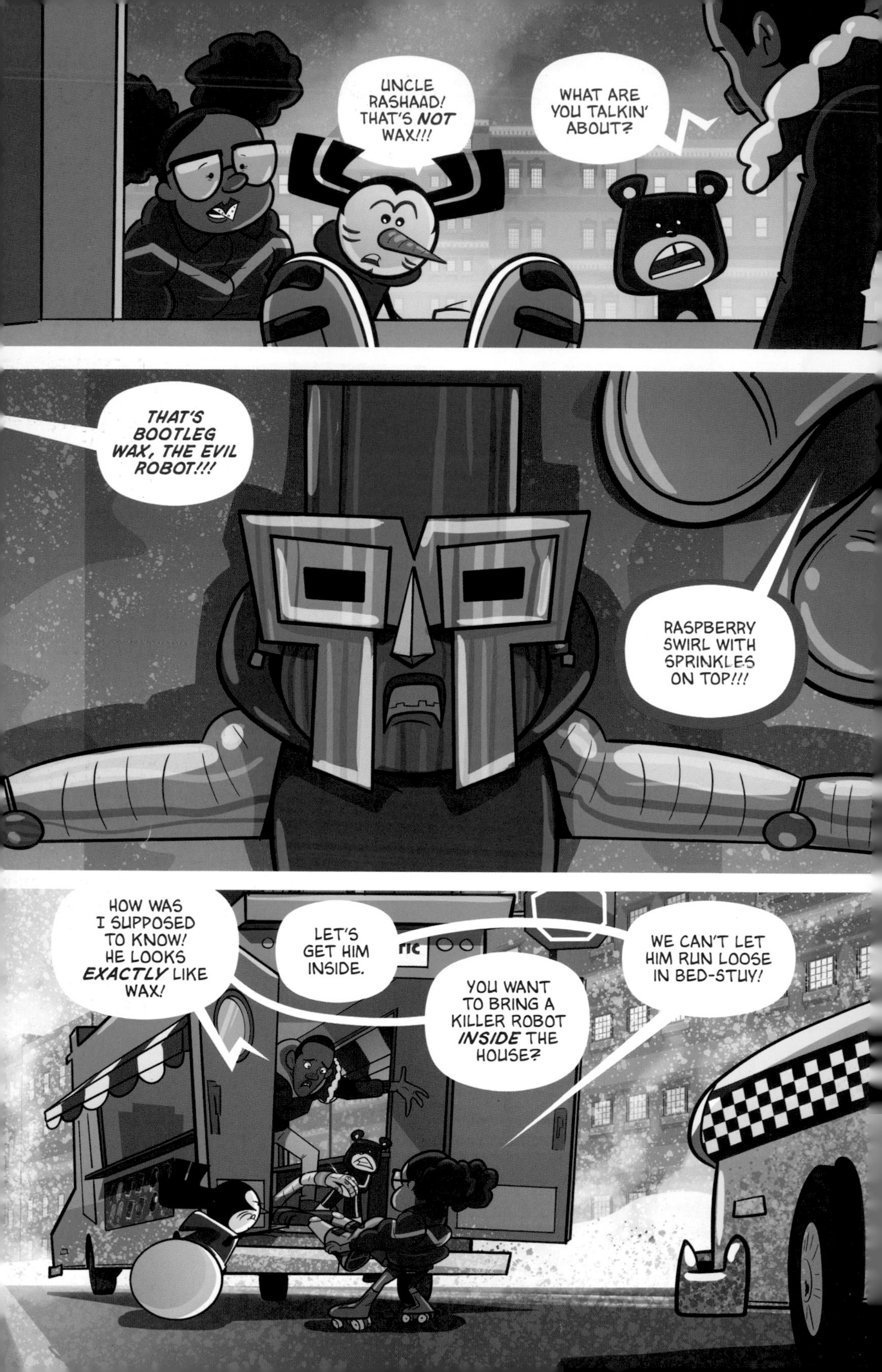
UNCLE RASHAAD! THAT'S NOT WAX!!!
WHAT ARE YOU TALKIN' ABOUT?
THAT'S BOOTLEG WAX, THE EVIL ROBOT!!!
RASPBERRY SWIRL WITH SPRINKLES ON TOP!!!
HOW WAS I SUPPOSED TO KNOW! HE LOOKS EXACTLY LIKE WAX!
LET'S GET HIM INSIDE.
YOU WANT TO BRING A KILLER ROBOT INSIDE THE HOUSE?
WE CAN'T LET HIM RUN LOOSE IN BED-STUY!

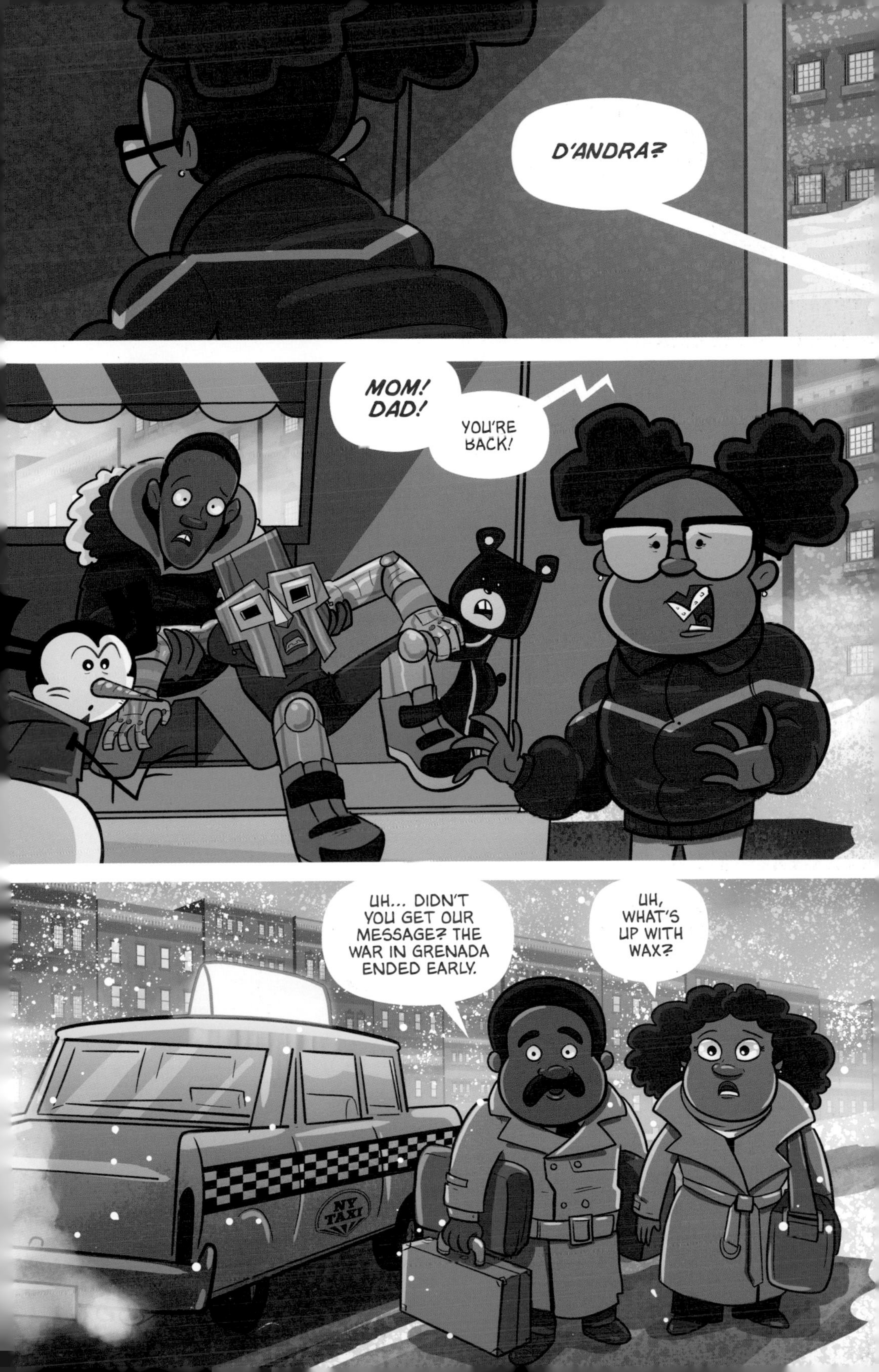
D'ANDRA?
MOM! DAD!
YOU'RE BACK!
UH... DIDN'T YOU GET OUR MESSAGE? THE WAR IN GRENADA ENDED EARLY.
UH, WHAT'S UP WITH WAX?
NY TAXI

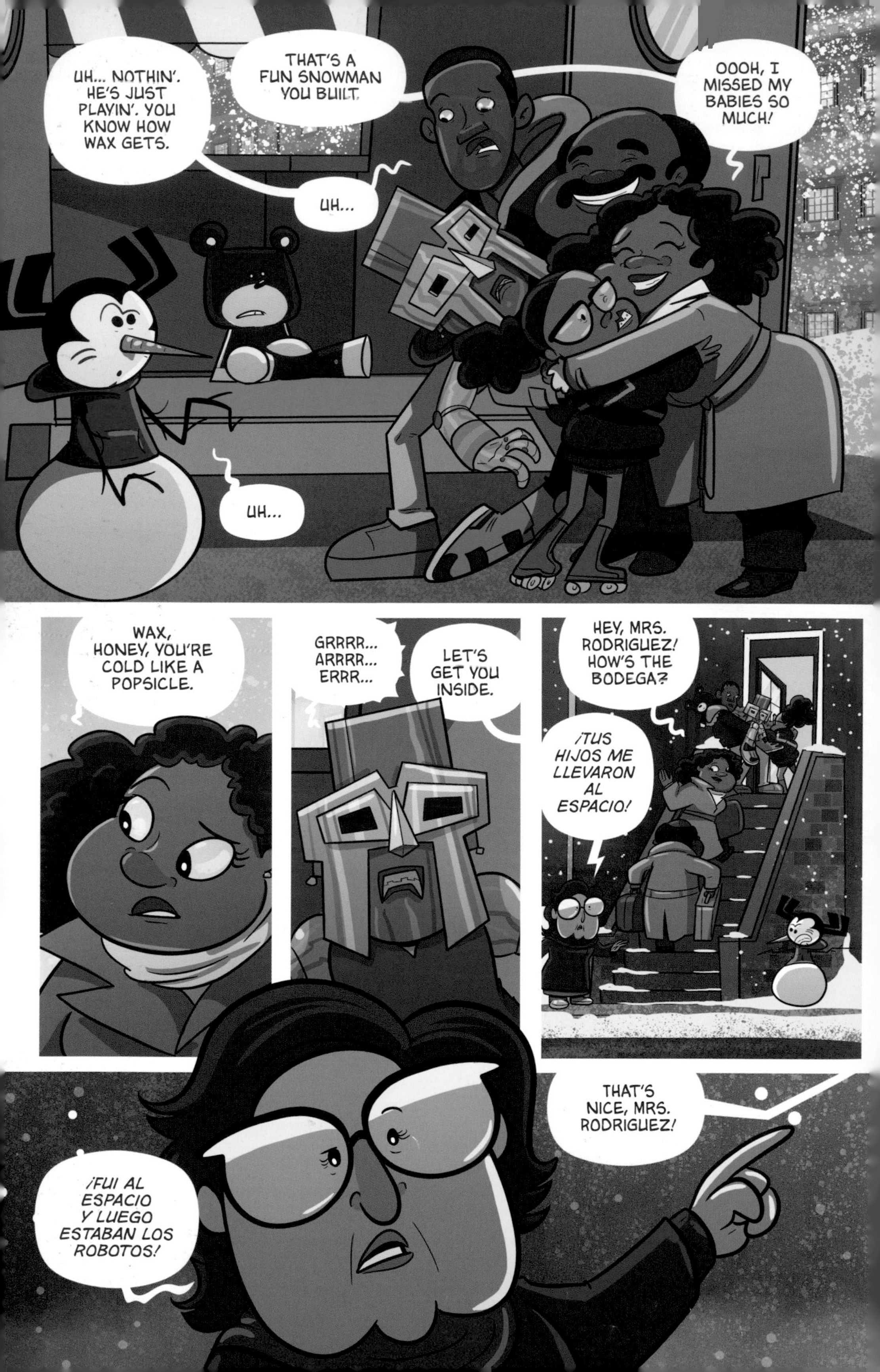

THAT'S A FUN SNOWMAN YOU BUILT.
UH... NOTHIN'. HE'S JUST PLAYIN'. YOU KNOW HOW WAX GETS.
OOOH, I MISSED MY BABIES SO MUCH!
UH...
UH...
WAX, HONEY, YOU'RE COLD LIKE A POPSICLE.
GRRRR... ARRRR... ERRR...
LET'S GET YOU INSIDE.
HEY, MRS. RODRIGUEZ! HOW'S THE BODEGA?
¡TUS HIJOS ME LLEVARON AL ESPACIO!
THAT'S NICE, MRS. RODRIGUEZ!
¡FUI AL ESPACIO Y LUEGO ESTABAN LOS ROBOTOS!

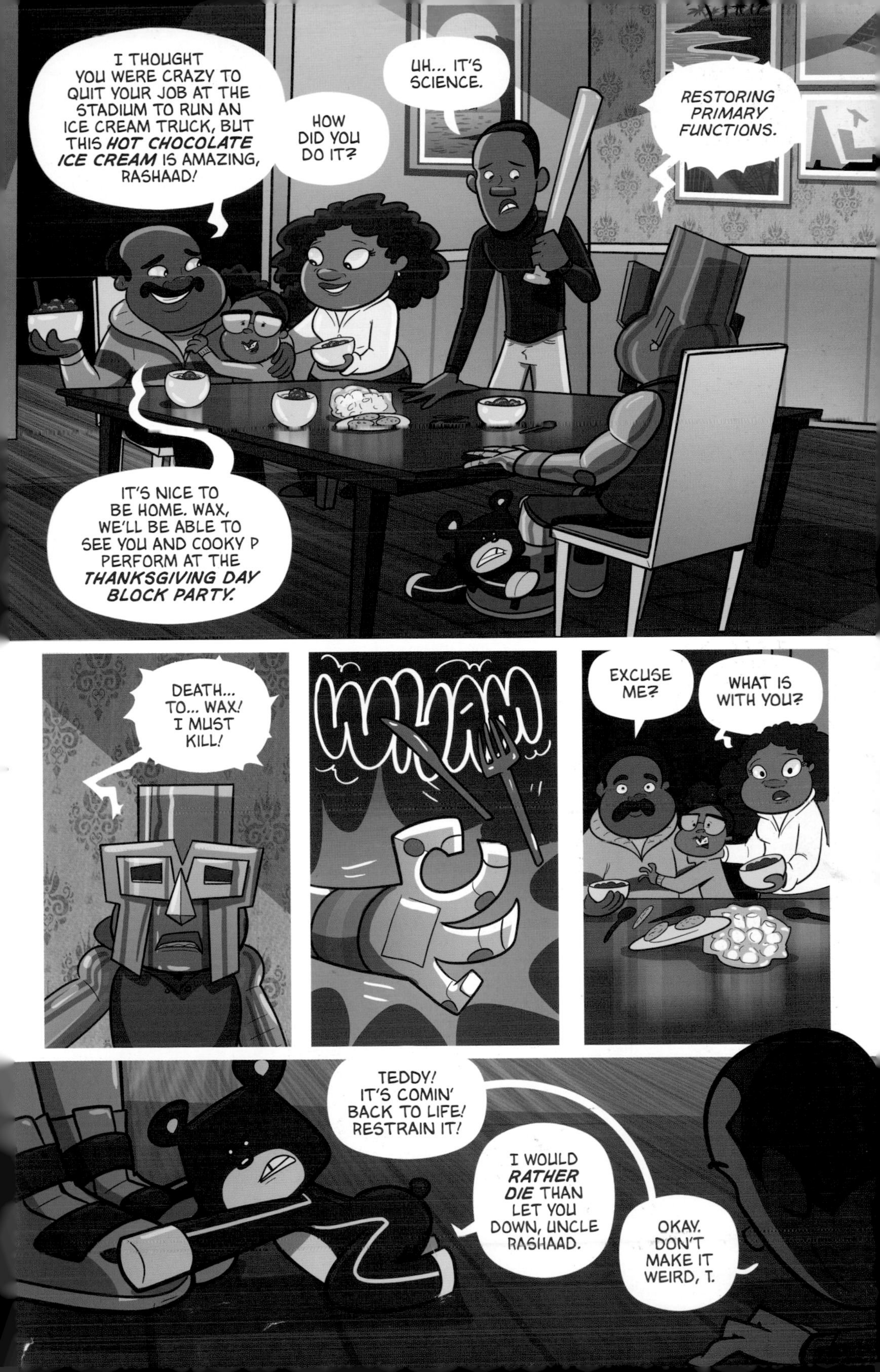
I THOUGHT YOU WERE CRAZY TO QUIT YOUR JOB AT THE STADIUM TO RUN AN ICE CREAM TRUCK, BUT THIS ***HOT CHOCOLATE ICE CREAM*** IS AMAZING, RASHAAD!
HOW DID YOU DO IT?
UH... IT'S SCIENCE.
RESTORING PRIMARY FUNCTIONS.
IT'S NICE TO BE HOME. WAX, WE'LL BE ABLE TO SEE YOU AND COOKY P PERFORM AT THE ***THANKSGIVING DAY BLOCK PARTY.***
DEATH... TO... WAX! I MUST KILL!
EXCUSE ME?
WHAT IS WITH YOU?
TEDDY! IT'S COMIN' BACK TO LIFE! RESTRAIN IT!
I WOULD ***RATHER DIE*** THAN LET YOU DOWN, UNCLE RASHAAD.
OKAY. DON'T MAKE IT WEIRD, T.

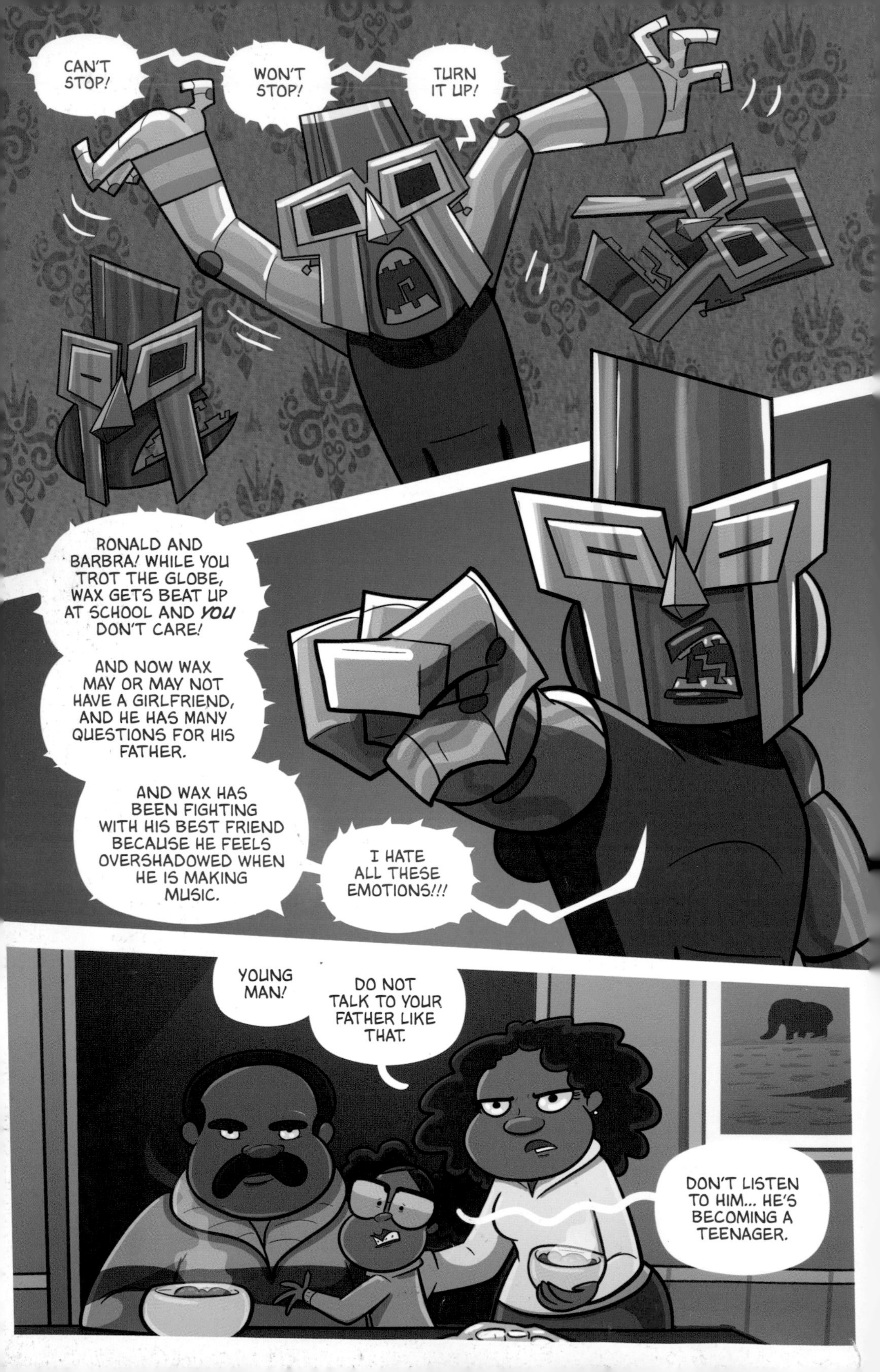
CAN'T STOP!
WON'T STOP!
TURN IT UP!
RONALD AND BARBRA! WHILE YOU TROT THE GLOBE, WAX GETS BEAT UP AT SCHOOL AND *YOU* DON'T CARE!
AND NOW WAX MAY OR MAY NOT HAVE A GIRLFRIEND, AND HE HAS MANY QUESTIONS FOR HIS FATHER.
AND WAX HAS BEEN FIGHTING WITH HIS BEST FRIEND BECAUSE HE FEELS OVERSHADOWED WHEN HE IS MAKING MUSIC.
I HATE ALL THESE EMOTIONS!!!
YOUNG MAN!
DO NOT TALK TO YOUR FATHER LIKE THAT.
DON'T LISTEN TO HIM... HE'S BECOMING A TEENAGER.

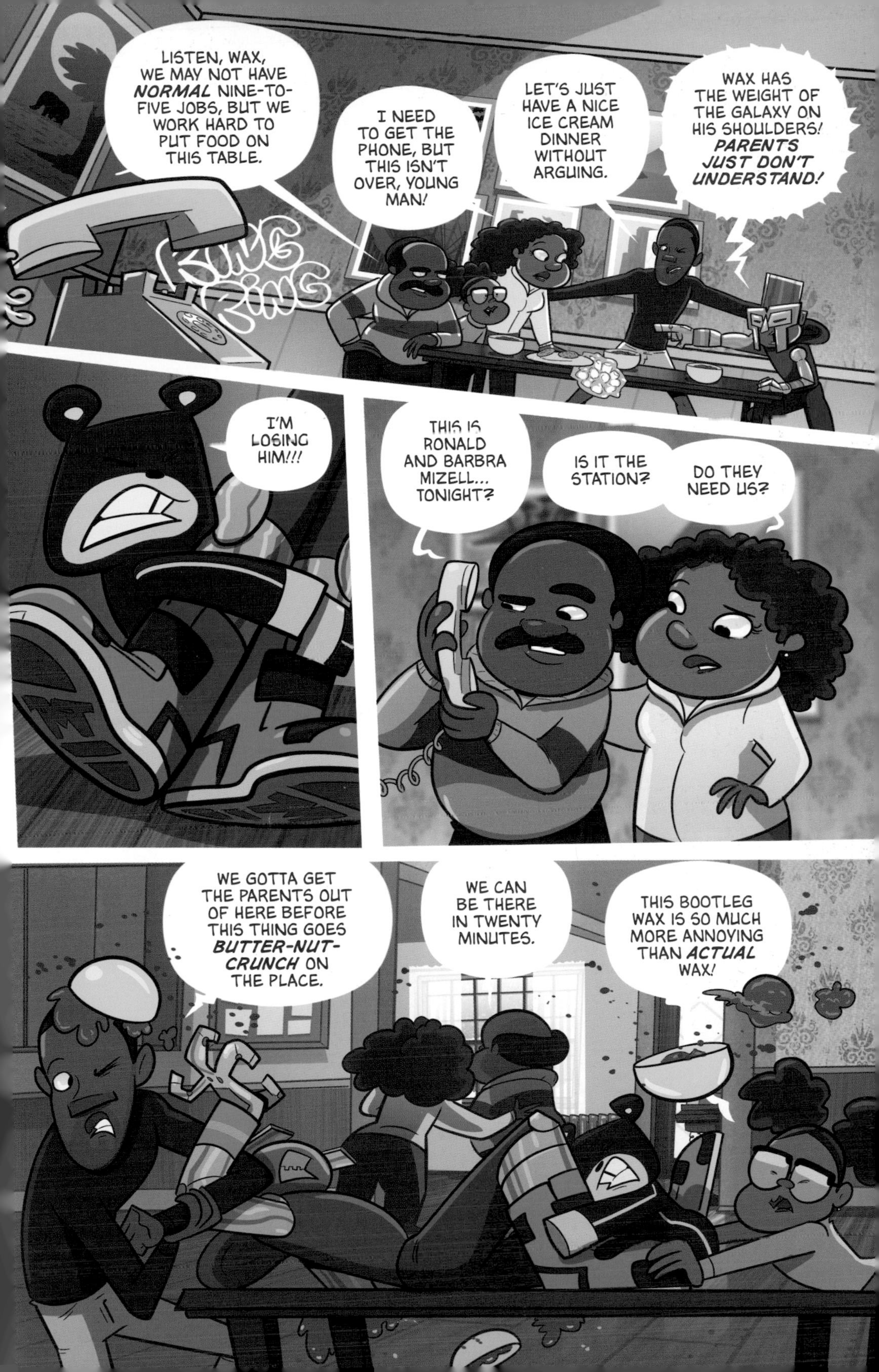
LISTEN, WAX, WE MAY NOT HAVE NORMAL NINE-TO-FIVE JOBS, BUT WE WORK HARD TO PUT FOOD ON THIS TABLE.
I NEED TO GET THE PHONE, BUT THIS ISN'T OVER, YOUNG MAN!
LET'S JUST HAVE A NICE ICE CREAM DINNER WITHOUT ARGUING.
WAX HAS THE WEIGHT OF THE GALAXY ON HIS SHOULDERS! PARENTS JUST DON'T UNDERSTAND!
RING RING
I'M LOSING HIM!!!
THIS IS RONALD AND BARBRA MIZELL... TONIGHT?
IS IT THE STATION?
DO THEY NEED US?
WE GOTTA GET THE PARENTS OUT OF HERE BEFORE THIS THING GOES BUTTER-NUT-CRUNCH ON THE PLACE.
WE CAN BE THERE IN TWENTY MINUTES.
THIS BOOTLEG WAX IS SO MUCH MORE ANNOYING THAN ACTUAL WAX!

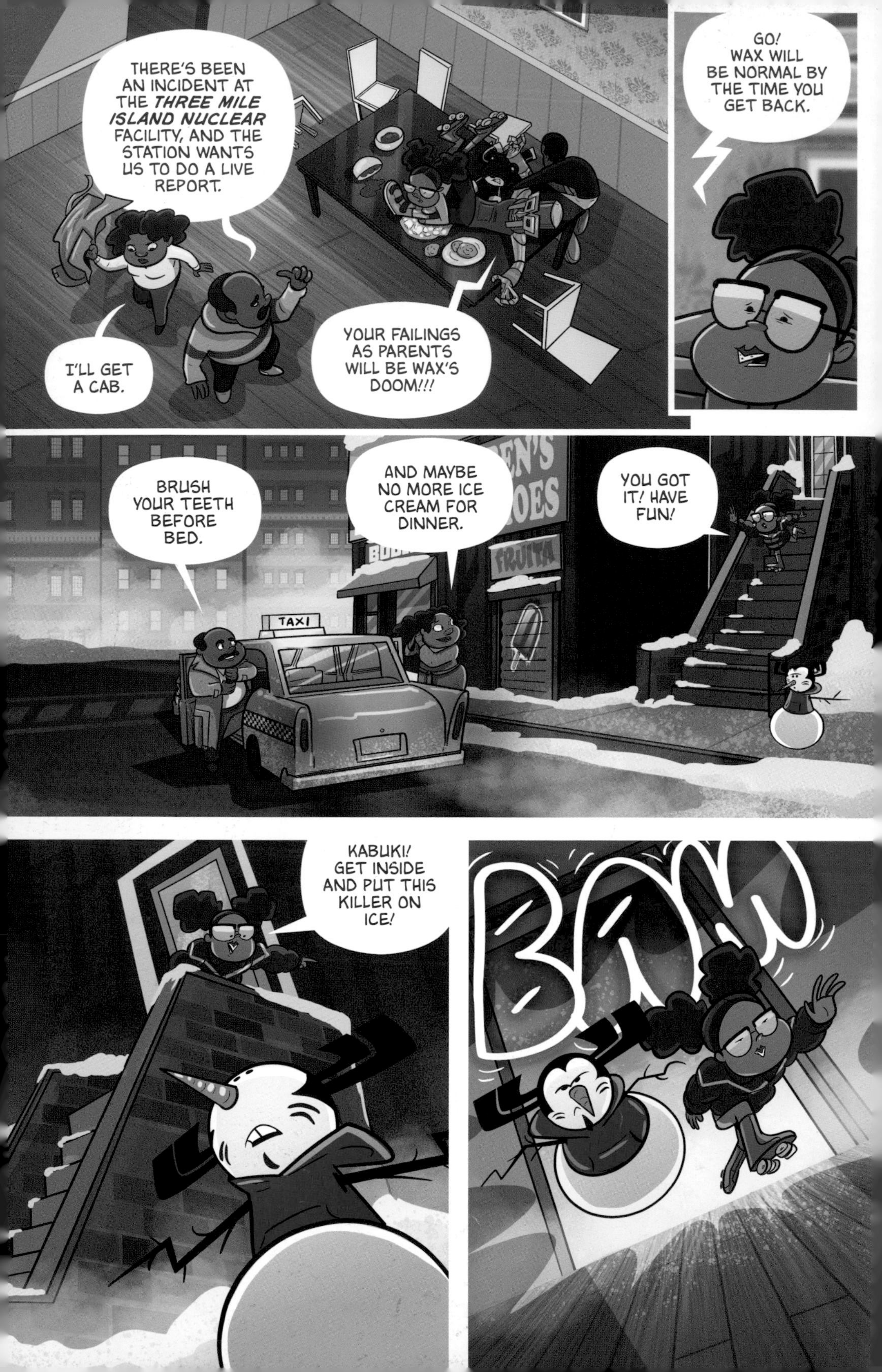
THERE'S BEEN AN INCIDENT AT THE *THREE MILE ISLAND NUCLEAR* FACILITY, AND THE STATION WANTS US TO DO A LIVE REPORT.
I'LL GET A CAB.
YOUR FAILINGS AS PARENTS WILL BE WAX'S DOOM!!!
GO! WAX WILL BE NORMAL BY THE TIME YOU GET BACK.
BRUSH YOUR TEETH BEFORE BED.
AND MAYBE NO MORE ICE CREAM FOR DINNER.
YOU GOT IT! HAVE FUN!
TAXI
FRUITA
KABUKI! GET INSIDE AND PUT THIS KILLER ON ICE!

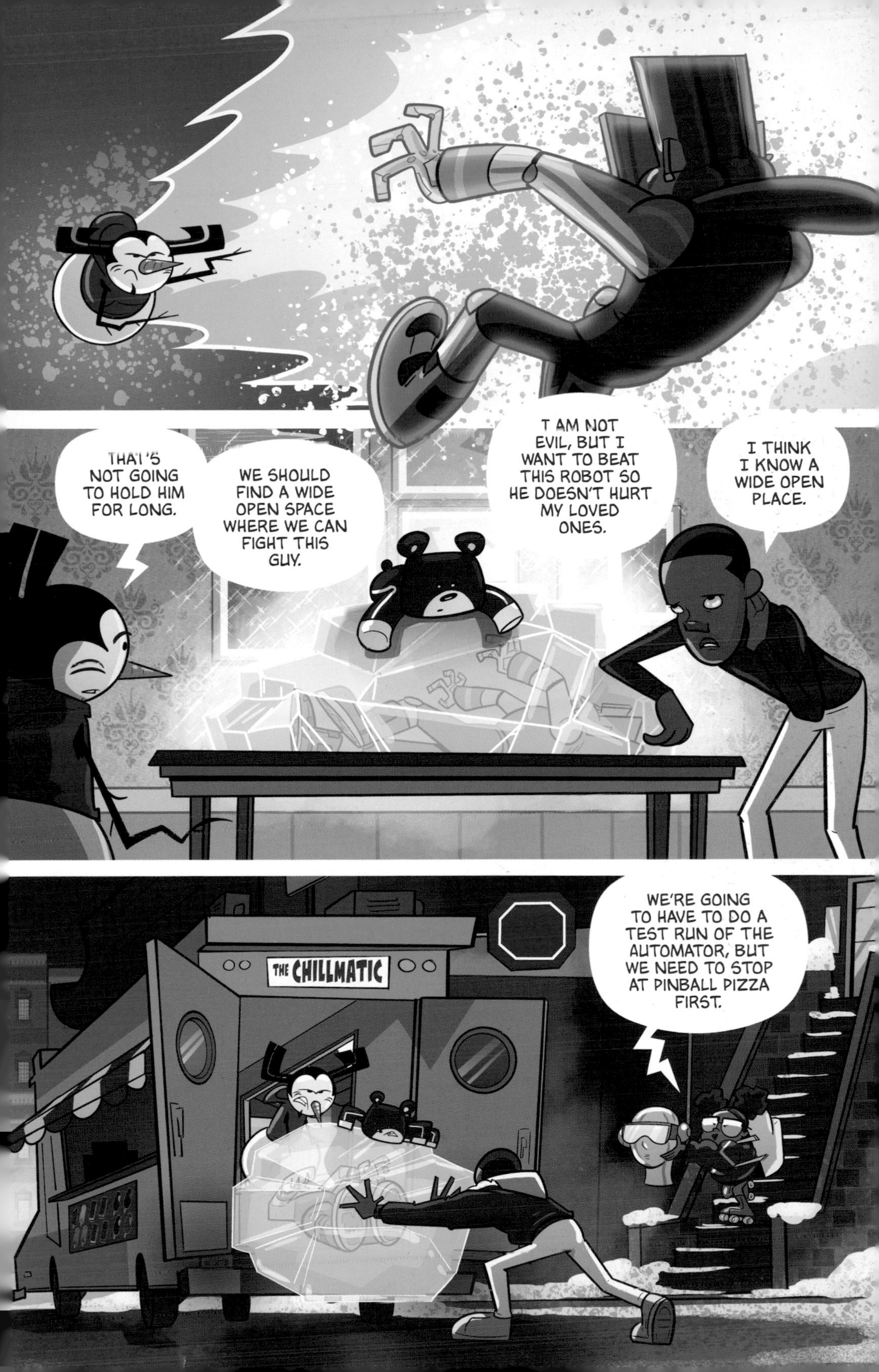
THAT'S NOT GOING TO HOLD HIM FOR LONG.
WE SHOULD FIND A WIDE OPEN SPACE WHERE WE CAN FIGHT THIS GUY.
I AM NOT EVIL, BUT I WANT TO BEAT THIS ROBOT SO HE DOESN'T HURT MY LOVED ONES.
I THINK I KNOW A WIDE OPEN PLACE.
THE CHILLMATIC
WE'RE GOING TO HAVE TO DO A TEST RUN OF THE AUTOMATOR, BUT WE NEED TO STOP AT PINBALL PIZZA FIRST.

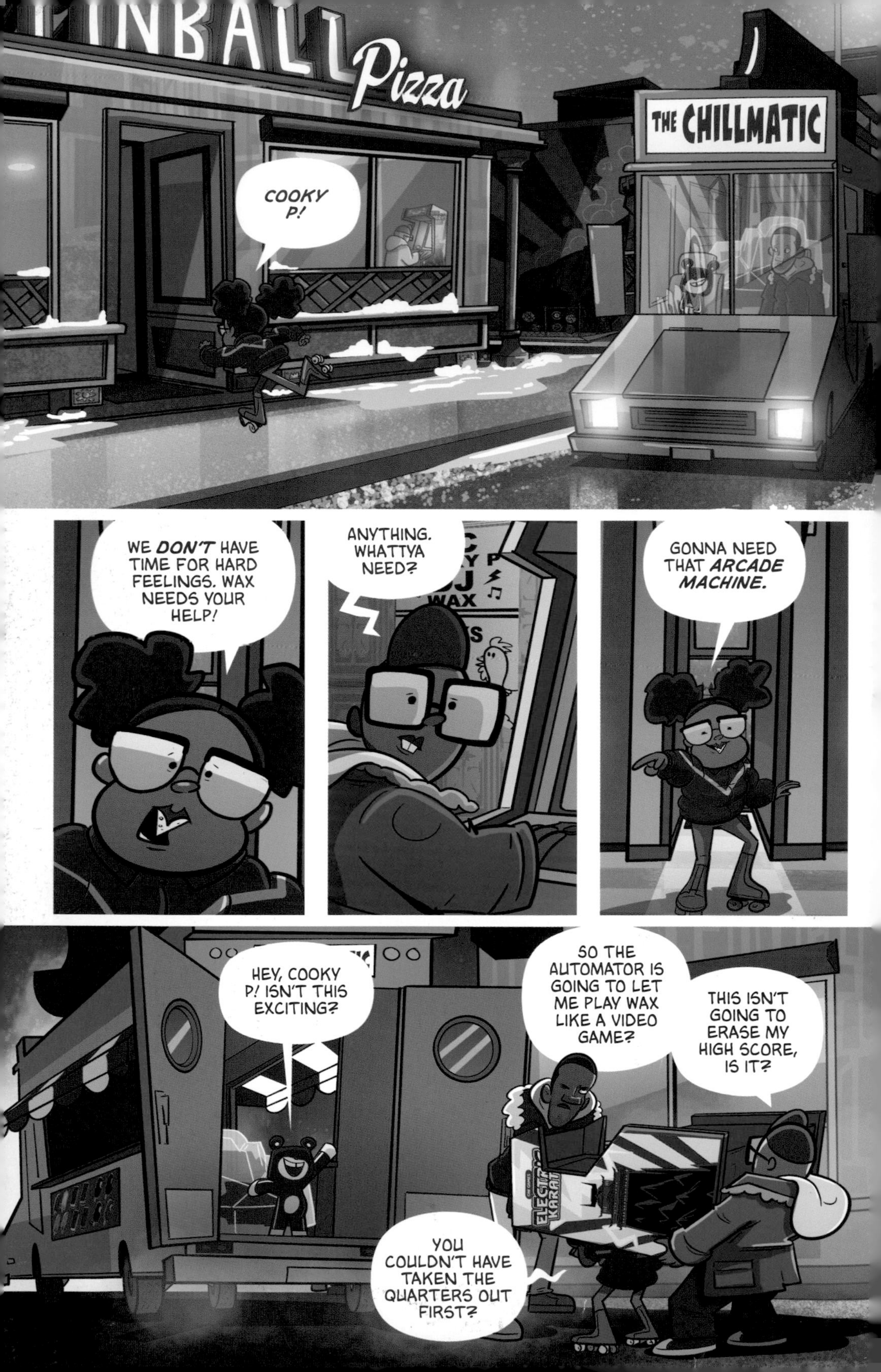
INBALL Pizza
THE CHILLMATIC
COOKY P!
WE DON'T HAVE TIME FOR HARD FEELINGS. WAX NEEDS YOUR HELP!
ANYTHING. WHATTYA NEED?
GONNA NEED THAT ARCADE MACHINE.
HEY, COOKY P! ISN'T THIS EXCITING?
SO THE AUTOMATOR IS GOING TO LET ME PLAY WAX LIKE A VIDEO GAME?
THIS ISN'T GOING TO ERASE MY HIGH SCORE, IS IT?
YOU COULDN'T HAVE TAKEN THE QUARTERS OUT FIRST?

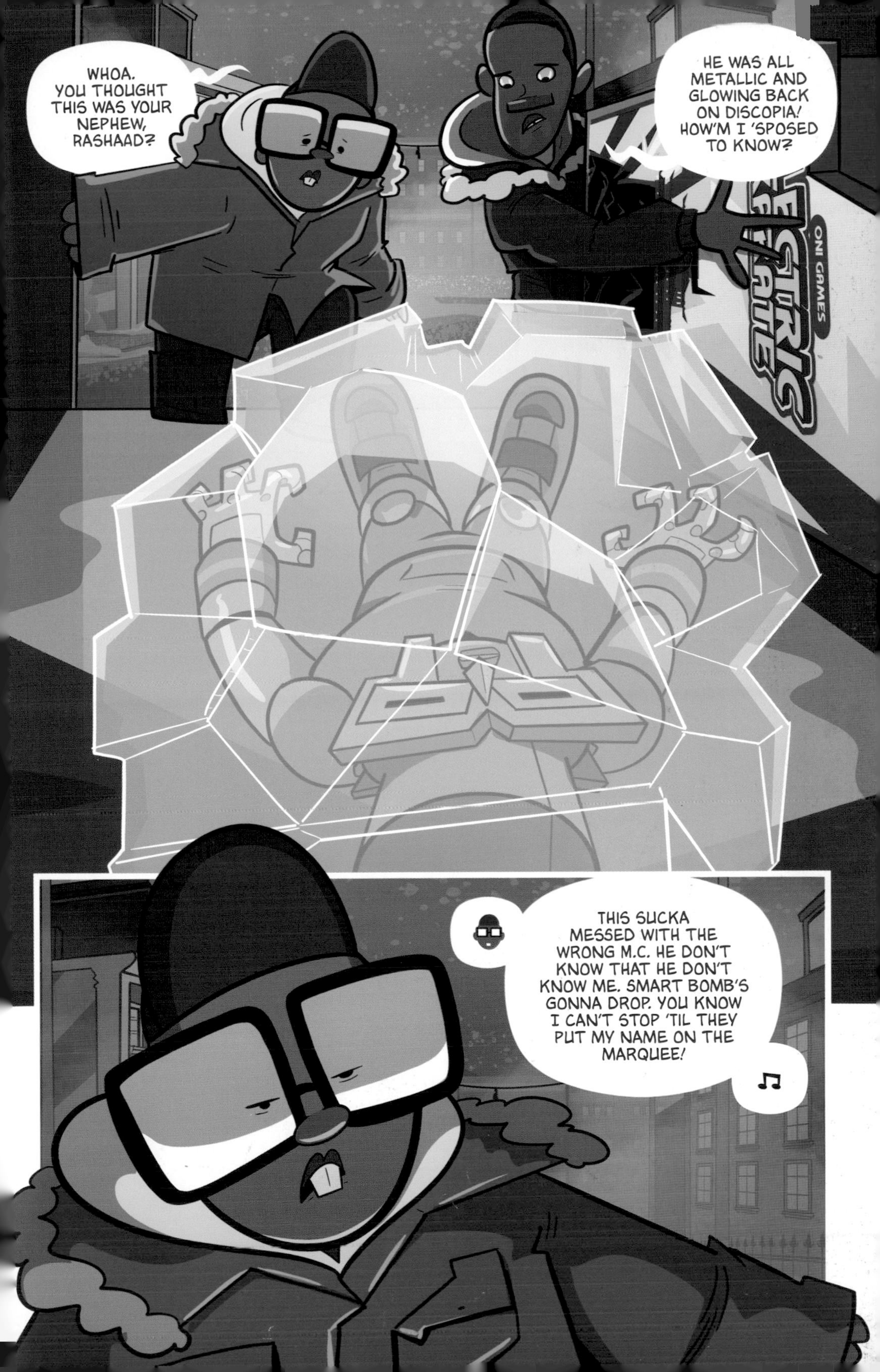
WHOA. YOU THOUGHT THIS WAS YOUR NEPHEW, RASHAAD?
HE WAS ALL METALLIC AND GLOWING BACK ON DISCOPIA! HOW'M I 'SPOSED TO KNOW?
ONI GAMES
THIS SUCKA MESSED WITH THE WRONG M.C. HE DON'T KNOW THAT HE DON'T KNOW ME. SMART BOMB'S GONNA DROP. YOU KNOW I CAN'T STOP 'TIL THEY PUT MY NAME ON THE MARQUEE!

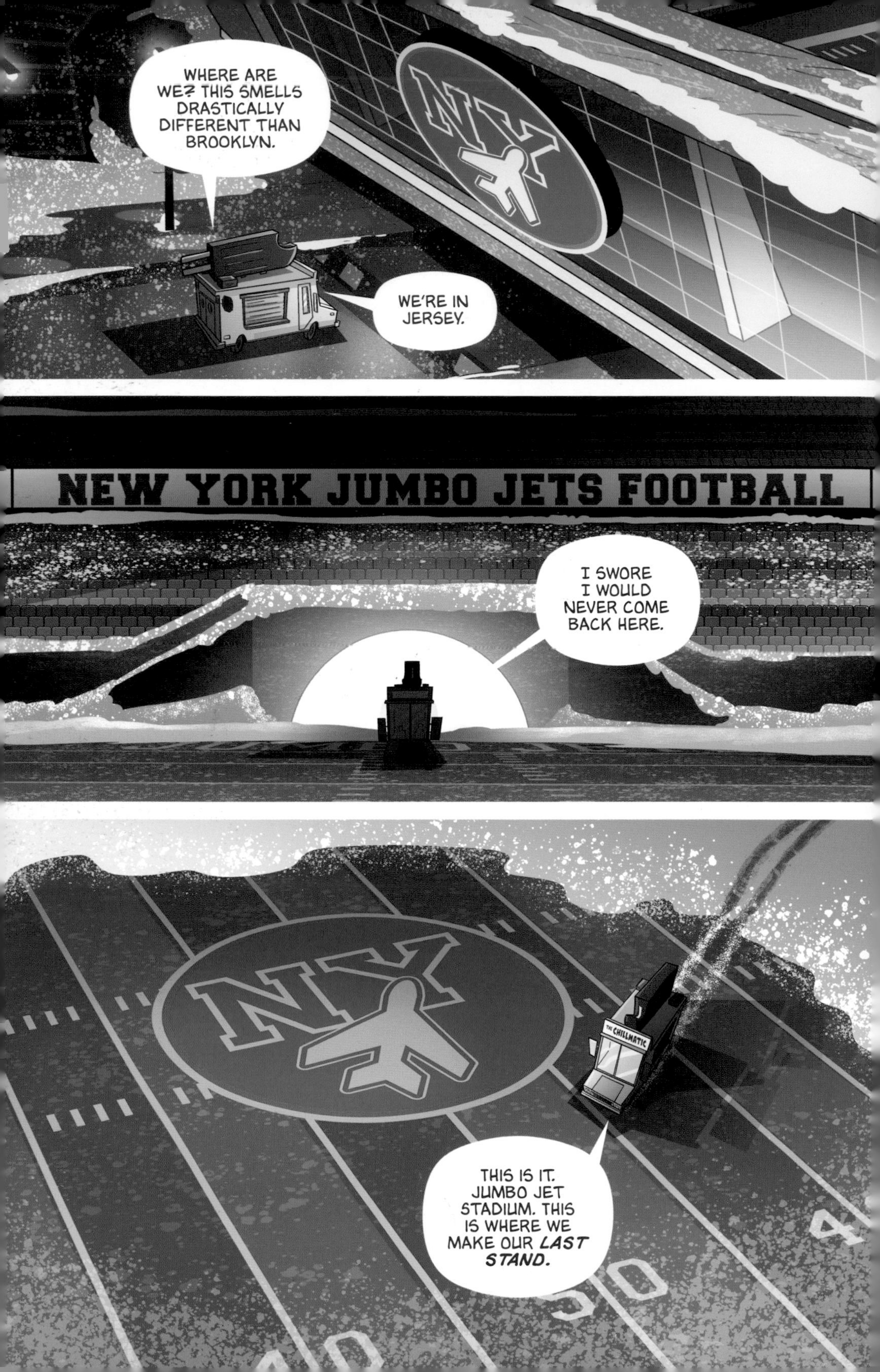
WHERE ARE WE? THIS SMELLS DRASTICALLY DIFFERENT THAN BROOKLYN.
WE'RE IN JERSEY.
NEW YORK JUMBO JETS FOOTBALL
I SWORE I WOULD NEVER COME BACK HERE.
THE CHILLMATIC
THIS IS IT. JUMBO JET STADIUM. THIS IS WHERE WE MAKE OUR *LAST STAND.*

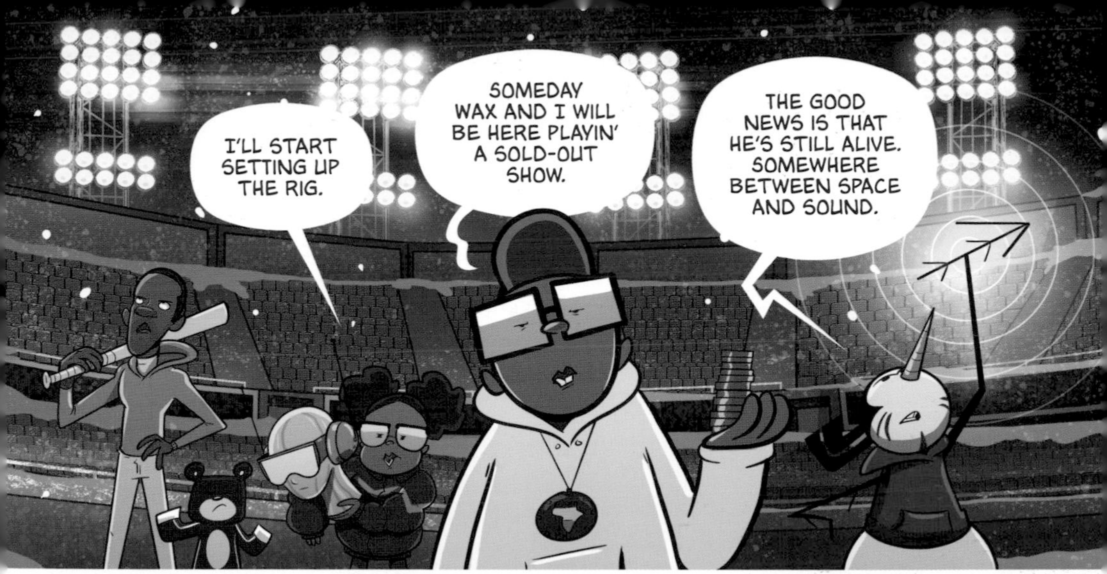
I'LL START SETTING UP THE RIG.
SOMEDAY WAX AND I WILL BE HERE PLAYIN' A SOLD-OUT SHOW.
THE GOOD NEWS IS THAT HE'S STILL ALIVE. SOMEWHERE BETWEEN SPACE AND SOUND.

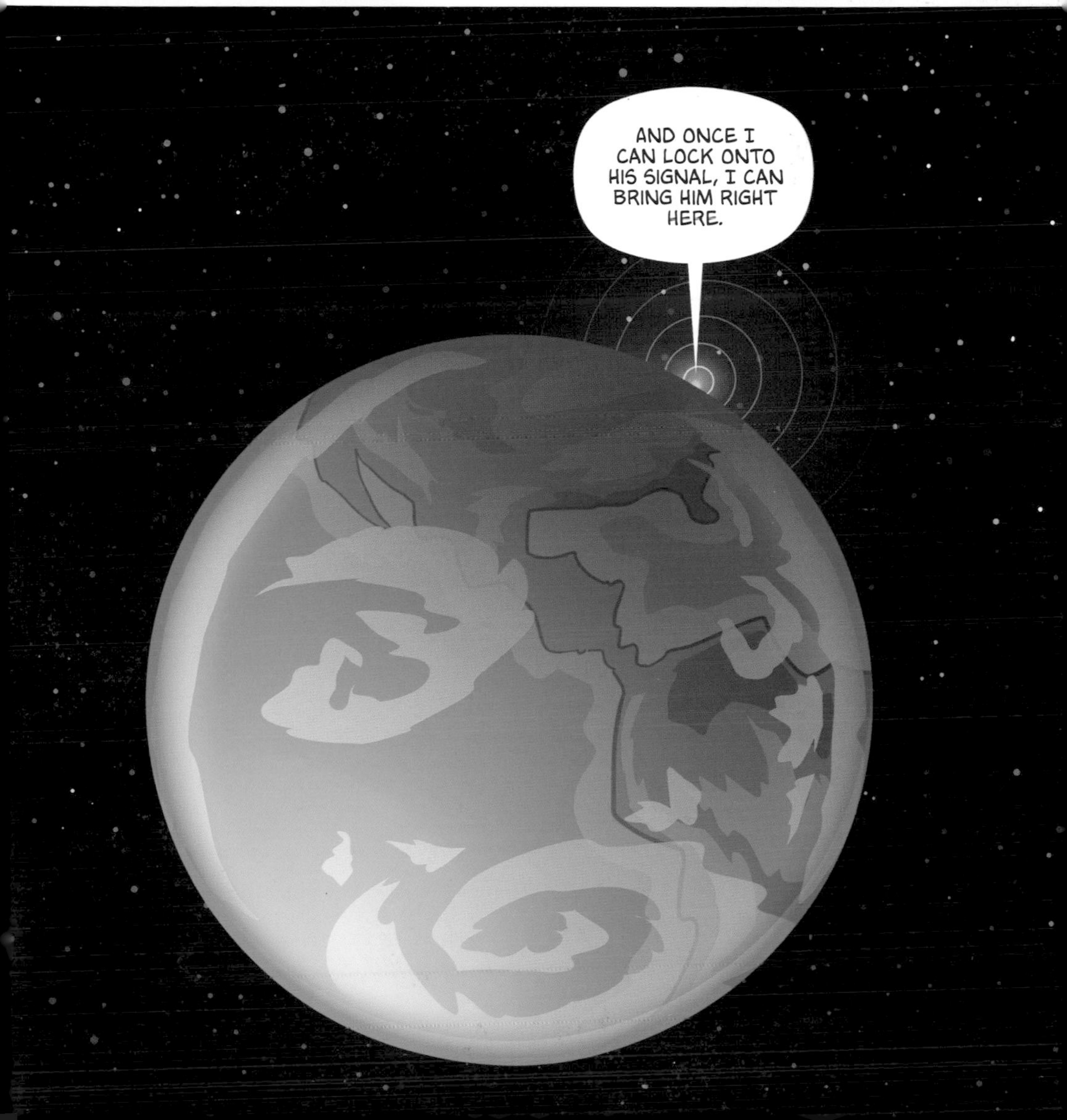
AND ONCE I CAN LOCK ONTO HIS SIGNAL, I CAN BRING HIM RIGHT HERE.

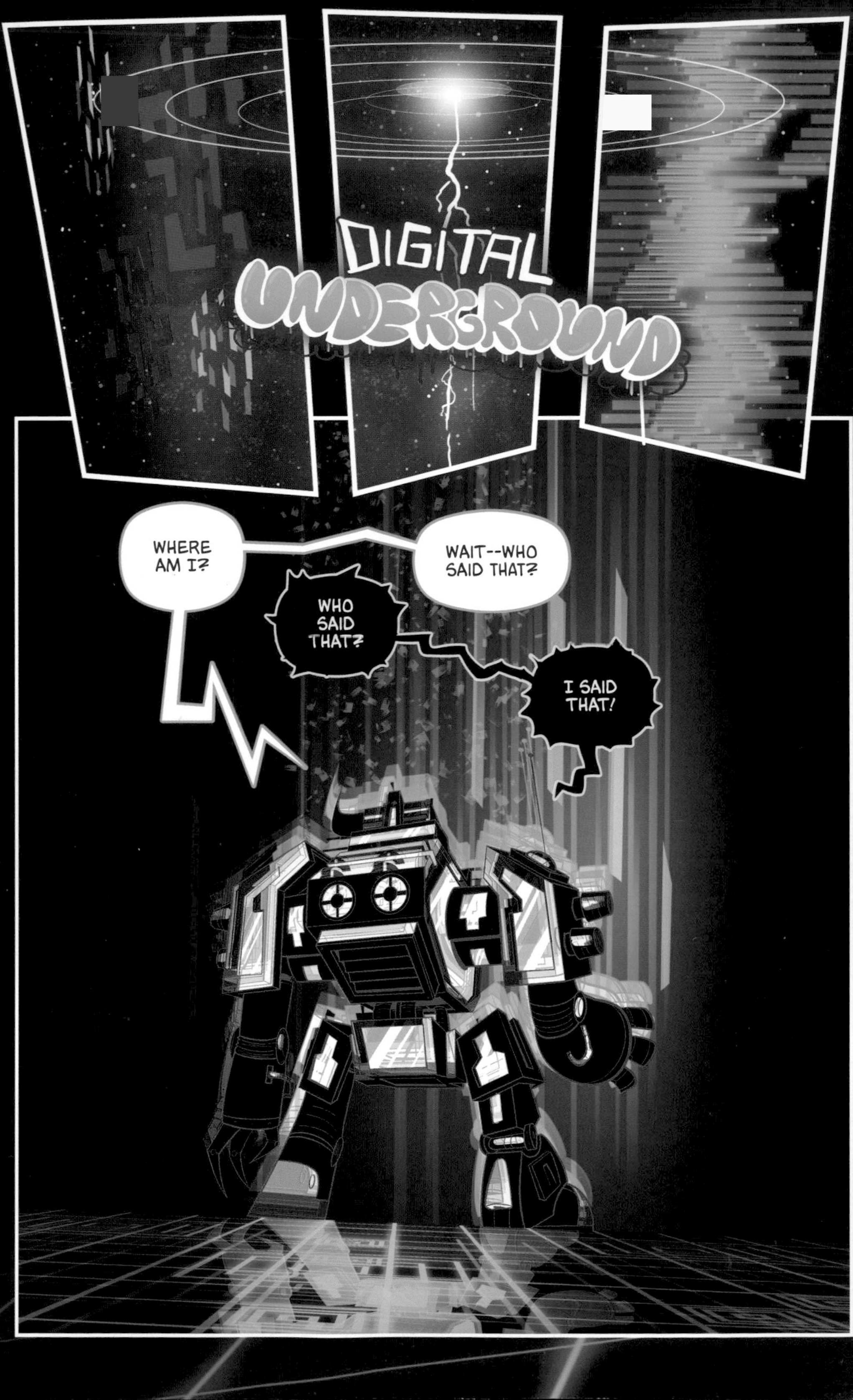
DIGITAL UNDERGROUND
WHERE AM I?
WAIT--WHO SAID THAT?
WHO SAID THAT?
I SAID THAT!

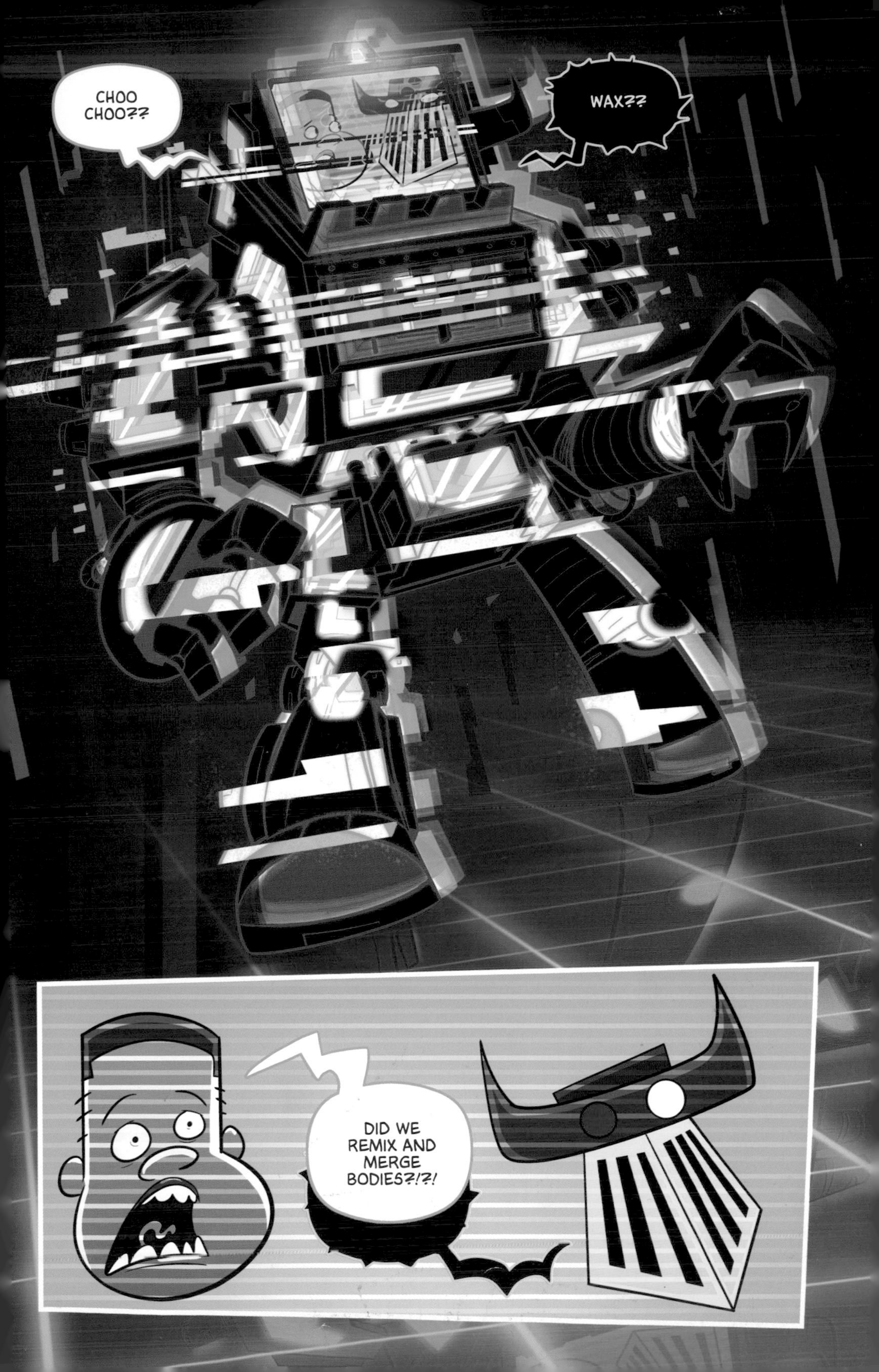
CHOO CHOO?!?
WAX?!?
DID WE REMIX AND MERGE BODIES?!?!

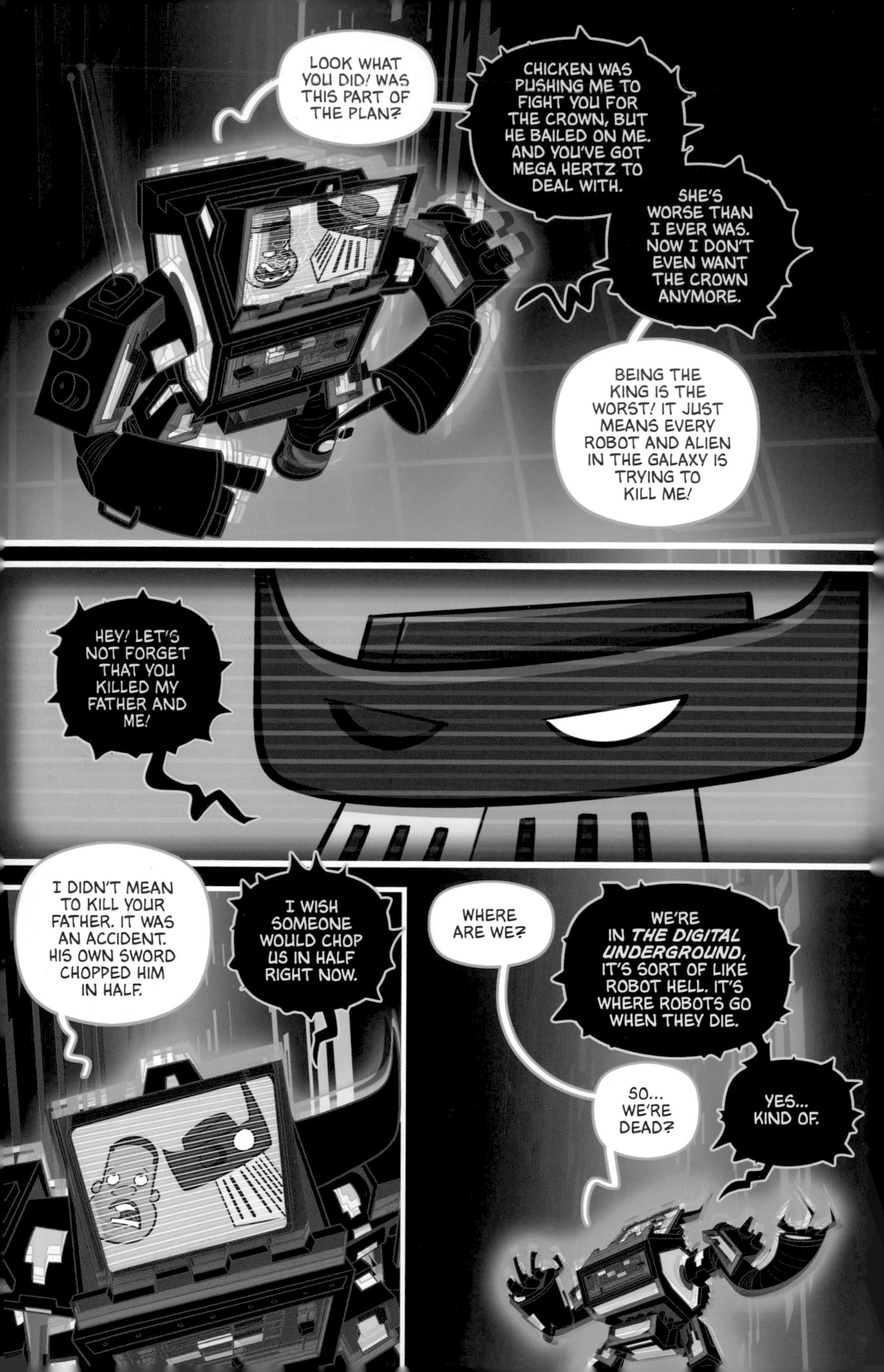
LOOK WHAT YOU DID! WAS THIS PART OF THE PLAN?
CHICKEN WAS PUSHING ME TO FIGHT YOU FOR THE CROWN, BUT HE BAILED ON ME. AND YOU'VE GOT MEGA HERTZ TO DEAL WITH.
SHE'S WORSE THAN I EVER WAS. NOW I DON'T EVEN WANT THE CROWN ANYMORE.
BEING THE KING IS THE WORST! IT JUST MEANS EVERY ROBOT AND ALIEN IN THE GALAXY IS TRYING TO KILL ME!
HEY! LET'S NOT FORGET THAT YOU KILLED MY FATHER AND ME!
I DIDN'T MEAN TO KILL YOUR FATHER. IT WAS AN ACCIDENT. HIS OWN SWORD CHOPPED HIM IN HALF.
I WISH SOMEONE WOULD CHOP US IN HALF RIGHT NOW.
WHERE ARE WE?
WE'RE IN *THE DIGITAL UNDERGROUND*, IT'S SORT OF LIKE ROBOT HELL. IT'S WHERE ROBOTS GO WHEN THEY DIE.
SO... WE'RE DEAD?
YES... KIND OF.

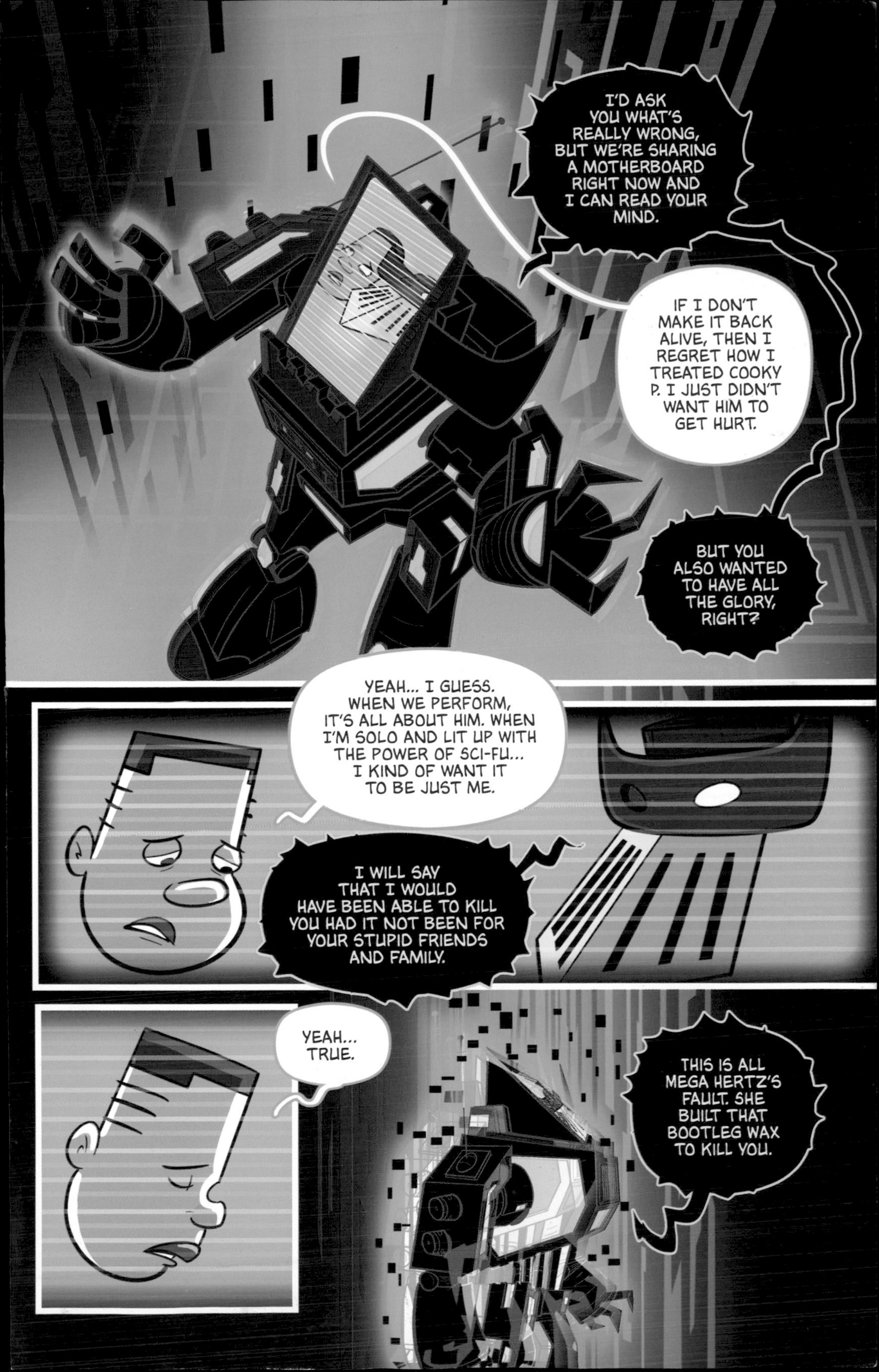
I'D ASK YOU WHAT'S REALLY WRONG, BUT WE'RE SHARING A MOTHERBOARD RIGHT NOW AND I CAN READ YOUR MIND.
IF I DON'T MAKE IT BACK ALIVE, THEN I REGRET HOW I TREATED COOKY P. I JUST DIDN'T WANT HIM TO GET HURT.
BUT YOU ALSO WANTED TO HAVE ALL THE GLORY, RIGHT?
YEAH... I GUESS. WHEN WE PERFORM, IT'S ALL ABOUT HIM. WHEN I'M SOLO AND LIT UP WITH THE POWER OF SCI-FU... I KIND OF WANT IT TO BE JUST ME.
I WILL SAY THAT I WOULD HAVE BEEN ABLE TO KILL YOU HAD IT NOT BEEN FOR YOUR STUPID FRIENDS AND FAMILY.
YEAH... TRUE.
THIS IS ALL MEGA HERTZ'S FAULT. SHE BUILT THAT BOOTLEG WAX TO KILL YOU.

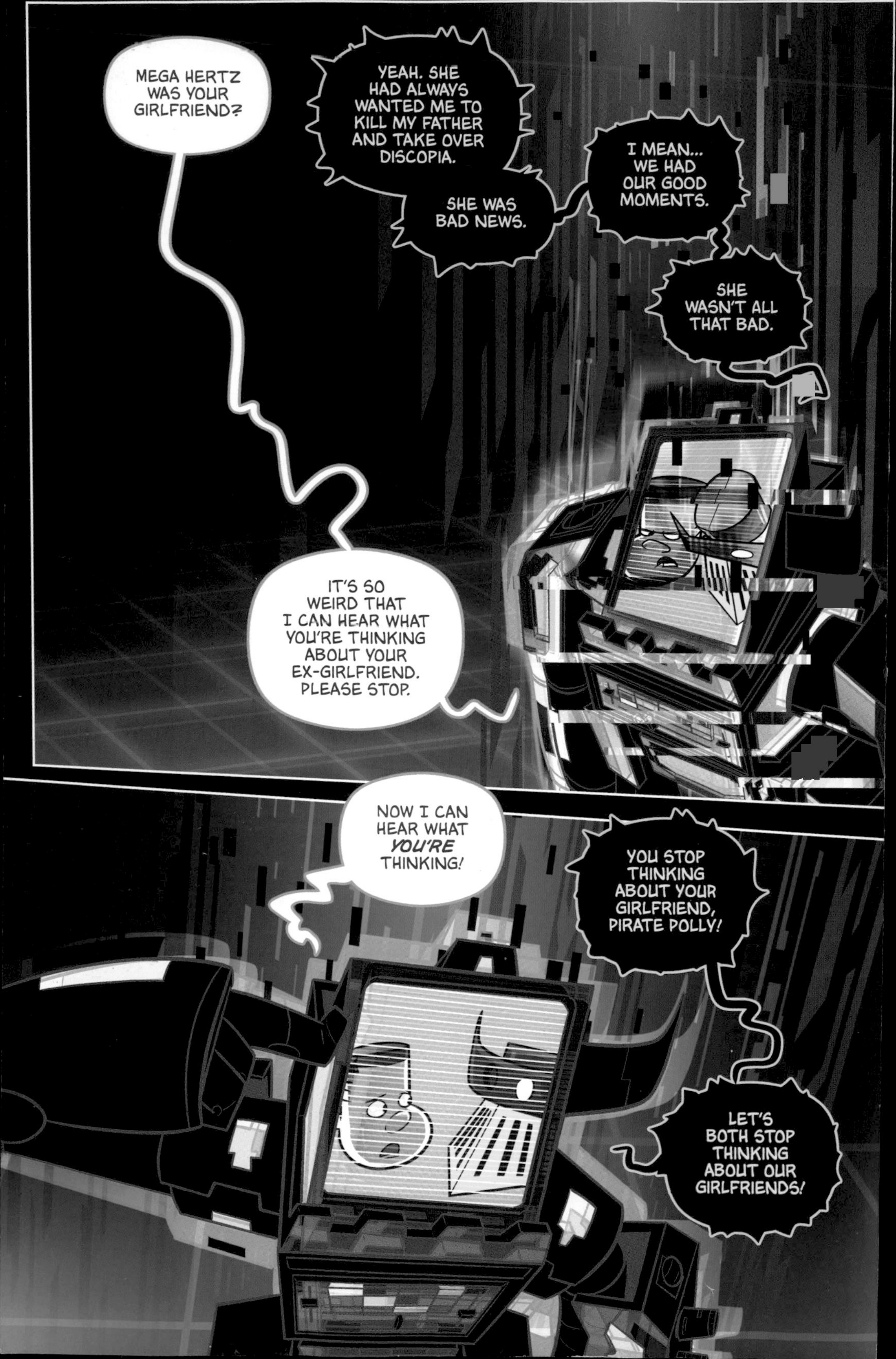
MEGA HERTZ WAS YOUR GIRLFRIEND?
YEAH. SHE HAD ALWAYS WANTED ME TO KILL MY FATHER AND TAKE OVER DISCOPIA.
SHE WAS BAD NEWS.
I MEAN... WE HAD OUR GOOD MOMENTS.
SHE WASN'T ALL THAT BAD.
IT'S SO WEIRD THAT I CAN HEAR WHAT YOU'RE THINKING ABOUT YOUR EX-GIRLFRIEND. PLEASE STOP.
NOW I CAN HEAR WHAT *YOU'RE* THINKING!
YOU STOP THINKING ABOUT YOUR GIRLFRIEND, PIRATE POLLY!
LET'S BOTH STOP THINKING ABOUT OUR GIRLFRIENDS!

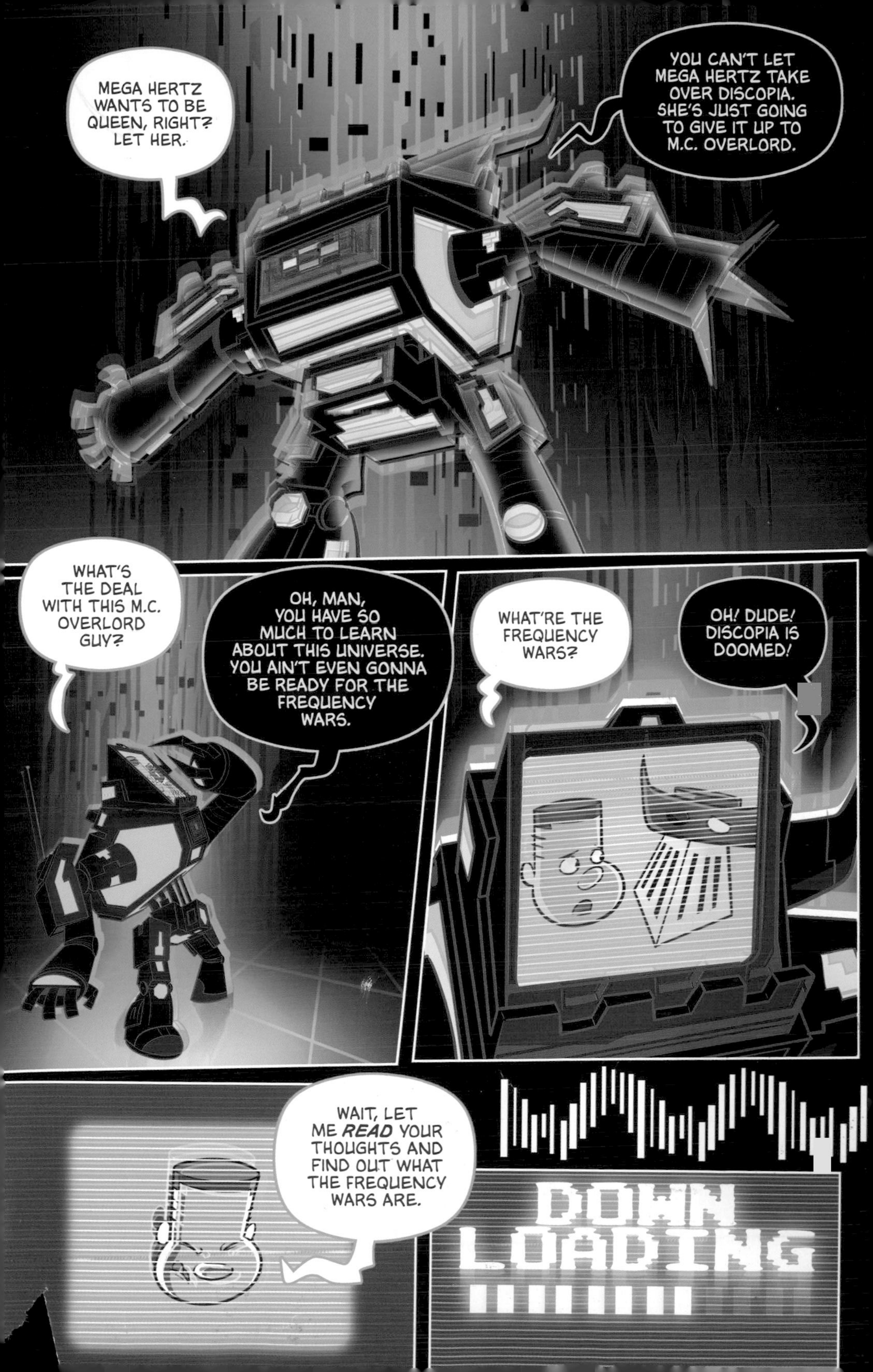
MEGA HERTZ WANTS TO BE QUEEN, RIGHT? LET HER.
YOU CAN'T LET MEGA HERTZ TAKE OVER DISCOPIA. SHE'S JUST GOING TO GIVE IT UP TO M.C. OVERLORD.
WHAT'S THE DEAL WITH THIS M.C. OVERLORD GUY?
OH, MAN, YOU HAVE SO MUCH TO LEARN ABOUT THIS UNIVERSE. YOU AIN'T EVEN GONNA BE READY FOR THE FREQUENCY WARS.
WHAT'RE THE FREQUENCY WARS?
OH! DUDE! DISCOPIA IS DOOMED!
WAIT, LET ME *READ* YOUR THOUGHTS AND FIND OUT WHAT THE FREQUENCY WARS ARE.
DOWN LOADING

DATA DOWNLOAD...

M.C. Overlord is an ancient celestial being who was created from all the elements of Hip-Hop.

He wants to control the spin of Discopia so that only his disciples can have the power of Sci-Fu.

Discopia is the crossroads of all intergalactic and interdimensional travel. Whoever controls Discopia will be able to create portals to any planet in the universe, making it easier to invade.

He wages a war with the robots every million cycles called the Frequency War. Sci-Fu Masters, Time Champions, and Robots all join together to fight M.C. Overlord.

If the robots win, then M.C. Overlord goes dormant since he cannot be killed. But if M.C. Overlord wins, then he will be able to take over Discopia and control all the robots.

▮▮▮ When the Frequency War ends, time is reset. Anyone who is not the King of Discopia or M.C. Overlord forgets that anything ever happened.

▮▮▮ It's up to the King of Discopia to teach their subjects of the upcoming war.

▮▮▮ The entire galaxy is doomed to repeat the Frequency War every million cycles.

▮▮▮ King Chug Chug has successfully fended off M.C. Overlord for the past five Frequency Wars, in part because he wields the Sword of Jamacles, which contains the souls of every Sci-Fu Master he ever killed.

▮▮▮ Now that King Chug Chug is dead and Discopia is in chaos, this would be the most dangerous time for M.C. Overlord to come out of hibernation.

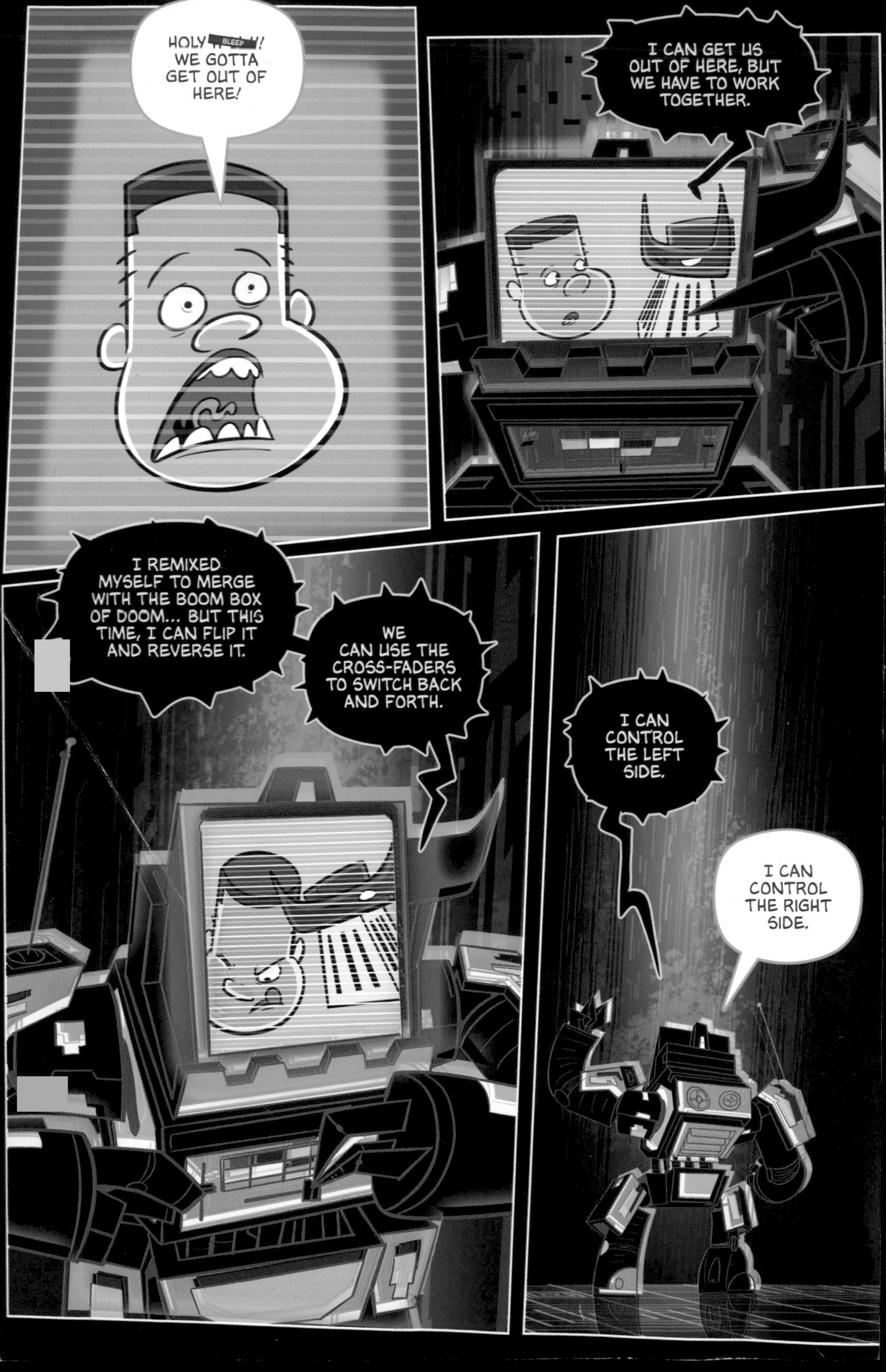
HOLY BLEEP! WE GOTTA GET OUT OF HERE!
I CAN GET US OUT OF HERE, BUT WE HAVE TO WORK TOGETHER.
I REMIXED MYSELF TO MERGE WITH THE BOOM BOX OF DOOM... BUT THIS TIME, I CAN FLIP IT AND REVERSE IT.
WE CAN USE THE CROSS-FADERS TO SWITCH BACK AND FORTH.
I CAN CONTROL THE LEFT SIDE.
I CAN CONTROL THE RIGHT SIDE.

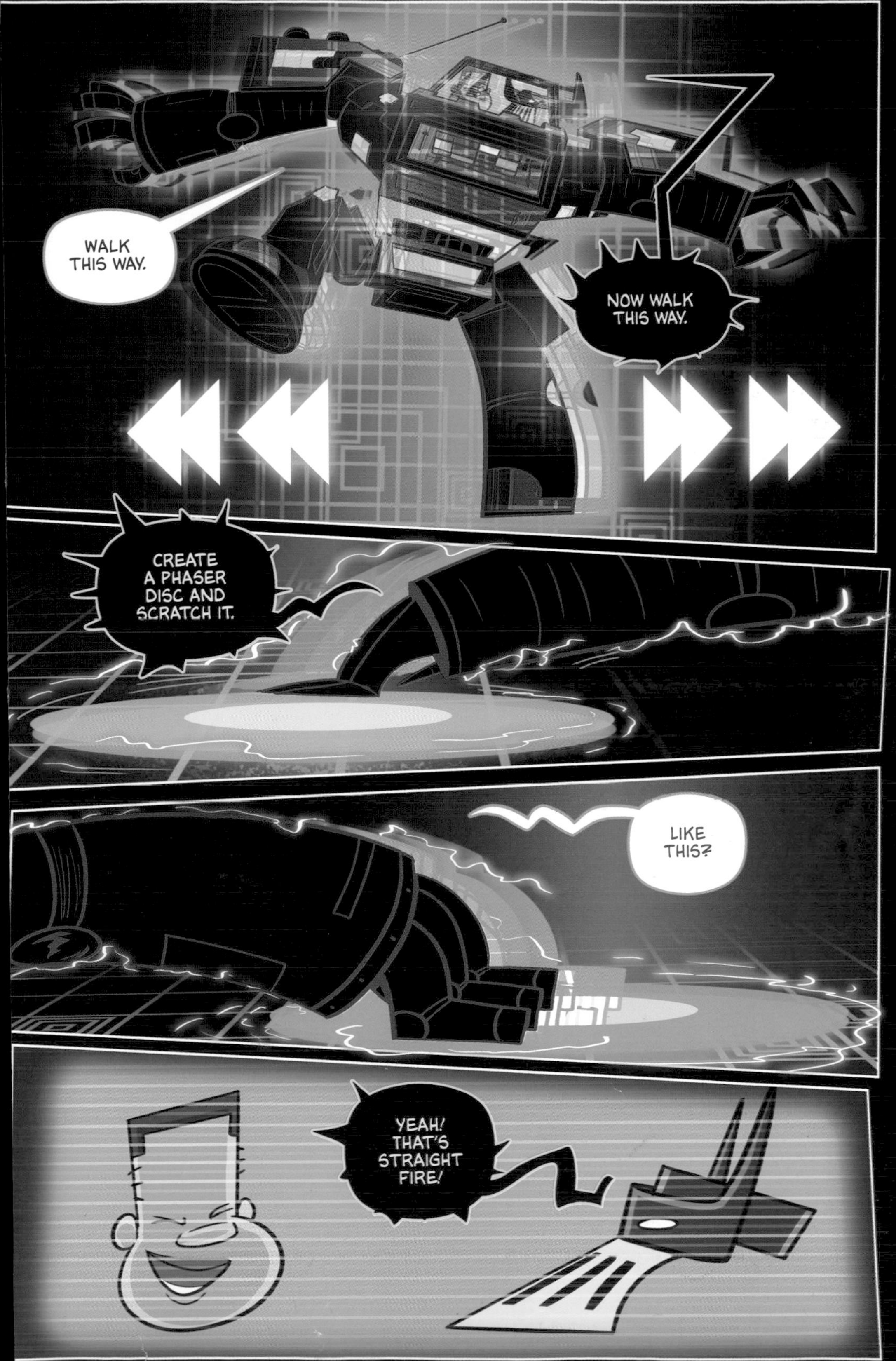
WALK THIS WAY.
NOW WALK THIS WAY.
CREATE A PHASER DISC AND SCRATCH IT.
LIKE THIS?
YEAH! THAT'S STRAIGHT FIRE!

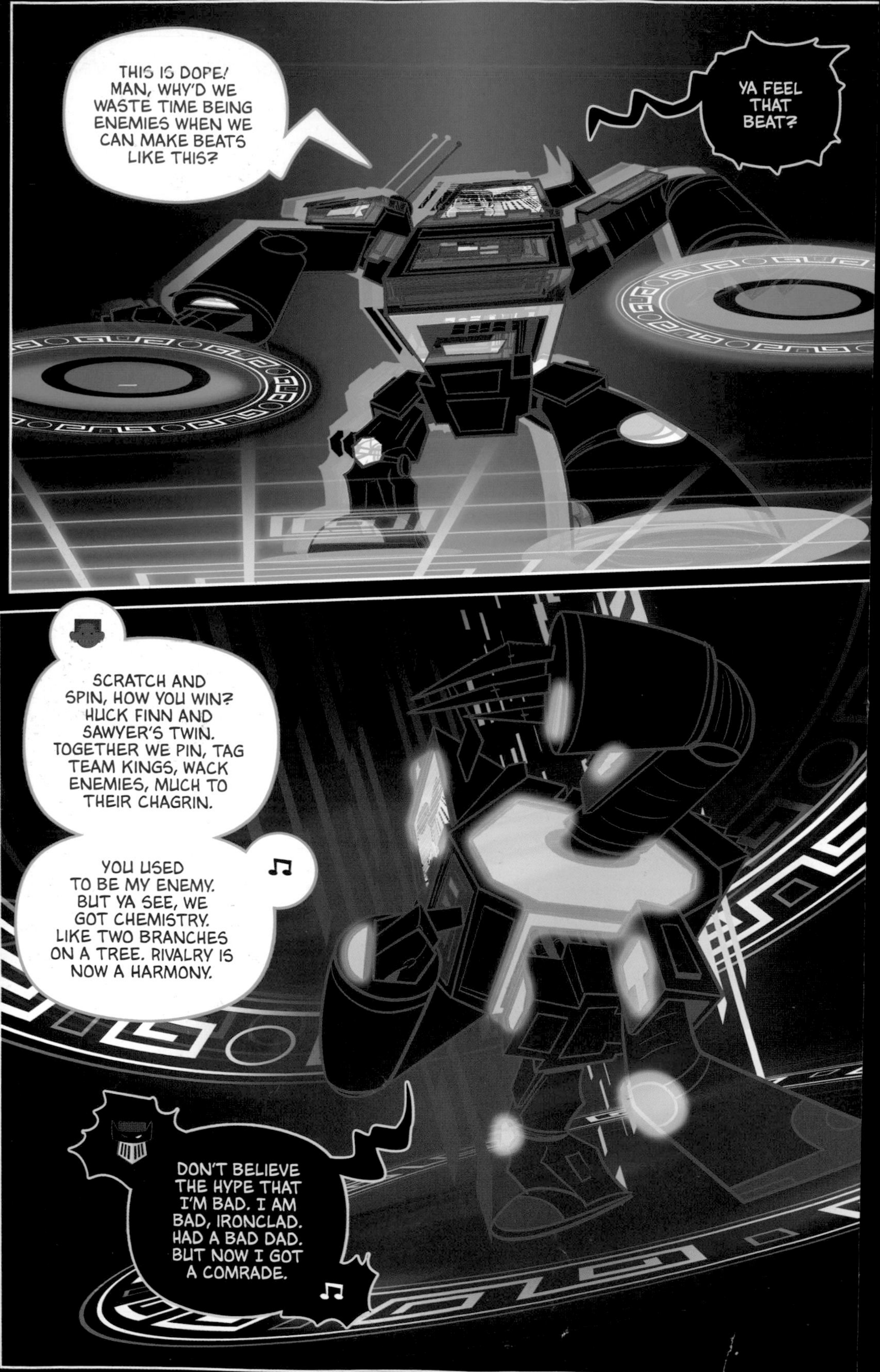
THIS IS DOPE! MAN, WHY'D WE WASTE TIME BEING ENEMIES WHEN WE CAN MAKE BEATS LIKE THIS?
YA FEEL THAT BEAT?
SCRATCH AND SPIN, HOW YOU WIN? HUCK FINN AND SAWYER'S TWIN. TOGETHER WE PIN, TAG TEAM KINGS, WACK ENEMIES, MUCH TO THEIR CHAGRIN.
YOU USED TO BE MY ENEMY. BUT YA SEE, WE GOT CHEMISTRY. LIKE TWO BRANCHES ON A TREE. RIVALRY IS NOW A HARMONY.
DON'T BELIEVE THE HYPE THAT I'M BAD. I AM BAD, IRONCLAD. HAD A BAD DAD. BUT NOW I GOT A COMRADE.

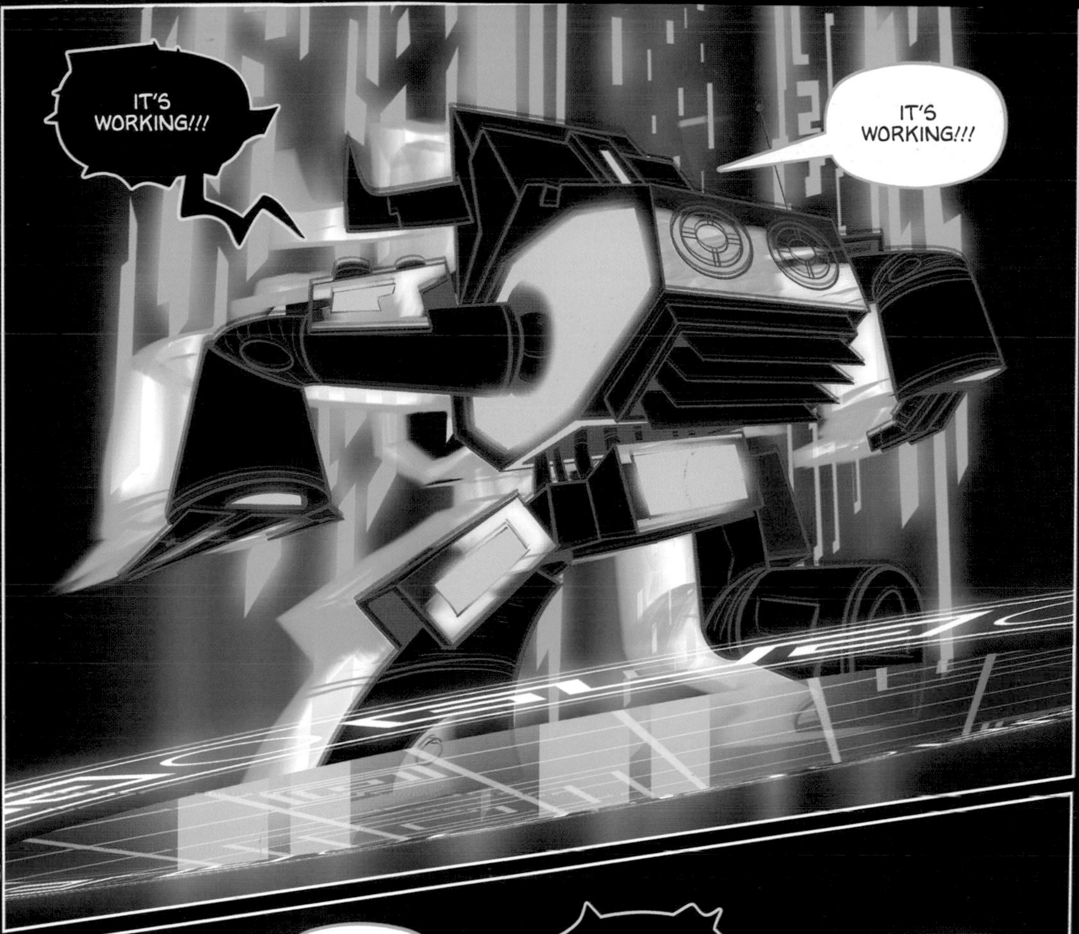
IT'S WORKING!!!
IT'S WORKING!!!

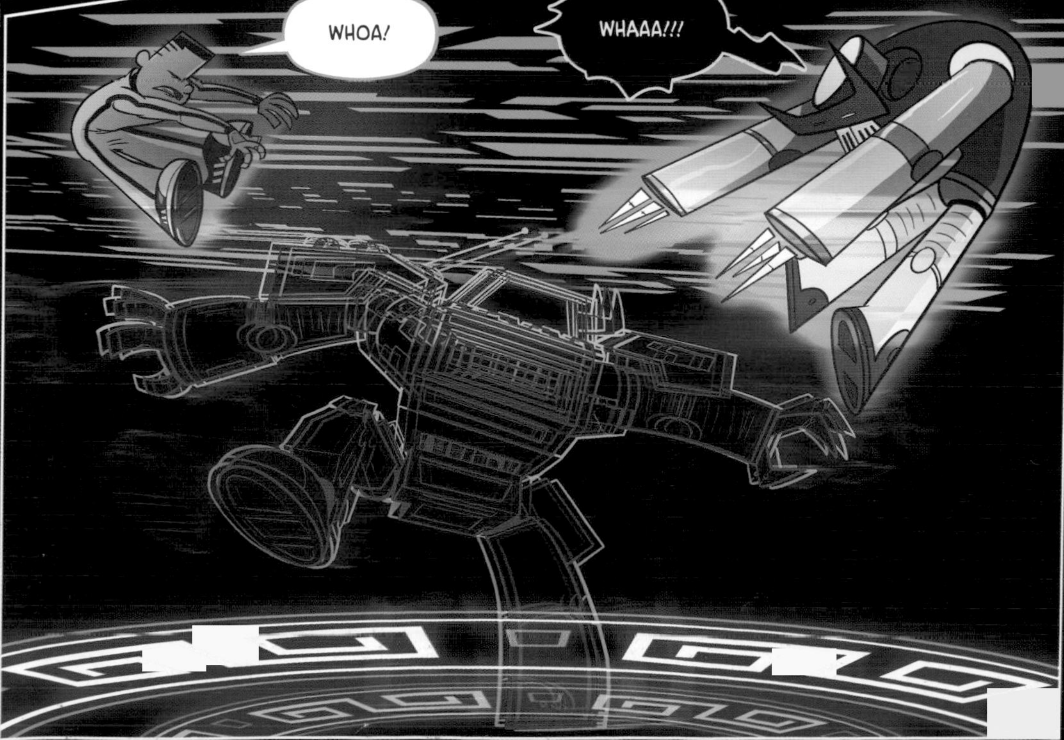
WHOA!
WHAAA!!!

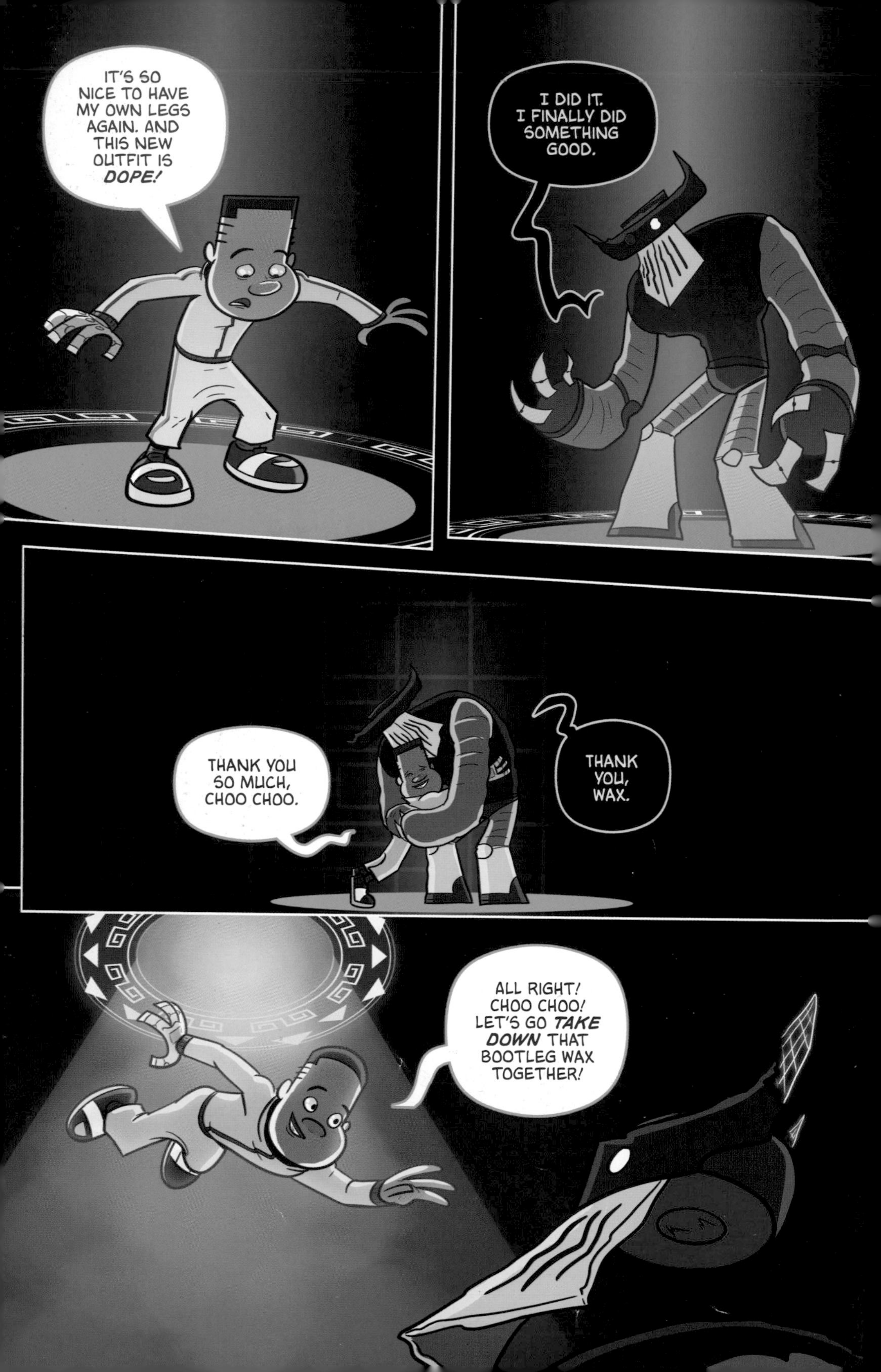
IT'S SO NICE TO HAVE MY OWN LEGS AGAIN. AND THIS NEW OUTFIT IS *DOPE!*
I DID IT. I FINALLY DID SOMETHING GOOD.
THANK YOU SO MUCH, CHOO CHOO.
THANK YOU, WAX.
ALL RIGHT! CHOO CHOO! LET'S GO *TAKE DOWN* THAT BOOTLEG WAX TOGETHER!

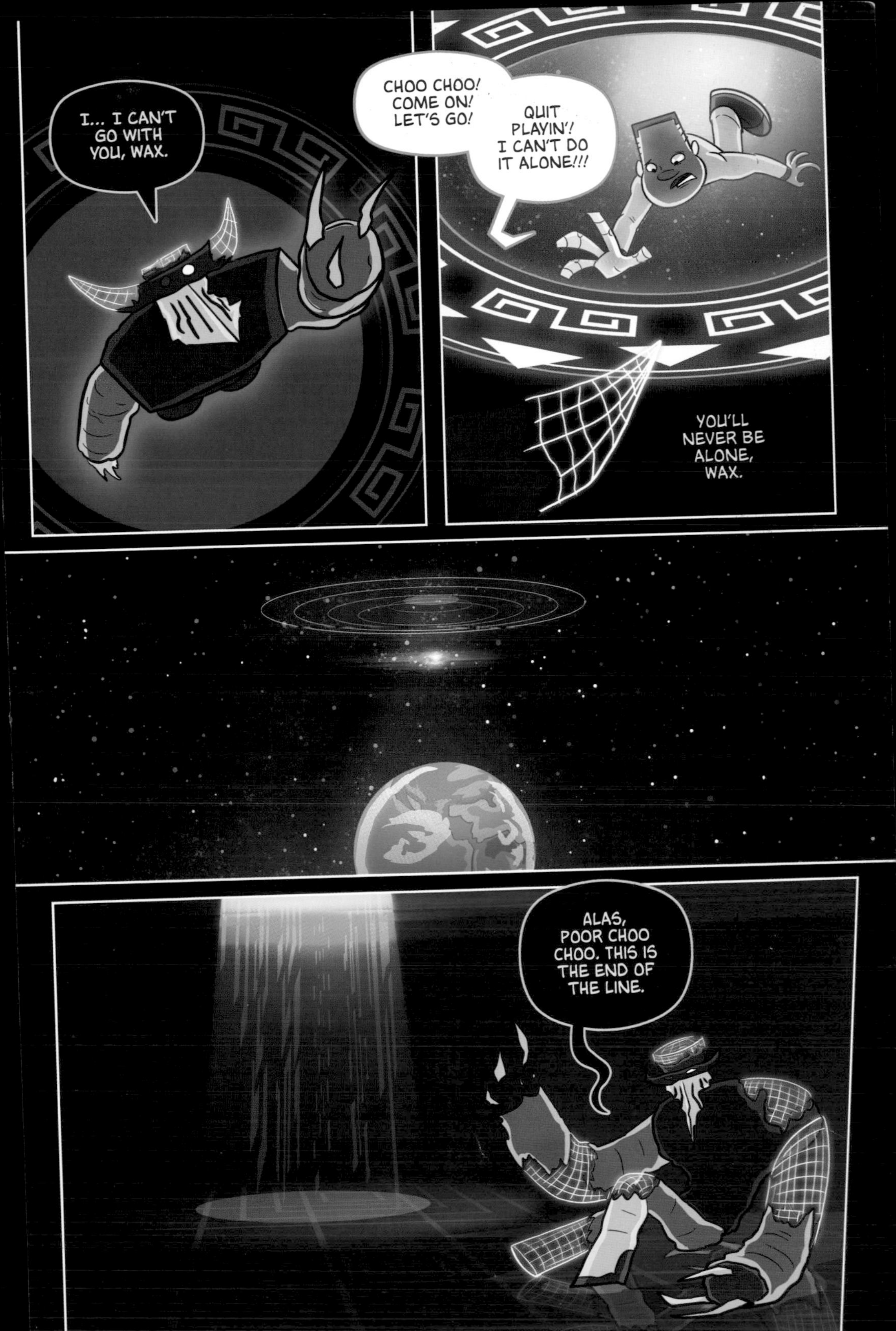
I... I CAN'T GO WITH YOU, WAX.
CHOO CHOO! COME ON! LET'S GO!
QUIT PLAYIN'! I CAN'T DO IT ALONE!!!
YOU'LL NEVER BE ALONE, WAX.
ALAS, POOR CHOO CHOO. THIS IS THE END OF THE LINE.

TRACK
5

REBIRTH OF WAX
(COOL LIKE DAT)

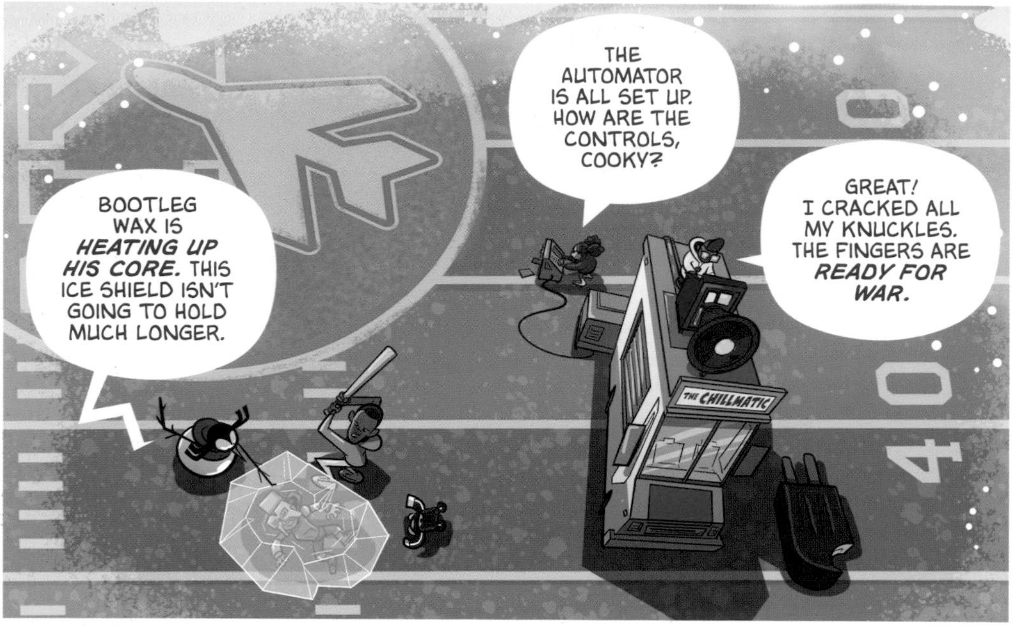
BOOTLEG WAX IS *HEATING UP HIS CORE.* THIS ICE SHIELD ISN'T GOING TO HOLD MUCH LONGER.
THE AUTOMATOR IS ALL SET UP. HOW ARE THE CONTROLS, COOKY?
GREAT! I CRACKED ALL MY KNUCKLES. THE FINGERS ARE *READY FOR WAR.*
THE CHILLMATIC

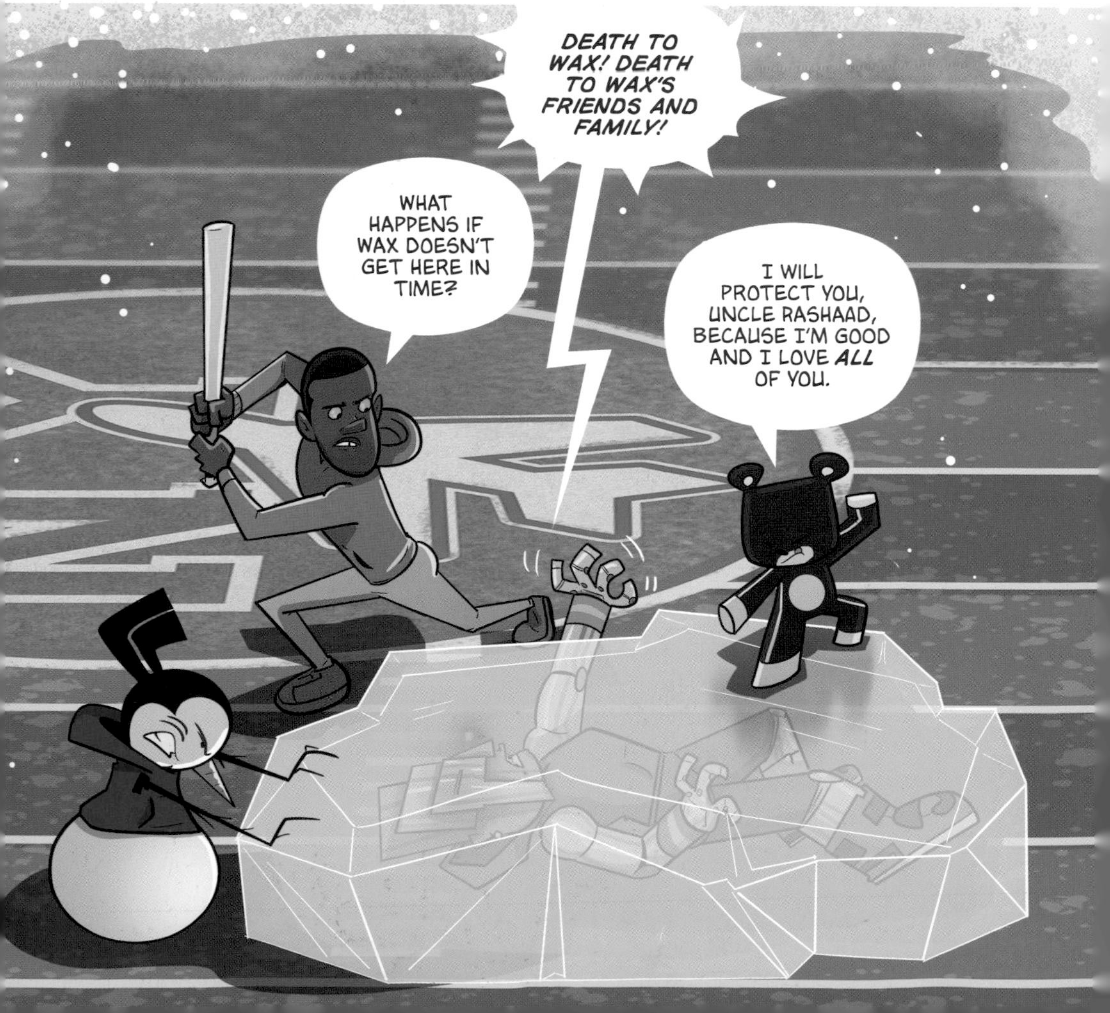
DEATH TO WAX! DEATH TO WAX'S FRIENDS AND FAMILY!
WHAT HAPPENS IF WAX DOESN'T GET HERE IN TIME?
I WILL PROTECT YOU, UNCLE RASHAAD, BECAUSE I'M GOOD AND I LOVE *ALL* OF YOU.

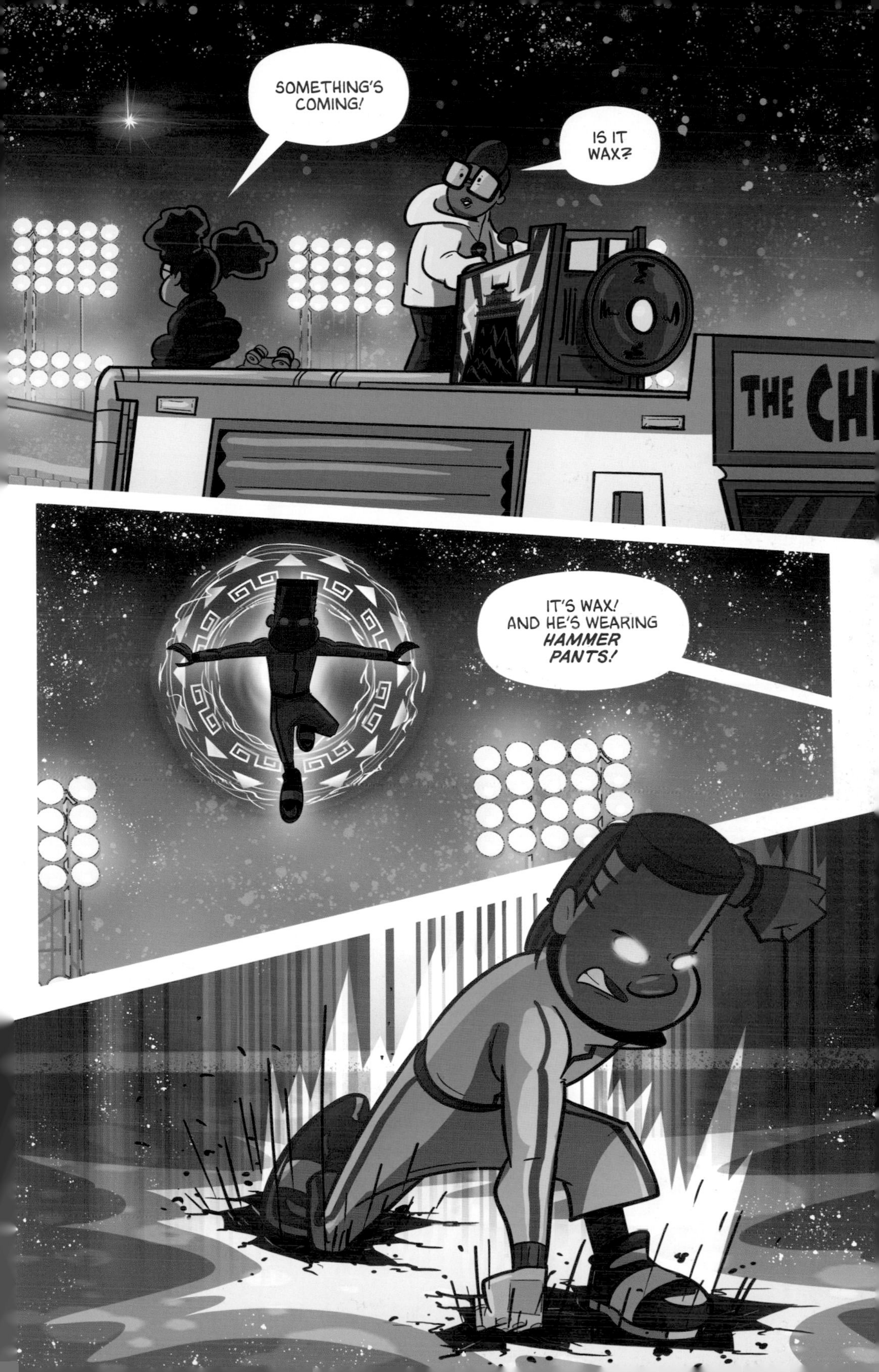
SOMETHING'S COMING!
IS IT WAX?
THE CH
IT'S WAX! AND HE'S WEARING *HAMMER PANTS!*

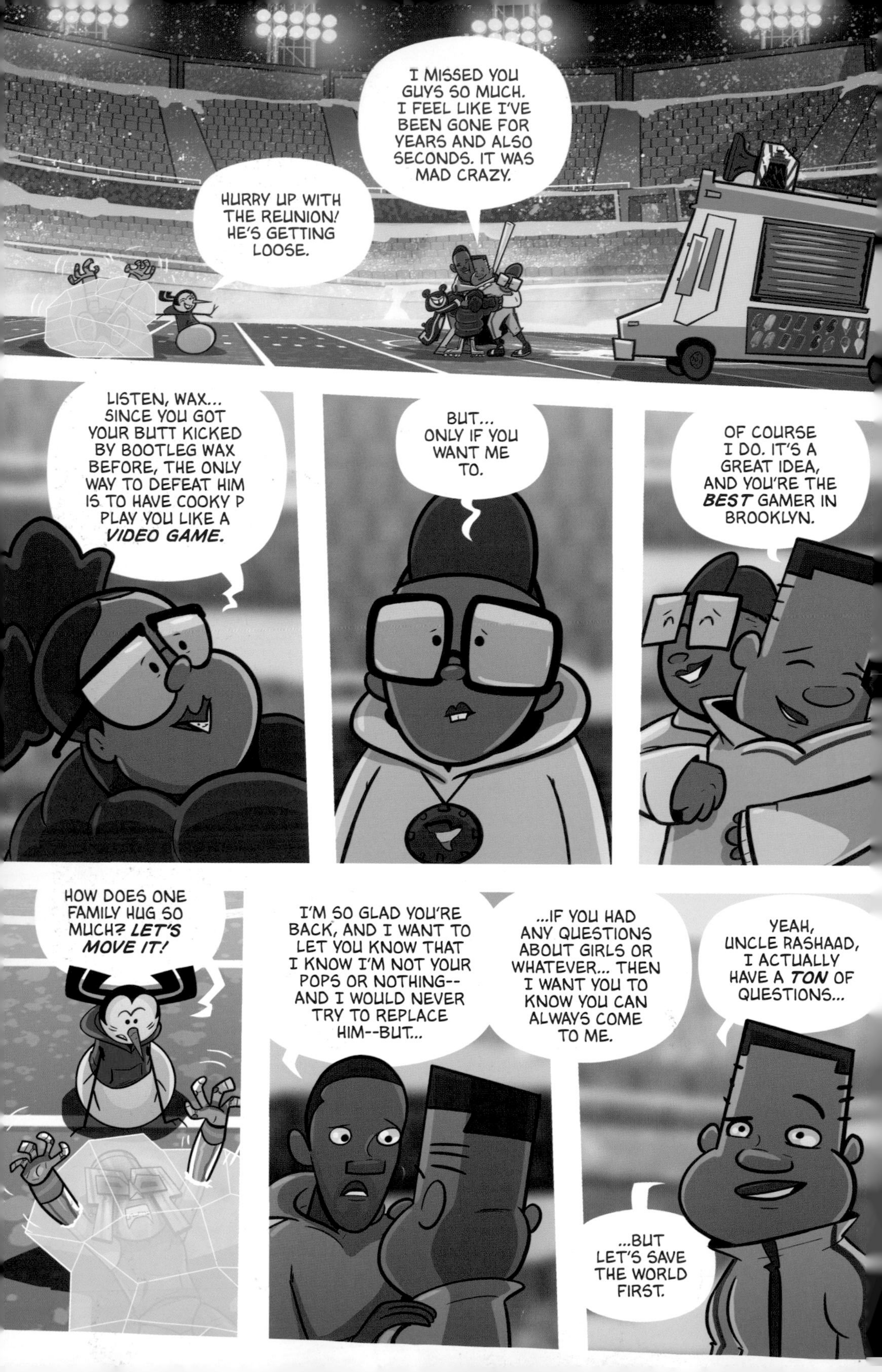

I MISSED YOU GUYS SO MUCH. I FEEL LIKE I'VE BEEN GONE FOR YEARS AND ALSO SECONDS. IT WAS MAD CRAZY.
HURRY UP WITH THE REUNION! HE'S GETTING LOOSE.
LISTEN, WAX... SINCE YOU GOT YOUR BUTT KICKED BY BOOTLEG WAX BEFORE, THE ONLY WAY TO DEFEAT HIM IS TO HAVE COOKY P PLAY YOU LIKE A *VIDEO GAME.*
BUT... ONLY IF YOU WANT ME TO.
OF COURSE I DO. IT'S A GREAT IDEA, AND YOU'RE THE *BEST* GAMER IN BROOKLYN.
HOW DOES ONE FAMILY HUG SO MUCH? *LET'S MOVE IT!*
I'M SO GLAD YOU'RE BACK, AND I WANT TO LET YOU KNOW THAT I KNOW I'M NOT YOUR POPS OR NOTHING-- AND I WOULD NEVER TRY TO REPLACE HIM--BUT...
...IF YOU HAD ANY QUESTIONS ABOUT GIRLS OR WHATEVER... THEN I WANT YOU TO KNOW YOU CAN ALWAYS COME TO ME.
YEAH, UNCLE RASHAAD, I ACTUALLY HAVE A *TON* OF QUESTIONS...
...BUT LET'S SAVE THE WORLD FIRST.

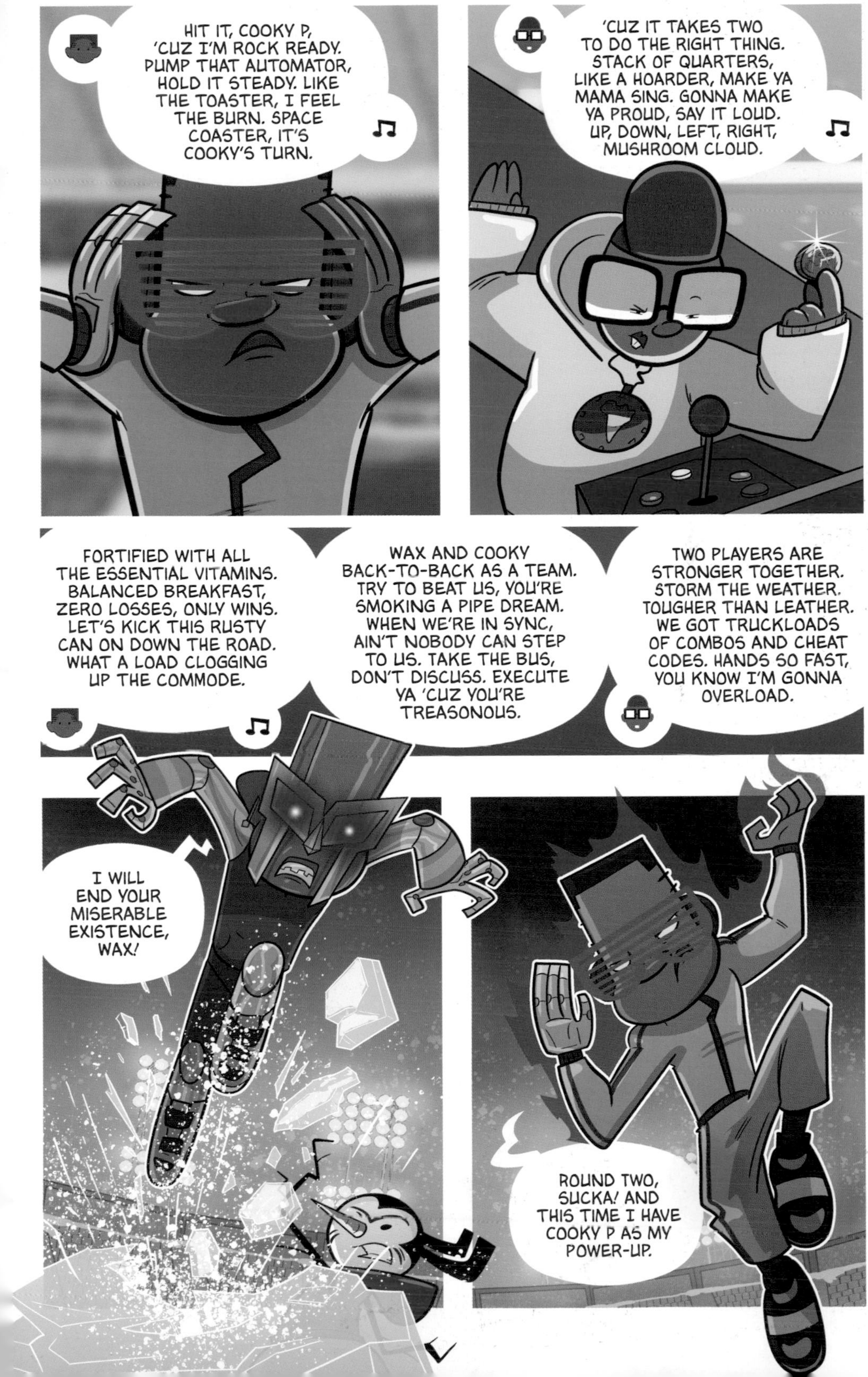
HIT IT, COOKY P, 'CUZ I'M ROCK READY. PUMP THAT AUTOMATOR, HOLD IT STEADY. LIKE THE TOASTER, I FEEL THE BURN. SPACE COASTER, IT'S COOKY'S TURN.
'CUZ IT TAKES TWO TO DO THE RIGHT THING. STACK OF QUARTERS, LIKE A HOARDER, MAKE YA MAMA SING. GONNA MAKE YA PROUD, SAY IT LOUD. UP, DOWN, LEFT, RIGHT, MUSHROOM CLOUD.
FORTIFIED WITH ALL THE ESSENTIAL VITAMINS. BALANCED BREAKFAST, ZERO LOSSES, ONLY WINS. LET'S KICK THIS RUSTY CAN ON DOWN THE ROAD. WHAT A LOAD CLOGGING UP THE COMMODE.
WAX AND COOKY BACK-TO-BACK AS A TEAM. TRY TO BEAT US, YOU'RE SMOKING A PIPE DREAM. WHEN WE'RE IN SYNC, AIN'T NOBODY CAN STEP TO US. TAKE THE BUS, DON'T DISCUSS. EXECUTE YA 'CUZ YOU'RE TREASONOUS.
TWO PLAYERS ARE STRONGER TOGETHER. STORM THE WEATHER. TOUGHER THAN LEATHER. WE GOT TRUCKLOADS OF COMBOS AND CHEAT CODES. HANDS SO FAST, YOU KNOW I'M GONNA OVERLOAD.
I WILL END YOUR MISERABLE EXISTENCE, WAX!
ROUND TWO, SUCKA! AND THIS TIME I HAVE COOKY P AS MY POWER-UP.

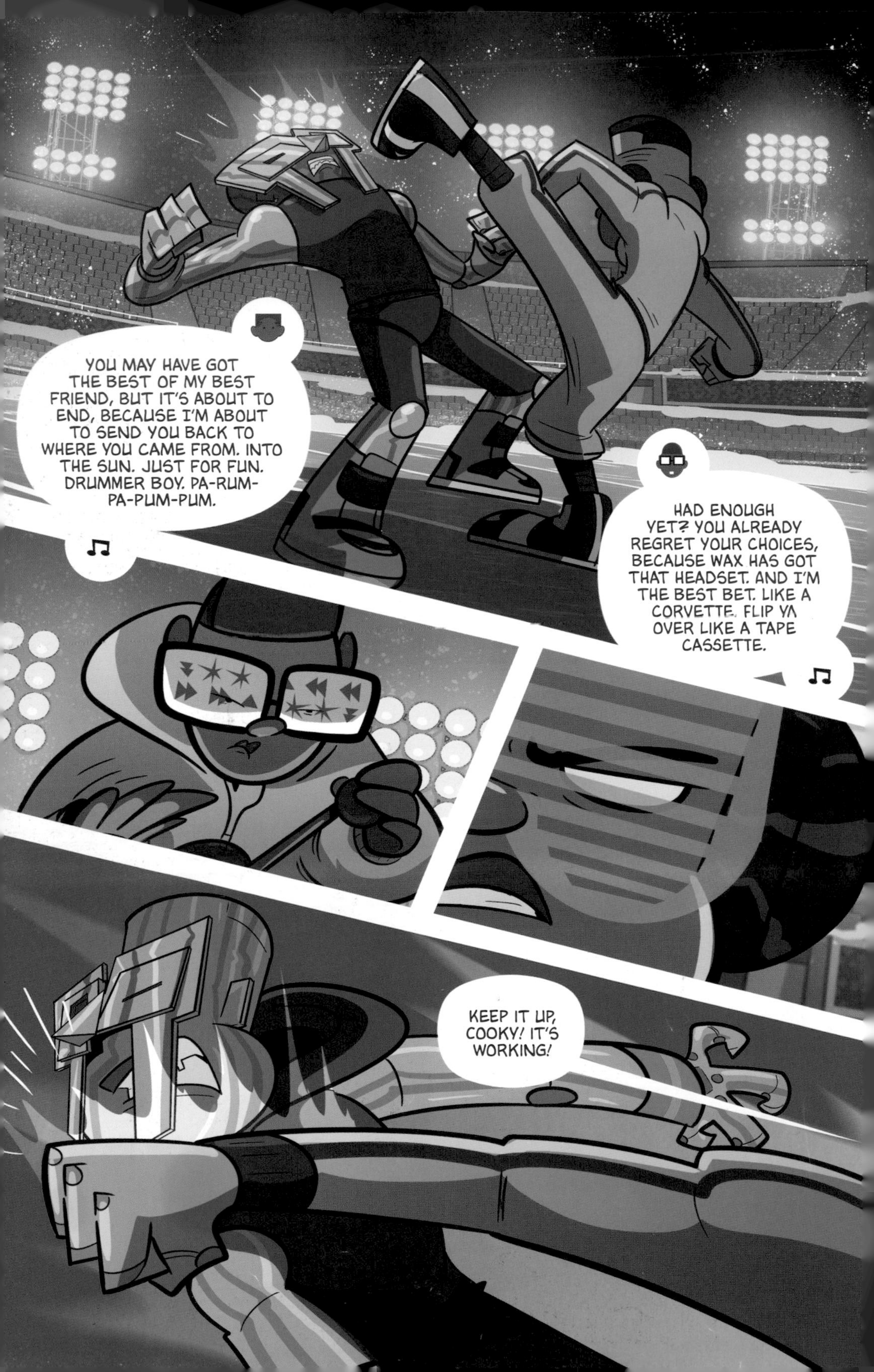
YOU MAY HAVE GOT THE BEST OF MY BEST FRIEND, BUT IT'S ABOUT TO END, BECAUSE I'M ABOUT TO SEND YOU BACK TO WHERE YOU CAME FROM. INTO THE SUN. JUST FOR FUN. DRUMMER BOY. PA-RUM-PA-PUM-PUM.
HAD ENOUGH YET? YOU ALREADY REGRET YOUR CHOICES, BECAUSE WAX HAS GOT THAT HEADSET. AND I'M THE BEST BET. LIKE A CORVETTE. FLIP YA OVER LIKE A TAPE CASSETTE.
KEEP IT UP, COOKY! IT'S WORKING!

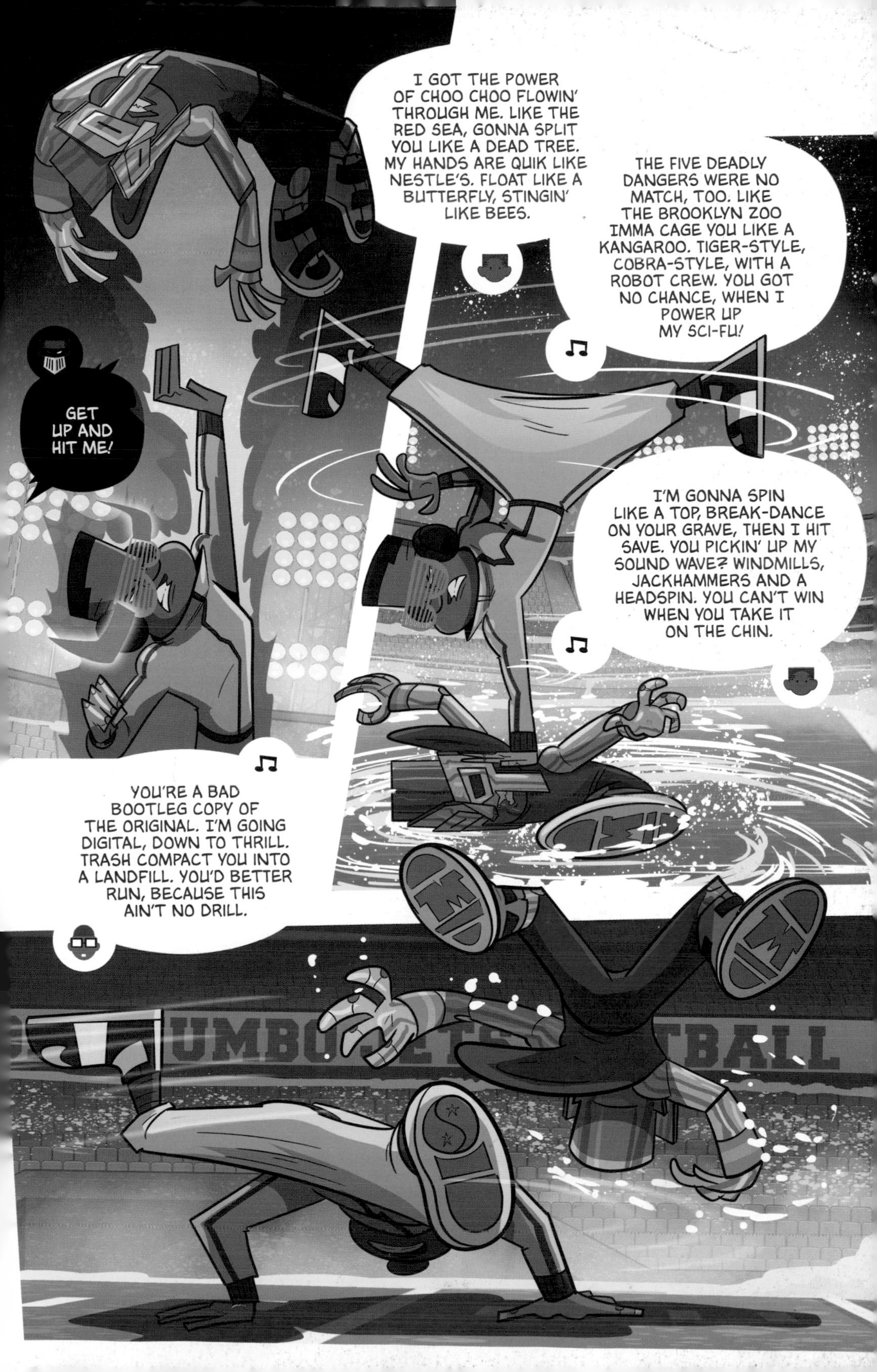
I GOT THE POWER OF CHOO CHOO FLOWIN' THROUGH ME. LIKE THE RED SEA, GONNA SPLIT YOU LIKE A DEAD TREE. MY HANDS ARE QUIK LIKE NESTLE'S. FLOAT LIKE A BUTTERFLY, STINGIN' LIKE BEES.
THE FIVE DEADLY DANGERS WERE NO MATCH, TOO. LIKE THE BROOKLYN ZOO IMMA CAGE YOU LIKE A KANGAROO. TIGER-STYLE, COBRA-STYLE, WITH A ROBOT CREW. YOU GOT NO CHANCE, WHEN I POWER UP MY SCI-FU!
GET UP AND HIT ME!
I'M GONNA SPIN LIKE A TOP, BREAK-DANCE ON YOUR GRAVE, THEN I HIT SAVE. YOU PICKIN' UP MY SOUND WAVE? WINDMILLS, JACKHAMMERS AND A HEADSPIN. YOU CAN'T WIN WHEN YOU TAKE IT ON THE CHIN.
YOU'RE A BAD BOOTLEG COPY OF THE ORIGINAL. I'M GOING DIGITAL, DOWN TO THRILL. TRASH COMPACT YOU INTO A LANDFILL. YOU'D BETTER RUN, BECAUSE THIS AIN'T NO DRILL.

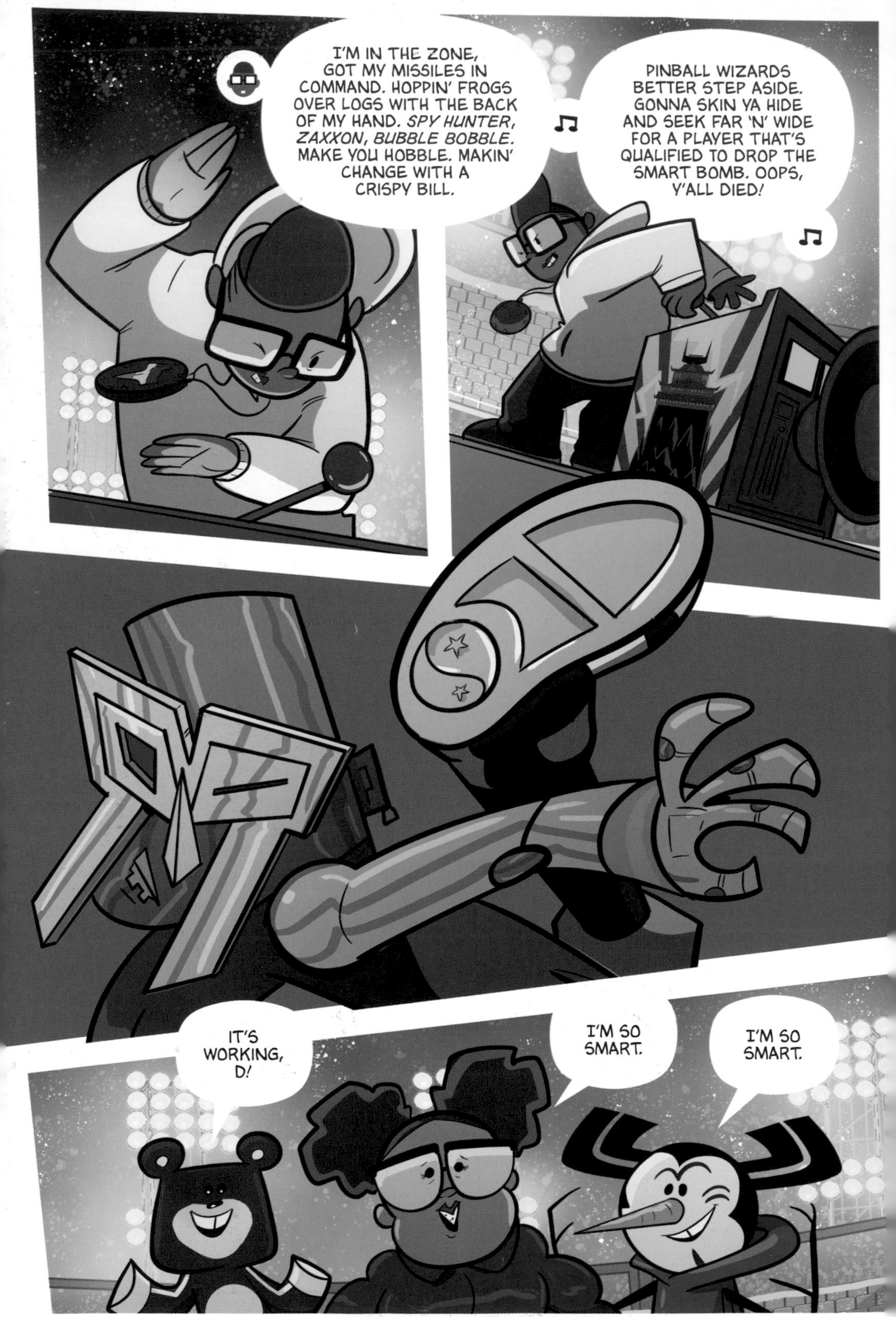
I'M IN THE ZONE, GOT MY MISSILES IN COMMAND. HOPPIN' FROGS OVER LOGS WITH THE BACK OF MY HAND. *SPY HUNTER, ZAXXON, BUBBLE BOBBLE.* MAKE YOU HOBBLE. MAKIN' CHANGE WITH A CRISPY BILL.
PINBALL WIZARDS BETTER STEP ASIDE. GONNA SKIN YA HIDE AND SEEK FAR 'N' WIDE FOR A PLAYER THAT'S QUALIFIED TO DROP THE SMART BOMB. OOPS, Y'ALL DIED!
IT'S WORKING, D!
I'M SO SMART.
I'M SO SMART.

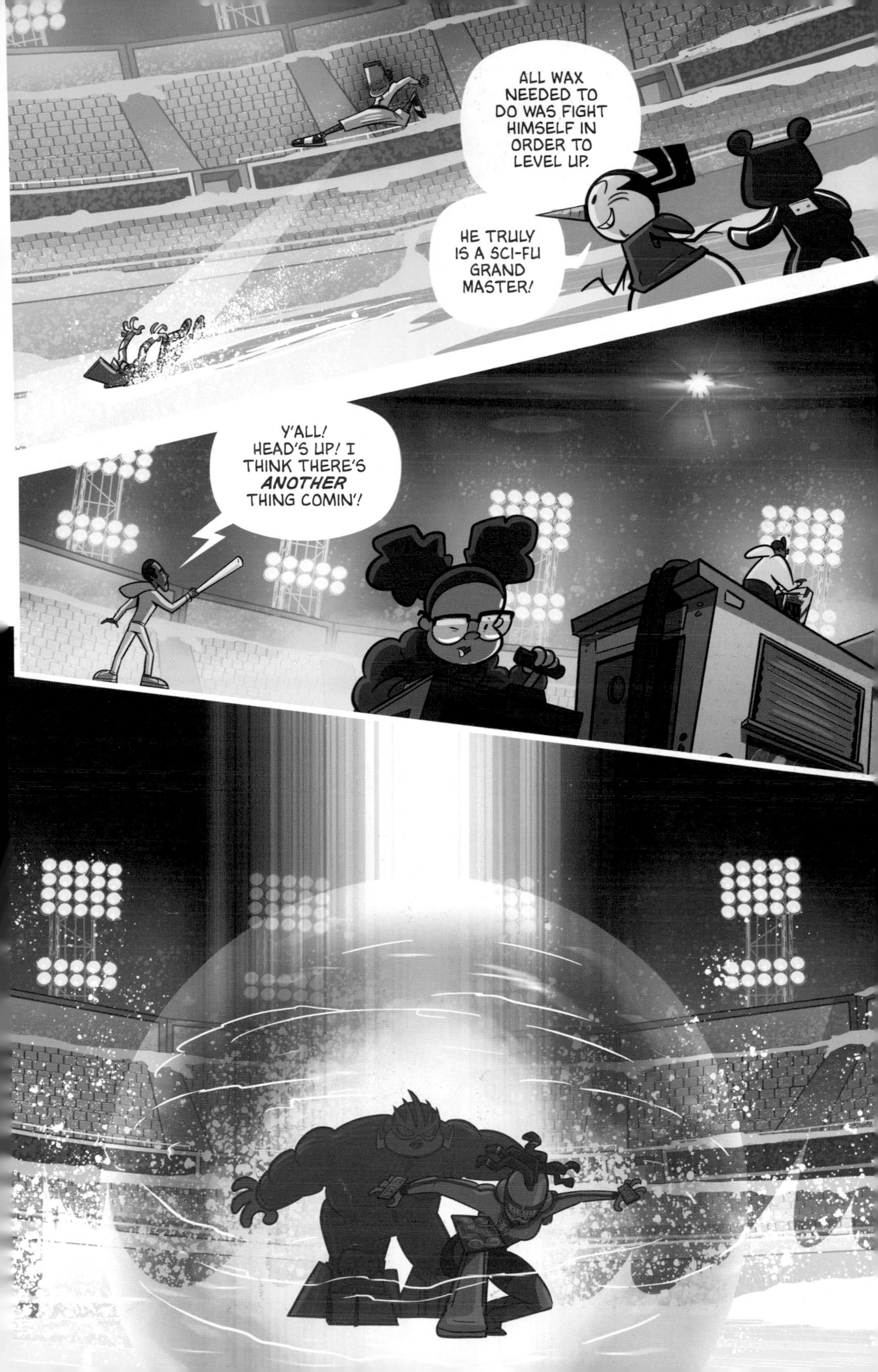
ALL WAX NEEDED TO DO WAS FIGHT HIMSELF IN ORDER TO LEVEL UP.
HE TRULY IS A SCI-FU GRAND MASTER!
Y'ALL! HEAD'S UP! I THINK THERE'S ANOTHER THING COMIN'!

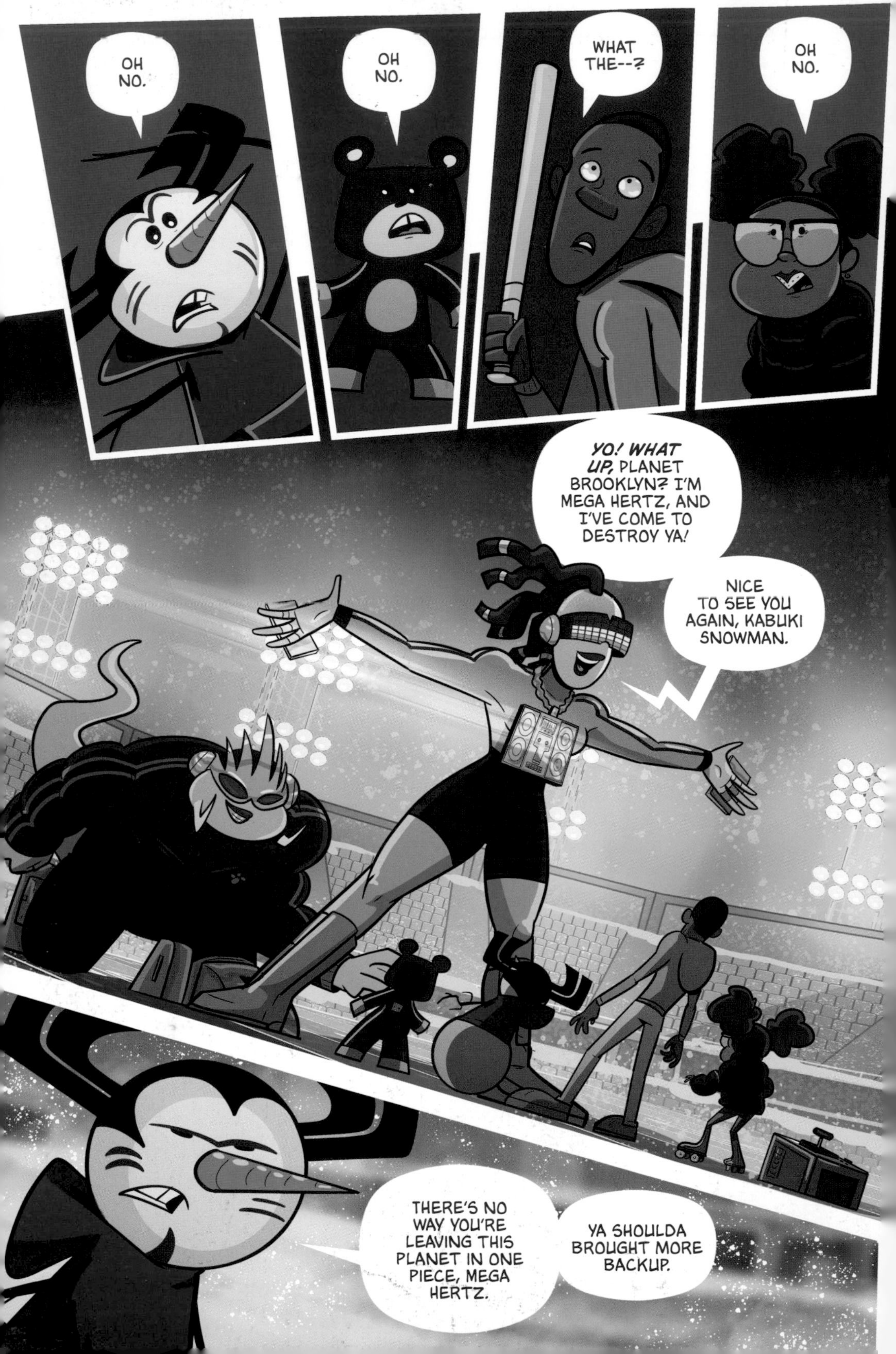
OH NO.
OH NO.
WHAT THE--?
OH NO.
YO! WHAT UP, PLANET BROOKLYN? I'M MEGA HERTZ, AND I'VE COME TO DESTROY YA!
NICE TO SEE YOU AGAIN, KABUKI SNOWMAN.
THERE'S NO WAY YOU'RE LEAVING THIS PLANET IN ONE PIECE, MEGA HERTZ.
YA SHOULDA BROUGHT MORE BACKUP.

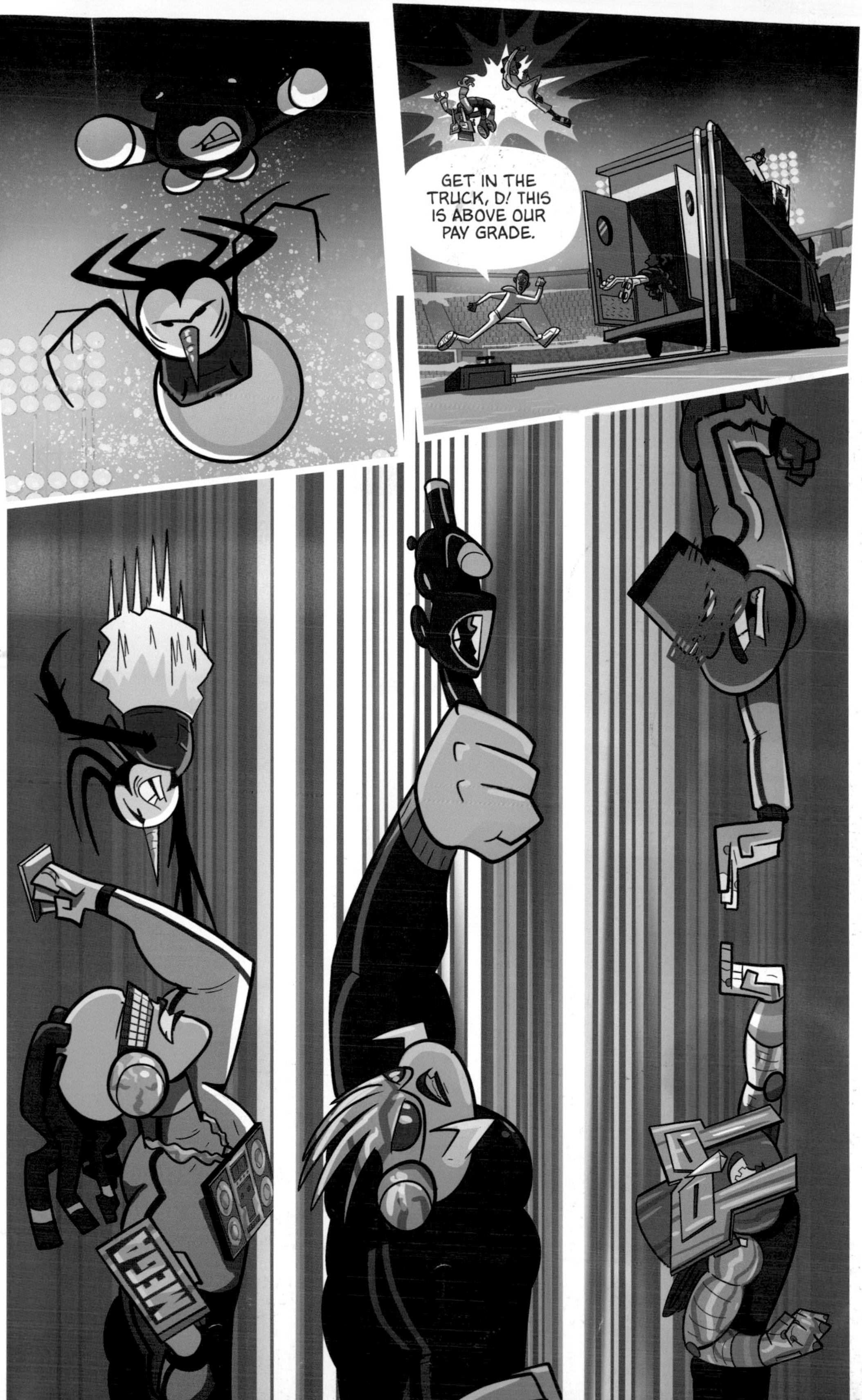
GET IN THE TRUCK, D! THIS IS ABOVE OUR PAY GRADE.

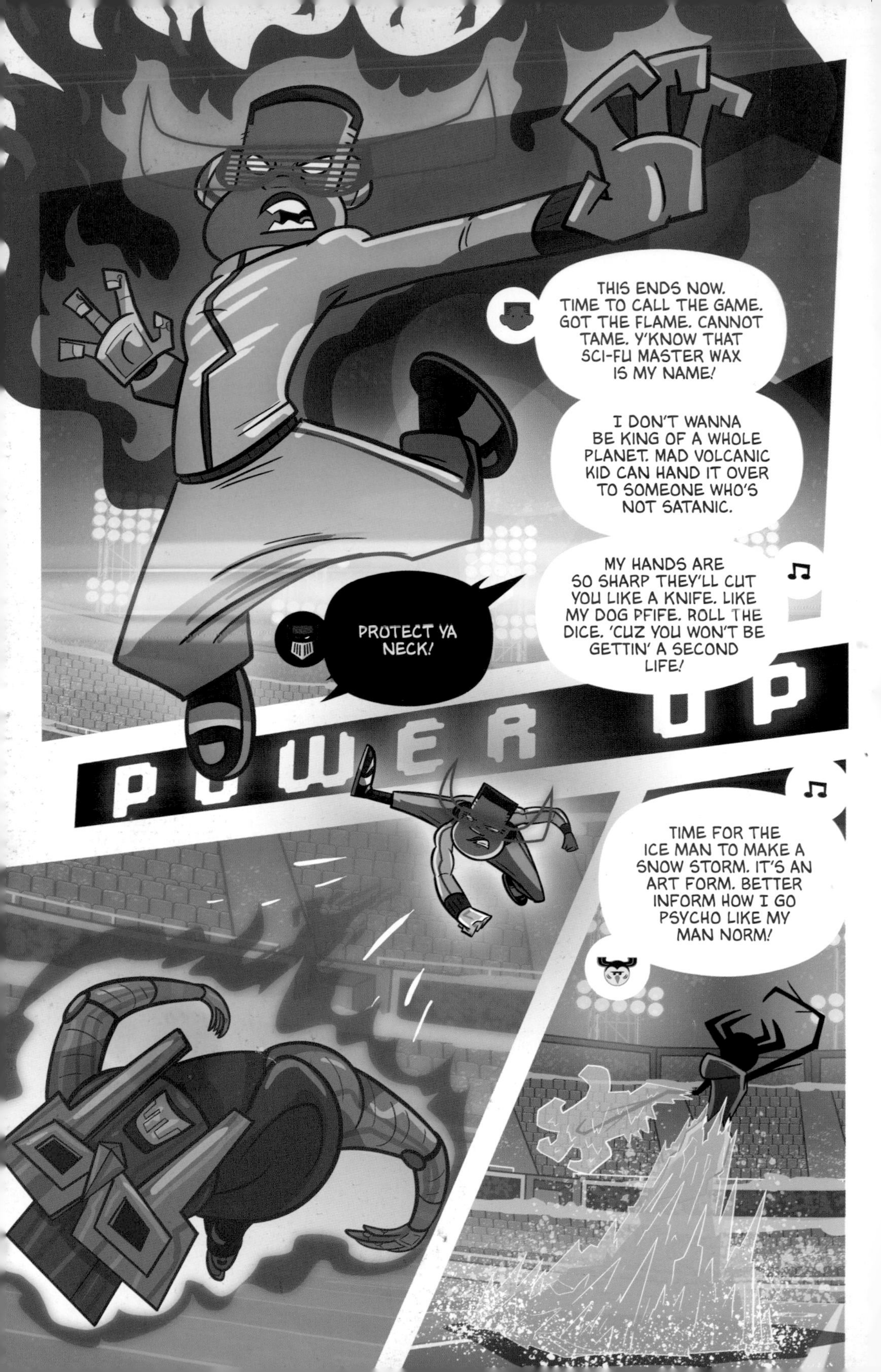
THIS ENDS NOW. TIME TO CALL THE GAME. GOT THE FLAME. CANNOT TAME. Y'KNOW THAT SCI-FU MASTER WAX IS MY NAME!
I DON'T WANNA BE KING OF A WHOLE PLANET. MAD VOLCANIC KID CAN HAND IT OVER TO SOMEONE WHO'S NOT SATANIC.
MY HANDS ARE SO SHARP THEY'LL CUT YOU LIKE A KNIFE. LIKE MY DOG PFIFE. ROLL THE DICE. 'CUZ YOU WON'T BE GETTIN' A SECOND LIFE!
PROTECT YA NECK!
POWER UP
TIME FOR THE ICE MAN TO MAKE A SNOW STORM. IT'S AN ART FORM. BETTER INFORM HOW I GO PSYCHO LIKE MY MAN NORM!

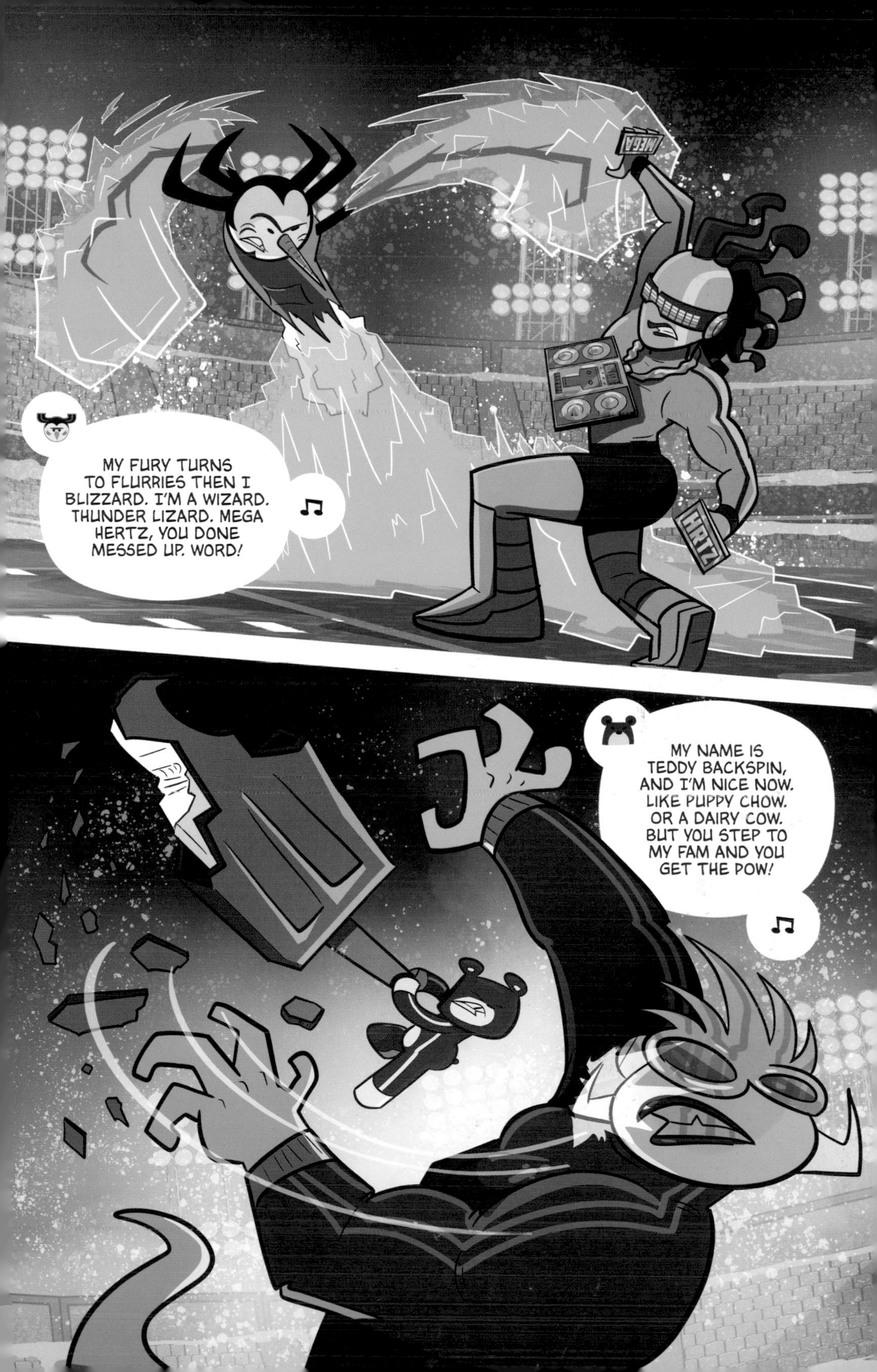
MEGA
MY FURY TURNS TO FLURRIES THEN I BLIZZARD. I'M A WIZARD. THUNDER LIZARD. MEGA HERTZ, YOU DONE MESSED UP. WORD!
HRTZ
MY NAME IS TEDDY BACKSPIN, AND I'M NICE NOW. LIKE PUPPY CHOW. OR A DAIRY COW. BUT YOU STEP TO MY FAM AND YOU GET THE POW!

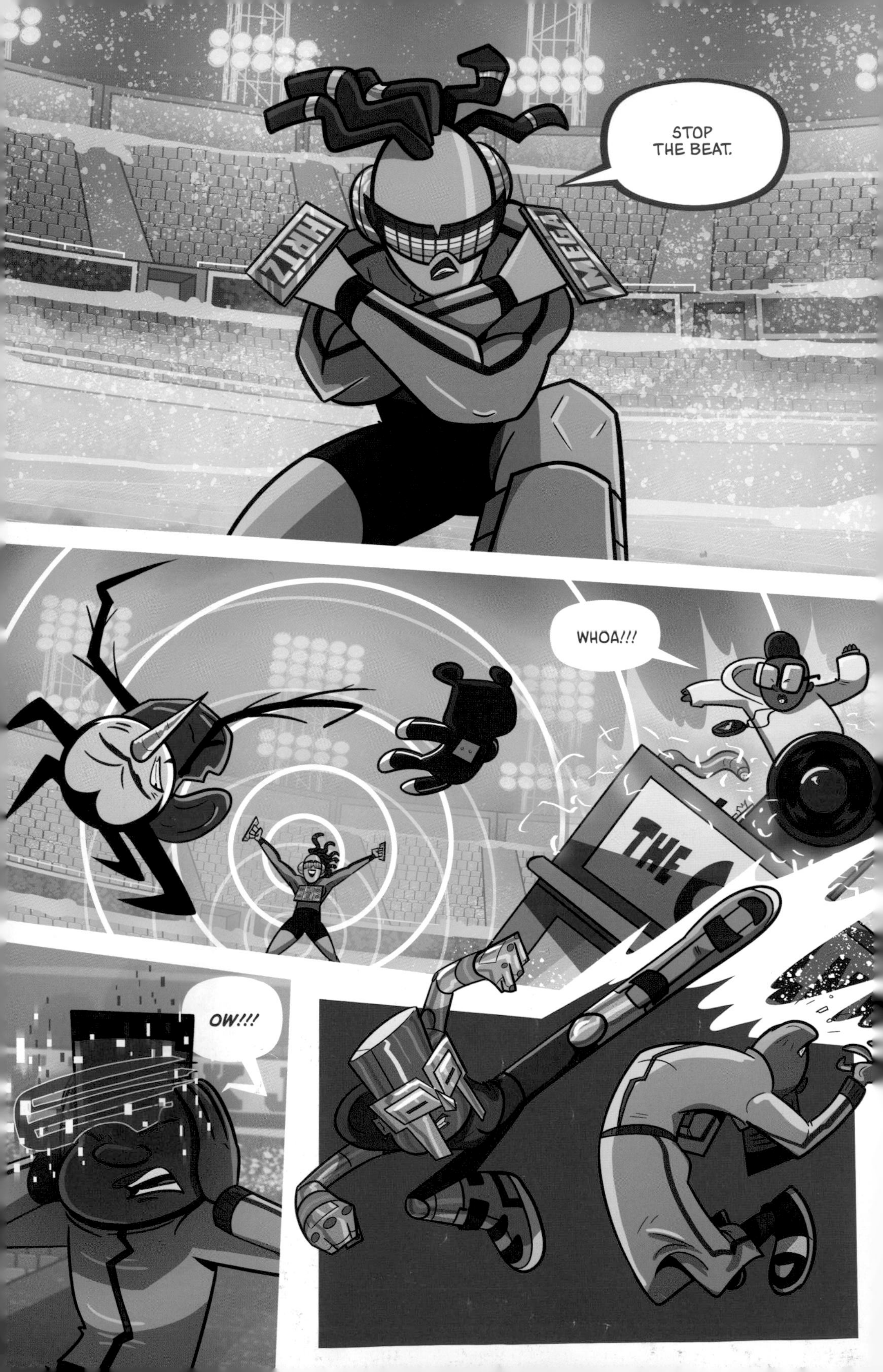
STOP THE BEAT.
HRTZ
MEGA
WHOA!!!
THE
OW!!!

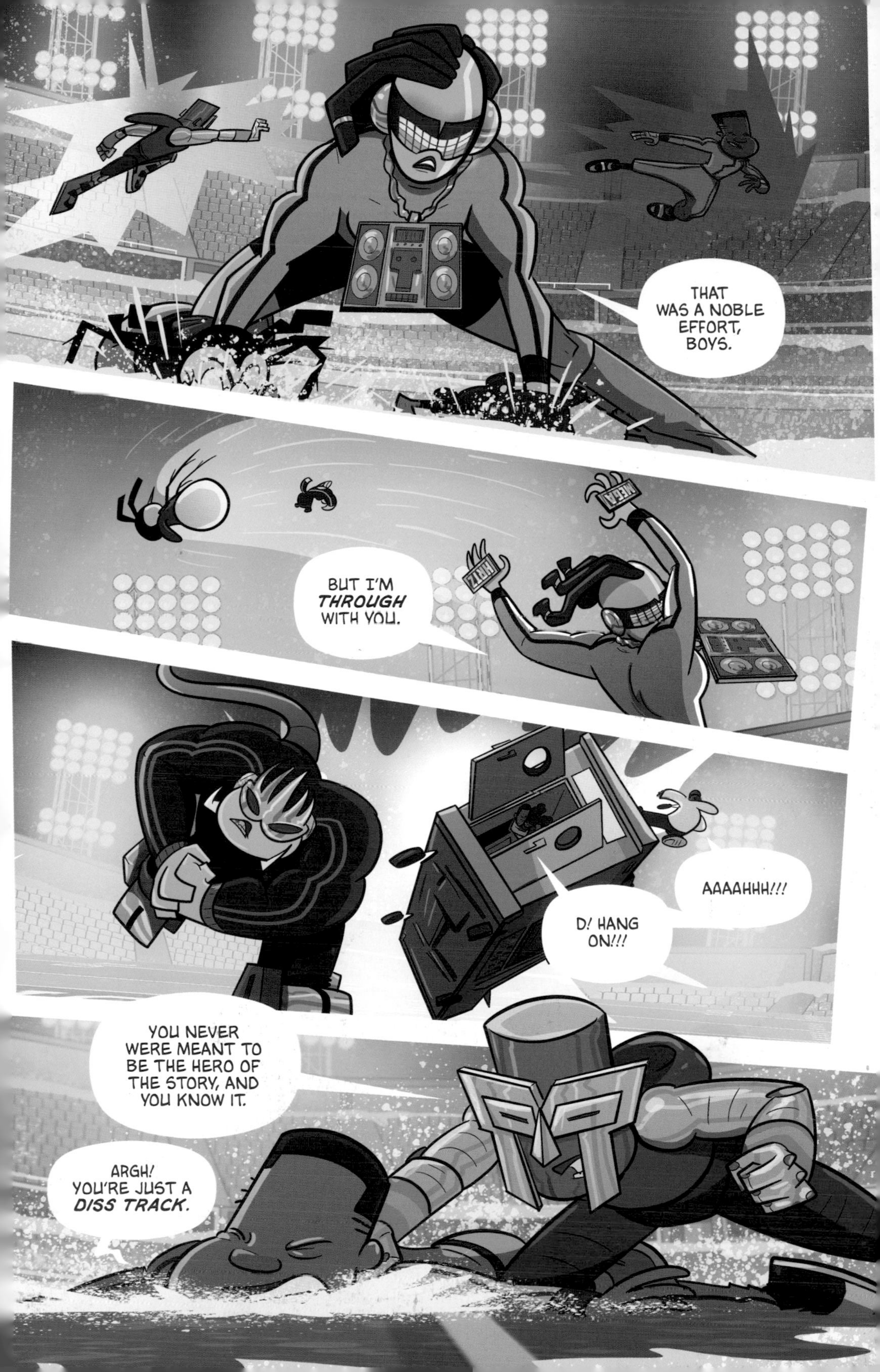
THAT WAS A NOBLE EFFORT, BOYS.
MEGA
BUT I'M *THROUGH* WITH YOU.
AAAAHHH!!!
D! HANG ON!!!
YOU NEVER WERE MEANT TO BE THE HERO OF THE STORY, AND YOU KNOW IT.
ARGH! YOU'RE JUST A *DISS TRACK*.

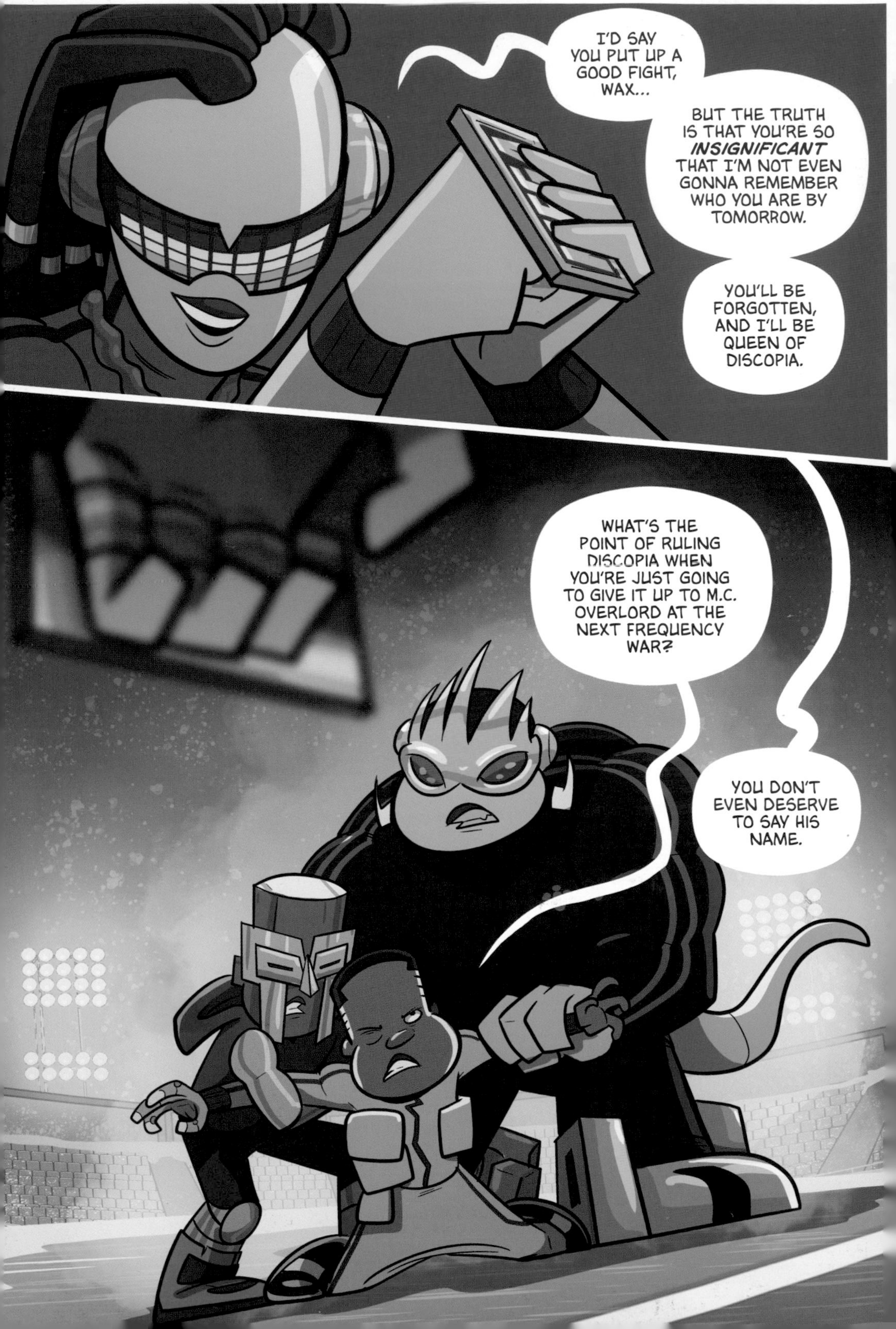
I'D SAY YOU PUT UP A GOOD FIGHT, WAX...
BUT THE TRUTH IS THAT YOU'RE SO *INSIGNIFICANT* THAT I'M NOT EVEN GONNA REMEMBER WHO YOU ARE BY TOMORROW.
YOU'LL BE FORGOTTEN, AND I'LL BE QUEEN OF DISCOPIA.
WHAT'S THE POINT OF RULING DISCOPIA WHEN YOU'RE JUST GOING TO GIVE IT UP TO M.C. OVERLORD AT THE NEXT FREQUENCY WAR?
YOU DON'T EVEN DESERVE TO SAY HIS NAME.

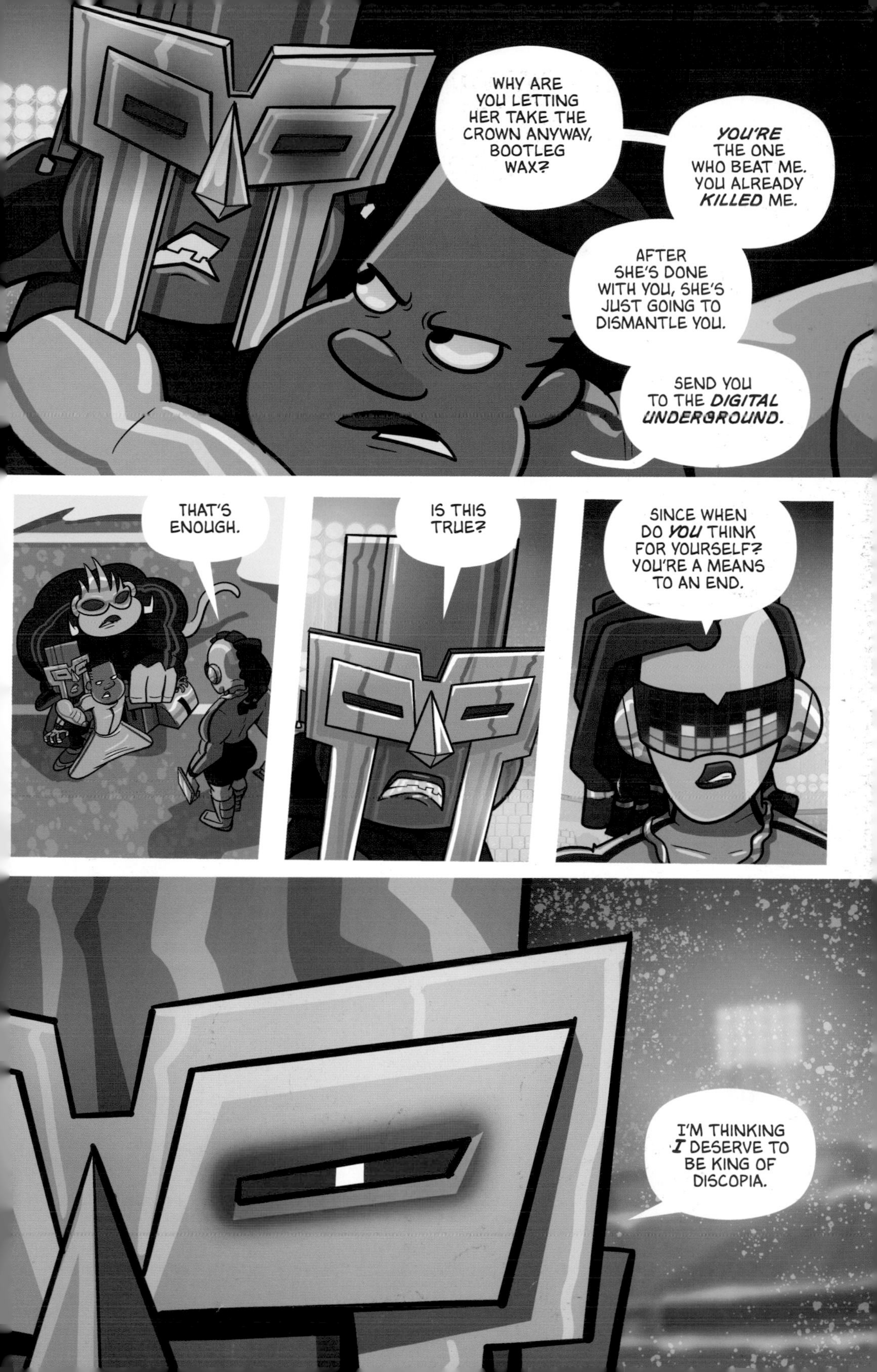
WHY ARE YOU LETTING HER TAKE THE CROWN ANYWAY, BOOTLEG WAX?
YOU'RE THE ONE WHO BEAT ME. YOU ALREADY *KILLED* ME.
AFTER SHE'S DONE WITH YOU, SHE'S JUST GOING TO DISMANTLE YOU.
SEND YOU TO THE *DIGITAL UNDERGROUND.*
THAT'S ENOUGH.
IS THIS TRUE?
SINCE WHEN DO *YOU* THINK FOR YOURSELF? YOU'RE A MEANS TO AN END.
I'M THINKING *I* DESERVE TO BE KING OF DISCOPIA.

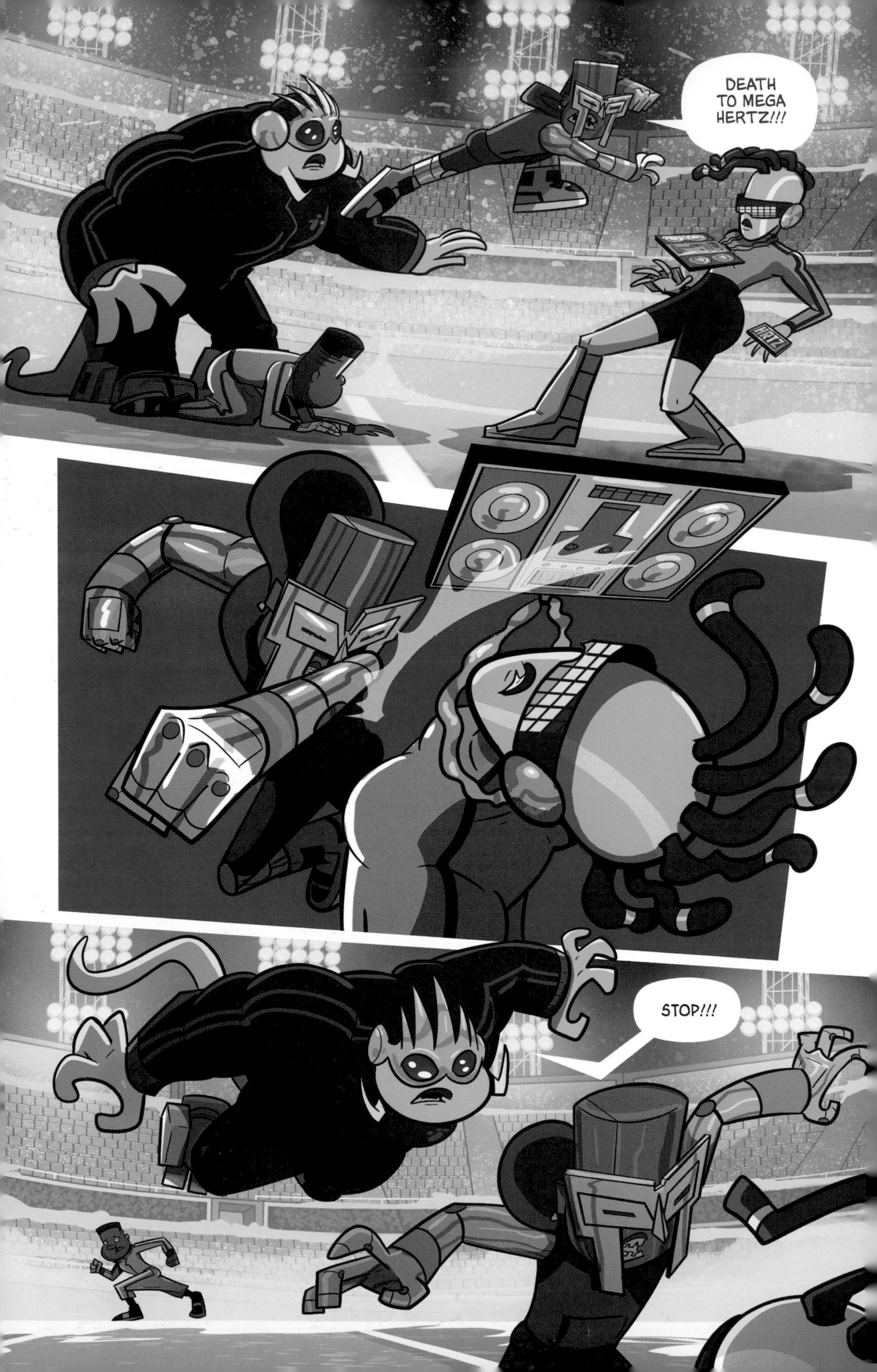
DEATH TO MEGA HERTZ!!!
HERTZ
STOP!!!

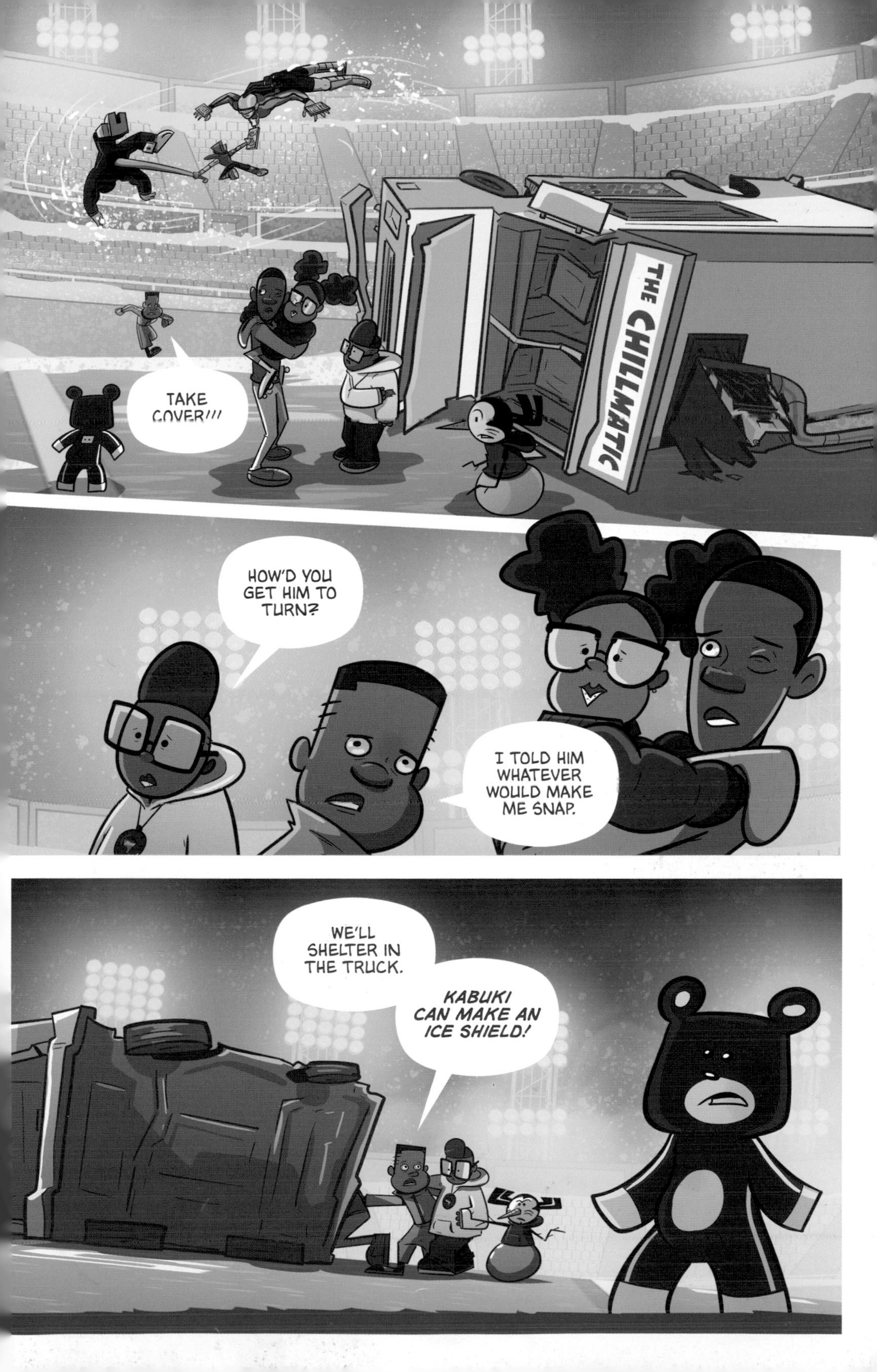
THE CHILLMATIC
TAKE COVER!!!
HOW'D YOU GET HIM TO TURN?
I TOLD HIM WHATEVER WOULD MAKE ME SNAP.
WE'LL SHELTER IN THE TRUCK.
KABUKI CAN MAKE AN ICE SHIELD!

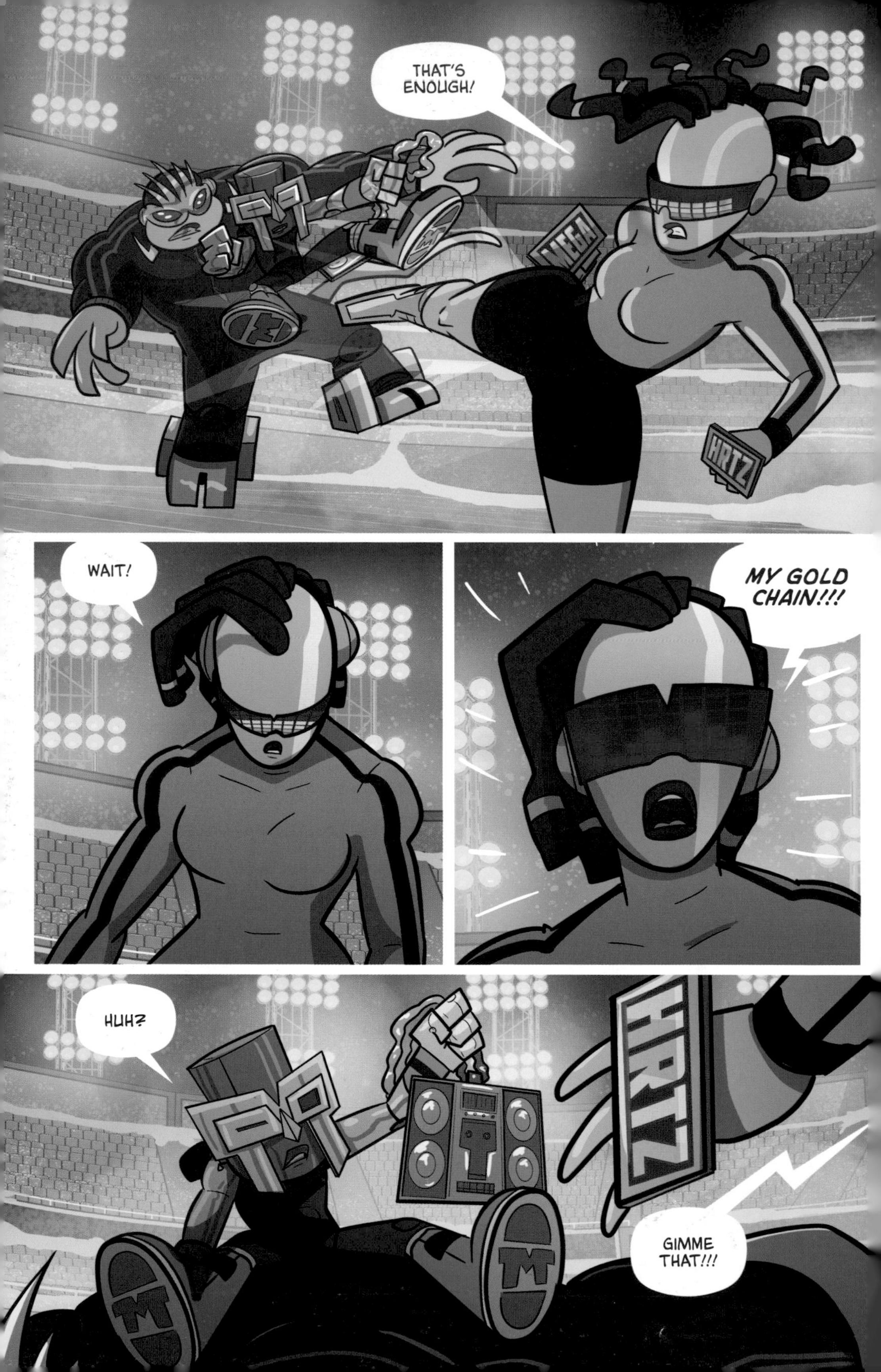
THAT'S ENOUGH!
MEGA
HRTZ
WAIT!
MY GOLD CHAIN!!!
HUH?
HRTZ
GIMME THAT!!!

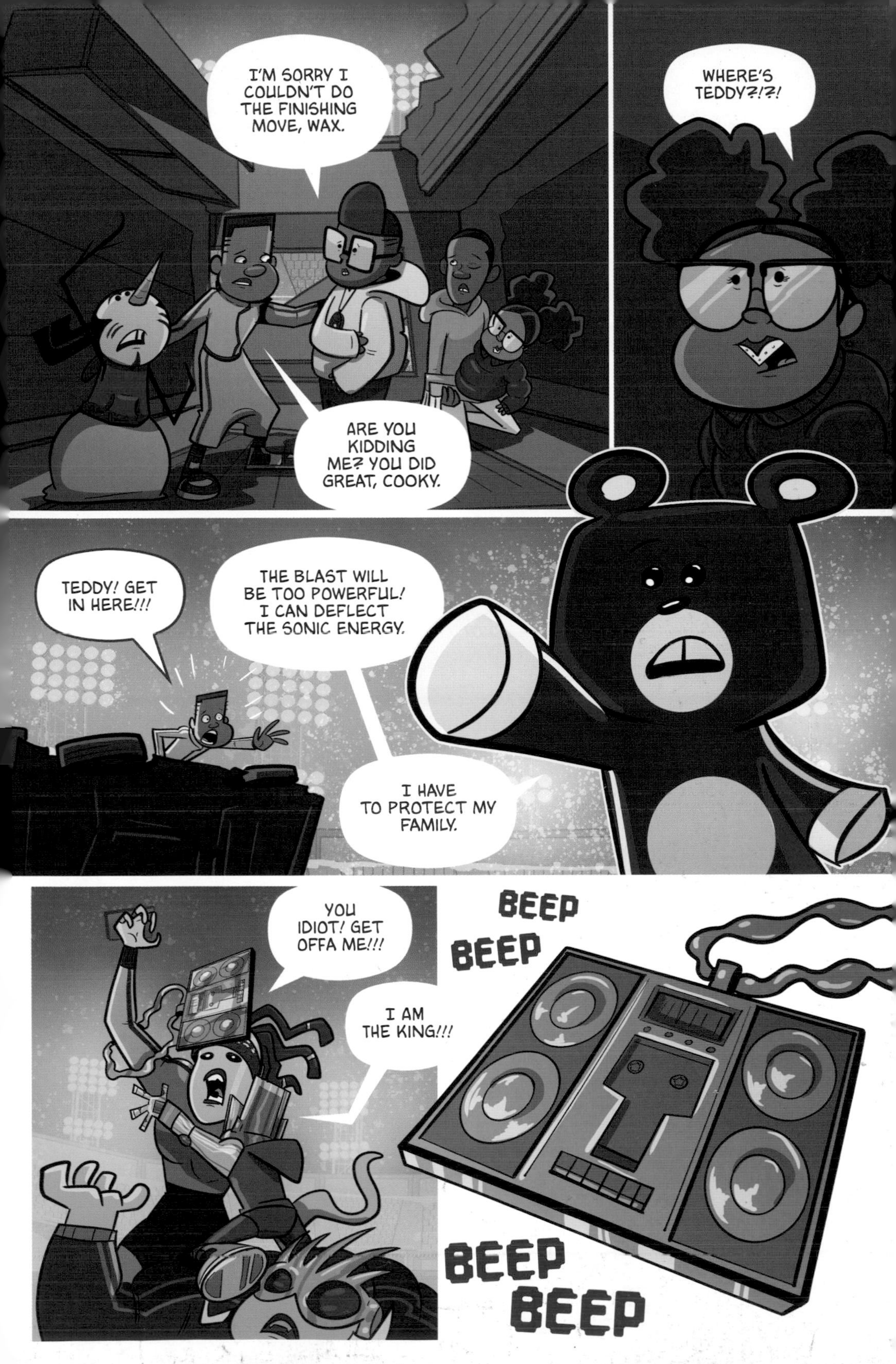
I'M SORRY I COULDN'T DO THE FINISHING MOVE, WAX.
ARE YOU KIDDING ME? YOU DID GREAT, COOKY.
WHERE'S TEDDY?!?!
TEDDY! GET IN HERE!!!
THE BLAST WILL BE TOO POWERFUL! I CAN DEFLECT THE SONIC ENERGY.
I HAVE TO PROTECT MY FAMILY.
YOU IDIOT! GET OFFA ME!!!
I AM THE KING!!!
BEEP
BEEP
BEEP
BEEP

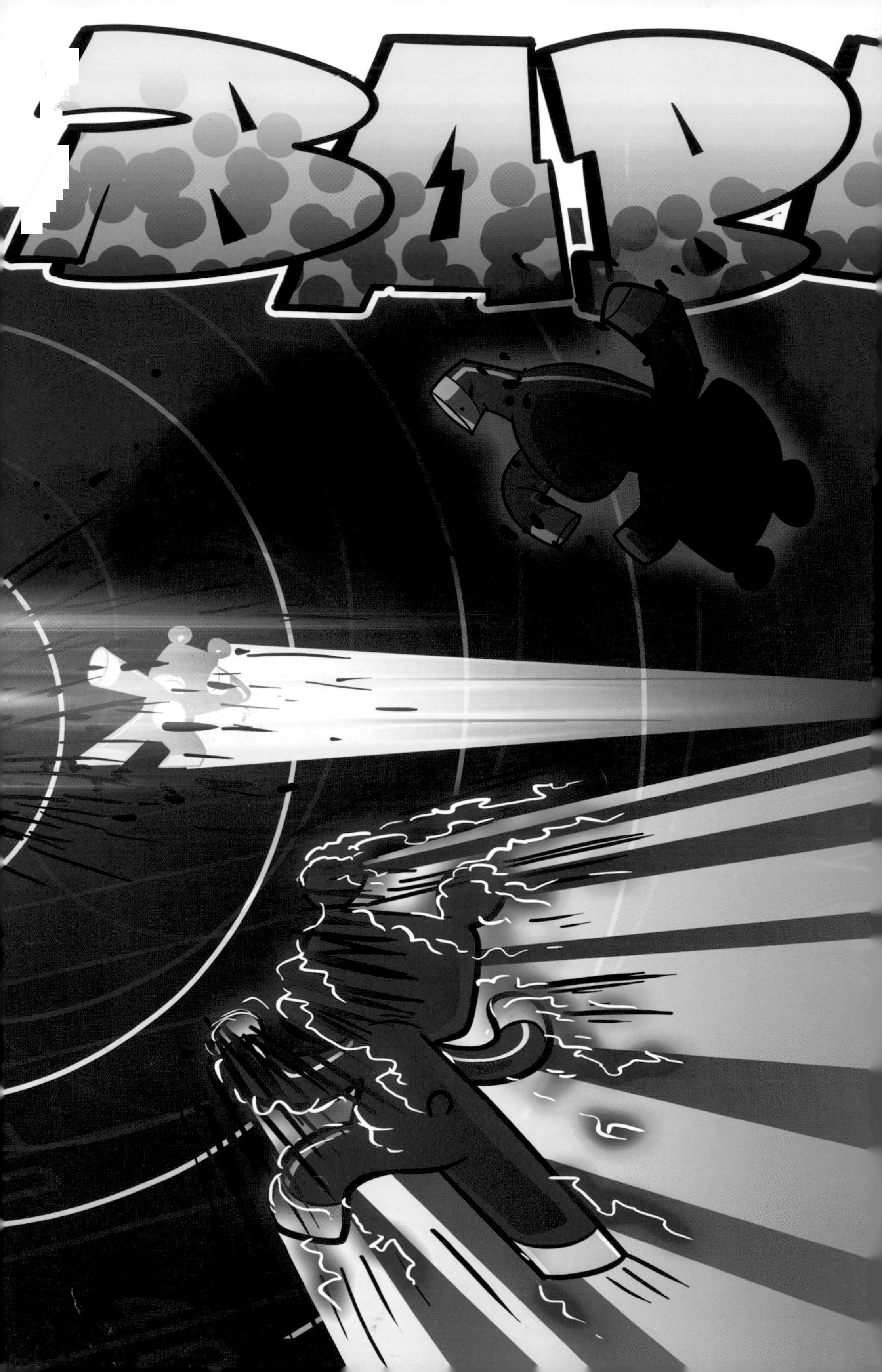

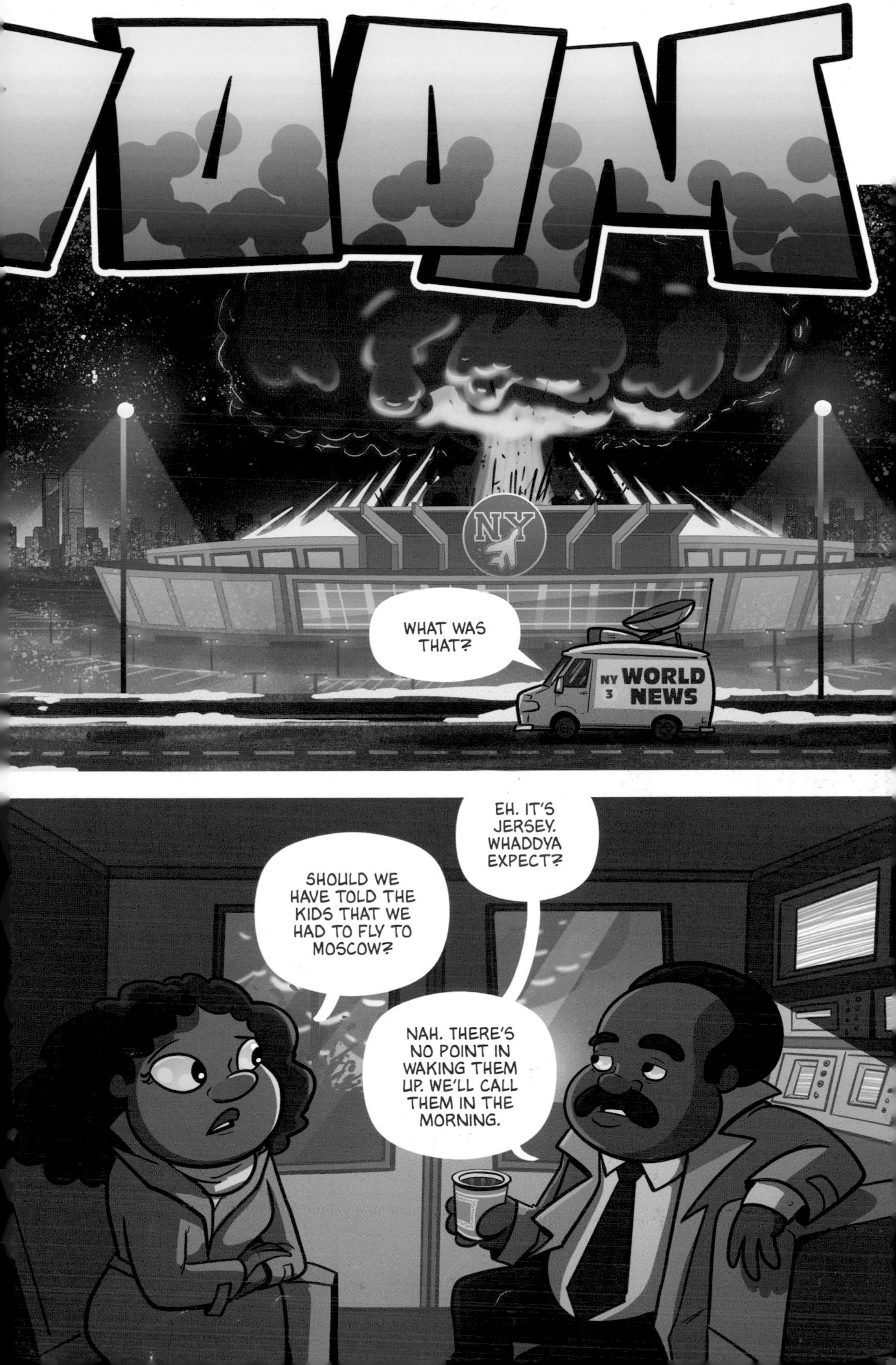
NY
WHAT WAS THAT?
NY WORLD NEWS 3
SHOULD WE HAVE TOLD THE KIDS THAT WE HAD TO FLY TO MOSCOW?
EH. IT'S JERSEY. WHADDYA EXPECT?
NAH. THERE'S NO POINT IN WAKING THEM UP. WE'LL CALL THEM IN THE MORNING.

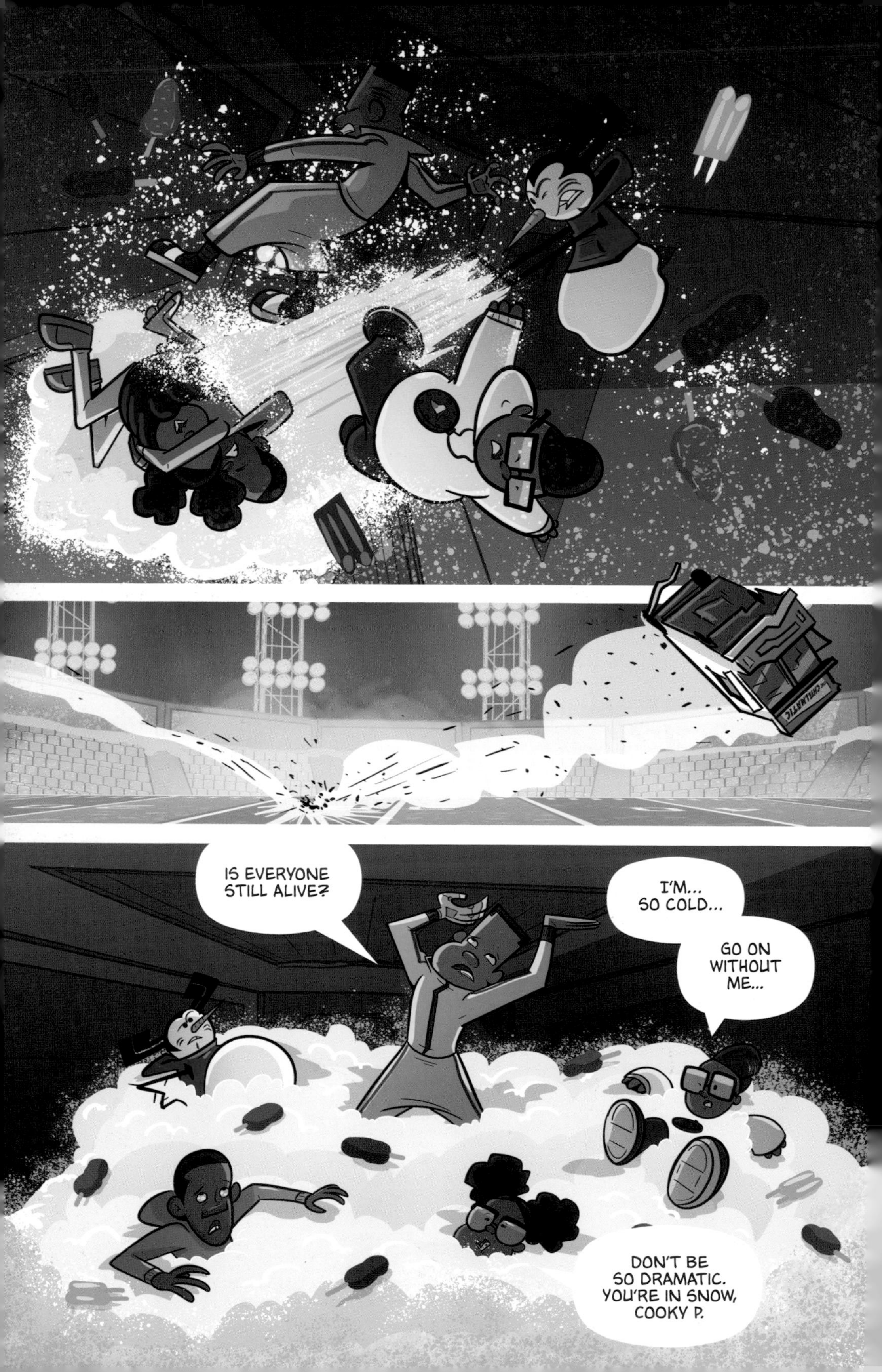
IS EVERYONE STILL ALIVE?
I'M... SO COLD...
GO ON WITHOUT ME...
DON'T BE SO DRAMATIC. YOU'RE IN SNOW, COOKY P.

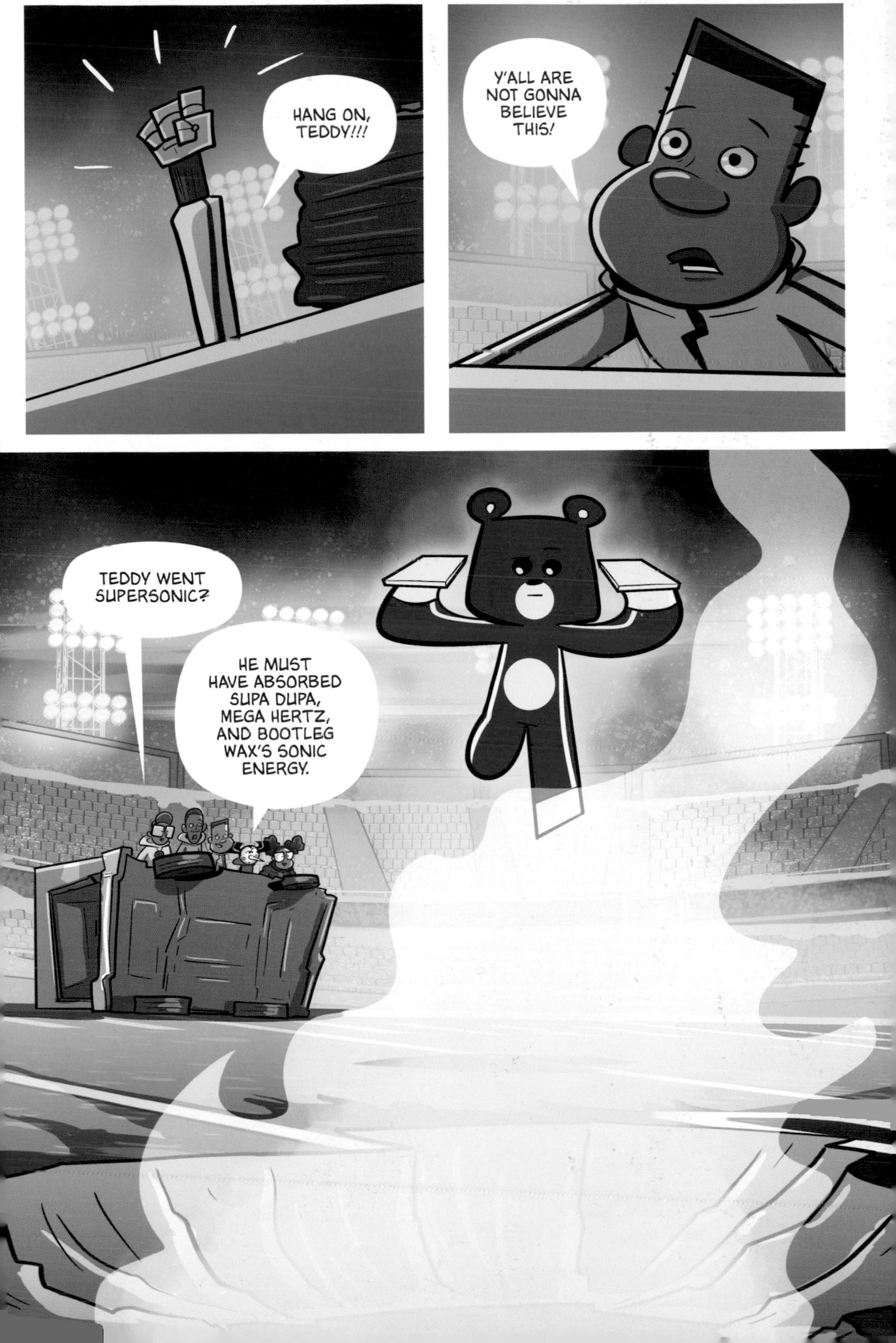
HANG ON, TEDDY!!!
Y'ALL ARE NOT GONNA BELIEVE THIS!
TEDDY WENT SUPERSONIC?
HE MUST HAVE ABSORBED SUPA DUPA, MEGA HERTZ, AND BOOTLEG WAX'S SONIC ENERGY.

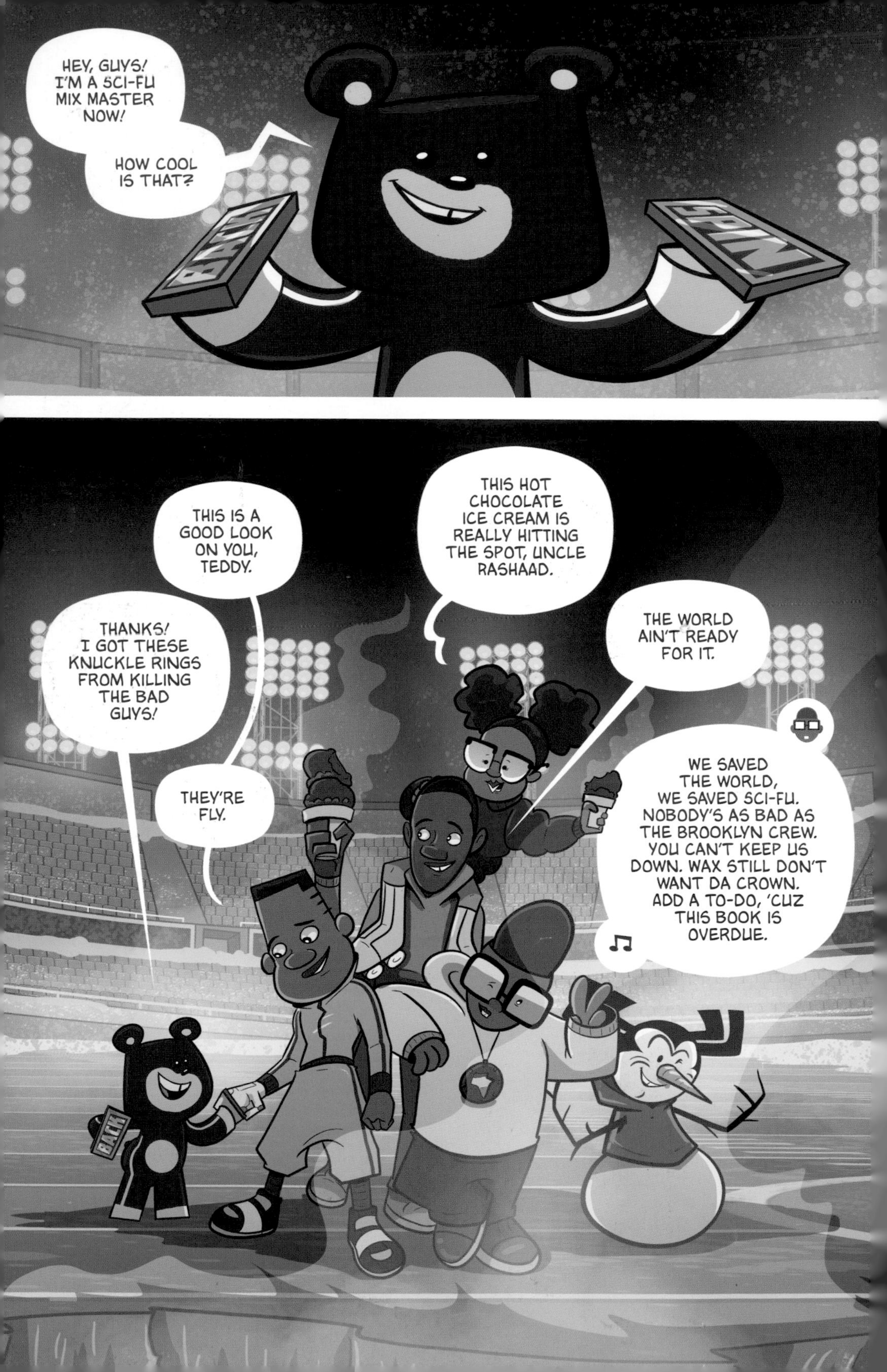
HEY, GUYS! I'M A SCI-FU MIX MASTER NOW!
HOW COOL IS THAT?
BACK
SPIN
THIS IS A GOOD LOOK ON YOU, TEDDY.
THIS HOT CHOCOLATE ICE CREAM IS REALLY HITTING THE SPOT, UNCLE RASHAAD.
THE WORLD AIN'T READY FOR IT.
THANKS! I GOT THESE KNUCKLE RINGS FROM KILLING THE BAD GUYS!
THEY'RE FLY.
WE SAVED THE WORLD, WE SAVED SCI-FU. NOBODY'S AS BAD AS THE BROOKLYN CREW. YOU CAN'T KEEP US DOWN. WAX STILL DON'T WANT DA CROWN. ADD A TO-DO, 'CUZ THIS BOOK IS OVERDUE.
BACK

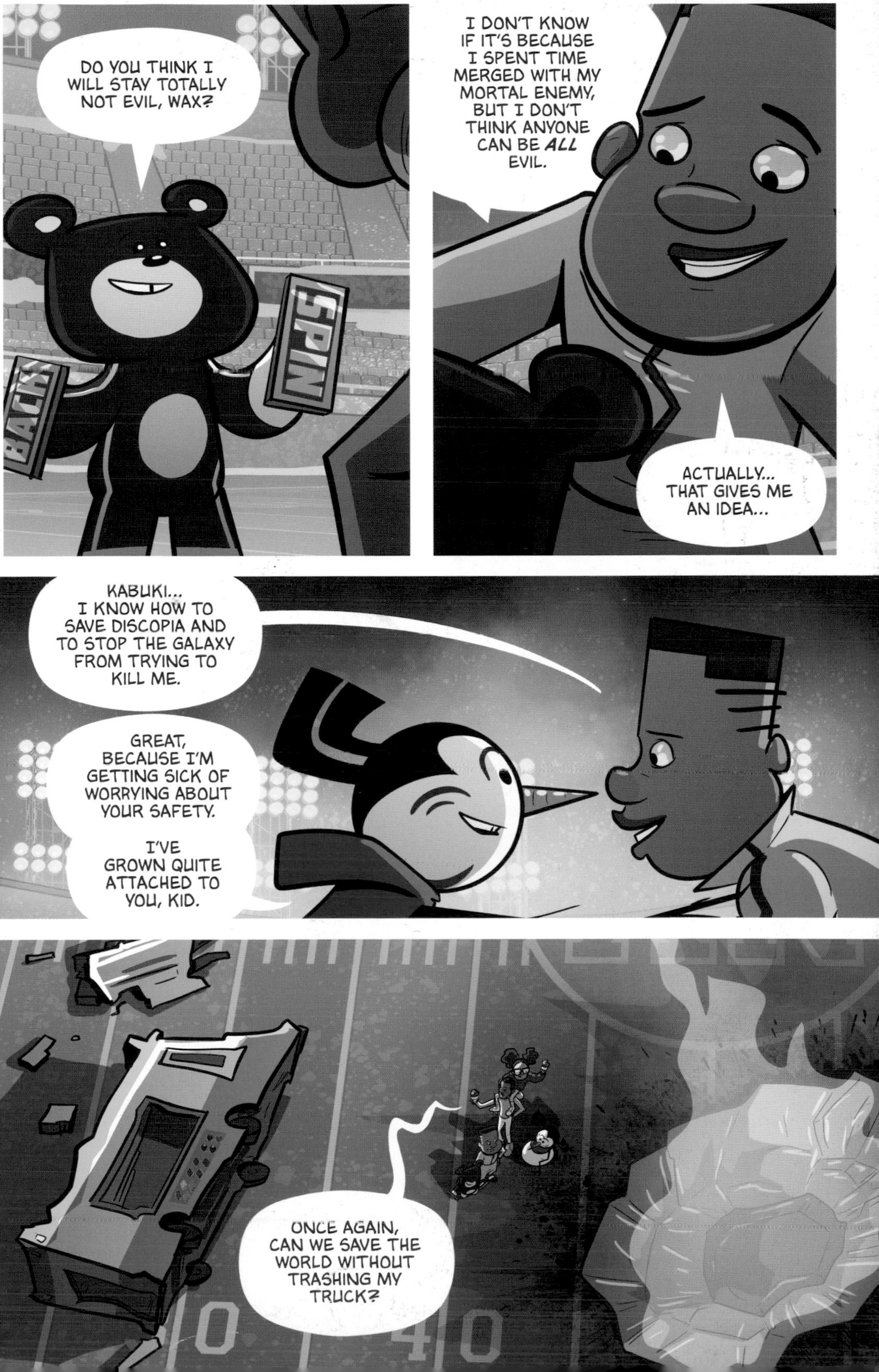
DO YOU THINK I WILL STAY TOTALLY NOT EVIL, WAX?
BACK
SPIN
I DON'T KNOW IF IT'S BECAUSE I SPENT TIME MERGED WITH MY MORTAL ENEMY, BUT I DON'T THINK ANYONE CAN BE *ALL* EVIL.
ACTUALLY... THAT GIVES ME AN IDEA...
KABUKI... I KNOW HOW TO SAVE DISCOPIA AND TO STOP THE GALAXY FROM TRYING TO KILL ME.
GREAT, BECAUSE I'M GETTING SICK OF WORRYING ABOUT YOUR SAFETY.
I'VE GROWN QUITE ATTACHED TO YOU, KID.
ONCE AGAIN, CAN WE SAVE THE WORLD WITHOUT TRASHING MY TRUCK?

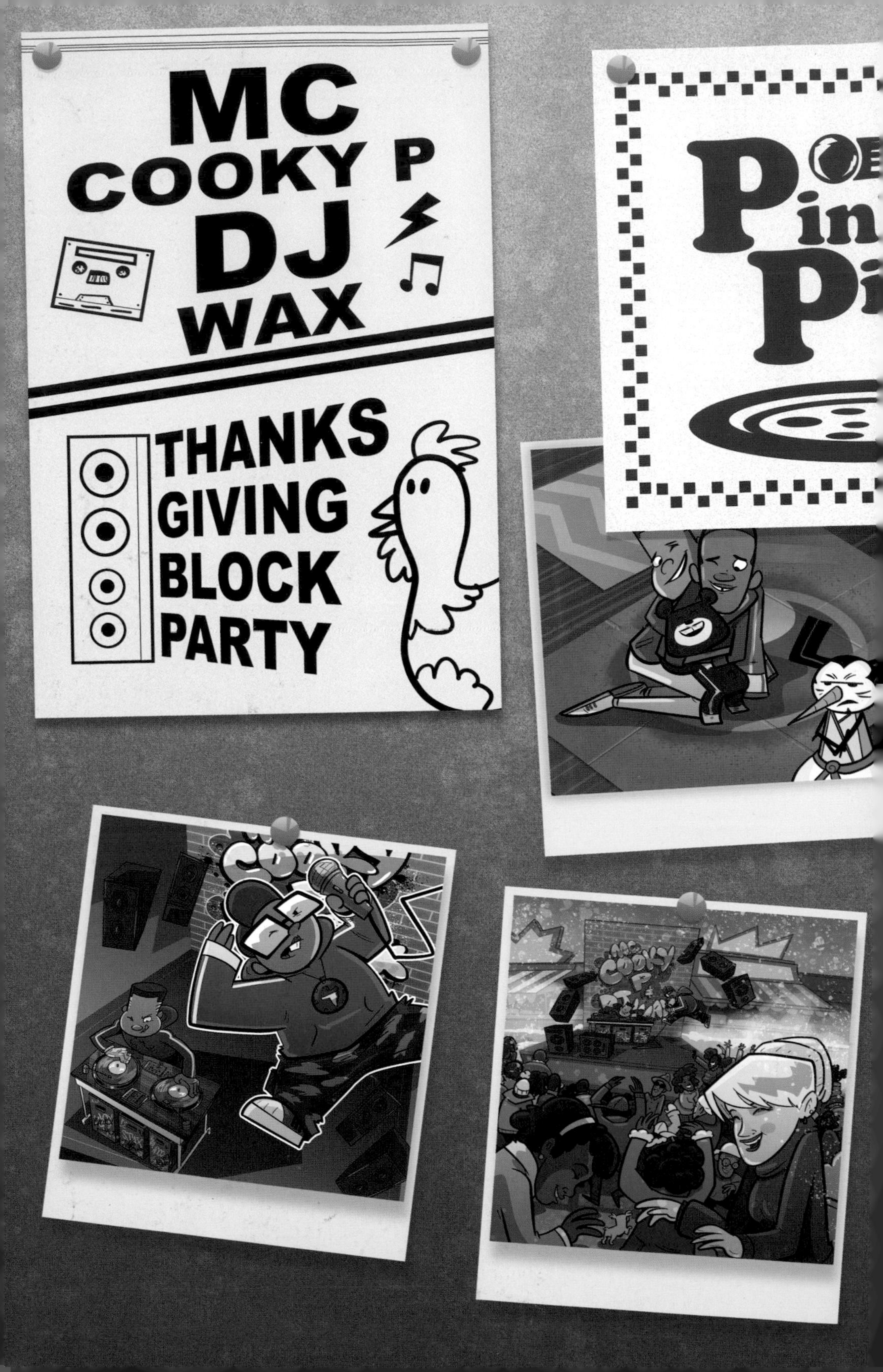
MC
COOKY P
DJ
WAX
THANKS
GIVING
BLOCK
PARTY

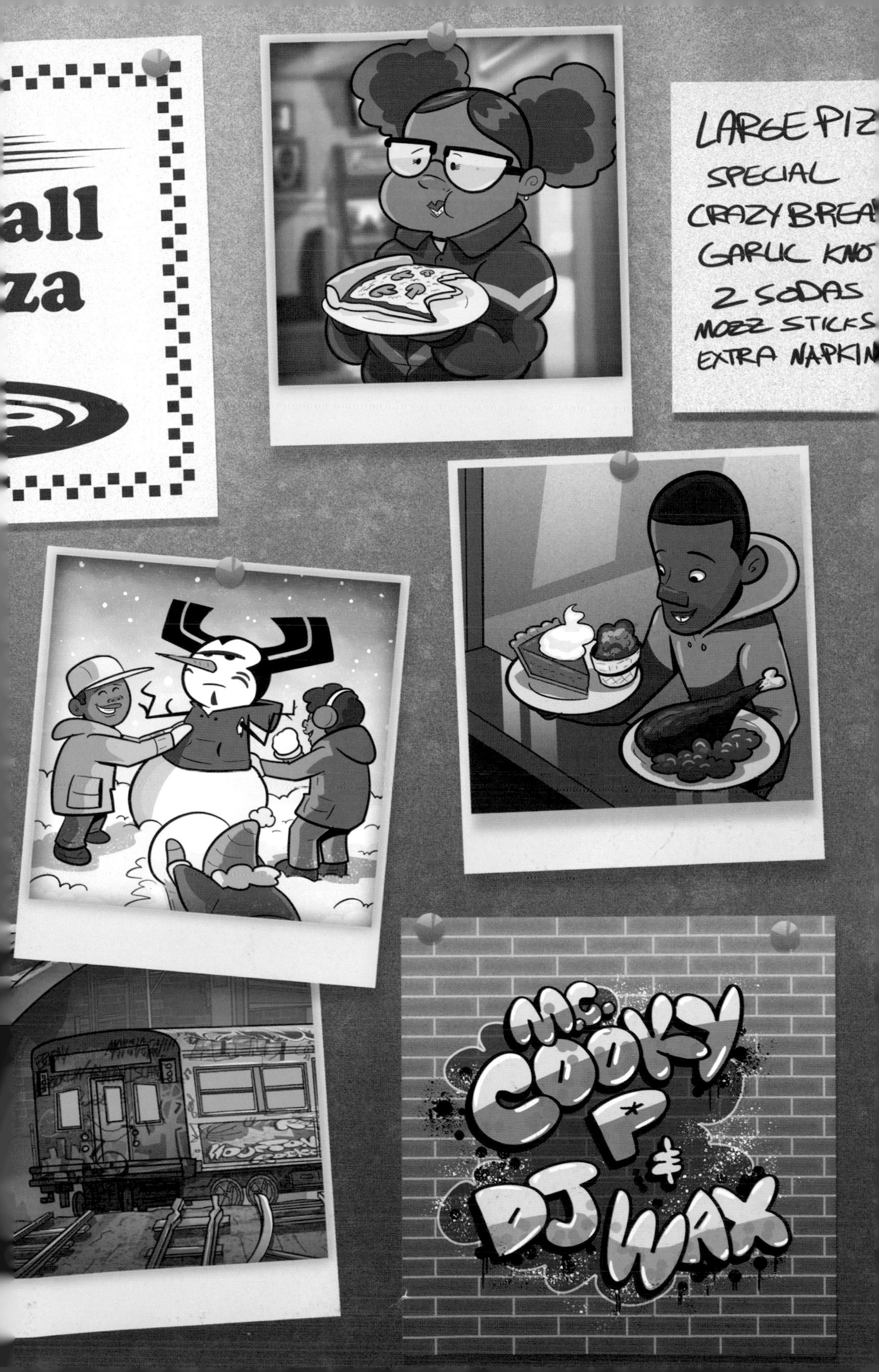
all
za
LARGE PIZ
SPECIAL
CRAZY BREA
GARLIC KNO
2 SODAS
MOZZ STICKS
EXTRA NAPKIN
M.C. COOKY P & DJ WAX

TRACK
6

DOWN WITH THE KING

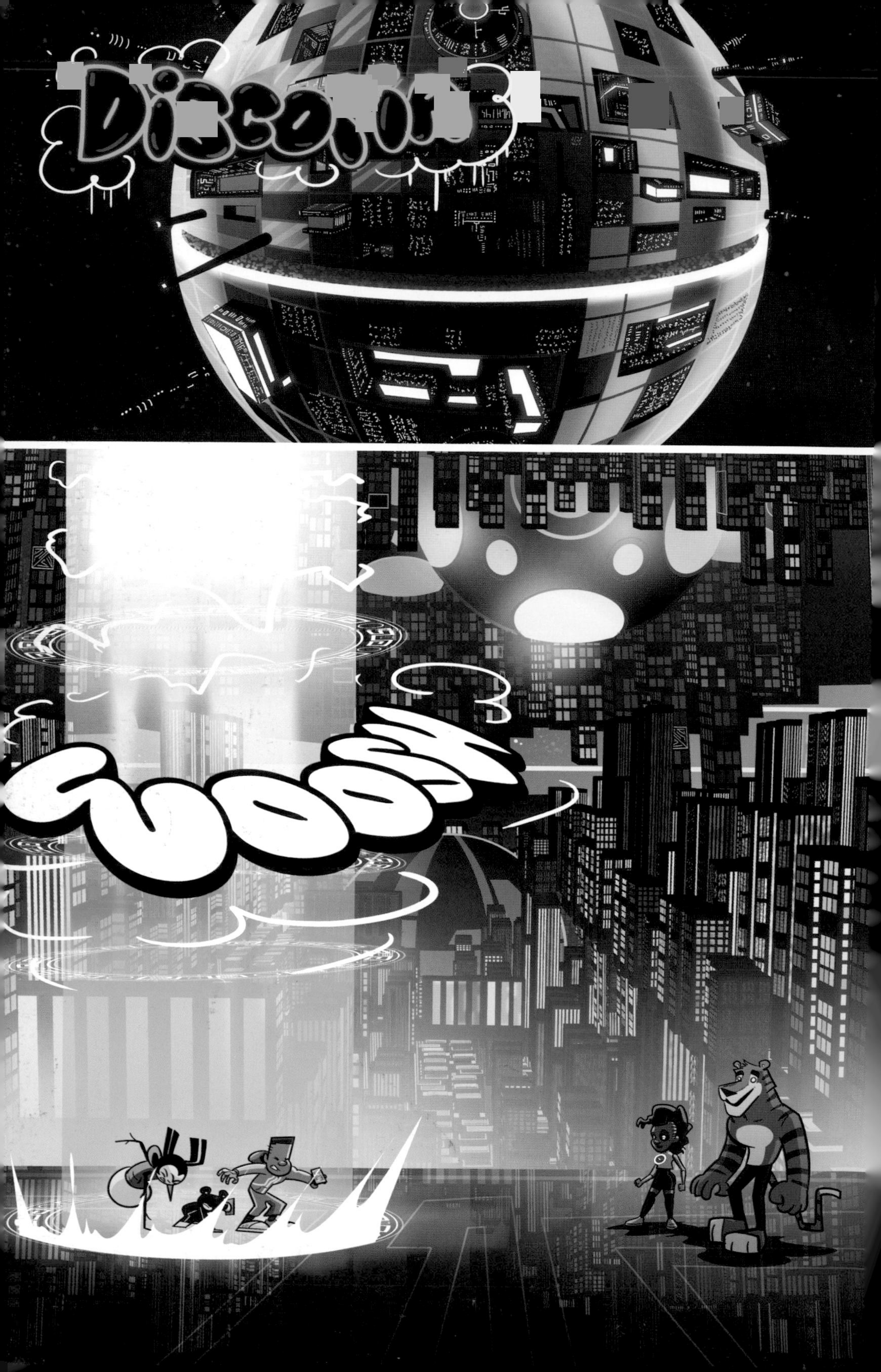

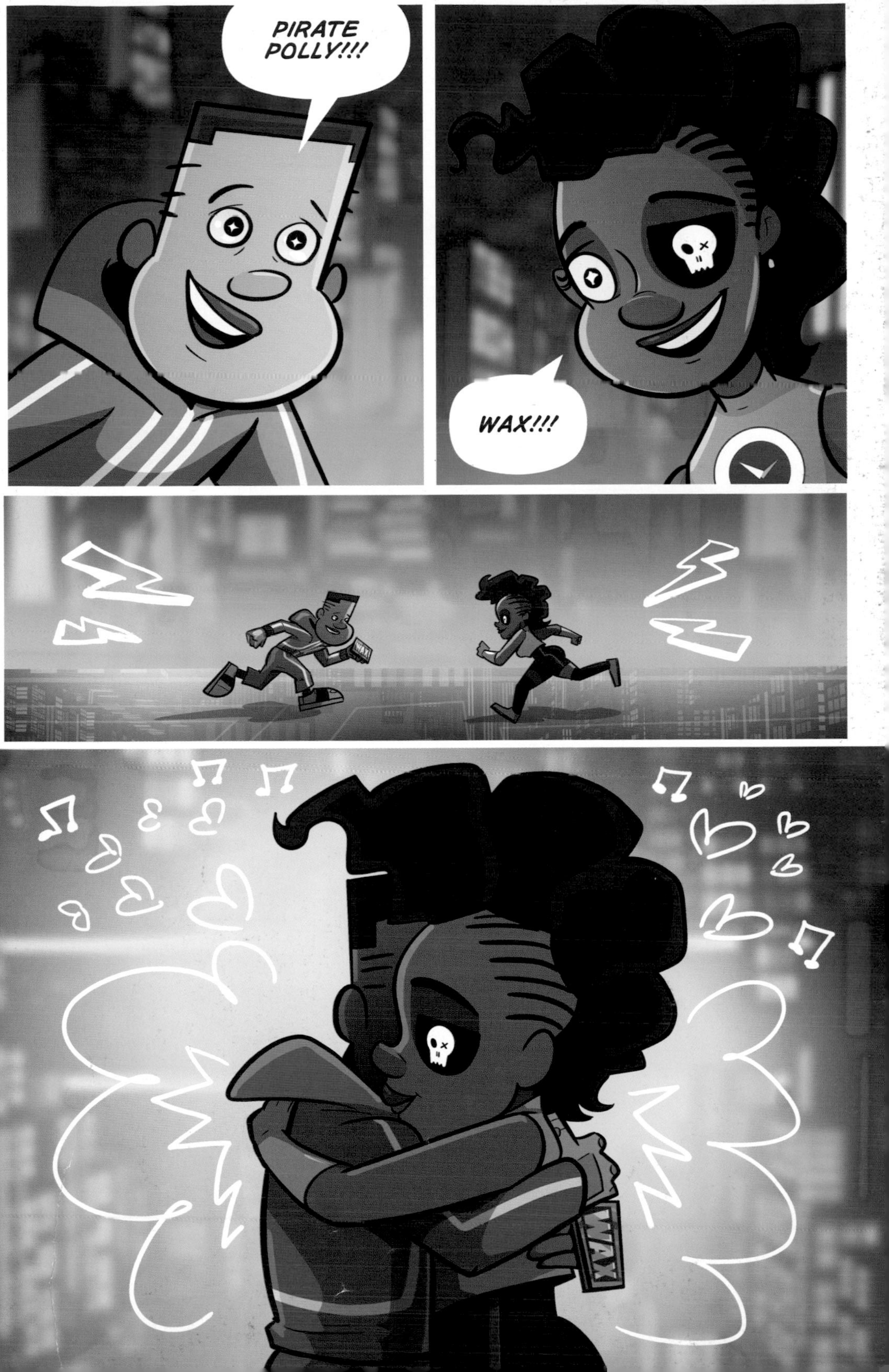
PIRATE POLLY!!!
WAX!!!
WAX
WAX

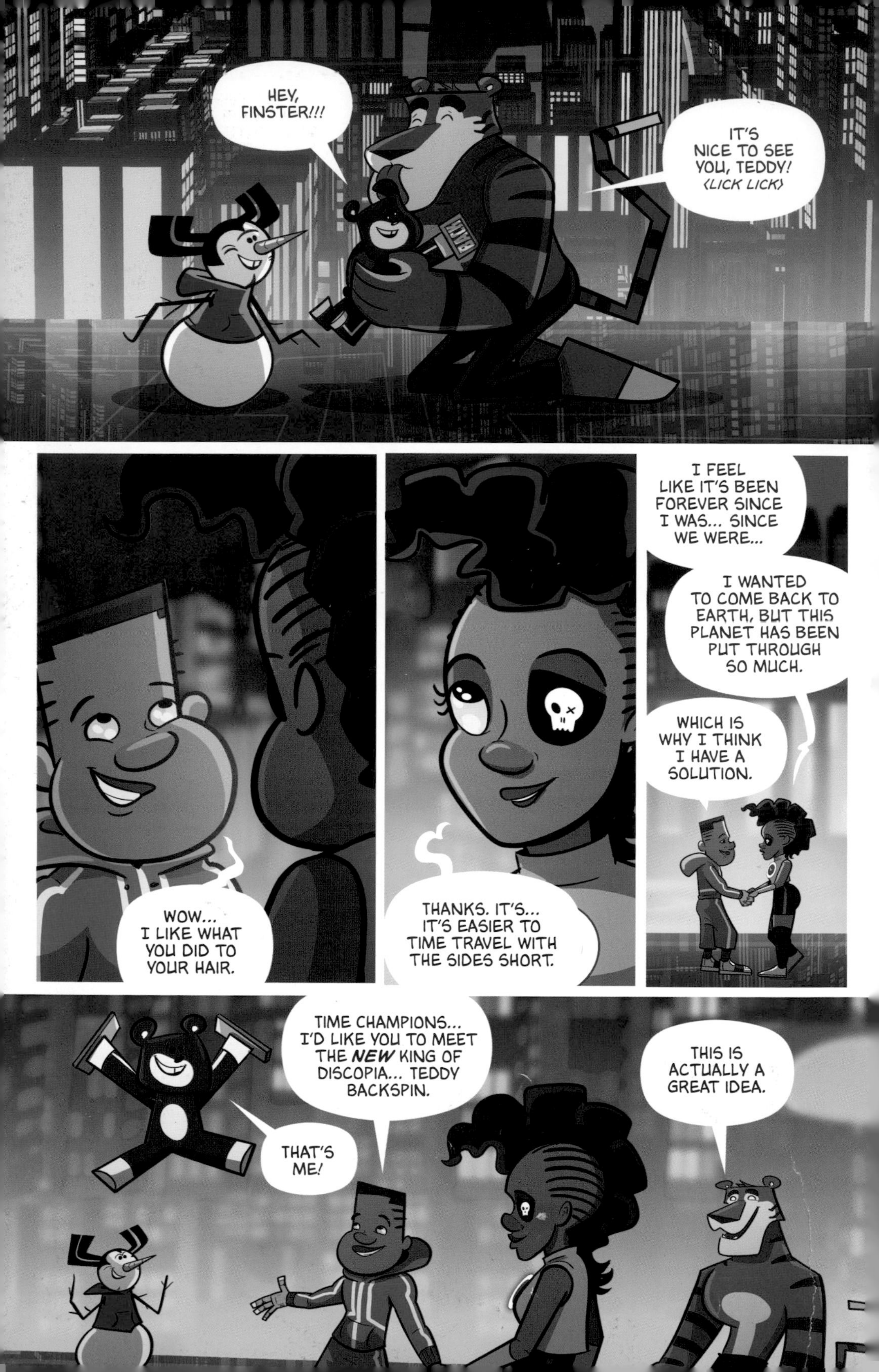
HEY, FINSTER!!!
IT'S NICE TO SEE YOU, TEDDY! ‹LICK LICK›
WOW... I LIKE WHAT YOU DID TO YOUR HAIR.
THANKS. IT'S... IT'S EASIER TO TIME TRAVEL WITH THE SIDES SHORT.
I FEEL LIKE IT'S BEEN FOREVER SINCE I WAS... SINCE WE WERE...
I WANTED TO COME BACK TO EARTH, BUT THIS PLANET HAS BEEN PUT THROUGH SO MUCH.
WHICH IS WHY I THINK I HAVE A SOLUTION.
TIME CHAMPIONS... I'D LIKE YOU TO MEET THE *NEW* KING OF DISCOPIA... TEDDY BACKSPIN.
THAT'S ME!
THIS IS ACTUALLY A GREAT IDEA.

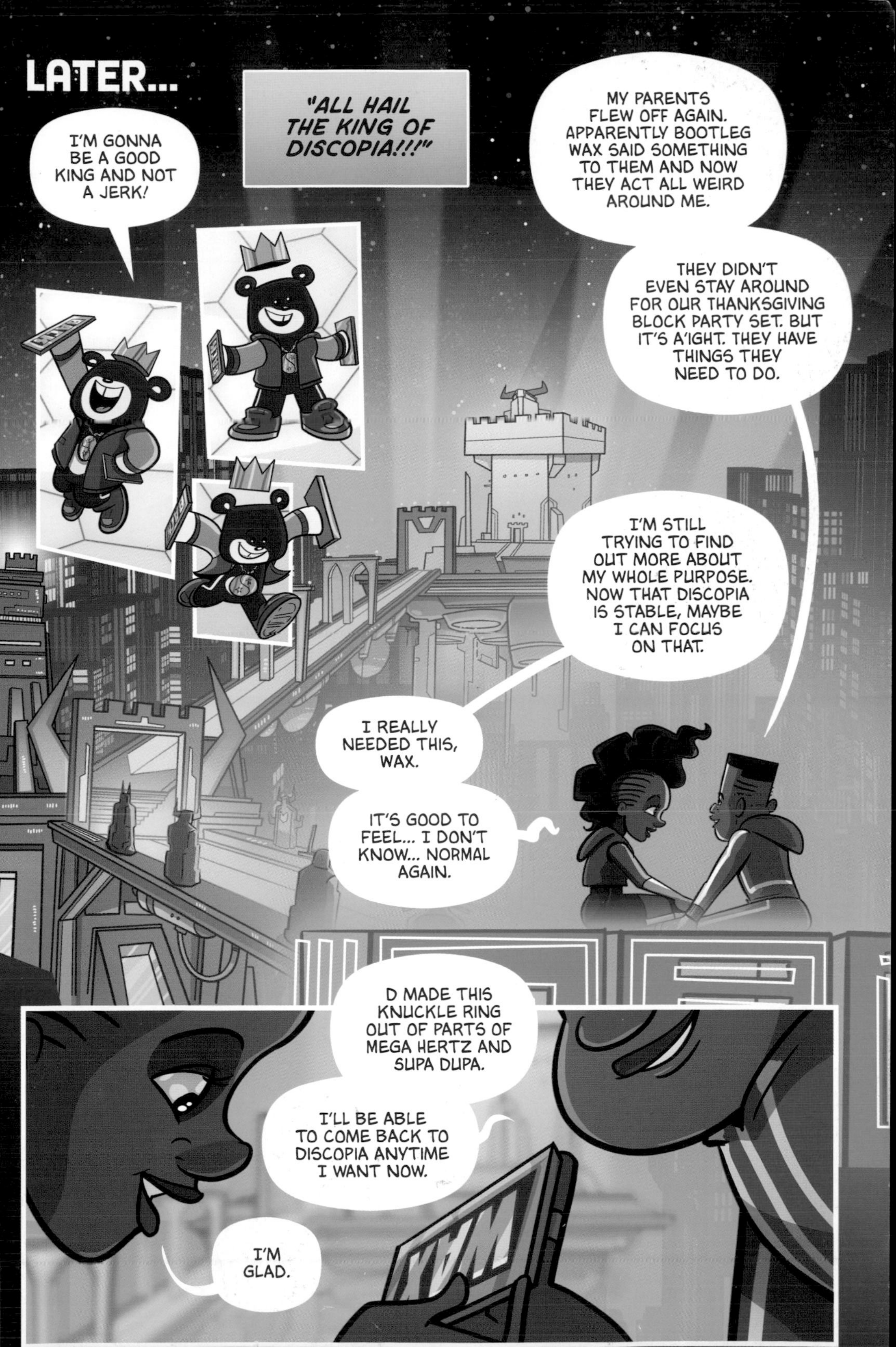
LATER...
I'M GONNA BE A GOOD KING AND NOT A JERK!
"ALL HAIL THE KING OF DISCOPIA!!!"
MY PARENTS FLEW OFF AGAIN. APPARENTLY BOOTLEG WAX SAID SOMETHING TO THEM AND NOW THEY ACT ALL WEIRD AROUND ME.
THEY DIDN'T EVEN STAY AROUND FOR OUR THANKSGIVING BLOCK PARTY SET. BUT IT'S A'IGHT. THEY HAVE THINGS THEY NEED TO DO.
I'M STILL TRYING TO FIND OUT MORE ABOUT MY WHOLE PURPOSE. NOW THAT DISCOPIA IS STABLE, MAYBE I CAN FOCUS ON THAT.
I REALLY NEEDED THIS, WAX.
IT'S GOOD TO FEEL... I DON'T KNOW... NORMAL AGAIN.
D MADE THIS KNUCKLE RING OUT OF PARTS OF MEGA HERTZ AND SUPA DUPA.
I'LL BE ABLE TO COME BACK TO DISCOPIA ANYTIME I WANT NOW.
I'M GLAD.
WAX

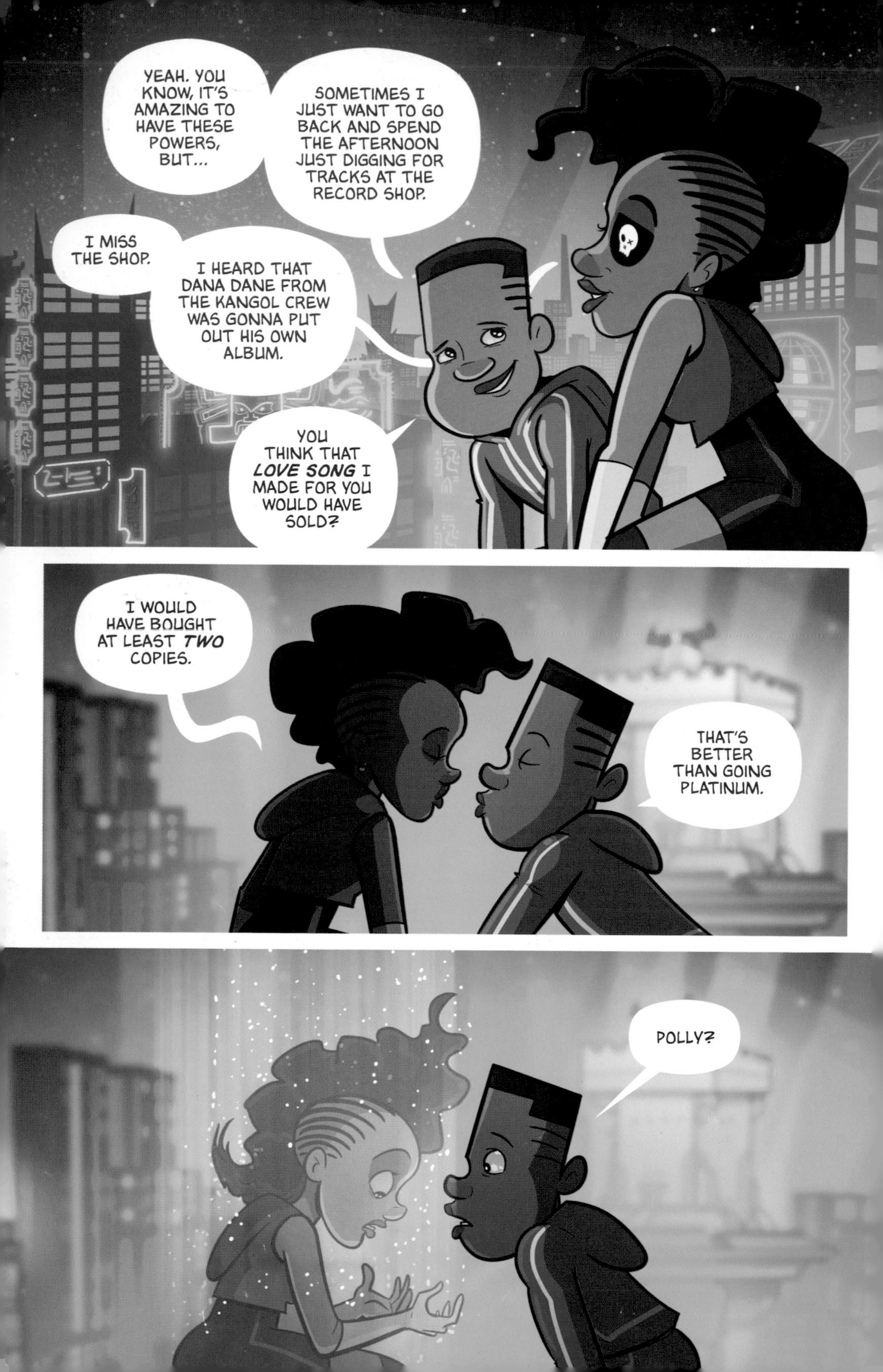
YEAH. YOU KNOW, IT'S AMAZING TO HAVE THESE POWERS, BUT...
SOMETIMES I JUST WANT TO GO BACK AND SPEND THE AFTERNOON JUST DIGGING FOR TRACKS AT THE RECORD SHOP.
I MISS THE SHOP.
I HEARD THAT DANA DANE FROM THE KANGOL CREW WAS GONNA PUT OUT HIS OWN ALBUM.
YOU THINK THAT *LOVE SONG* I MADE FOR YOU WOULD HAVE SOLD?
I WOULD HAVE BOUGHT AT LEAST *TWO* COPIES.
THAT'S BETTER THAN GOING PLATINUM.
POLLY?

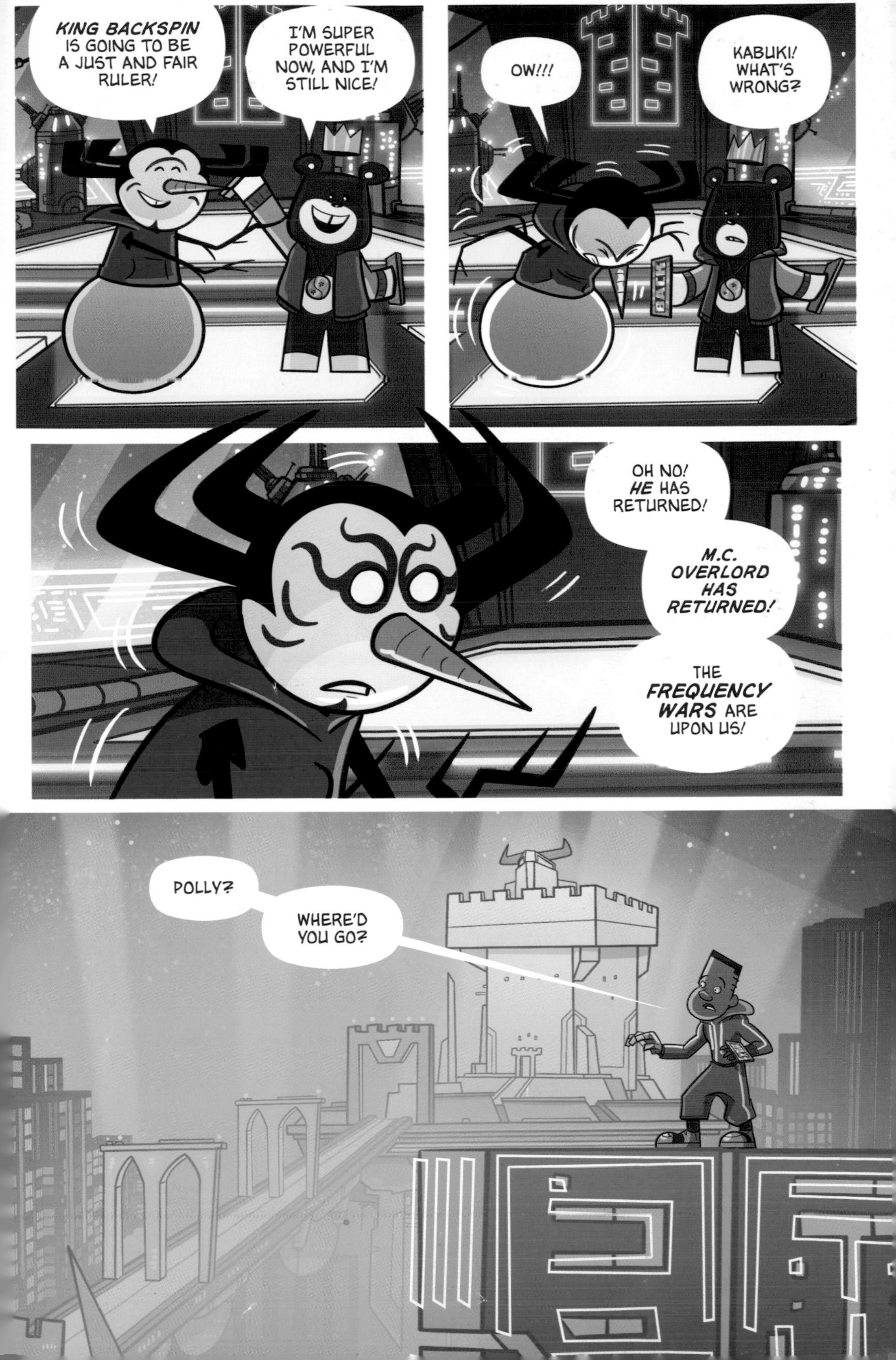
KING BACKSPIN IS GOING TO BE A JUST AND FAIR RULER!
I'M SUPER POWERFUL NOW, AND I'M STILL NICE!
OW!!!
KABUKI! WHAT'S WRONG?
BACK
OH NO! HE HAS RETURNED!
M.C. OVERLORD HAS RETURNED!
THE FREQUENCY WARS ARE UPON US!
POLLY?
WHERE'D YOU GO?

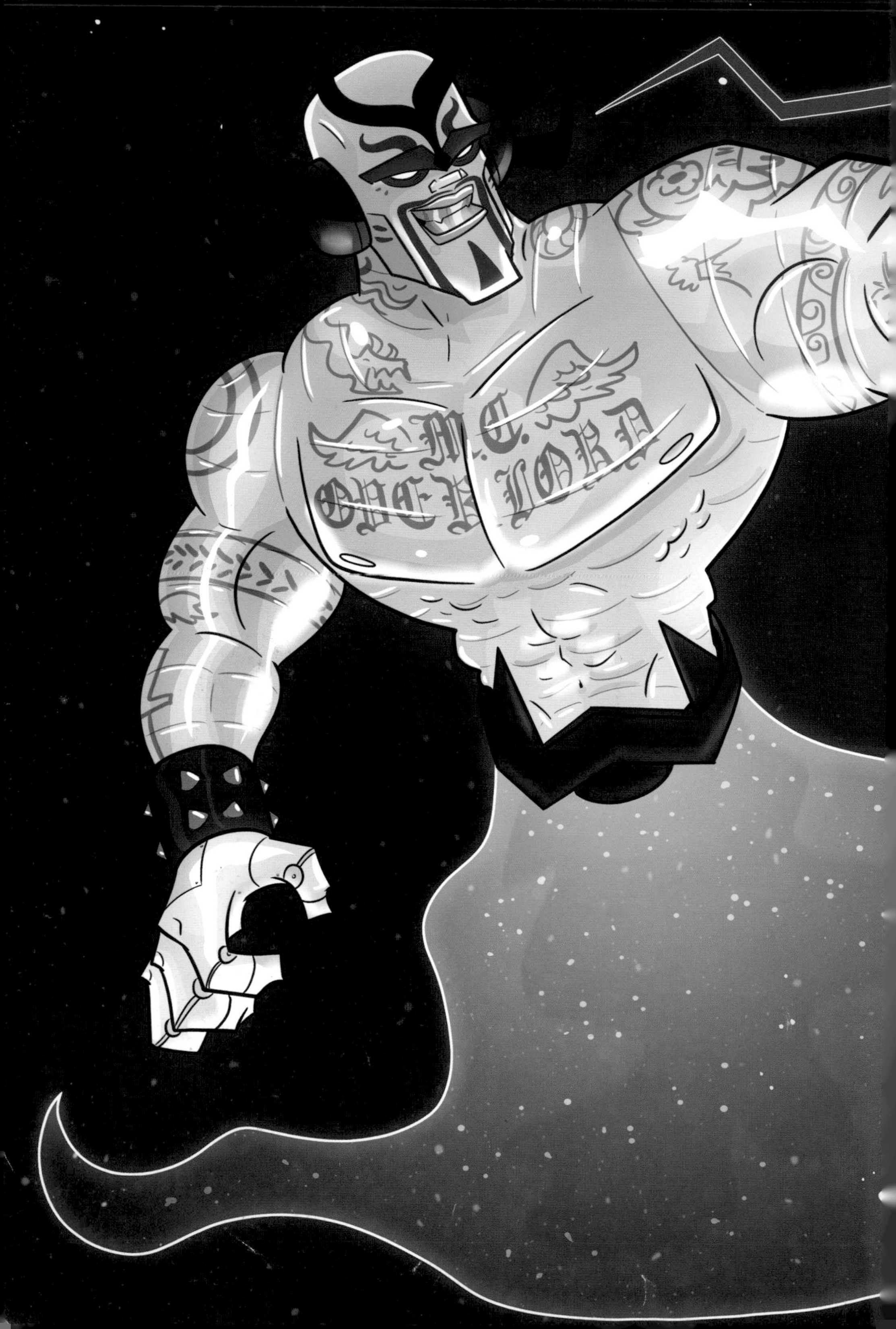
M.C.
OVERLORD

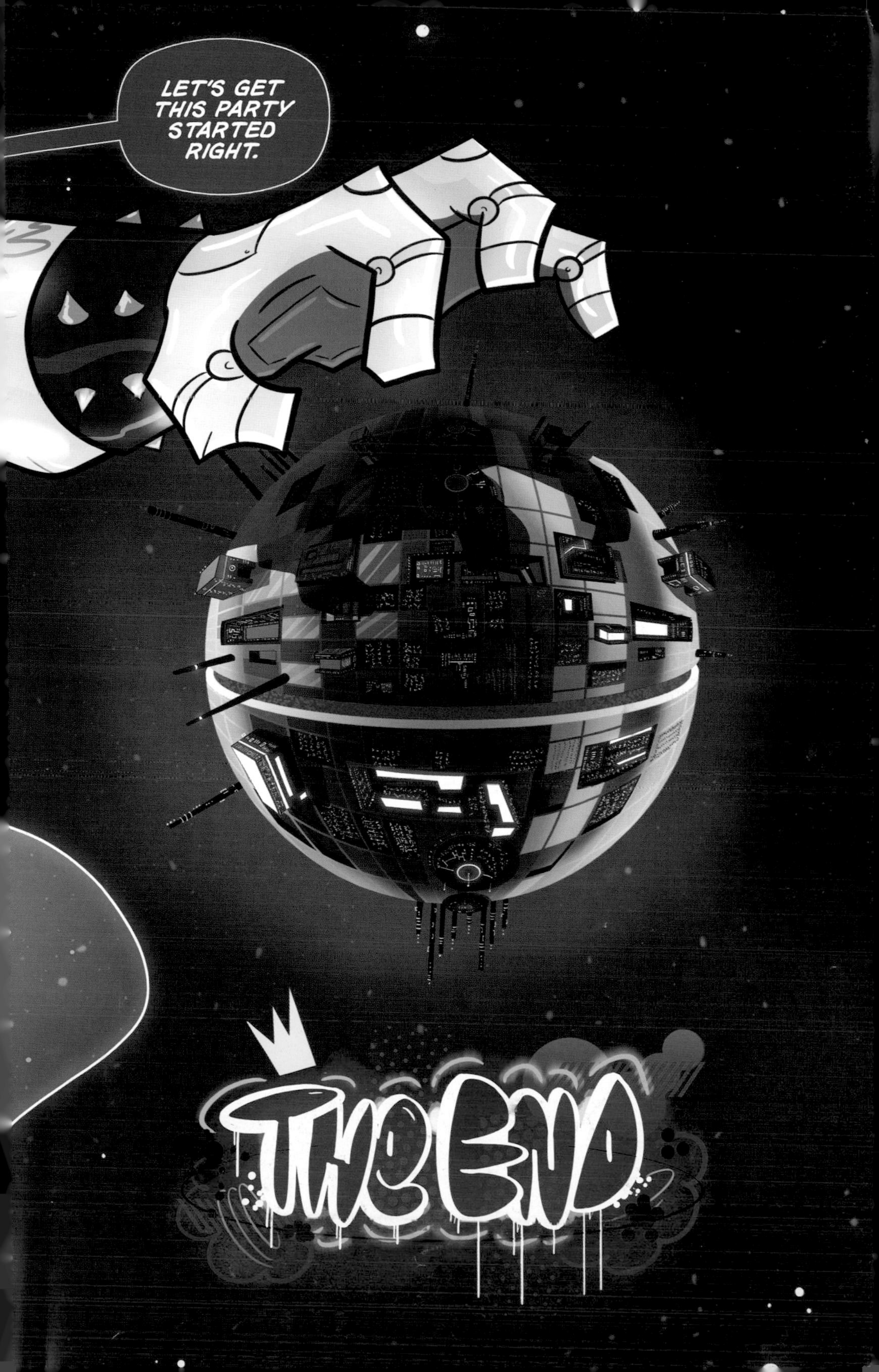
LET'S GET THIS PARTY STARTED RIGHT.
THE END

SPOTIFY PLAYLIST

CURATED BY KENNY KEIL

A DATE _____

- IT TAKES TWO Rob Base & DJ E-Z Rock
- PAID IN FULL Eric B & Rakim
- LYTE AS A ROCK MC Lyte
- ESCAPISM Digable Planets
- CAN I KICK IT A Tribe Called Quest
- YOU GOTS TO CHILL EPMD
- MAKE THE MUSIC WITH YOUR MOUTH, BIZ Biz Markie
- FRIENDS Whodini
- DROPPIN' SCIENCE Marly Marl & Craig G

B DATE _____

- THE CHOICE IS YOURS Black Sheep
- BEYOND THIS WORLD Jungle Brothers
- HARD TIMES Kurtis Blow
- TALKIN' ALL THAT JAZZ Stetsasonic
- SET IT OFF Big Daddy Kane
- BROOKLYN'S IN THE HOUSE Cutmaster DC
- DOIN' DAMAGE JVC Force
- SOULFLEXIN' KMD
- EXPRESS YOURSELF N.W.A.

A DATE _____

- GO CUT CREATOR GO LL Cool J
- THE POWER Chill Rob G
- HEY YOUNG WORLD Slick Rick

B DATE _____

LISTEN AT
HTTP://BIT.LY/SCI-FU

SPECIAL THANKS TO:

Grace Scheipeter
James Lucas Jones & Charlie Chu
Eileen Anderson
Bucky & Bosco
Ludmilla y Gerardo
The Hoodis Gang
The Warfield Posse
The Pueblitz Boys
Chris Cerasi
Desiree Rodriguez
Angie Knowles

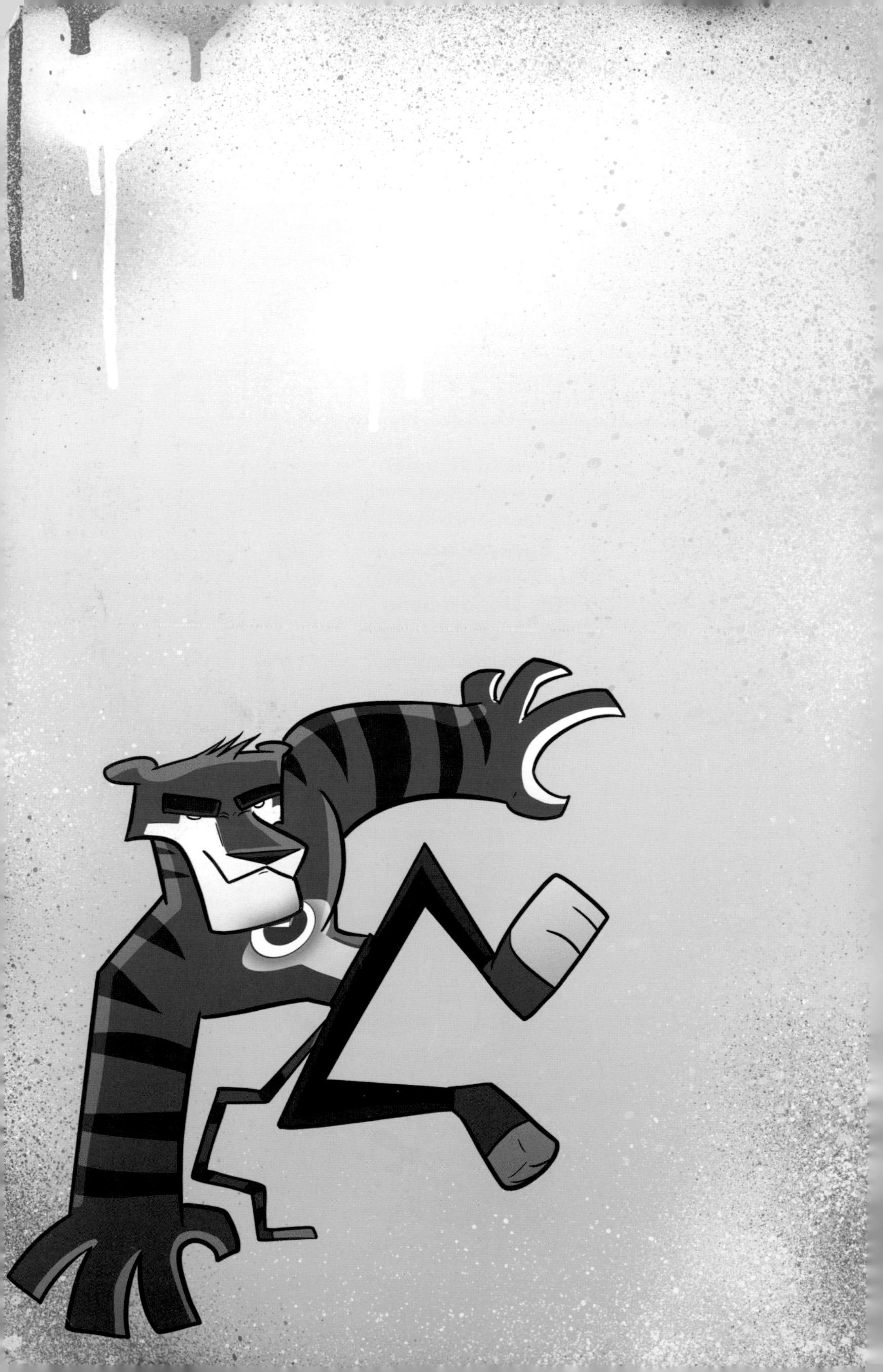

YEHUDI MERCADO

Yehudi Mercado was born in Mexico City and grew up in Houston, Texas. He fell in love with hip-hop at an early age. After college, Yehudi worked in video games and eventually became an art director for Disney Interactive, where he co-wrote and art-directed the *Guardians of the Galaxy* mobile game. His graphic novels include *Chunky, Hero Hotel, Rocket Salvage, Fun Fun Fun World,* and *Sci-Fu.* Yehudi was the artist on the Epic Original graphic novel *Cat Ninja.* Yehudi created a narrative podcast based on his graphic novel *Hero Hotel* for the Pinna Network. He has two adorable dogs named Bucky and Bosco, and usually sneaks one of his pets into his books.

MORE BOOKS FROM YEHUDI MERCADO!

Sci-Fu: Kick It Off

AVAILABLE NOW!

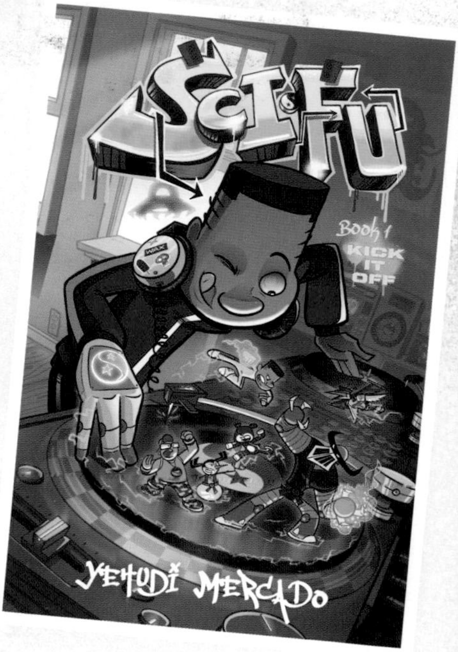
SCI-FU
Book 1
KICK IT OFF
YEHUDI MERCADO

Thirteen-year-old Wax's life may not be perfect, but that doesn't stop him from spinning some of the sickest beats on their Brooklyn block... But he's a better DJ than he thinks. One night, while making a mixtape for his crush, Wax scratches the perfect beat and responds to an interstellar challenge that transports him and the entire block to the robot-filled planet of Discopia. Mistaken by the locals for a master of the futuristic, sound-bending martial art known as sci-fu, Wax finds himself on the wrong side of a showdown against the Five Deadly Dangers and their leader, Choo Choo.

With help from the sci-fu master Kabuki Snowman and Wax's crew—including his best friend Cooky P, his sister The D, and even his crush, Pirate Polly—Wax has to become a sci-fu master or risk losing Earth forever!

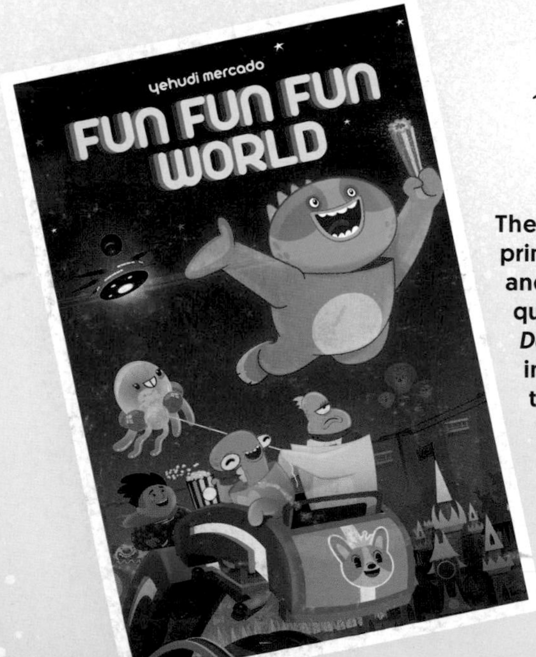
yehudi mercado
FUN FUN FUN
WORLD

Fun Fun Fun World

AVAILABLE NOW!

The *Devastorm 5* is an alien warship whose prime directive is to seek out planets to invade and conquer in tribute to the almighty alien queen. The only problem is that the crew of the *Devastorm 5* is led by Minky, the worst captain in the whole imperium. In a last-ditch effort to be taken more seriously, Minky convinces the crew to conquer Earth once and for all. Ground zero for operation "Conquer Earth" is a defunct amusement park called Fun Fun Fun World, overrun by cats and hiding a major secret. Will the crew of the *Devastorm 5* be able to complete their mission?